Becoming Shadows

Book 3 Shadows of Synd Series
by E. Abraham

Copyright © 2023 Emilia Abraham

This is a work of fiction. Any similarity to places or persons, living or dead, is entirely coincidental. All ideas and characters are

that of the author and should not be reproduced, stored, or transmitted in any form without the written permission of the author.

Sharing is caring, but not for pirates. Be a friend, not a pirate.

All rights reserved.

ISBN-13: 979-8-9857684-6-6

For the readers who wore the mask so long they forgot who they
wanted to be.

iii

And to Emily—for calling me a cunt, all while making this book
the best it could be.

A Special Note

Within Becoming Shadows there are many different kinks that are used within BDSM, and while this is a fictional book, it also mirrors reality to an extent. I have a lot of research in variousforms to help me in understanding both for myself and for my books. However, this is not a how-to guide. Becoming Shadows is still fictional, and should be treated as such. There are creative allowances given the situations and circumstances within this fictional city that do not translate to real life. That being said, please do not recreate the scenes in this book without doing researchfor yourself. It is important that safety and consent is paramount when engaging in this type of play. I've listed many of the kinks below to help better prepare you, the reader, for what you will expect when reading Becoming Shadows, along with the trigger warnings.

Happy Reading!

Trigger Warnings:

Attempted Murder

Death/Murder

Death of parent (mentions of cancer briefly-not on page)

Physical Abuse (not by MMC)

Misogyny

Kidnapping

Emotional Abuse

Stalking

Violence

PTSD induced Panic Attacks/Anxiety

Criminal Activity

Content Warnings:

Explicit language

Adult sexual Scenes

Light BDSM:

Choking, bondage, edge play, sensory deprivation, CNC, primal play (minimal), anal play

Chapter One

Hawk

I can't remember the last time I fucked.

I'm not holding out for the perfect woman to walk through the door. I also haven't been going out of my way to find anyone either. The last year has been a shit show, with little time for finding someone to fuck, much less seeking out something more. Now, I'm so exhausted by the end of the day I barely have enough energy to take off my boots before I fall into bed. Complaining about it won't change a damn thing though, so I keep my mouth shut.

"You want another one, Hawk?" Trigger asks, tipping an empty glass toward me.

"Yeah, one more," I say, gazing around at the half-finished bar.

The Night Slayers burned down the last one, but Trigger set up shop here, kept the name, Trigger's, the same, and kept doing business as usual.

"You sure? You look like you're about to fall off the stool. How much sleep you gettin' these days?"

"None of your fucking business, Trigger. Pour the drink," I snap.

The last thing I need is a babysitter. It may be his bar, but I outrank him in the club. At this point, I'm running shit around here, since Ryker Helms, our president, is out of commission after being shot. I can't blame him for how fucking exhausted I am. I should ask for help, but I'm in so deep I can't pass anything off. Doesn't mean I can't take my shitty attitude out on them though. Perks of being the vice president of a motorcycle club.

"Your fucking funeral," he mutters, passing me another beer.

My phone buzzes and I pull it out to read Helms's latest text complaining about the house next to his. It used to house the previous vice president and his kids before the attempted coup ten years ago, and it needs to be finished. It hasn't been at the top of my priority list, and now he's bitching. Mac, his woman, has a friend coming to town and apparently, she needs her own place to stay. Mac refuses to say when her best friend is actually coming and it's starting to piss me off. I don't blame the woman for wanting her own space, away from Helms and Mac. They recently found each other after ten years, fought the demons following Mac, and fell in love again. Now they're making up for lost time.

I rub at the ache in my chest. I'm happy for them, but it's not easy watching them live out the life I wish I had. Being around them is both amazing and disheartening when I think about it. They've been reconnecting all over the damn house, which isn't something I like thinking about when I eat there.

The tinkling of the bell above the door floats over the hum of the other bikers. Peering over my shoulder, I watch a woman with a sheet of blonde hair trip inside, and I whip back around. Trigger gives me a look from halfway down the bar, then turns to the newcomer. She settles a couple seats from me, and I casually glance her way. I can't put my finger on it, but she feels familiar. Subtly studying her, I realize there's no way she lives here.

Reaper territory isn't very large, and most people from Synd don't travel up this way. We're tucked away at the north end of the city, occupying a couple dozen city blocks. Crossing from Synd into Reapers area is like entering a new world. She's definitely not from around here. I would've noticed her.

I track her as she tips her head back, laughing at whatever Trigger is saying. He slides a drink in front of her, rapping his knuckles on the counter before going to talk to Doc, our sergeant at arms, who's tucked away in his usual corner at the end of the bar.

"Excuse me?" The woman's voice flows over me, and goosebumps scatter across my arms. Peering at her from the corner of my eye, I find her staring.

I tense, the sense of familiarity hitting me again. "Yeah?"

"Sorry, I was wondering if I'm allowed to be here?" Her brows pull together, nose scrunching.

"Why wouldn't you be allowed in here?" I ask, turning fully to face her.

Her skin flushes, traveling from her neck to settle on her cheeks. "Well, I realize this is—" She leans in, whispering. "—motorcycle club area."

I rub my hand across my mouth, hiding the grin threatening to pop out. "And?"

She huffs. "I don't know the laws. I don't want to break a rule that I didn't know was there in the first place."

"What do you think we're going to do if you do break a rule you didn't know about?" I ask, raising an eyebrow.

Her mouth parts as she stares over my shoulder. I don't know what the hell she's doing, but I'm worried I broke her brain. I might have just played into all her worst fears of what an MC is like. She clearly knows nothing about the Reapers. Her eyes find mine again, and a flush splashes across her cheeks.

Squaring her shoulders, she says, "I think you would be benevolent and understanding of the fact I'm not from around here and have no idea what the correct protocol is for coming into an establishment in a motorcycle club's..."

"Territory. I don't know about benevolent, but we don't punish people for mistakes like that. We're not that scary. You're allowed to be in here. We're not going to stop you from getting a drink. And we call it an MC. Or the Reapers. That's our club's name."

"Oh, I got that," she snorts, waving her hand at the various flags hanging on the walls. "I didn't know if I was allowed to say the name. All these groups have different..." She waves her hand. "Whatever."

She bites her lip and my eyes flick down. Her mouth pulls into a smile before she ducks her head. Trigger walks toward us, but I pin him with a glare, and he pivots, scuttling away. I don't want him pulling her attention back to him. Her straight blonde hair swings, covering her face as she turns back to the counter, resting her arms on the bar. She's short, toes barely touching the rod at the bottom of the stool.

"What brings you to Synd?" I ask before taking a sip of beer.

"I'm visiting a friend. She's busy though, probably in bed by now since it's so late."

I glance at the clock, seeing it's barely midnight. This is early for most of us. In fact, this is about the time bikers start pouring in or set out to deal with shit for the Reapers.

Glancing over my shoulder, my gaze flows over the various groups gathered inside. There are more outside, taking advantage of the late summer night. A prospect walks in, propping the front door open with a brick. Nick isn't a bad kid, but he thinks he's more important than he is. He's a cocky asshole most of the time, but I haven't had the energy to bust his ass about it.

A couple more prospects follow him. I narrow my eyes when he spots the woman three stools down from me and a grin spreads across his face. Most women who come here are members' old ladies. They'll grab a prospect's nuts and twist if he hits on her. This woman, though, is fair game. I slide off the stool and gather my beer before settling next to her.

"Oh, okay," she mumbles, pinching the skin on her knuckles.

"We don't need to keep talking, but the guys who just walked in won't bother you if I'm sitting next to you."

She peeks over her shoulder then whips back around. "Thanks. I mean, we can keep talking, if you want. Don't feel like you have to entertain me. I just didn't want to go back to the hotel yet. What's your name?"

She's babbling, her voice tighter than before. I don't want to run her out of Trigger's, but Nick won't leave her alone if I move back.

"Do I make you nervous?"

"No. Sort of. Not you," she says, turning wide eyes to me. "I'm not used to a place like this. Newbie here, remember?"

"Just a regular bar. More bikes out front is all. In fact, this might be the safest bar for you. Nick"—I throw a thumb over my shoulder—"is harmless, but beautiful women make him annoying."

A blush creeps across her cheeks again. "Well, thanks for saving me from being annoyed to death. Are you from around here?"

I grin into my beer. Something holds me back from revealing anything about my life. The mystery is more fun than dumping everything about myself.

"Here and there. I'm here now. Why didn't you want to go back to your hotel yet?"

"I was sitting there, mindlessly watching TV and couldn't handle being stuck inside anymore. I figured I'd come out and see if there was anything I could find."

"What are you looking for?"

Her hands flutter before settling in her lap and she tucks her head to her chest to hide behind her hair. "I don't know yet. Guess I'll know when it comes along."

I glance over my shoulder again to glare at the others milling about. A couple of them are circling closer, but they back off when they catch my eye. Trigger raps his knuckles on the bar, and I swing around.

"He bugging you, miss?"

She laughs, smothering the musical sound behind her hand. "No, he's saving me from turning down overzealous suitors."

"A regular knight in shining armor, huh?" Trigger smirks. I shake my head, glancing out the window. The rumble of bikes rattles the glass and a dozen guys pull out of the lot on their way to a deal.

I startle when her small hand rests on my arm.

"A lifesaver, for sure," she giggles.

Trigger nods to my half-full beer. I shake my head, hoping this night ends better than it began. I wouldn't mind the distraction of a hot fuck to take my mind off the stress of the MC. I'm not convinced she's looking for that type of fun time, though. Her tone has a flirty edge to it, but she doesn't seem like the kind of girl who trolls for random dick at a bar. In fact, she seems innocent. It might be her button nose, or the spattering of freckles across her cheeks. Her bright blue eyes *are* dancing with mischief. The corners of her eyes crinkle and a dimple appears on her left cheek when she smiles.

"You need another, sweetheart?" Trigger asks, and she peeks at me from under her lashes. I shrug, waiting for her to decide.

"No, thank you. I'm all set. How much do I owe you?"

Her hand slides off my arm and a shiver runs down my spine. Spinning, she digs in the purse she has slung over the back of the stool. Trigger gazes at me, brows disappearing under his mop of hair, and I shake my head. He'll put it on my tab. The MC pays out for the inner circle every month anyway.

"Don't bother. Beautiful women don't pay," he snickers, and I glare.

"Are you sure? I have some money." She pulls out a wad of cash and I cover her small hand with my own.

"Best not flash green around. Wouldn't want someone to get the wrong idea there, *léaró dóchais*," I mutter. Trigger snorts at the phrase rolling off my tongue before strolling away again.

"Duh. That was stupid. Sorry." She tucks it back in her bag as she mumbles to herself.

"No big deal. The regulars won't bother, but there's always a few stragglers in here. They wouldn't care about how things would turn out."

She sighs, wrapping her hands around her glass. "Getting robbed isn't what I was looking for."

Her face shutters and she looks miserable. I don't know how to salvage this. My window of seduction is swiftly closing, and I have to act fast if I want to spend more time with her.

"I'd save you if they tried. White knight and all that. Kind of in the job description." I smirk, ducking my head to catch her deep blue eyes.

A small smile forms on her lips, the dimple reappearing. Maybe this night won't be a complete bust after all.

"What else is in the job description for white knights? I've never met one before."

I tap my finger on my glass, and I feel her gaze tracing the tattoos on them before following them up my arms and finally settling on my face.

"Riding around on a white steed, saving damsels in distress, ya know, regular knight stuff."

She giggles and turns toward me. "And you can wield a sword, right?"

"Course. Question is, can *you* handle a sword?"

Her mouth falls open, then snaps shut. I watch the emotions flit across her face, but they're too fast to decipher. She bursts out laughing, and I can't help but grin.

"Does that line actually work?"

I shrug. I don't normally flirt, so I don't have any practice. The women I sleep with are down for the release, maybe looking for a romp with the tatted bad boy who rides a motorcycle. None of them catch my interest long enough to try to flirt. This woman is like the good girl you meet at one of those fancy parties the Kings are always going to. I wouldn't be surprised if she came from money.

"What did you call me before? What does it mean?" she asks, tapping a finger against her glass.

"I can't tell you. Secret knight language," I murmur.

"Listen, I'm going to be completely honest here..." she starts before pursing her lips.

I hold my breath, but she stares into her empty glass. "You going to finish that sentence? Or should I guess what you're thinking?"

Her spine straightens before she spins on the stool. "I've never done this before, but I've had a shit day. Actually, a pretty shitty couple of months. So, I'm trying something new. Do you wanna come back to my hotel room?"

I slide off the stool, gesturing her to the door. "Lead the way."

Chapter Two

Willow

My stomach is a riot of butterflies. Can butterflies even riot? I don't know, but my fingers tingle, and my heart races. I don't think I've ever been this nervous before. The tall, dark biker's hand swallows mine as he tugs me out the door. I don't even remember the name of the place.

I hope no one recognizes me later. I'm sure Mac goes here. I didn't intend on going into Reaper territory, but when the driver asked me where I was headed, I couldn't think of anywhere else.

I've never been to Synd, and I left Rima in a hurry, hopping the last train out, without doing any research on what was here. The hotel I'm staying at isn't the nicest, but at least I don't feel like I'm going to get kidnapped going through the lobby. Robbed maybe, but not kidnapped.

A thrill crawls its way up my spine when I glance at the guy pulling me along. He's at least a foot taller than me, not that it makes him tall. I barely top five feet. I shouldn't have misled him, but when I walked into the bar, something came over me. Playing up my ignorance on all things MC seemed like the best way to start a conversation with him.

I snort, and he glances over his shoulder, raising an eyebrow. I shake my head, throwing a half smile his way. A couple bikers hanging around outside start hollering at him and he flips them off, tugging me until I'm to his side.

"You okay riding?" he asks, his smoky voice washing over me and I shiver.

"Riding what?"

We stop in front of a motorcycle, the neon light glinting off the chrome. I take a step back, eyes widening.

"I only have my bike. I've got this, if you want." He drops my hand and reaches for the helmet hanging off the side.

"I've never rode...ridden...um, I've never been on one."

My stomach turns, but not with butterflies. Now it's a raging swarm of wasps, intent on making me puke all over this ridiculously hot man.

"Not hard. All you have to do is hold on to me. Oh, and lean into the curves," he smirks, his green eyes twinkling.

"But...but there's nothing between you and the road. What if you fall? What if a tire blows? What if someone hits you?"

Trying to calm my racing heart, I bounce on the balls of my feet. I always refused when Mac urged me to get on a bike. Eventually she stopped asking.

"I'm not going to fall. If a tire blows, I'll deal with it. No one is going to hit me, because I pay a-fucking-ttenion. You'll wear this helmet. Oh, and don't pass out. I'd rather not have to scrape you off the road," he says, handing me the flimsy plastic I'm supposed to trust to protect my brain.

"What?" I whip my head up, hugging it to my chest.

"Kidding." He throws his leg over the bike, planting his feet on the gravel.

I scan his body, taking in his thick muscles and strong jaw. The nerves I had before when I propositioned him come back full force, right along with the desire. I didn't lie, I've never done this type of thing before.

I don't know his name. I don't know what he does. I don't even know if he's actually in the Reapers. The only people I've heard Mac talk about are Ryker and Hawk, and I'm banking on this guy being a random member I won't see much of, if ever. Mac and I haven't exactly had a lot of time to catch up. I shove the helmet over my head, hoping my hair doesn't get too staticky.

"How do I get on?" I ask, my voice muffled. He tugs me forward, adjusting the strap under my chin. His fingers brush my throat and I tremble.

"Step here"—he points down—"then swing your leg over. Don't fall off the other side."

I roll my eyes as he faces forward and grabs the handles. I plant my foot right where he said, hopping on the other to get some momentum. I might be psyching myself up. Both my hands are on the seat, inches away from his ass, looking extra delicious in those jeans. I tear my eyes away, focusing on getting on this thing. It's huge compared to me. I'm afraid my legs aren't long enough to sit properly, but I've seen little kids do it, so I should be able to as well.

He reaches back to grab my hand, and put it on his shoulder. I squeeze tight before launching my leg over. As my ass plops down, he grips my thigh, stopping me from sailing over the side just like he warned, and I swallow the gasp trying to escape. When he squeezes my leg, another flood of desire engulfs me, settling straight between my legs. This was an excellent idea. I've never had a one-night stand, but if I can manage to not die on the way there, I am here for it.

"You actually have to hold on to me. Remember, no scraping you off the road," he says.

He tenses as I slide my arms around his waist, fingers dipping under the leather vest he's wearing. There are patches and numbers all over the back. I stare at them, instead of looking around. I don't want to know when we take off. My stomach can't take it.

He pushes the kickstand up, then balances. The rumble of the engine is loud, even through the helmet. The vibrations are like nothing I've ever felt before, and I have more than a few toys that vibrate at home. When he eases forward, we lurch and I yelp, gripping his waist tighter.

Before I know it, we're flying into the night, and I start muttering prayers to whatever god I can remember. I don't want to get scraped off the road any more than he wants to deal with that mess. Thankfully, I told him the address before we left. Even if I didn't have the urge to faint, he'd never hear me over the wind whistling past us.

After five minutes, my muscles relax, and I'm able to at least peer around a little. Still not entirely a fan when we have to stop, but he doesn't seem to mind my nails digging into his skin. A curve appears ahead, and he leans, guiding my body with his. When we tip a little more a scream escapes me, and I thump the helmet into his back as his shoulders shake.

It feels like forever, but then he pulls into the hotel's parking lot. The doors are on the outside, so maybe this is actually a motel. Whatever. It was cheap and they took cash. I only have to stay here one night anyway. I thought it looked okay when I got here, as the sun was setting. Now it looks ominous, like there could definitely be a drug deal going on out back and a porno being shot next door.

"Are you sure you should be staying here? It's a little sketchy," he asks after he turns off the bike. I'm struggling with the helmet strap, trying to find the clasp when he knocks my hands out of the way and unclips it, pulling the helmet from my head. As I expected, my hair stands on end, swirling around my face and defying gravity. He smooths it down, sending a shiver through me, before stepping back.

"It's only for one night, but it didn't look this bad during the day. Not going to lie, I'm kind of glad you're here. That van gives me the creeps." I point to the white vehicle with no windows on the sides and his eyes follow.

"Yeah, we're going the long way around that one." He clips the helmet back on the hook before grabbing my hand and tugging me along.

"Should you leave your bike out like that?" I ask, glancing back.

I stumble on a crack in the parking lot and he catches me, wrapping an arm around my waist to hold me up. As he presses me against his hard body, a worm of self-doubt slithers in.

"I'm not worried."

I rummage around in my purse and pull out an actual metal key. This place doesn't even have automatic locks. It does have three deadbolts inside, though. My hand trembles when I stick the key in the lock, and I angle my body so he doesn't notice. I can't tell if it's nerves or anticipation rolling through me. I've never had the quintessential bad boy interested in a romp in the hay with me, and now I'm wondering if I can live up to whatever fantasy he's conjured in his head.

I shove open the door, having found out the hard way it sticks. My toe catches on the threshold and I tumble through. As he catches me from behind, a high-pitched laugh bubbles out and I press my lips together when he releases me.

"Sorry, I'm a little clumsy."

He raises an eyebrow before glancing around the dingy space. The furniture looks like it's straight out of the 80s, complete with an old tube TV. There are approximately seventeen channels on it, all showing absolutely nothing. I don't expect us to be doing a lot of binge watching though.

I wring my hands, confused on what to do now. I figured picking up a guy at a bar would be easy. I'd show I'm interested and we'd go someplace. I'd board the beef bus and then...actually I have no idea what happens after. Does he stay and cuddle? Do I ask him to leave? If he asks for my number, I might jump out the window. Do I say, "Thanks for churning my butter, hopefully we never cross paths again"?

Shit. How do I act if I do meet him again? I mean, I *did* go straight into Reaper area—territory—and pick up someone in a biker gang. I shake my head. There's no reason to think I'll be spending any time with any of them.

I've known Mac for five years now, and I've only been to Vipers' headquarters once. She always told me it wasn't a place I could go. Her brother runs the Vipers, but she said she doesn't have the authority to let me hang around. She keeps me in the dark about most things with the MC. I don't even know if other bikers run their shit the same way the Vipers do.

I'll probably spend most of my visit with Mac in the city. The worst that'll happen is seeing him in passing. It'll be awkward, but we'll survive, I'm sure. As long as I don't have to admit to Mac I knocked boots with one of the Reapers, I can handle it. Maybe.

"This is...nice," he chokes out, scanning the room.

"It's only for a night." *Like us.*

He nods, pressing his lips into a thin line. I take advantage of his distraction to scan his body. Staring, I see how ridiculously hot he is. The sharp angle of his cheekbones, the fullness of his lips, his broad shoulders tapering down to a trim waist covered in jeans that only accentuate his ass. I swear to all things holy, I am going to climb this man like a tree.

He seems like the kind of guy who throws a girl on the kitchen table, or takes them on the back of his bike to do the deed. Those fantasies always feel like they'd be thrilling in the moment, but then I'd end up banging my elbow on the corner of the table. The one time someone tried to bang me in the shower, I slipped. It wasn't very sexy to say the least. I'm too short for crazy excursions in random places anyway. There's never enough height or length or whatever to get to the finish line.

Most of the time I don't care, but it'd be nice to actually experience being on top and have an explosion of pleasure. It's why I don't usually date men as tall as this guy. Less of a shock when I refuse to stuff the muffin on the kitchen table. I rear back, realizing I've been staring for a whole minute ogling him and thinking about riding his pony express.

"We don't have to do this, you know," he says, gruffness lacing his tone.

"No, I want to. I just haven't done it before." I wrap my arms around my waist, squeezing, hoping to settle my stomach.

"Wait, you haven't done *what* before?" Panic overtakes his face as his eyes widen.

"Oh, no! I've had sex before. I just haven't done the whole one-night thing." I don't know if calling this a one-night stand is okay, but it's out there now.

Relief floods his face. "If you want to stop..."

"I don't. If I do, I'll let you know."

He gives me a look I can't decipher. I may not do this type of thing, but I'll definitely stop him if I'm uncomfortable.

He stalks forward, and I drop my hands to my sides as my eyes dart around, finally settling on his face. He smirks, hands gripping my waist, and a thrill runs through me as his thumbs sneak under my shirt to circle my hip bones. Warmth seeps into my skin, and tingles bounce around my body.

I take a deep breath, giving into the sensations he's dragging from me. I may not know how to have a fling with someone, but I certainly know how to fuck. I drag my hands down his chest and slip my thumbs into his waistband, before yanking him closer. Tipping my face up, I stand on my toes when his mouth swoops down, taking my lips.

I expected fireworks. I didn't expect an explosion. His hand ghosts along my side until it reaches my hair, twisting around the strands. He tugs, angling my head, so his lips can glide along mine. I dart my tongue out, licking at the seam of his lips and then his own is dueling with mine.

He guides us backward until my shins hit the bed frame, and then we're falling. He catches himself on his elbows, but our mouths stay fused together. He'd suffocate me if he dropped on top of me, and I run my fingers under his shirt, scraping his hot skin with my nails.

Before I can register what's going on, my shirt is whipped over my head. His own follows as he sits back, fingers wrestling with his belt before shoving his pants down and kicking them off. I lift my hips to shimmy out of my leggings, thanking all that's holy I decided to opt for comfort over style. He bats my hands away, peeling the fabric from my legs, leaving me in only a black thong and lacy bra. His gaze travels down my body, leaving goosebumps in their wake.

I don't have the full tits and grabbable hips Mac does. I like my body, but I've had men walk away at this point in the game. My mystery man's green eyes are on fire, though, blazing a path along my flushed skin.

I sit up, grabbing the waistband of his boxers and yank him on top of me again. The jeans may have highlighted his ass, but they hid what he is packing in them. He's hard, grinding into me, while his mouth nips down my neck.

My bra pops off, and he shoves the cups up, squeezing my tits together to nuzzle them. A moan leaves me, and I grip his hair to keep him from moving on. When he swirls his tongue around a nipple, my hips buck. I bend my knees, if only to draw him closer and an ache builds in me. My body flushes and trembles when he moves to the other bud while rolling the nipple he abandoned between his fingers.

Usually, my nipples aren't this sensitive. Whenever I'm with someone I let them play, but it's more for them than me. Maybe they just don't know how to get my engine going though, because this man knows exactly what he's doing to drive my body further along the lust express. He's still sucking on my skin when his hands drop, and his hips lift to pull my thong off. His boxers join the rest of our clothes strewn about the room, and I finally see him.

He freezes while I stare at his cock. I'm not one to examine the nether regions of men, since most of them aren't all that pretty, but his is hard to miss. I'm not going to write sonnets dedicated to it, but he's definitely beyond what I've seen before. Wiggling up the bed, I clamp my knees together. He ducks, pulling an obviously extra-large condom out and rolling it on. Thank god, since I'm pretty sure I would have fucked him bare without a second thought.

Crawling onto the bed, he pushes my knees a part to kiss along my thighs. His tongue darts out and licks right up the center, flicking my clit. My entire body spasms, and I whimper. My pussy clenches as he presses kisses up my stomach, then nips at each nipple before settling between my thighs, his tip nudging into my core. Then he stops, gazing down. I pull my knees up again, and he slips further into me.

"Please," I beg, squirming beneath him.

He surges forward, thrusting into me and I gasp, fingernails digging into his arms. He rolls his hips while I adjust to his size, and with each shallow thrust, a bolt of pleasure pulses through me. When I can't take it anymore, I wrap my legs around his waist. My heels barely reach to hook on to each other, but I manage. Burying his face into my chest, he groans.

My legs fall to the sides as he kneels, latching on to my hips before pounding into me. I dig my fingers into the sheets, holding on while my climax builds. A cry of frustration spills from my lips when he stops and pulls out completely.

Grabbing my ankles, he flips my body, the smell of bleach and sex filling my nose as my face is buried into the sheets. I yelp when he grabs my hips again and yanks my ass up in the air. Groaning, he slams back in, the new angle sparking a flame in my gut and another moan leaves me.

He leans down, covering my body with his to whisper in my ear. "You didn't think I would leave you unsatisfied, did you?"

I shake my head, an unintelligible noise escaping me.

"I'm going to ruin you for anyone else," he growls, slamming into me with every word. I shudder, pushing back to meet his thrusts. His fingers pinch my nipple before finding my clit. He presses and rolls until I'm thrashing under him, my orgasm hitting me hard. He sits back to grip my hips again, and fucks me through the fireworks flashing behind my eyelids. The coil in my stomach is already tightening again.

"Be a good girl and come for me again," he grunts, driving into me harder and faster. His words spark another explosion and I cry out.

His chest covers my back, before his arm wraps around my waist. I can't remember the last time I went twice in one go. Sex doesn't last long enough, usually. But this man seems like he could go for hours and leave me a purring mess of contentedness. He slows, blowing out a breath through gritted teeth. I spasm around him again and he grunts.

He grabs a pillow and shoves it under my stomach before easing my hips down. Turning my head to the side, I can just make out his rugged face, a feverish look in his eyes as they sweep over my body. He digs his fingers into my ass, thrusting into me again. I don't have it in me to do more than moan into the scratchy hotel sheets. He's muttering something, but I can't hear the words over the roaring in my ears.

I push back, meeting his thrusts, our gasps filling the room. I tumble over the edge again, a weightlessness enveloping me, as he groans long and low, cock twitching inside me as he finally erupts. His nails digging into my ass send another wave of ecstasy through me, and I whimper. As he collapses, he holds his weight on his elbows before pressing a kiss to my shoulder.

"Was that what you were looking for, *léaró dóchais*?"

A sigh is my only answer.

Chapter Three

Hawk

The sheets beneath me are scratchy and reek of bleach. The exhaustion from earlier in the night has settled into a bone-deep satisfaction. I roll my head, looking toward the bathroom where the woman disappeared ten minutes ago. I assume she's cleaning up, but there's no sound coming from the room. She *did* say she didn't understand how one-night stands worked. Does she think she has to hide in the bathroom until I leave?

I clear my throat, pushing myself up to gather my clothes. Spinning around, I look for the garbage can. Honestly, I don't do this sort of thing often either, although sometimes a one-night stand is easier, especially right now. My life is enough of a mess without adding more drama. She's already made it clear this is for one night, and I'm fine with that. The more I think about it, the more I wonder who I'm trying to convince.

I finally find the garbage under the sink, which is right outside the bathroom. I contemplate knocking, but I don't want to freak her out more. I pull my clothes on before sitting on the mussed-up sheets. We didn't even get the thin comforter off before I was pounding into her.

Pulling out my phone, I find three texts from Helms, each one more ridiculous than the last. It's after two in the morning, but his sleep has been messed up since he was shot. Oftentimes I'll have fifteen messages from him when I wake up.

Five minutes later I'm still staring at his texts, waiting for the mysterious woman to reappear. The shower isn't going. The toilet hasn't flushed. The sink is outside the room, so she's not using that. My chest tightens and I wonder if I fucked up. She was enthusiastic and definitely enjoyed it, unless she's a very good actress. I mean, she could be, since I know nothing about this woman other than the sounds she makes when I'm inside her. I don't even know her name.

A thought tickles my brain reminding me how familiar she looks, but I swear I've never met her before. She isn't from around here, but maybe I met her in Rima, when I was growing up. The thought sends a shiver down my spine.

I'm not going to sit here all night. I doubt she wants me to stay, and I certainly don't want her to hide in the bathroom until morning. I push myself up, and find a pad of paper before scribbling a note on it. Seems weird to thank her for the fuck, but I don't want her thinking I skipped out without a word. Glancing once more at the bathroom door, I listen for any indication she's about to come out. It stays closed though, so I grab my jacket, locking the door before I walk out.

The night is cooler now, but not by much. The creepy van is gone, but my bike is where I left it. No one would dare steal it unless they have a death wish. We're close enough to Reaper territory everyone would recognize the decals on the saddlebags.

I swing a leg over my bike and head for home, the knot in my stomach sticking with me the whole ride. I don't know if I made the right decision to slip out without a word. Maybe I should have knocked, or at the very least called out to her. I shake my head as I skip up the stairs of my front porch. No reason to keep worrying about things I can't change.

You could go back.

Nope. I'll never see her again, so it doesn't matter. In hindsight we should have talked about it, but I won't make a fool of myself chasing after her, even though I might want to. I barely know her and I have no time to pursue anything anyway. Best to leave it be.

A pounding on my door has me bolting upright. I fumble with my phone, finding it's barely past seven. Four hours is not enough sleep, especially now. I stretch, easing my tight muscles as the pounding continues. It'll be Helms and I'm not ready to face him yet. He's going to toss a shit ton more on my already full plate. Eventually he'll come barreling in, shouting, whether I answer or not, so I slide off the bed and pull last night's pants on before shuffling down the stairs.

"What?" I grunt as I rip open the front door.

"Hello to you too, asshole," Helms says, shoving past me.

Following him into the kitchen, I collapse on a stool at the breakfast bar. My house is small with no space for a dining table. It's only me here, so I don't mind. I don't have what Helms has. He has MacKenzie now, filling up his space, making his house more like a home. He wanted me to move in next to him, in the old VP's house, but I don't need all that space. More hassle than it's worth.

"Did you need something?" I ask as he digs in my fridge. I don't know what he's expecting to find. I mostly eat at his house, so there's only condiments and cheese in there.

"Couple things. Have a good night?" He glances over his shoulder, raising an eyebrow.

"Busy. The drop went fine. Tank is trying to expand, set up some new routes. Trigger is wanting to put in a hot tub in the bar, so he's pissed at me." I drop my head on my arms and close my eyes.

"He can't have a fucking hot tub."

"Why do you think he's pissed at me?"

I yawn, wishing I could kick him out. This is the problem with him being both my best friend and my president. He gets double the respect from me, and I never want to piss him off. I didn't have anyone to rely on for a long time, and I'm not going to fuck up my friendship with him because I'm tired. He slams the fridge door shut before leaning against the counter.

"Heard you were busy with something else after that. Care to share?"

"No. What did you need to tell me?"

"Fine. Be an asshole. Those contractors you hired? They're shit. I thought I told you to get the Raines' house fixed up? Kenzie's friend is supposed to be in town any day now and she's got no place to stay."

I jolt upright, wide awake now. "What the fuck did the contractors do? They were supposed to be done with the kitchen and master bedroom by now, plus the flooring. I went by there two weeks ago and it was on schedule. Mother-fuckers." My mind starts listing all the shit I need to deal with. "When is her friend coming?"

"Don't know. Willow said she was trying to find the right time to come from Rima, whatever that means." He rolls his eyes as he pulls out his phone.

I tense as his words filter past the lingering exhaustion. My stomach knots as I watch him swipe at the screen. There has to be hundreds of Willows in Rima. There's no way Mac's Willow is the same one I know. The coincidences would be astronomical.

Memories flash through my mind, and I slam my eyes shut, trying to calm my racing heart. The teenage Willow of my past swims up from the depths of my mind, a tiny wisp of a girl, looking much younger than I assumed she was. I never met her in person, but the media loved her. Just looking at her, you knew she came from money, never having to work a day in her life. They can't be the same girl.

"I can't do everything at once. I'll get to dealing with the Raines' house when I've got the rest of the shit fixed with the roads. They're almost done, but there's something going on with the lights."

"I hope you're not keeping shit from me. I am capable of running the Reapers, ya know." Helms glares, crossing his tattooed arms.

"I've told you everything you need to know," I say.

"Not the same thing, dick. I'm not an invalid. We need to start transitioning back to normal."

Mac comes waltzing into the room as if she owns the place, and I scowl.

"Morning, Hawk. You a little sleepy today?" she asks, smirking.

"Fuck off. I've been working my ass off, and your asshole boyfriend woke me up at this ungodly hour for a bunch of bullshit that could have waited. You need to keep a leash on him."

I just want to go back to bed. My dreams were filled with the mysterious blonde woman from last night. I'll be using our time together as inspiration in the shower for quite a while. Not like I'm going to go searching for someone else to ease the tension.

"I'm going to start taking on some things you've been doing. Help ease the load. Contrary to what Kenzie thinks, I am capable of doing my fucking job," Helms says.

"Oh, you are?" She spins to face him, a sly grin on her lips. "So, you don't need help showering anymore?"

"If you two are going to start fucking, I'd rather you not do it on my counter. Especially while I'm here."

Neither of them notices. They're too busy eye-fucking each other. I don't have the mental strength to deal with their lovey-dovey shit this early in the morning.

Mac's phone rings, stopping them from making the situation more awkward. When she answers it with a screech, Ryker and I wince.

"Willow St. James. What do you mean you're already in town? When did you get here?"

Her mouth is still moving, but the roaring in my ears drowns her next words. No. I must have misheard. There's no way Mac's friend is Willow fucking St. James. Of all the fucking people in Rima, Mac has to be friends with that rich bitch. How they even met in the first place is beyond me. Willow St. James is an elitist, rolling around the upper set of Rima's society. Their worlds couldn't be further apart.

My vision blurs, and I slam my eyes shut, but the same vision of Willow when we were young swims into view again, conjuring up images from my past. I gag, reliving the worst time in my life. I'm pretty sure my hands are numb, but I push to my feet anyway.

"Hawk," Helms's voice rumbles in warning.

"I'm fine. I have things..."

My brain scrambles to find an excuse, anything to get me far away from here before I lose it entirely. I shouldn't take my bike, but an itch scurries down my leg, begging me to get far away. I shouldn't. This is my home, but the urge to run, like every time before, is so strong it almost sends me crashing off the stool.

"What just happened?"

"Nothing. I'm fine. You gotta go."

He nods, searching my face, but I turn away. The room shrinks, and the need to get out overwhelms me. I try to keep my steps measured, but when I hit the stairs, I scramble up them. Slamming my bedroom door open, I brace my hands on my knees as I suck in deep breaths. The mess I found myself in wasn't Willow's fault, but her family represents everything I lost. Everything that was ripped away from me.

Creaking on the stairs pulls me from my thoughts, and I straighten right before a knock rumbles through my room. I spin, and pull it open to reveal Doc. He used to be a therapist or psychologist or something so he's usually a good person to spill to, not that many of us do. He's got a way of ferreting out feelings and making me confront them dead-on before I even realize what he's done. I'd rather not deal with him today.

"Helms said you needed to talk?" He raises an eyebrow, scanning me from head to toe.

"I'm fine," I wheeze, still trying to get enough air in my lungs to slow my racing heart.

"Hawk, you'd better start talking, or I'm going to drag your ass back downstairs and force you to deal with whatever bullshit you're hiding from Helms and Mac."

I shake my head, staring at my bare feet. I can't tell them. Mac will defend her friend, say Willow had nothing to do with it, and I should let it go. She'd be right. Willow didn't have anything to do with what happened to me, but I'm not about to spill my past if I can help it. Helms will side with Mac. It's a lose-lose situation no matter what I do.

I understand the hierarchy has shifted since Mac came back into his life. I don't begrudge her for it, but I refuse to leave the one place I've felt like I actually belong. And that's what I'd probably have to do if I told them about what Willow's father did to me. I cross my arms, feeling sanity seep back in.

"I'm fine. The last couple of weeks, hell, the last couple of months haven't been easy. Lots of stress is all. I'm going to get dressed and go for a ride, then I'll get back to dealing with shit. We've got a meeting tomorrow. Make sure everyone is there."

He's silent for so long, I wonder if he's planning on staring at me until I confess. I won't, but that wouldn't stop him from trying to pull the last dredges of memories from me. Eventually, he tilts his head as he presses his lips into a thin line.

"I'm calling bullshit. When you're ready to talk about it, I'm here."

I think about denying it, but Doc's past makes him extremely adept at sniffing out lies. There's no way he'll buy whatever shit I shovel at him. I don't know why I thought I could get away with it in the first place.

I nod, avoiding his eyes to glance over his shoulder. I can see the kitchen over the banister and I spot Mac standing there, concern lining her face. I want to think she'd understand if I told her about the shit Willow's father pulled, what he did, but I won't put her in that position. I won't make her choose. Not only because I'm pretty sure she'd pick her friend, but also because I'd rather not lose another person in my life. I won't let anyone take anything more from me than was already stolen.

Chapter Four

Willow

The bright light from the morning sun wakes me. The curtains in this hotel are flimsy, just like everything else. I should have stayed somewhere a little less shitty, but I didn't want to spend more money than I needed to. The fact I left Rima with the small amount I had stashed away was ballsy enough. Now, I don't know if I can go back without a shitstorm waiting for me. I need to conserve the cash I have, and blowing it on a fancy hotel room isn't in the budget.

I wonder if I made the right decision. I've never had the option to get away before, so I don't know if I would have done this years ago. This time around, I was backed into a corner and couldn't see my way out.

I'm pretty sure my stepfather was gaslighting me when I came to him with my concerns. He wasn't my first, second, or hell, my eighty-seventh choice to ask for help, but with Mac gone, I didn't have anyone else. He brushed off my worries, told me to stop being paranoid and to grow up. I snort when I remember I'm twenty-six. I'm plenty grown, with nothing to show for it.

Most would say I've led a privileged life, after my mom married the prestigious Judge Joseph Merrick. They'd be wrong. Sure, I didn't have to worry about a roof over my head, but that was about it. In fact, I'm pretty sure he threatened to kick me out more than a couple of times. Having money and having security are two very different things.

I used to dream about being back in the shitty apartment my mom rented for us, barely making ends meet after Dad died. She thought all our problems were solved when Joseph came into our lives. Mom never understood I would have traded the clothes and status in a heartbeat to go back to the way things were. She wanted a better life for me, and gave up hers in my stead.

My phone buzzes, pulling me from my thoughts. I snatch it up and grin when I see Mac's name flashing across the screen.

"What's up, honeydew?" I say, sitting up. The bed frame creaks, something I didn't notice last night with my hot knight. I blush, remembering the positions he had me in. I'm not a prude, but that was the hottest sex I've ever had. Thinking back on it, maybe I am a prude.

Mac laughs, making me grin again. "I can't figure out if I want you to stop calling me that, or if it's still funny."

"Still funny. You're the one who said you had melons for thighs," I say.

"Whatever. I talked to Blue. It's a no-go on the car. I don't want you taking a service here, so we're bringing someone to pick you up. Don't fight me on this, Willow. I know you don't want to get on a bike, but he's very responsible and an excellent rider. He'll make sure you don't end up getting scraped off the road. Plus, he's hot." Mac squeals, her muffled voice scolding Ryker. "Sorry. You'll think he's hot. I think he's average. Nothing like squeezing your thighs around a tight ass to make you forget there's nothing between you and the road."

I bite my lip, keeping to myself my late-night ride from the bar. I don't want to tell her I went into Reaper territory. She was pissed enough when I told her I got in last night and didn't call. I'm definitely not going to tell her I hooked up with one of their bikers. A shudder overtakes me, imagining her reaction.

"That's fine. I'm a big girl. I can handle it. But how are we going to get my bags?"

"Shit, that's right. How attached are you to your suitcases?" Men's shouting voices seep from her end, then abruptly cuts off.

"I mean, they're just a couple duffle bags." I eye the two black bags, hoping she doesn't comment on the fact I don't have actual luggage. To my eyes, it's obvious

I was in a hurry when I packed. Although, Mac grew up in a different world, so maybe she won't even realize.

"Perfect. So, Ryker and I will lead Hawk to the hotel, and we'll just get them on the bikes. It'll be fine. If all else fails, I'll call Sam to come meet us. She'll be grumpy if I wake her up this early though, so we'll try this way first. Be ready in thirty." She hangs up before I can answer.

My stomach rolls, wondering if this Hawk guy could be the man from last night, but I push away the thought. It would be too much of a coincidence. Another twinge hits me when I make it to the bathroom, remembering how I hid from him.

I don't regret anything. When I made it to the bathroom though, my emotions were all over the place. I haven't slept with someone since I broke up with my ex-boyfriend six months ago. The guy last night was nothing like him. Half the time I had to fake it with my ex, while some random biker got me off three times in less than an hour.

I huff out a laugh as I get in the shower. As the water washes away the sweat from last night, I close my eyes. I thought about taking one when I was hiding out, but there wasn't any products and I couldn't bring myself to do it. Once I plucked up enough courage to leave the safety of this small space, he was gone.

The door was locked, sheets still rumpled, air smelling of sex. He left no trace of who he was other than the used condom languishing in the trash. I don't know what I expected, but I didn't think he'd bail without saying anything. I still don't know how to feel about him taking off without a word, but maybe that's the way these things are supposed to go.

The water turns cold five minutes in, and I rush to finish. I'm shivering by the time I step out. Hopefully, wherever Mac has me staying has hot water. I don't know if I can deal with cold showers for however long I stay in Synd.

Throwing one of the bags on the small desk, I pull on clothes over my damp skin. I can't bring myself to bother with makeup. My hair is still dripping when the handle jiggles and I freeze, eyeing the door. All three deadbolts are flipped, but someone could break it down if they were strong enough.

"Willow, open up!" Mac's muffled voice rings out.

I let out a heavy breath, finally able to move my feet to swing it open.

"What the hell? Why didn't you just knock?" I scowl.

"What would be the fun in that? Plus, I needed to make sure you weren't being an idiot in this part of town. Seriously, could you have picked a sketchier motel?" She barrels inside before stopping in the middle of the room to scan the space.

"It was only for one night. I'm fine." I roll my eyes, throwing the last of my stuff in the bag.

"Well, let's get out of here. This place is giving me horror movie vibes. Did you check for random holes in the wall?"

She pulls me into a hug, and I'm dwarfed. Mac is at least eight inches taller than me. I feel like a child being hugged by her, but I'll never turn one down. She's the only one I get them from these days.

"Are we leaving or are you going to keep smothering me?" I ask, voice muffled by her shirt.

She pushes me backward. "Shut it. I missed you. You'll have to tell me everything your dick of a stepdad has been up to lately. Oh, and why you didn't feel the need to tell me you were in town last night instead of this morning."

She pins me with a glare, and I grin while blushing. Part of me didn't want to bug her so late, just like I told mystery man, but partly because I wasn't sure she'd be okay with me showing up unannounced. I didn't want her to feel obligated to take me in, even for the night. At least if she said I couldn't come this morning, I could get right back on a train. Maybe I'd ride the rails all the way to some random place I've never heard of before. Anything to get me away from the shit going down in Rima.

"Sorry?"

"Whatever, whore. Oh, this is Ryker." She gestures behind her, and I lean to see around her body. "Be nice," she mutters to him.

I try to wipe all emotion from my face, but I'm pretty sure he notices my stunned expression. Not only is this guy a hulk, he's also pretty hot. His eyes are the brightest blue I've ever seen. Between his rugged face, tattoos running up and down his arms, and the leathers, I don't think I've ever seen someone more intimidating. He looks like he stepped straight out of a biker movie. Mac says he's a big teddy bear, but I'm convinced that's only for her.

Doubt floods me. Maybe I shouldn't have come. I ran on a whim and there's enough going on in my life that if my problems follow me here, I might be fucked. The president of the Reapers doesn't look like he has a sympathetic bone in his body. Sure, he helped Mac, but he's in love with her. From what she says, he's been in love with her for years. I'm not even close to important enough to protect. This was my last resort, but now I'm rethinking all my plans.

I startle when Mac's hand wraps around my arm. "You okay?"

"Sorry, yes. I'm fine." I glance at Ryker as he comes up next to us. "You're tall."

I laugh nervously. Anything to cover my inner-turmoil.

"Am I tall or are you short?" Ryker says, smirking. He glances at Mac and his face morphs. I swear his entire demeanor transforms as his eyes soften and the smirk turns into a smile. I never understood when people said they wore their heart on their sleeve, but here's the evidence right in front of me. A pang runs through my chest, and I rub the spot, trying to ease the ache. Jealousy turns my stomach, but I shove it down. I'm happy for Mac, and I won't let her think otherwise.

"Oh, I am short. A curse most days, but at least I can shop in the kid's section for shoes."

Mac laughs, gathering my bags. I reach for them, but they're yanked from her hands by Ryker, who stalks out the door with them.

"He's a little overprotective. Come meet Hawk. He's nice. You'll like him. How long are you staying? Did fuckface kick you out? How is Rima? Any word on the Night Slayers?"

She pops off the questions rapid-fire as she pulls me from the room. I'm used to her not waiting for answers. Most of the time we don't have long enough to sit around and chit-chat. Either she's being pressured to come home or I'm being followed. It's never fun to hang out when we know someone is watching us.

"Are you sure he's okay with..." I stop, staring at the man leaning against the bike across the parking lot. He's parked in the same spot he was last night. My random one-night stand. My sexy mystery man. My absolutely nothing since he slipped out without a goddamn word.

I thought I was okay with it, seeing as how I hid in the bathroom for twenty minutes, but now I'm pissed. He could have knocked. He could have called out. He could have waited. Instead, he slipped out like a thief in the night, as if what we did was dirty. I'm surprised he didn't leave some money on the nightstand.

He's scowling, as if he'd rather be anywhere other than here, picking my ass up.

You and me both, buddy.

He obviously didn't think he'd be seeing me again either. Good. I shouldn't be the only one feeling awkward. He can't be upset with me though. I didn't do anything wrong. It's not my fault we're in this situation. We both knew what we were getting into.

He probably didn't think you were Mac's friend, while you knew he was in the Reapers.

Mac is halfway to him before she realizes I'm not moving. She glances over her shoulder, giving me a look and gesturing me to hurry up, and I force my feet to start walking.

I try to wipe my face blank, but based on his nostrils flaring, I don't think I pull it off. He's not hiding anything, but now I'm really not going to admit to Mac I slept with this guy. She'll never let me live it down. Or she'll push to get us together. I cough, cheeks blazing.

"Willow, this is Hawk. He's going to give you a ride. Don't worry, he's really safe and won't dump you, so you don't have to be nervous. Promise," Mac says when we reach him. Her head whips back and forth, waiting for either of us to speak.

"Hi," I whisper, giving him a little wave.

He grunts in response before turning to his bike and unclipping the helmet I wore last night. He shoves it at me, forcing me to grab it before it can hit the gravel. The asshat still hasn't met my eyes.

Mac leans in, whispering, "Sorry. He's been acting weird today. Do you two know each other?"

I shake my head, watching as he swings his leg over and starts the bike. I didn't realize how loud the engine was last night, but now it's deafening. Hawk stares straight ahead, even when Ryker calls out to Mac. She gives me a confused smile before skipping toward him.

I watch as she walks across the parking lot and hops behind him. My eyes are still tracking them as they pull away and spin out of the lot. I don't know what to say to this man. Sure, we talked last night, but that was flirty banter. I don't think that'll work now. I could make a joke about him being my white knight, but I think if I open my mouth I might puke.

"Get on," he grunts.

I stare at the seat, contemplating how to respond. Clearly, he's regretting our night together. Or maybe he's just regretting the fact he has to be around me again. Maybe what I thought was an amazing experience was terrible for him.

"You're not just a member, are you?"

"What do you know about that shit?"

"Not much. Mac said she was keeping me in the dark 'for my safety'." I don't mention all the things I've picked up along the way. That'll only complicate this more.

"Are you getting on or calling a car?" He drops his chin to his chest, still refusing to look at me.

I scan the parking lot, nerves building in my stomach. When he revs the engine, I whip my head back. The dickhead is kicking up the stand and rolling forward, as if he'll leave me here.

"Wait," I shout over the rumbling, and stumble toward him. "You're not going to leave me here, are you?"

"Those are your options, St. James. You ride with me or you call a car. I guess you could always walk, but I don't advise it."

"I don't know why you're being such an asshole." I'm tripping after him as he circles around the lot. I probably look like an idiot. "Would you fucking stop? My fucking god."

"Such a mouth, geesh," he says, but at least he stops.

I push the helmet over my still wet hair, finding the strap still fits perfectly. I put my hand on the seat again, hesitating for a minute as I eye his shoulder and the bike jerks forward. Silently cursing him, I switch my hand to his shoulder, and his muscles flex under my fingers. Launching myself over the seat, I almost slip off the other side. His hand doesn't stop me this time, and a pang hits my chest.

I knew running into him was a possibility and I assumed it would be awkward, but this is a whole other level. I thought I could handle the fallout of a one-night stand. Now, my one night of fun, of freedom from everyone else dictating my life, is imploding right before my eyes. Why I thought I could handle this shit is ridiculous, looking back. I wanted one goddamn night of fun and this is what I get for it? I could handle the embarrassment, but he's treating me like I'm the problem, like I planned this or something.

Huffing, I realize I'm pissed. Fuck him if he thinks he's the only one this affects. I'll ignore his shitty attitude for now, but if he pushes me, I'm not holding back. I'm sick of getting kicked around and walked all over. If I have to take a stand, it might as well be with him.

Chapter Five

Hawk

My palm itches to reach back and steady Willow as she settles on the seat, just like I did last night. Resisting the urge, I squeeze the handles tighter. I hold still, trying to will away my raging hard-on.

When Ryker told me I was coming with to pick up Willow St. James, I almost refused. I should have, especially now that I know the woman I fucked last night is one and the same. Of course, my life couldn't be easy. The minute I gave in to my urge for a release, I fucked it up.

There's no reason for her to recognize me from Rima. We've never met—not officially. We didn't run in the same circles when we were younger. She was too rich, too smart, too important to associate with someone like me.

"You have to hold on to me. Remember, no scraping you off the road," I say, my words sending a pang through my chest.

I brace myself for the feel of her arms circling my waist, but my muscles twitch when she slides them around me. I push the kickstand up and balance. I'm trying to ease into it, but we still lurch forward, and her hands gather fistfuls of my shirt, nails digging into my skin. She's muttering something, but between the engine and the helmet, I can't make out the words.

I open the throttle as we ease on to the road. Typically, this is my favorite time of day to ride with traffic being sparse this early in the morning. I wish I was outside the city limits, blasting over the road, but I don't think Willow would appreciate the detour.

Taking a corner, I lean with the bike, and she yelps. The helmet bangs between my shoulder blades and I grin.

In this moment, I'm not reliving the past or remembering the consequences I'll have to face because of my night with the woman currently clinging to me. Right now, I'm enjoying the thrill of sharing this ride, this sense of freedom with someone else.

Ten minutes later we're pulling into Ryker and Mac's driveway. We barely stop before Willow slides off the side. I shoot my hand out to catch her so she doesn't stumble into the hot engine, but she rips her arm away. She's still struggling with the clip on the helmet when I turn the bike off and dismount. I watch her for another minute until her muffled curses fill the space between us. She pushes the shield up, her blue eyes blazing when they find mine.

"Would you like some help?" I ask, raising an eyebrow.

"It's stuck," she huffs.

"It's not stuck. You're just not pushing the clip in."

I reach out and bat her hands away. She sucks in a breath when my fingers brush her throat, just like last night. I undo the clip quickly before tucking my clenched fists behind my back. I try to keep the tremor from my fingers, but can't. My mind is warring with my body—one wanting to forget and the other refusing to wipe the images of her writhing under me away. Her hair doesn't stick up this time and another pang shoots through my chest. I don't know if I'm relieved or disappointed to be honest.

I didn't want to walk away last night. For some reason, I thought this woman was exactly what I needed in my life. My stomach rolled the entire ride home, remembering how I left her. I fought the urge to go back while I tossed and turned in my empty bed. I don't know if it would have changed how I felt had I known who she was.

Willow thrusts the helmet into my chest, waiting until my hand closes over the edge before stomping off. I don't know why she's so pissed. She's the one who knew she was fucking one of the Reapers, while I had no idea she had any ties to us. She said she'd never had a one-night stand, so maybe she assumed she'd never see me again. I certainly thought that's what would happen.

She pivots when she reaches the bottom of the stairs. "You don't get to be mad at me."

I clip the helmet on the hook and straighten, crossing my arms. "Who said I'm pissed?"

"Your actions are speaking much louder than your words."

I don't know where the flirty banter from last night went, but in her place is a raging viper.

"All I've done is give you a ride." I smirk.

She snorts, gazing down the street. "Don't be an ass. I didn't do anything wrong. I wasn't the one who slipped out like we did something dirty."

I wipe my face, remembering the reasons why I can't associate with her more than absolutely necessary. Clearly, she's harboring regret at how we ended things, but she'll have to deal with those on her own. I can't afford to get caught in her web. Even if I could forget the family she comes from, rich girls like her never last long with bikers like me. Add in the fact she's Mac's friend and the cards are stacked against us.

"Depends on your definition of dirty, but don't worry, St. James. We won't be repeating past mistakes. Have fun explaining shit to Mac." I don't even bother to mention the note I left.

I'm gone before she can recover, her reply lost in the rumble of my bike. I don't have a destination in mind, but I turn into my own driveway a few minutes later anyway. Doc's and Ryker's bikes are parked out front. The last thing I need is a lecture. They can bitch among themselves. I swing back around and ride to Trigger's.

Trigger lifts a hand when I settle on the same stool I occupied last night. I reach over the bar to grab a beer, flipping him off when he scowls. It's not even close to noon, yet I'm posted up at the bar, avoiding everyone. The place is still a mishmash of the old space it was before the Night Slayers burned the old bar down and whatever Trigger wants it to be now.

"What the fuck is wrong with you?" Trigger asks, pulling me out of the dark cloud swirling around my head.

"Nothing," I grunt.

"Doesn't look like nothin' Looks like you're running from somethin'."

"Fuck you, Trigger." I take another swig.

"Do I need to call Prez? Have him knock some sense into you? This about that woman last night? Should I call Doc and have him make you talk about your feelings?"

"I'm fine. I just need a break. Are you going to keep being a shithead or leave me be?" I snarl, bracing my hands on the bar.

"Fine, be a dick, but I'm still calling Doc."

He turns, pulling his phone from his pocket and following through on his threat. The last thing I want is to be ambushed by him and his asinine assessments of my mental state.

I hop off the stool, leaving the beer where it is, when Doc's hand lands on my shoulder, pushing me back down. He's huge and regardless how soft-spoken he is, he's more than capable of keeping me right where he wants me. It's the reason he's our sergeant at arms and general enforcer. Most members don't mess with him.

"How the hell did you get here so fast?" I grumble, grabbing my beer. Trigger sets another one down for Doc, smirking.

"I was already on the way. Helms may have told me about your interaction with Mac's friend earlier."

He settles in, leaning on the bar. I'm not about to explain myself, so I lean forward too and drink.

"You talking about the woman from last night? That what he's all twisted about?" Trigger asks, making my stomach tighten.

Doc waves him away, then turns. "How do you know Willow St. James?"

"I don't."

"Then why the hell wouldn't you introduce yourself? Talk to her? She's going to be here awhile, ya know. Not exactly the way you want to start."

I snort. "She doesn't need to introduce herself. I don't really care what she thinks of me. Just because she's here, doesn't mean I have to interact with her."

"Okay. What the fuck is going on with you? She's attractive. Is that it?"

I knew I was going to catch shit, even before I showed up at her motel this morning. There have to be thousands of Willows in Rima, but of course Mac's friend has to be *that* Willow.

I doubt there's a person in my hometown who doesn't know who she is. Not surprising the other Reapers don't recognize her. Her daddy isn't very well known outside his city. The fact I fucked her last night adds a whole other layer to my conflicted feelings. The only way I'll get any peace is if I shut this shit down now.

"I don't give a flying fuck if she's the most beautiful fucking woman in the whole goddamn world. I wouldn't go near her with a ten-foot pole. I'll put up with her for Mac's sake, but don't expect me to bend over backwards to be nice to that viper."

I push back from the bar, and when Doc doesn't stop me, I twist, intent on getting on my bike and riding as far as I can get with the remaining daylight.

I jerk to a stop when I spot Mac's stormy face. I can just make out Willow tucked behind, her blonde hair swinging forward to cover her face. Her small hand wraps around her friend's arm before tugging her back.

My face turns stony, staring down a murderous Mac. I refuse to apologize, whether I'm terrified of her fiery temper or not. This is one of the few things I won't budge on. I've made my decision and I'll stand by it. Mac can rail at me all she wants. I will never grovel at Willow St. James's feet.

I swing around and grab my beer, walking to a booth in the back. This is Reaper territory and as vice president, I have the right to be here. I try to push down the guilt swirling in my stomach, but it's useless. I feel like a fraud. I don't want to feel anything, but can't stop reliving her beneath me, ecstasy stamped on every inch of her body. I wish I could be apathetic, but between the guilt and the memories of the judge's face glaring down at me from his bench, damning me before I even had a chance, I won't be able to accomplish apathy.

There's too much shit standing in the way for me to forgive Willow, even if she didn't do anything wrong. Shaking my head, I rub at my eyes as doubt clouds my mind. I'm so fucking confused.

Trigger slides in the other side of the booth, resting his elbows on the table and I turn to watch Mac and Willow make a quick exit. There aren't many people around, especially this early in the day.

Before the Night Slayers burned down his bar, a lot of the locals under our protection would come to eat at his place. Now it's mostly members, since there's no food. We're rebuilding, but it's not a quick job. I've been fighting with contractors so they don't gouge us, but I'm running out of threats. I'll have to reach out to the Kings to see if they have anyone else we can use. Helms wants the Raines' house finished, but he doesn't understand it's not an overnight project. Just because Willow wants to stay there, doesn't make the situation urgent—not to me.

"We going to talk about you being an ass?" Trigger asks.

"I'd rather not."

"Did you meet her before last night?" The easiest thing to do is lie, but I doubt I can keep my contempt for her family under wraps for long.

"I've never met her before, but I know who she is now."

"Well, that explains something. What happened last night? She break your heart?" He chuckles.

If only it were that simple. I inhale slowly, trying to steady my racing heart as memories rush back to me. Her whimpers echo through my mind and I shake my head. I slam my eyes shut, but all I see is her smiling face, calling me her white knight.

"No. Last night, hell, even what I know about her, isn't worth the words. Definitely wasn't that sort of thing though. Don't go pushin' shit around about her and me. In fact, keep your opinions to your fucking self. And don't fucking tell Helms I left here last night with her."

The last thing I need is everyone gossiping about us. Even though I don't want to have anything to do with her, I don't want anyone thinking she's something she's not. And with our recent past, people will want to talk. The least I can do is head shit off at the pass.

Tank stomps through the door, doing a double take when he spots me before hurrying to the other side of the room. Apparently my little tantrum got around quickly. Or maybe he's in the shit with the prospects.

"Prez isn't going to be very happy with you. You know how he is with Mac. I imagine he's going to be pretty protective of her friend too," Trigger says, as if I need the warning. Helms has already been up my ass about not pissing Mac off.

"I'm well aware. I plan on staying as far away from her as possible."

Chapter Six

Willow

"Leave it alone, Mac. He knows I'm Willow St. James. He's going to blame me for something I had nothing to do with, all because he hates my stepfather. Not much I can do about it. This kind of thing happens more than you'd think." I slump onto the bed.

I've known MacKenzie for over five years, and I'll never be able to repay her for being my friend. She was there when I went through all the shit with Joseph, my stepfather, encouraging me to set boundaries and eventually giving me a safe person to run to. I'd be on the streets if my family ever found out I was cavorting around Rima with her. My stepfather doesn't bother with the Vipers, labeling the bikers as annoying gnats. Having me hang out with them though, would be a blow to his reputation. If he paints them as a school-yard gang, others won't take them seriously. Can't have a stain on his precious city. I roll my eyes at the thought.

"Is Hawk from Rima? Maybe that's how he knows who I am, or knows Joseph."

"I think so. Still, it's not right. Are you sure you've never met? Hawk isn't the type of guy to judge you by your family. You'd think he would get to know *you* before he started spouting shit."

My stomach turns as I track her pacing back and forth in the spare bedroom I stashed my bags in. I told her I wasn't going to intrude on their space, but she insisted I dump my stuff here before checking out the house next door. I feel weird, taking over an entire freaking house, but Mac isn't concerned. Ryker merely grunted when I thanked him.

"Calm down. It's not a big deal. He can hate me all he wants." My words turn to ash in my mouth. "I'll just stay out of his way as much as possible. Not like I wanted to see him again anyway." I grimace. I don't know how I'm going to accomplish that, but hopefully we won't be forced to interact much.

"I don't like it." Mac collapses on the bed next to me and we both lie back, staring at the sunbeams dancing over the ceiling. My fingers find hers, lacing them together.

"I missed you," I murmur.

"Me too. Was it bad?"

"It wasn't fun, that's for sure. The Night Slayers were burning buildings and terrorizing people. Joseph kept bellowing about those dirty bikers every chance he got. I thought he was going to pressure the commissioner to call in a SWAT team to push everyone out. I kept trying to call you, but you never answered. I'm really glad you're okay. I don't know what I would have done if something happened to you."

"You're a good friend, Willow," she whispers.

"You're my only friend, so safe to say I'm going to keep you around as long as I can." I giggle. "You're the only one willing to put up with me."

"You just haven't met the right people. You'll like Sam. She can be your friend too," she says, but a knot forms in my stomach.

"It's going to change though, isn't it? You're going to stay here and live happily ever after, and I'm going to have to go back to that shithole." My heart skips a beat. "Sorry. I swear I'm happy for you. I shouldn't be complaining."

Mac grins. "I'm happy for me too, but you can complain all you want. Unless you want me to bitch you out..."

A soft knock on the door has my head swiveling as it inches open and Ryker's head pops in.

"What the hell are you two doing?" he asks, narrowing his eyes.

"We're talking. It's what normal friends do," Mac laughs. I expect her to jump up, but she stays beside me. Maybe it won't be so different.

"I'm pretty sure neither of you are normal."

"Hey, you don't even know me yet. I could be exceptionally normal." I frown.

"You're friends with Kenzie. You can't be normal if you're friends with her," he snickers.

"Good point," I say.

Mac smacks my arm before swinging off the bed and rolling her eyes. "Get ready so we can go eat. I'm starving."

I turn away when she reaches him, not willing to intrude on their time. I never know where to look when people start all the lovey stuff. Mac laughed at me the first time I turned away when a couple started making out right in front of me. Apparently, PDA isn't an issue for most people. Plus, I didn't come here to rain on their parade. I'm happy for them, but it doesn't mean I'm not a little jealous.

I shut my eyes as they close the door, and Hawk's face floats through my mind. My blood heats and my cheeks burn. Hawk is not the person I should be imagining in a romantic way. We had one night that he's now pissed about for reasons unknown. I'm going to move on with my life. Was it probably the best night of my life? Yes. Do I want a repeat? Maybe. Do I wish I would have come out of the bathroom sooner? Yeah, I really wish I would have. Maybe things would be different now if I had. I fucked up, but I'm not going to let him get away with treating me like shit either.

I shake my head, vowing to push his shitty attitude aside and enjoy the respite from the last few months in Rima. I never told Mac how long I planned on staying. Extended is such a fickle word. She'd let me stay for months if I asked. I wonder how much pull Hawk has and if he'll try to kick me out before long. I'll ride this train as long as I can, because I can't go home. My stepfather isn't the only reason I need to be far away from Rima.

I yank clothes from my bag. They're wrinkled, but I wasn't worried about folding shit when I skipped town. I change before throwing my hair into a ponytail. It's stringy since I didn't brush it. Hell, I didn't even dry it before I was flying down the street on the back of Hawk's bike. I don't know how Mac's hair always looks so perfect, regardless whether she's done anything to it or not.

I skip to the door and my stomach growls, reminding me I haven't eaten since I left Rima.

"You okay?" Ryker's voice has me stumbling back, almost tripping over my feet.

"Holy shit. You scared me." I laugh, pressing a hand to my chest.

"Sorry. Are you okay?"

I tense when I meet his bright blue eyes. Mac tried to warn me he was intense, but I didn't think him simply looking at me would be so powerful. Shit, I've been staring at him like a creeper for too long. My eyes widen, trying to remember what he asked me. Shit.

"I'm good. Long day." I smile, but he narrows his eyes before nodding. He gestures me to go ahead of him and the thought he might push me down the stairs races through my mind as I take the first step, but I shake my head. Ryker isn't going to attack me. He's not going to hurt me. He's not going to kill me. If I repeat it enough, my mind will accept it and I won't be skittish around him.

"Of course you look fucking amazing," Mac huffs as I reach the bottom. I step to the side quickly to let Ryker pass.

"I'm wearing jeans, not a freaking ball gown."

"Still look hot."

I roll my eyes. "Still have no ass, but thanks."

"Not all it's cut out to be, sweetie. Trust me."

Ryker snakes an arm around her waist. I'm pretty sure he's squeezing her butt.

"I happen to like your ass," he says.

She giggles and I wander away, still not ready to deal with their affection. The living room is cozy, not as big as I imagined. Photos line the mantel and I stare at the middle one, filled with a group of laughing kids frozen in time. There's another photo of Ryker and Mac in front of his bike. I spot Hawk, grinning, in another frame with a bunch of bikers. I swear his entire face is transformed, closer to the man I met last night. Gone is the scowling asshole. He looks happy, like he couldn't ever imagine a better place than here.

"That's some members from a year ago, right before the Guild came in trying to take over. A lot of them aren't here anymore," Mac says.

I glance over my shoulder. "Like dead or...?"

"People don't leave an MC. At least in our kind of clubs. The only reason Ryker let my dad leave is because it was right after Ryker's dad died and Ryker took over. No one wanted to fight anymore."

"Ryker didn't want you to stay?"

A flash of pain crosses her face and I wish I could stuff the words back in my mouth. "We've never really talked about it, have we?"

I shake my head. "You don't have to tell me."

"No. It's okay. Ryker was doing what he thought was best. Maybe he was right. If I had stayed, we might not be together now. I'm trying to be okay with what we have instead of living with the what-ifs," Mac says. She glances toward the kitchen where Ryker disappeared. He's wiping down the counter, though it looks spotless.

"Is he okay?" I ask.

"Yeah. He cleans when he's got something on his mind. Don't worry about it. Let's go to lunch. I can hear your stomach from here."

She links her arm with mine, calling to Ryker. I reach for my purse by the door, but she yanks me past. Ryker's footsteps pound on the porch stairs behind us and Hawk materializes from the side of the house, waylaying him. He doesn't look in our direction, but there's a frown on his face. I swear to god, his cheekbones were chiseled from some type of stone. What do they say? Chiseled from marble? Something like that.

Mac pulls my attention back by yanking me to sit on the bottom of the stairs. I watch Ryker and Hawk wander toward their bikes in a heated conversation.

"Are we not talking about why you're avoiding shit?" she asks.

"What shit?" I murmur, praying she didn't find out I slept with Hawk.

"Hmm, like how you came to Synd without any warning? I'm not complaining, but you clearly took off from Rima without a second thought."

"I may have gotten into an altercation with Joseph. He's not happy with me, so I took a little break." I hold my breath, hoping she doesn't ask more questions.

"Well, shit. He going to send someone after you? I'll have to warn Ryker if that's the case."

I shake my head before glancing at the pair. "I'm sure it'll be fine."

"Willow, are you sure you're okay? He isn't hurting you, is he?"

I wave away her questions. "My illustrious stepfather is an asshole, but he's not that kind of asshole. He's more of a 'cut you off and leave you destitute' rather than 'cut off your fingers and leave you fingerless.' You know how he is."

"I do, but I also know there's a thin line between controlling and psycho. I want you to tell me if he crosses it, okay?"

A shiver runs down my spine. I open my mouth, ready to spill all my secrets, but snap it shut when I notice Ryker and Hawk, making their way toward us.

"For sure, but I swear it's fine. I mean, he's still a dickbag, but it'll be okay. I might be disowned after this, but it'll be worth it. I hate being put on display, like I'm a show dog," I say, bitterness seeping into my tone.

"Well, you're more than welcome to stay here as long as you'd like. Hawk's been fixing up my childhood home. It's not great, but it's livable. You can always stay here with us. I figured you'd rather be there, since I know how you get about sharing space." She smirks.

"And listen to you two bury the sausage? No way. I'll stay there, as long as there's no snakes." I brush my hands down my arms, smoothing out the goosebumps as I imagine them slithering over me.

"You two ready to go?" Ryker calls.

I expect Hawk to take off, but he stays right where he is, planted next to his bike. I thought we'd be taking a car, but only the motorcycles are out front.

"Uh, Mac? Are we taking those?" I point to the hulking machines. I figured after the incident this morning, plus the one at the bar I wouldn't have to see Hawk much. He made it clear he wants nothing more to do with me.

"Yeah. I tried to borrow Blue's car, but he needed it. Sorry. I'm sure Hawk will be on his best behavior. Ryker talked to him. Honestly, he's a really good guy. I'm sure once he gets to know you things will be better. Maybe you'll even..." She wiggles her eyebrows.

I swallow the nervous giggle threatening to escape. This is going to be just great.

Chapter Seven

Hawk

Three times in one day is too much for my cock. At least the first time I got relief. Now, I'm being forced to schlep prissy Miss St. James around like a chauffeur. I'm following Helms, Willow's arms wrapped tentatively around me. I assume she's getting used to riding, since she doesn't have a death grip on me. As she leans back, throwing off the balance in the process, I wrap my fingers around her wrist and yank. Her chest hits my back, helmet bouncing off my shoulder blades. I grit my teeth. It's not worth scolding her for it. She'd never hear me over the wind anyway.

I almost keep going when Helms pulls into The Flaming Skillet's parking lot. Of course he came here. He probably did it on purpose, just to piss me off. I contemplate going home, but I won't let this woman run me out of my own territory.

I hop off the bike as soon as I park, not waiting for the others. Willow barely drops her arms before I do, and she ends up tilting to the side and stumbling. I shoot out a hand, but yank it back before I touch her. I wonder if I can get away with sitting at a different table.

Once inside, I hold up four fingers to the server before she can greet me. Eyes widening, she takes in my face and grabs the menus before hurrying off to a booth. I'm about to say something, but she tosses them down and then bolts for the back, black hair whipping around, before I open my mouth. I sit, knowing I'm going to be forced to sit next to Willow.

Willow stutters to a stop, eyeing both sides of the booth. Glancing around, I search for Helms and Mac. Willow starts to slide in across from me, but twists at the last second, falling on the seat beside me. She lets out a small "oof" as I slam my elbows on the table, hanging my head so I'm not tempted to stare.

After a whole minute of blessed silence, she clears her throat. "Do you like being the vice president?"

"Why the fuck do you care?" I snap.

My head drops to the table, inwardly cursing myself for answering. Do not engage—my number one rule when it comes to dealing with her and I've already broken it. The less I talk to her, the less I'll relive last night.

"I don't know why you're so pissed. I'm not the one who gallivanted off into the night without a word," she hisses.

"I'm not the one who hid in the damn bathroom for a fucking hour," I snarl.

Her head whips around, mouth falling open, but she snaps it shut when Helms and Mac slide in the opposite side.

Mac immediately starts prattling on about the menu, oblivious to the tension swirling around us. Helms isn't as unobservant though. His eyes are fixed on me with a frown splashed across his face. I'll hear about it later, but he won't say anything in front of St. James.

Willow sweeps a menu toward me, but I don't bother with it. I'm here enough that everyone knows my name, food, and position in the MC, which is precisely why I didn't want to come here in the first place. Hopefully I can get through this and still come back later. I spot our server and mutter a curse, and I catch Willow pursing her lips.

"Well hey there, Hawk. Long time, no see," Mia grins, rolling her eyes from me to the others before zeroing in on Willow. I'm suddenly very happy I took the inside. Mia doesn't have many boundaries, even more so since I made the mistake of sleeping with her two years ago. I've told her it wouldn't go anywhere, but it doesn't stop her from flirting.

"Mia," I grunt.

"Oh, I know you," Mia says, leaning toward Helms, practically in Mac's lap. The server smashes her tits together, giving him what she thinks is a sultry smile.

"Back the fuck up," Mac snarls.

A snort leaves me, followed closely by Willow's giggle which she smothers with her hand. I glance at her and she catches my eye. Staring at each other, her smile slowly fades and I rip my gaze away to glance out the window as my stomach turns. I can't afford to give in to the feelings swirling inside me. I need to remember all the reasons she's off-limits, starting with her stepfather.

"My bad, girl. I see you." As annoying as Mia is sometimes, she doesn't get in another woman's business. "So, what are we having?"

The rest order but Mia just nods to me before flouncing away to the back. Helms stares at me and I raise an eyebrow and thus the silent conversation between us starts. He pushes me to engage with Willow and I tell him to fuck off. The girls are embroiled in some asinine conversation about the server's outfits and whether they're from the 40s or 50s. When they fall silent, Helms's eyes call me an asshole before turning to Mac.

"Why didn't you order?" Willow asks.

"Don't need to," I mumble.

"You come here a lot then?"

"Yes."

"That's nice. Having a place to go where they know what you want must be nice. Oh, and they probably ask about you, worry when you're not here for a while. That must be nice."

"Stop." It's the only thing I can think to say to get her to stop saying the word "nice". I'd rather have Helms silently berating me than listen to her force conversation between us.

"Sorry," she whispers before turning away. My chest tightens, hearing the tears in her voice. She clears her throat and I sneak a glance from the corner of my eye as she plasters on a fake smile, looking toward Mac.

I shouldn't feel bad, but I do. Last night shouldn't change the way I feel about her, but it does. It's not even her I'm pissed at. We left things weird, but I don't blame her for hiding in the bathroom. I should have done something different.

Who her family is shouldn't dictate who *she* is, but separating her from them is hard. Judge Merrick ruined my life, derailed it completely, costing me everything. Sure, it led me here, to the Reapers, but I'll never get back what I lost because of him. I'll never get back what I could have been.

"We need to talk to one of the Kings or Byrns. See if they've got anyone else for contractors," I say, capturing Helms's attention.

"What else is wrong with the contractors we have?"

"They're all shit. Half the time they don't show up. So, it's either fire them or kill them and I figured you wouldn't appreciate a bunch of bodies floating down the river, leading straight back to the club."

Willow twitches, her arm brushing mine. Goosebumps erupt on my skin and I suppress a shiver.

"You thought right. We can't afford the cops coming around again. The shit with the Night Slayers already has us on their radar and I'd rather not have to get Shane involved. I told Alex to lean on the commissioner to get them off our back, but I haven't heard from him in a few days."

"I'll text him. See what's going on. They get rid of Munther yet?"

Helms shakes his head. "I imagine he's easy to placate. Only reason they'd keep his ass in the seat."

"That and the fact he's not smart enough to try to fuck them over like Alan did. I doubt the Wraith wants to take out another commissioner."

"Does that type of thing happen a lot?" Willow mutters.

I snort, causing Helms to glare, as if I'm the one responsible for scaring Mac's friend. I assumed Willow knew how an MC does things, with her associating with Mac whose brother runs the Vipers in Rima and operates much like we do. I don't understand how she can have a friend like Mac and not see how we run our part of the city. Shit goes down and we take care of it. We're not out here offing random people, but we protect our own, plus the innocent bystanders who live in our territory. When someone crosses us, we deal with it, though that doesn't happen often. It helps that our territory isn't very large, only taking up a couple dozen blocks on the north side of Synd. I can't imagine dealing with the large swaths of area the Kings and Byrns are responsible for.

"You remember how Dante kept saying you weren't allowed to come by? This was the reason. He didn't want you caught up in shit, not only because of, well you know. But you saw what the Night Slayers did to Rima. Sometimes the MC has to shut shit down so it doesn't spread. Hawk isn't going to go around strangling construction workers because they're not rebuilding Trigger's fast enough." Mac laughs.

"Course." Willow shakes her head. "The Night Slayers are gone, by the way. Whoever was left packed up and skipped town pretty quickly. I went by to see if I could find Dante, but that one guy said he wasn't back yet. Have you heard from him?"

Mac grimaces. "Shouldn't have done that, Willow, but I did get a cryptic text message. I swear if he took off to some tropical island to have an extended vacation, I'm going to sic Hawk on him to wring his neck." Mac mimes strangling her older brother.

"You make me sound like a serial killer." I rub a hand over my mouth to hide my grin.

Willow tenses and I tip my head to the side to find her staring at the table, hands wringing in her lap. The bell above the door chimes, and she whips her head around, blonde hair almost slapping me in the face. I rear back and follow her gaze. A couple teenagers stumble in, elbowing each other and laughing. Willow's shoulders relax and then she squeaks, jumping when Mia drops a plate in front of her.

"What the hell did you order?" I didn't mean to say it so loudly, but the words hang in the air between us, as I eye her plate.

"Corn beef hash. Have you had it before? It's delicious. I hope they made it right. A lot of places under cook it or burn it. It needs to be crispy, crunchy, but still have enough softness to it. A lot of people don't like it because it's salty."

"Or because it looks like dog food," I mutter before stuffing eggs in my mouth to give me an excuse to stop talking. The smell of her food hits me then and I gag. Snatching up my water, I gulp half the glass before slamming the cup down. Then my lungs try to eat themselves and I end up inhaling the liquid.

"Are you okay?" Willow's small hand lands on my arm, but I yank it away.

Feeling her skin on mine is too much. It reminds me of how soft she felt under me, how she tasted of sunlight, and the whimpers falling from her lips when I was deep inside her. I suck in a breath, immediately regretting it when I catch a whiff of her food again.

"Sorry," I mutter, directing my apology to Mac. She looks appalled and I don't blame her. My mind is ping-ponging between wanting Willow and wanting to be as far away as possible.

Willow pulls her plate away, almost hanging off the edge of the booth. I huff, tipping my head back. I need to get my shit together. I need to deal with her being around. Ignoring her isn't going to work. I'm not going to be able to stop myself from wanting her. One-night stands were all well and good—until now.

The only thing I want is to bend her over the booth and sink into her again. I want to throw her over my shoulder and ride off while she slides her hand to my cock. I want...I want to stop this line of thought, since all it's doing is making me hard again.

"Didn't you order over easy eggs?" I mutter, glancing at her plate of un-touched scrambled eggs.

"Oh, um, yeah? It's fine," Willow says.

"But you ordered something and didn't get it. Where's your sausage?"

"I like bacon too. It's not a big deal." Willow's cheeks flush, as she tips her head forward, hiding her face behind her hair.

I don't acknowledge Helms's stunned look as I lift my hand to catch Mia's attention. Her hips sway as she comes around the counter and up to the table. I look away, not wanting to encourage her.

"What do you need, sweetie?" Mia asks, leaning against the table.

"You fucked up her order," I growl, pointing to Willow's plate.

"Oh, no idea how that happened." She smirks.

"Fix it, Mia. Now."

"Don't get your panties in a bunch, geesh. I'm sure she'll be fine with what she's got, won't you?"

"She won't. Get her what she ordered." I stare at Mia until she straightens, an understanding flashing in her eyes. She nods before hurrying off to the kitchen.

"You didn't have to do that. I was perfectly fine," Willow hisses.

"Fine isn't good enough."

I don't know why I'm fighting this. It shouldn't matter. I shouldn't get involved in her shit. The fact she was just going to choke down what they put in front of her, though, is too ridiculous to ignore. I imagine Mia did it on purpose.

"Willow doesn't like to fight," Mac says, eyes fixed on her own plate.

"That right?"

Most of our short time together has either been fighting or fucking. Maybe I bring out a side of her Mac rarely sees. The thought sends a thrill through me.

"I'm not a big fan of confrontation, for reasons I'd rather not talk about," Willow says through gritted teeth.

"Well, now at least you'll have what you wanted in the first place because of Hawk," Mac says, widening her eyes. "Say thank you."

Shit. I should have just kept my fucking mouth shut.

Chapter Eight

Willow

I stare at Mac, begging her to drop it. Between Ryker and MacKenzie, we're going to end up either killing each other or falling into bed again. I smother a snort, tucking my chin to my chest. There's no reason I should be thinking about sleeping with him.

I'm going to ruin you for anyone else.

And damn if he wasn't right. Apparently, I was looking in the wrong places before. I'm still pissed he walked out, but I could do with another round. Everyone is gaping at me, while my shoulders shake. This is completely the wrong response, both to my thoughts and to what Mac demanded from me.

"Thank you," I gasp.

I swallow causing a bubble to get caught in my throat and then I'm choking. Drinking doesn't help. I'm pretty sure it makes it worse. Suddenly, Hawk slaps me on the back and the bubble descends.

"What the fuck was that?" Ryker barks. Mac is halfway out of the booth, hands reaching out.

"Holy shit, that hurt." I groan before taking another drink. "I had a thing in my throat. It's fine. I'm fine."

Hawk hovers over me, half standing. My back stings where he hit me, but I'm not going to complain. I'm pretty sure he just saved my life or something. Probably not, but it felt like I was dying.

"This is the weirdest fucking meal I've ever been to," Hawk mumbles under his breath, settling back in his seat.

"Get used to it," I whisper. "They're intent on shoving us together, and I'm not exactly normal."

He gives me a look, but I go back to eating. There's no reason I should elaborate. Better he knows I'm a weirdo from the get-go. Then whenever he's forced to be around me, he won't be surprised. Shit like this happens all the time. I'm a klutz, mostly tripping over my own feet. My life has been a shit show from the beginning.

In fact, I should be in therapy. Most of the time I'm convinced no one wants me around and they're merely putting up with me. The first time Mac asked me to hang out, I cried. No one ever invited me to anything unless they wanted something from my stepfather or were chasing his clout. When Mom married him, I didn't understand what was so important about being a judge. I soon found out Judge Merrick has a lot more reach than a normal person should.

"Seem normal to me," Hawk mutters.

His plate is almost empty, while I have yet to receive half of what I ordered.

Maybe I can salvage something if I can keep him talking. "What's with the server?"

He swallows, waiting so long I think he's going to ignore me, when he says, "Made the mistake of sleeping with her once. She'll figure it out."

"Figure what out?"

"That she shouldn't be a bitch to you."

I don't know how to respond to that, so I focus on my food. The rest start talking, but I keep my head down. A plate of over-easy eggs and sausage appears at my elbow. I look up to thank the server, but she's already halfway back to the kitchen. I stab the sausage, ignoring the fact it's probably too hot, and shove the end in my mouth. There's a gagging noise next to me and I swing my gaze to Hawk. He's beet red and coughing.

"What?" I ask around my food.

"Nothing. Just...knock it off." He coughs again, burying his face in his hands.

"No idea what you're talking about." I shove the other end in my mouth and Mac begins to laugh. "What?"

"Oh, sweetie. I love you. Never change," Mac giggles.

"Mmmk," I mumble before shoving the rest in. It's good, the spices exploding on my tongue.

Hawk was right. This is the weirdest meal I've attended too. And I was there when the mayor's wife got called out for sleeping with the police commissioner's son. That was probably the best luncheon I've ever been to. For once I could sit back and watch the drama unfold and not worry about the backlash from Joseph.

"So, what are we doing the rest of the day?" I ask, eyeing Mac.

"Ryker and I have some things we need to take care of. In fact, we have to go to Rima. We're leaving tonight—be gone a couple of days." Mac pouts, an apology in her eyes.

"I knew I should have called. I can...uh...I can just go back too. No biggy."

I can feel my body coiling tighter. My heart races, and my palms start to sweat. I drop my fork before wiping my hands on my jeans to erase the anxiety. I have enough money I could stay at the motel a couple more days. I could hop on a train and go somewhere else—anywhere else. It hits me that I can't go back to Rima, regardless what I just said to Mac.

He'll find me for sure then, if my stepfather doesn't first. Joseph doesn't think *he's* a problem. No, Joseph thinks my being followed is nothing to worry about. He kept reassuring me that it was some man who was only interested in me to get to him because he's a judge. Joseph didn't see the latest "gift" left by my secret admirer though. I shiver and my stomach flips.

"You can stay here."

I expect the words from Mac, but they come from Hawk. I was trying to keep my emotions under wrap, but he must have noticed. He's giving me a look between concern and annoyance.

"Of course, you can stay here! I know you need a break, Willow. We'll be back in a couple of days—a week tops. We're just bringing Maddox back to the

Vipers. Blaze said they'll keep him there until Dante shows his face again. Hawk can keep you company," Mac chimes in with a smile, like she's solved all our problems.

Hawk's face says something different. The concern vanishes from his eyes, replaced with suppressed rage. I don't know what his problem is, but we're going to have to address it soon if he's going to be forced to play babysitter.

"Change of plans, Kenz," Ryker says, staring at his phone. "We have to leave now. Like, right now."

Mac scrambles from the booth and Ryker follows. She leans down, gathering me in her arms and hugging me tight. I cling to her, trying to hold back the tears and hide the tremors in my hands.

"It'll be okay. Call me if you need me," she whispers before pulling back, waving as she walks out the door. I scan the diner only finding an old couple in the corner glaring at the group of teenagers a few seats over from them.

I spin back and stab another sausage to shove that one in my mouth too. I should move to the other side of the booth, but my appetite followed Mac out the door.

My eggs have gone cold. There's no way I'm choking them down, so I mix them up with the fork. I swallow before I've finished chewing the sausage and almost choke again.

Hawk hasn't said a word, but I get the feeling he knew this was happening long before I did. I don't think he realized he'd be looking after me though. Or maybe he didn't and he's just as blindsided as me.

"You don't have to hang out with me. I can just do whatever," I mutter before draining my glass, and he grunts. "We can go. I'll get the check."

I look around for our server, Mia, but she's disappeared.

"We don't need to pay. Finish your food." He pulls out his phone, set on ignoring me.

Picking up my fork, I stare at my plate, but my stomach rolls. This whole trip feels like a waste and I haven't even been here long, and I doubt it's going to improve with time. I just wanted to get away from my stepfather's controlling ways. I wanted to get away from the feeling of someone watching me every time I stepped out of my house. I wanted to get away from the creepy presence leaving gifts for me on the doorstep.

Joseph kept telling me they were nothing—that I was bound to attract attention based on his position, but I couldn't shake the feeling it was something more than an ardent fan seeking my attention. The last "gift" scared me enough to come here. If I can spend a little time away, the gifts will disappear, right along with the itching feeling between my shoulder blades.

"I'm not hungry anymore. Can we go?" I whisper.

I'm not able to hide the tremor in my voice or my hands, so I fold them in my lap and clamp my lips together. I could walk out, but that would be rude. Hawk is my ride home, and I don't want to piss him off enough that he'll leave me.

I'm slowly beginning not to care anymore. I haven't even known this man for forty-eight hours, and I don't know where I stand with him. One minute he's gagging over my meal and the next he's demanding they make my order right. He's going to push me until I snap.

"Fine, but I'm not getting you food early just because you didn't finish your lunch," he snarls as I slide from the booth.

"Okay, boss," I say, sarcasm dripping from my voice. He rolls his eyes as he throws some cash on the table.

At least he tips.

The bell above the door chimes again and my hairs whips across my face as I strain to see. A dark-haired man stands at the front door, head tucked to his chest. I tense, craning my neck to check out the window. I see a fancy car in the lot, which has my stomach cramping. I thought once I made it out of Rima, my nerves would settle, but if anything, I'm jumpier.

My breath hitches when his head lifts before scanning the small space. I step back, tucking myself behind Hawk. He's at least a foot taller than me, so I can easily hide my frame behind his.

"What the hell are you doing?" he snaps, glancing over his shoulder.

I shrug, forcing a small smile on my face. He scowls, grabbing my hand and pulling me toward the door. He stops suddenly and I stumble into his back. Dropping my hand, he looks down at his own palm before his forest green eyes burn into mine. He swings around, and the dark-haired man lifts a hand to Hawk. They must know each other. A whoosh of air flows from me as Hawk snatches my hand again. I hope I don't puke all over them.

"Mason," Hawk rumbles. They shake hands, but Hawk doesn't drop mine.

"Hawk. We need to meet later. I've got some shit for you to go through." Mason's voice is gravelly, as if he doesn't use it a lot.

I make a note to ask Mac what they're putting in the water around here. Every person I meet seems to be hotter than the freaking sun. Most of the men I have to associate with are classically handsome, but they know it, using their good looks to their advantage to get whatever they want. These men, though, look like they could either fight or fuck you with zero hesitation.

"Helms is starting to deal with some of that shit again, but he's in Rima for the week," Hawk answers, glaring at the hostess when she starts toward them. She glances at Mason, rolls her eyes and stomps away, combat boots clomping across the tiles. They're so at odds with her 1950 uniform, I grin, giddiness easing some of the tension in my shoulders.

"That's fine. It's just some distribution issues. It'll keep." Mason leans around him, raising a brow.

"This is Willow. She's Mac's friend. Just visiting. Won't be staying long."

Mason's brows disappear beneath the dark hair falling over his forehead. "Nice to meet you, Willow. Enjoy Synd."

Hawk nods before tugging me out the door. I wave, giving Mason a polite smile. When I trip over the threshold and Hawk grabs my arm, steadying me.

"Stop it," he snaps under his breath.

"Stop what? If you weren't yanking me everywhere, maybe I could keep my feet underneath me," I snap, tugging from his grasp.

He runs his fingers through his hair, then laces them with mine. I have no idea why he's insisting on holding my hand, especially when his bike is right there. It's not like we're on a date or something. Last time...well, last time was different.

"You would have gone through the glass if I wasn't holding onto you, so I wouldn't complain if I were you."

"Not true," I sniff, flushing. He's probably right, but how he knows I'm that much of a klutz is beyond me.

"Just get on the bike. The sooner I get you back in Reaper territory, the easier I'll breathe."

As he hands me the helmet, I can't tell whether he doesn't want to be seen with me or if he's nervous. I open my mouth to ask, but snap it shut when I spy him scowling. Shoving the helmet on I fumble with the clip before clambering behind him. At least I didn't almost fly off the side this time.

I smile, then jump when the bike rumbles to life. Wrapping my arms around him, I lace my fingers together over his stomach, which twitches under my palms. He can act like he hates me all he wants, but I'd put all the cash I have stashed away in my bag his body doesn't agree. If I play my cards right, maybe he'll stop being an ass, and we'll end up greasing the loaf again. Hell, as long as he keeps his mouth shut, I'd fall straight into his bed in a heartbeat, and I don't know what that says about me.

The rest of the ride is spent arguing with my nether regions on why it would be a terrible idea, but as we cross the line into Reaper territory, I push it from my mind, if only for my sanity.

Chapter Nine

Hawk

"Shut the hell up, Doc," I say into the phone, my mind still sifting through Willow's reactions at the diner yesterday.

He's cackling, giving me hell for having to play babysitter. I fell right into Helms's trap. He told me they were going to Rima, but he made it seem like a far-off trip, months from now. The cryptic text he sent me after they left the diner proves he has ulterior motives.

"Did Helms at least tell you why he went now?" Doc asks, his voice echoing down the line and through the bathroom of Mac's childhood home. I've been stuck here for two hours, trying to install a fucking shower door.

"I thought they got a lead on Dante, but I'm not so sure anymore."

I swing the door shut and then open it again. I'm pretty sure it won't fall off and shatter, but it's been a while since I've done this type of thing.

"Why's that?" The rumble of a bike rolls down the line, drowning out the rest of his words. I grab my phone, sliding down the vanity, legs splayed wide.

"I think he did it to force Willow and me to get along," I mutter.

Trigger may not be a gossip, but there were plenty of people at the bar the other night. They saw us leaving together. They'll come to their own conclusions on what we are to each other. And Helms is bound to hear shit sooner or later.

As pissed as I am Helms left me to deal with the meeting alone so soon after saying he was going to start leading again, at least it gives me more time to figure out how I'm going to tell him I fucked his woman's friend. He already knows I got laid, if his sly looks the next morning were any indication, but he'd probably float me if he knew it was Willow I picked up at the bar.

"May have heard a rumor about you two. I don't know what the hell is going on, but I suggest you figure it out before he gets back. Someone's bound to tell him about you guys." He hangs up before I can answer.

Heaving my body up, I check the time, seeing I've been here for two hours trying to make the place livable. I asked Willow last night if she was going to stay at Helms's, but she just scrunched her nose. I don't blame her. Staying in someone's house while they're not there is weird. At least it's only a short walk to headquarters either way.

Mac's childhood home, right next door to Helms's place, hasn't been tended to in years. The whole project took a backseat while I was getting the rest of our territory back in order after the war with the Night Slayers. I'm impressed the contractors I hired got as much done as they did before they were pulled away to other projects, even though they fucked it up.

I pack up the tools I brought, tucking them in the corner of the closet in the bedroom. The contrast between the new floors in the bedroom and the cracked stairs leading downstairs is glaring. At least the kitchen is done. The sun porch at the back of the house is drafty, and I make a note to call someone to install new windows in the whole house.

Stepping onto the back deck, I scan the trees in the morning sun. It's already hot, the day promising to be humid. Glancing at Helms's back porch, I step back into the house's shadow when I spot Willow, mug in hand and feet propped up on the railing while reading a book.

I didn't expect her to be up so early. She seems like the kind of girl to sleep in until ten and then complain the day got away from her. I shake my head, trying to reorder my thoughts. I don't know anything about this woman—not really. Just because she comes from money doesn't mean she's like every other rich bitch I came across in my youth. Her connection to Judge Merrick suggests otherwise.

I shuffle down the stairs and make my way over. Doc is right. I need to force the conversation with her or it'll never happen. I'm not trying to sneak up on her, but she still yelps when my boots hit the wooden stairs, coffee splashing over the rim. She leans forward, setting the mug down before wiping her hand on her shorts.

"Shit, that's hot," she mumbles, shaking out her fingers.

I bound up the rest of the stairs before snatching her hand in mine to examine the red splotches. She gapes at me, but I keep my gaze fixed on her skin. It's not injured, not really, but I brush my thumb across her fingers.

Goosebumps erupt along her arm, and I finally lift my gaze to her wide blue eyes. Staring into them, I see they're not truly blue, but shot with green as well. She slowly blinks as her tongue darts out, wetting her bottom lip. The move pulls my eyes down to her mouth and I remember how she melted under my touch.

I should drop her hand but instead I say huskily, "We need to run this under water."

Pulling her up, I tug her into the kitchen. Her fingers contract in mine and I clutch at her hand. I don't know what I'm doing, but for some reason I can't stop.

I flip on the faucet before pushing her hand underneath the spray. She gasps, trying to pull free, but I step behind, holding her still. Her trembling body is crowded between the counter and me. Closing my eyes, I dip my head, breathing in the fresh scent of her shampoo. It's probably some flower I can't pronounce, but it's intoxicating nonetheless.

"I think it's okay now," she whispers, shutting the water off. I'm still holding her wrist, and I can't make myself let go. The voice in the back of my head screams to step away, but my feet won't move. I didn't want to walk away two nights ago either.

My cock doesn't care if she's connected to my past and my mind is starting to agree. I dip my head lower, grazing her neck with my nose and her head tilts to the side. I press a kiss behind her ear, finally making up my mind.

"Are you still mad at me?" I murmur before nipping at her lobe.

Her body spasms, pressing her ass into my cock, and I swallow a groan. This woman is an addiction for me, one hit and I'm hooked. I've never been this drawn to someone before. Since the moment Willow walked through the door of Trigger's she's felt like more.

"I should be." She gasps as I keep up my assault on her flushed skin.

"Why?" I latch onto her lobe again and she lets out a soft moan. Scraping my teeth along it before releasing her flesh, I skim my hand to her hip.

"You left," she murmurs and her eyes fly open. "And you called me a viper." There's an edge to her voice.

"I shouldn't have said that," I confess.

"That's not an apology. Are you sorry you said it or because you got caught?"

I rest my chin on her shoulder. "I shouldn't have said it in the first place. There are many things I could use to describe you, but a viper isn't one of them."

"Then why say it at all?" she cries, spinning around to face me. I straighten, watching the flush creep into her cheeks. She crosses her arms, glaring.

"I know who you are," I mutter, tucking my hands in my pockets. "I know who your father is."

"Stepfather," she corrects, nostrils flaring.

"Stepfather. Him and I aren't on good terms," I say through gritted teeth. Just the thought of Judge Merrick and the shit he's gotten away with over the years sends a bolt of rage through me.

"Well, that makes two of us then."

I scan her face for the lie. I don't find it. She's staring over my shoulder, lost in thoughts I can't read. Something flashes in her eyes, but she blinks it away before I can decipher what it is. I plant my hands on the counter, boxing her in, and her arms drop.

"I shouldn't have been an ass to you. But I'm not apologizing for leaving. You locked yourself in the bathroom. What the hell was I supposed to do?"

Her mouth falls open, shock spreading across her face. I can't resist the temptation of her plump lips and I capture her mouth with mine, swallowing her gasp. I push my body into hers, delving a hand into her hair to grip her neck. Her tongue sweeps across my lips and I'm lost.

Wrapping my arm around her waist I pick her up and spin us around. I set her on the island before stepping between her legs. My hand snakes under her shirt, caressing her soft skin. When her hands grip my shoulders, nails biting through the fabric, a tremor runs down my spine. Our mouths are fused together, tongues dueling. She tastes like damnation and salvation and temptation and redemption. My emotions are in upheaval, trying to settle on what I feel.

My phone blares and I jerk back, hands falling away from her body. Her chest heaves and our panting fills the quiet space until my ringtone sounds again. I pivot before stalking past the laundry room and out the back door as I pull out my phone. Helms's name flashes across the screen and I scowl.

"What?"

"We're staying longer. You're going to have to hold down the territory until we get back," he says, wasting no time in derailing my entire life.

"Why the fuck are you staying longer? I thought you were just checking on the Vipers and dropping dickface off? What the hell happened?"

"Not sure. Looks like the Night Slayers have disbanded for good. Half their territory is burned to the ground. We've got a lead on where Dante is, so we need to run it down. You can handle shit. I trust you. I need you to do something though," Helms says, Mac's voice ringing out in the background. It sounds like they're at Vipers' headquarters, but I can't be sure.

"As if I'm not doing enough, but sure, lay some more shit at my feet why don't you," I grunt.

"Shut the fuck up. I don't pull rank with you, Hawk. Don't make me start. You need to keep an eye on Willow. And not just check up on her every once in a while. Mac's got a feeling."

I lean against the rail, gazing into the muted hallway of his house and barely making out Willow's silhouette right where I left her, bowed head with hair cascading over her shoulders.

The longer I stare, the more I feel like I made a mistake. I should have left well enough alone. I forgot she's not just Willow St. James. She's also Mac's friend. I can't start something with her, only for us to part again later. Mac would kill me.

"What kind of feeling?"

I remember her tensing at the diner yesterday. She became a puddle of fear when we ran into Mason Byrns. I tracked the terror skittering across her face. She tried to hide her reactions, but I saw them. Willow is in trouble. Some real deep shit. The question is, what type of hell is she running from?

"Something about her stepdad. Dick? Mick?"

"Joseph." I watch as Willow jumps from the counter, wandering around the island, like she's not sure what to do with herself.

"Whatever. Mac thinks he might come after her. Willow doesn't seem that concerned, but Mac would feel better if she knew you were watching out for her."

I grunt, knowing I would be doing that anyway—whether she's in trouble or not, she's still staying in Reaper territory. I'm responsible for everyone here. I'm not going to let anything happen to her, though I have to keep my distance. No more cornering her in the kitchen and kissing the shit out of her.

"Yeah, I got her. Anything else?"

"Hawk," he growls. "You're going to have to stay with her unless you can convince her to go to your place. If you wanna crash at my house, you can. Whatever it takes to keep your eyes on her twenty-four seven."

"You've got to be fucking kidding me. She's a grown ass woman, Helms. She doesn't need a babysitter," I bellow.

Willow's head whips toward me, and I leap down the stairs, stalking back to the Raines' house. He can't be fucking serious.

"Remember the last time I left a woman in danger alone? I'm not going to have a repeat of that. I'm not risking Willow getting kidnapped or some shit to protect your delicate sensibilities. Get your shit together and do your fucking job."

He hangs up as I reach the sun room. Scanning the space, I find more holes. I'm stuck trying to figure out how the hell I'm going to fix this place without any goddamn help. It should be the least of my problems, but for some reason, I can't focus on anything other than the broken wood under my feet. What the fuck am I going to do now?

Chapter Ten

Willow

"Fuck," Hawk yells, lifting his fist like he'll punch the wall. The tension rolls off him as he leans his forehead against the wood instead, fist thumping next to his head.

I crouch, stepping backward carefully. I wasn't trying to eavesdrop, but when I heard him bellow my name, I figured I should ask what the hell is going on. I texted Mac, but she just said to trust Hawk. Not much of an answer. What if they know something I don't? What if there's some danger lurking in the shadows and I won't see it until I'm sucked inside? The threat might not even have anything to do with me.

I doubt whoever was following me in Rima came all the way here to continue their pursuit. I'm loathe to call them a stalker. They might border on the creepy side, but nothing has happened to warrant real paranoia.

Whatever Mac is worried about probably has nothing to do with me, and I just inserted myself in their world, expecting them to take care of me. I should leave, go back to Rima. Or hide out in some random-ass town until my body stops reacting to every small thing.

I take two more steps, eyes trained on Hawk's back, praying he stays where he is until I can slip away. I'm not what one would call stealthy, though. I've never been able to keep my feet underneath me. Now, more than ever, I hope I can make a quick getaway without breaking my ankle.

I make it another three steps when I trip over a log sitting next to a fire pit I didn't notice. Arms flailing, I fall in slow motion, clamping my mouth shut, intent on swallowing the squeal begging to be let out.

Fortunately, I land on my ass. Unfortunately, a pain shoots through my tail bone, forcing a soft yelp from my throat. Leaning forward, I rest my elbows on my knees. I swallow, blinking so my tears don't fall, but it doesn't work. I bury my face in my hands, gritting my teeth.

Knees crash next to me and Hawk's hands run over my legs, poking and prodding along the way. I kick, trying to dislodge him, but he won't let go. His hand easily circles my ankle and a shiver runs through me, remembering how he flipped me on my stomach at the motel.

"Stop it. I'm fine. Stop babying me." My words are muffled by both my hands and tears.

I hate this. I hate feeling like I'm consistently making mistakes. I hate that I can't stop making a fool of myself in front of this man. I hate that he makes me feel all these emotions and yet I can't figure him out.

"I'm not babying you. You fell on your goddamn ass, Willow. What were you even doing sneaking around?"

I peek between my fingers, watching him stare off into the trees and run his fingers through his hair. Dropping my hands, I keep my face hidden behind my hair. I'm sure he knows I was crying, but no reason to give him proof. He'll only think I'm weaker than we both know I am.

"I wasn't sneaking around. I heard you talking about me and I was going to ask you what was going on. Then I thought better of it." I heave myself up, then dust off my jeans. My hands come away black with soot and I scowl down at my soot-stained palms.

"You don't need to worry about it. It's being taken care of," he grunts, standing so he's towering over me.

"I need to go change. Wash my hands. I'll see you around, Hawk."

I'm sure he can hear the dejection in my voice, but I don't care anymore. This whole trip was a bust. None of it was worth it. Even the amazingly hot sex doesn't make up for the shit show I'm in and I haven't even been here a whole two days. I need to remember the reasons I came in the first place: to get away from Joseph and give my secret admirer time to move on.

Instead of letting me go, he follows. Glancing over my shoulder, I scowl. Once we reach the porch, I'm ready to scream, but I bite my tongue. I slam the door in his face before he can barrel through, but he settles in my vacated chair to pick up the book I left. I contemplate stomping out there to get it back, but pivot into the house instead. It's not worth another fight. Maybe he can learn something if he reads it. Although, he certainly doesn't need to read the smutty bits. He has quite the handle on that area.

Mac's presence is everywhere in the house. Ryker doesn't seem to care if she takes over his space. An ache rips through my chest and I press a fist where the twinge radiates from. I'm happy for her, but the thought she'll stay here forever, so far away from Rima and me, is hard. Mac is my only friend and she's moved on—to a new city, a new life, and new friends.

Once I'm in the spare bedroom, I realize there isn't a bathroom up here, unless I'm willing to walk into their room, which feels weird. I'll have to go back downstairs. I mumble under my breath as I grab another pair of shorts. I don't want to stay in this house. I feel like I'm intruding in their space, even if they're not here. I should just go home.

Back downstairs, with new shorts and clean hands, I peek out the back door at Hawk who's still reading my book. I lean against the door frame and clear my throat.

"You don't have to babysit me. Like you said, I'm a grown-ass woman."

"You're in Reaper territory, staying in the Prez's house. That makes you my responsibility while he's gone." He doesn't even bother turning around.

"I don't even have a car here, so where am I going to go? I'll just sit outside and read. Or watch TV or something."

"You going to tell me what you're running from?" He flips the page, as if he's actually carrying on a conversation while reading.

"Who says I'm running from anything? I wanted to visit my friend."

"Mac isn't here, yet you still are. So, stands to reason you're hiding out in Synd. Question is: from what... or who?"

His voice is calm, almost detached, like he doesn't care either way. He's only asking because it could affect his precious MC. I shake my head at that thought. Of course he doesn't care about me. We don't even know each other.

"Fine"—I run my hand through my hair—"I needed a break. You said you know who my stepfather is, so you understand why that's necessary."

"I do. I also know there's more to it than that. Why don't we get this over with so I know what I'm up against," he grunts, lumbering to his feet and spinning to lean against the railing. He crosses his arms, finger still stuffed between the pages to keep his place.

"You're not up against anything. I can handle myself. Like I said, I don't need a babysitter."

Shit. I can feel my face flushing. I should have kept my damn mouth shut.

He raises an eyebrow. "Willow, I'm going to need you to stop dodging the question."

"I may have had an altercation with Joseph. I thought it best I wasn't around for a bit. That doesn't mean I'm running or hiding. I just need a break." Swallowing hard, I wrap my arms around my waist and open my mouth to confess more, but snap it shut when he scowls.

"Well, be my guest then." He sweeps his hand out, gesturing between us. "Glad we could be your vacation spot for the summer. I'm sure it's hard to get away from such a difficult life."

"You don't know the first thing about me," I cry, grateful I didn't reveal more.

"I know that delicious noise you make when I'm deep inside you. I'd say that's enough."

My mouth falls open as he smirks, then sets my book down. What an absolute asshole. I can't believe I said he was a white knight. Clearly, he was hiding his asshole so he'd get laid. I wish I had a comeback, but his words only send a shiver through me, forcing my mind to relive the images of him flipping me over and pounding into me the other night and then kissing the shit out of me not twenty minutes ago. What the hell was I thinking, letting him touch me again? And I wanted a repeat as long as he kept his mouth shut? Fuck.

"What the hell do you want from me?" The words tumble from my mouth.

There's no reason I should care what he wants. I should do whatever the hell *I* want, tell him to get the fuck out, say I want nothing to do with him. I'm not bold enough though.

I wish I could channel Mac's confidence. She doesn't take shit from anyone. She can shut someone down and they actually listen. I've never had those traits though. This is the most I've ever stood up to another person. I'm always afraid I've fucked things up. I'm worried how people will see me. I assume I'm the one in the wrong. I shouldn't, but I can't turn it off. The feeling that people only interact with me because they don't want to hurt my feelings constantly lives inside of me.

He stares at his feet for so long, I'm convinced he won't answer. Maybe he doesn't know either. Maybe he's just as lost as I am. I can't believe I've only known this guy for two days and I'm already trying to define the relationship.

This isn't a normal situation though. After being friends with Mac for so long, I understand life in the MC is never easy or normal. There always seems to be one crisis after another to deal with. Life runs fast and hard for them. Still, she tries to keep me away from most of it. I've picked things up along the way, just not enough to be comfortable using them around Hawk. I never imagined I'd be in the thick of their world, though.

"It doesn't matter what I want. Helms told me to keep an eye on you, so that's what I'm doing," he says to his feet, frowning.

"So, I'm a job. Okay. Fine. But that doesn't mean you have to be in my back pocket." I step into the dark hall and mutter, "And you sure as hell don't need to corner me in the kitchen."

He tips his face up, a small smile playing on his lips. I eye my book, wondering if he'll stop me from grabbing it. I can lock myself in the spare room and read the day away. After the weirdness of the last couple days, it sounds like the perfect plan.

"I'll be next door."

He's dropped the book and is gone before I've processed what he said. I watch as he lopes across the yard, disappearing into the sun room attached to the back of Mac's old house. I snatch up my book before closing myself in the house.

As I pass the front door, a chill runs down my back. Staring at the wood, I eye the lock. The metal is cool in my hand as I turn the knob to peek outside. No one is out front, of course.

I stop short when I spy the flower petals scattered innocently at the top of the stairs next to a stem stripped of all color. Shoving the door closed, I slam the lock home as my heart threatens to beat from my chest. I scramble to the back door, tumbling into the wall in my haste. Turning that lock too, I peer out the back windows at the trees innocently swaying in the summer breeze.

I slide down the wall before burying my face in my hands. It could be nothing. Anyone could have left them there. In fact, the flowers might not even be for me. Maybe someone left them for Mac. Hell, maybe Ryker gave them to her and they somehow were trampled on. No reason to panic. I pull in a deep breath and hold it until I let it out in a whoosh. Flowers are nothing.

Flowers are how it started before, the voice in my head whispers, sending a shiver through me as my stomach knots.

I push to my feet, gathering up the book I dropped during my mad dash to lock the back door. When I reach out for it though, I notice my trembling hand.

I snatch up the paperback before racing up the stairs. I'm going to do exactly what I told Hawk I was going to: stay in the house and wait for Mac to come back. If my secret admirer did find me... I'll cross that bridge when I come to it. I might have to run, but not yet.

Chapter Eleven

Hawk

"At what point did you assume we wouldn't find out you fucked up our job?" I bark into my phone.

I pace the sun room, wood creaking under my boots. It would be just my luck to put my whole damn foot through a soft spot, but if I stop moving, I'm liable to march back to Helms's place and throw Willow's ass out the door or on the bed. The whole exchange we just had threw me off and I'm spiraling. She flipped from being scared to flabbergasted to a brat in the span of seconds, and I have no idea how I'm going to deal with her.

The contractor on the other end laughs, like I won't put his ass in the ground. There aren't many companies in town to work with, but one less in business won't matter. I hang up before he pisses me off any more. I hesitate for a total of five seconds and then call Alex.

"Hawk, how's it going, man? Heard you got a new friend up there. She cute?"

"Sam know you're salivating over another woman, King, or should I inform her you aren't as loyal as she thinks?"

He barks out a laugh. "Sam's the one who told me she was hot, at least according to Mac. She's not the jealous type. Besides, she'd cut off my balls before I ever got far enough to cheat on her. Not that I would. One in a million, man."

"Whatever. I need some help," I snap. Now that I'm in this conversation, all I want is to be out of it. I shouldn't have called, but I don't have the time nor the inclination to deal with shitty workers.

"Woman help? I got you. See, what you need to do is go from the belly button..."

"I can find the fucking clit, Alex. I need help with a contractor who's fucking us over."

I swing around, spotting Willow and she freezes.

"What?" I growl at her, watching her eyes narrow.

"Huh?" Alex asks, and now I'm having two conversations at once. Fuck my life.

"Hold on, Alex." I pull the phone away. "What do you want?"

"Don't expect me to give references on whether you can find the clit. I'm sure your lady friends are very happy about that. I just need to know if there are flowers planted around here."

"For fuck's sake, you interrupted me to ask about fucking flowers? Why the hell would I know anything about that shit?" I holler.

She opens her mouth but snaps it shut before spinning around and marching back to Helms's house. Alex wheezes on the other end of the phone, and I'm pretty sure I catch Sam giggling in the background.

"Shut the fuck up."

"Oh, you are fucking screwed, Hawk. Listen, don't fight it too long. Fucking the feisty ones is an experience you should never pass up," Alex laughs. Sam's cry of outrage follows. Fucker put me on speaker.

"I'm not going to fuck her." *Again.* "Are you going to help me with the contractor? They've been fucking us over ever since we dealt with the Night Slayers, and I haven't had time to get in a pissing contest with them. They told me they did a bunch of work, Tiny, our treasurer, paid them, and I find out today they didn't do shit. Dumbass laughed when I told him we'd be paying him a visit. We need someone to finish this job."

"Well, Shane got someone over to help with the businesses up there, but the only residential company we have in our pocket you just fired. We've never had a problem with them, so I could lean on them, but we'll cut 'em loose if they're fucking with you. Maybe try Byrns? He's got a few."

Of course, I can't get anyone reliable. We usually don't have someone we use regularly, so we've never had a problem like this before. I don't know what the fuck to do. Last time I talked to Byrns he was four whiskeys deep and yelling at me about blowing shit up. He wasn't angry with me in particular, but I took the brunt of his wrath. He's been all over the place since he woke up from a coma to his territory falling apart around him.

"Maybe sic Sam on them. If you get any leads, let me know. This house is a death trap, but Willow is set on staying here. She's not exactly used to living in squalor and I'm not about to get my ass chewed because a spoiled brat can't handle not having a working sink."

"Uh, you wanna talk about your distaste for Willow? Or are we just going to ignore the fact you just totally shit on her?" Alex asks and I hear a door close on his end.

I want to snap back, tell him to stay the fuck out of my business, but I can't keep doing this shit. I need to get the fuck over the fact that she's rich. Willow hasn't done anything. I need to stop shitting on her because of a number in her bank account. It's an excuse anyway.

"We have a complicated history," I mumble, not willing to admit I might have taken things too far.

"You've known her for two fucking days. How complicated can it be?"

I tip my head back, staring at the sagging ceiling. "We may have slept together before we knew who the other person was. And I also grew up in Rima."

Alex whistles, then is silent so long I wonder if he'll say anything or just leave me to wallow in this shit alone.

He snorts before muttering, "Well, that might be a little complicated. You tell Helms?"

"Fuck no, I didn't tell him. He'd tell Mac and she'll bust my balls for sure. I can't afford—" I freeze, rethinking how much I'm revealing. "I shouldn't be the one to tell them anyway. Willow is Mac's friend."

"Uh, sure, but you're also Mac's friend. So..."

"I'm not telling them. I'm not about to go airing Willow's business. Plus, he wants me to keep an eye on her. An exceptionally close eye apparently."

Alex chuckles. "Oh, you're totally fucked."

"What's that supposed to mean?"

"Two days and you're already in this deep? You better get your head on straight about her. Especially if you're going to have to protect her."

I scoff. "If I knew what the hell I'm protecting her from, might be easier. She won't tell me shit about what's going on other than a fight with her stepfather—who happens to be a judge."

"Hawk, pull your head out of your ass and figure out what you want. Then do your fucking job."

He hangs up and I let out a deep breath. My instinct is to rage or deny how drawn I feel to her, but Alex is right. I need to get my shit together and do my job.

I stomp over to Helms's back porch, but I'm stopped short when the door won't open. I take another deep breath, wanting to break the damn door down, but I knock instead. There's a crash from inside and my heart leaps into my throat. Pounding on the door, I bellow Willow's name. She yells something, but I can't make it out.

I can't see anything from the small window, so I rear back and ram my shoulder into the wood. It creaks, but doesn't break. I plant my feet ready to smash into it again when it pops open, revealing Willow. A riot of blond hair swirls around her head highlighting a bump on her forehead. She glares as she rubs her elbow.

"Were you going to break the door down? Dammit, Hawk. I don't have the money to replace a whole goddamn door."

My mouth falls open, glancing over her shoulder to see into the gloom. "What happened to your head?"

Her hand brushes over the knot forming and winces. "Nothing. I just...nothing. I'm fine."

I plant my hands on my knees, sucking in deep breaths. For all I bitched about how she wasn't really in danger, my reaction isn't normal. At least for someone I just met. My heart is pounding, my stomach is rolling, and I can't get enough air in my lungs.

"Are you okay?" Willow's hand brushes my shoulder, but then she yanks it back as I peer up at her, taking in her flushed face. She smooths back her hair to pull it into a ponytail.

"We have to figure this shit out. But first"—I straighten, gesturing her inside—"tell me what the hell happened to your head. I'm guessing there's no ax murderer in the house chasing you around?"

She snorts, but doesn't budge from her spot in the doorway. "I was just a little startled. I tripped. It's fine."

I bring my hand up and she twitches back, a wariness in her blue-green eyes. Brushing a finger over the knot sends a shiver through her, but I will my body not to react. It doesn't work. I tilt my head, spying her red elbow, but there aren't any bruises.

"What was your question about the flowers?"

"Oh, nothing. Does Ryker buy Mac flowers?" Willow glances toward the Raines' house.

"Not that I've seen, but I'm not in their business like that. He's not the flower buying type, though."

"Okay, what did you need?"

She still won't look at me and I guide her eyes back to mine with a finger on her chin. Something close to fear flashes in her eyes before she blinks it away.

"I shouldn't have been a dick to you. You were right. I don't know anything about you. Not really."

"That's not really an apology," she whispers.

"That's about all I can manage."

She nods, trying to look away again, but I keep her eyes on mine. The longer I stare, the more I see the edge of fear in her eyes. No matter if I think she's in trouble or not, she's clearly concerned. The question is, what is she afraid of? What is she actually running from?

I need to focus on how it will affect the Reapers, but I'm not about to kick her out. The fallout of another woman coming in who we need to protect is something we need to know, but forcing her to leave isn't our style.

"What are you staring at?"

I sweep a finger across her nose. "Freckles."

A shiver runs through her body. "We should probably..."

I wait, but she stays silent, mouth slightly parted. I sway but drop my hand at the last second and step back. Whatever this draw is toward her, I can't make a move and figure things out until I know the whole story.

"What are you really up against, *léaró dóchais*?" I ask, tucking my hands in my pockets.

Somehow this woman has lit a spark inside me, a glimmer of hope that's hard to smother. The reasons I have for staying away are slowly becoming less important, less terrifying, less daunting.

"I don't know," she whispers, ducking her head.

"You need to figure that out. And then you need to tell me."

"Why do I need to tell you?"

"Because you're in Reaper territory. We protect whoever is here. You're here, so I need to know how to protect you."

Her arms wrap around her waist. "Okay."

She doesn't look convinced. In fact, she looks like she's going to run. I don't know where she'd go. Mac would blame me if Willow left and then Helms would kill me. My first thought is to lock Willow away, keep her where she's safe. I shouldn't feel this strongly about her though. I shouldn't want her this much.

"Don't," I breathe.

She lifts her eyes to mine. "Don't what?"

"Mac wouldn't be very happy if you skipped town," I murmur. It's not what I want to say, but it's all I can admit at this point.

"Would you be happy if I left?"

Chapter Twelve

Willow

Shit. I should have kept my damn mouth shut. Of course he wants me to leave. Neither of us thought we'd see each other again. He's made his intentions clear: he'd like to fuck me again, but nothing more.

"Never mind," I mumble as I turn, intent on fleeing into the house.

I stumble over nothing and I expect Hawk to catch me, to say something, and I slow. Once I'm through the door though, I realize what I'm doing and pick up my feet.

There's no reason for him to stop me. The liability for the MC is enough. I shouldn't expect him to care whether I stay or leave, other than how it'll look for him in Mac's eyes. I get it. I shouldn't have come here. With the red tulips showing up on the front porch, I'm more convinced than ever. I should run.

If he's followed me here, I'm putting everyone helping me in danger. I freeze at the thought.

I never took the threats as seriously as I clearly should have. If he *is* a stalker, then it stands to reason he might have tracked my phone. I jump when it starts vibrating, like an omen echoing through the space.

I clear my throat before slipping it from my pocket. It's still buzzing and Joseph's name flashes across the screen. Relief floods me before I'm doused with another wave of anxiety.

Lifting a trembling finger, I swipe the screen. He's yelling before I've even lifted it to my ear.

"...ungrateful brat. This is unacceptable. I don't know who the hell you think you are, but you'd better get your lazy ass back here. I expect you to be here and play your part. I knew I should have dealt with you years ago. Stop being a fucking slut and get your ass back to Rima."

He hangs up before I have a chance to respond, not that I would. Numbness seeps into my limbs. I can see my fingers curling around the phone case, but I can't feel them. Forcing my feet to move further into the house, I grip my phone tighter. His tirades used to upset me. I would spend hours trying to figure out how to "be good." Whatever that meant. It didn't take me long to find out nothing I did was ever good enough. After I stopped trying to get his approval, I moved on to crying. Every time he'd cut me down, the tears would come, forcing me to hide away until I could face him again. Then, he'd yell at me for that too.

Now, I couldn't give a shit. My entire body shuts down until he's done spewing whatever filth spitting from his mouth. My stepfather is a hateful, spiteful person and I will never be good enough in his eyes.

I don't care. I'm not a failure, or lazy, or a slut. I no longer believe his insults, but I wonder how much I've internalized. How much trauma do I carry inside without even realizing it? How loud is his voice in my head? How much influence does he have on my reactions to situations that have nothing to do with him? I shudder, afraid of the answers.

I pull a bottle of water from the fridge before twisting off the cap. The plastic bottle slips from my grasp when Hawk clears his throat behind me. It bounces across the floor, spraying water all over me and the rest of the kitchen.

"Shit," I mutter, grabbing a towel to mop up the mess. There's too much for just this small piece of fabric, especially with me soaked as well, but I refuse to turn around and acknowledge him. He probably heard everything and now he's going to pity me. Although, with the way he reacts, maybe he'll agree with Joseph.

I'm so exhausted. The last six months have been a slow descent into hell and I don't know how much more I can take without breaking. The last straw would be Hawk agreeing, or hell, not saying anything at all. The silence would be deafening, digging its way into my heart.

A large towel plops beside me while I'm on my knees.

"Thanks," I murmur, avoiding his eyes.

Another towel joins it and Hawk drops next to me, swiping it across the tiles. "He always like that?"

"Like what?"

"An asshole?" Our arms brush, both of us going for the cupboard, but I yank away and focus on the floor.

"That's a stupid question. You said you knew him."

"I didn't realize he was like that with you," he murmurs. I sneak a glance at him, but his eyes are fixed on the floor.

"I told you we had more in common than you thought. I know you think I'm some rich goody two-shoes who doesn't have a care in the world. I'll be the first to admit I have more than other people, but that doesn't mean shit is easy or simple or I have some perfect life."

I shouldn't have said any of that. I should have kept my damn mouth shut, but for some reason I can't seem to help myself around Hawk. Maybe I just need to vent.

Mac would listen, but I feel like I'm burdening her with my problems. Plus, she would want to save me. I don't want someone to save me. I just want someone to tell me whether I'm overthinking everything, whether I'm making the right decisions. I want someone to help me deal with Joseph. I want someone to figure out how to get whoever is stalking me to leave me alone.

Fuck, maybe I do want someone to save me.

"I told you I shouldn't have said those things. You can't help who your mom married," he says gruffly.

"Yeah, well..." I don't know how to finish, so I clamp my mouth shut.

"Well what?"

"I don't know." Swiping the last droplets of water from the fridge before I snatch up both our towels, I march into the laundry room. I should start a load, but after the shit from the last couple days I need a nap.

"We need to figure out how to be around each other."

His voice echoes from the kitchen and I contemplate hiding in here, hanging out with the washer and dryer. The last thing I want to do is have another conversation, especially with him. It's exhausting. Everything is exhausting lately. I can't hide though, especially if I want to change my sopping clothes.

"No, we don't," I call, brushing a finger over the cool metal of the washing machine. "We'll just pretend the other person doesn't exist." A pang hits my chest and my fingers go numb again.

"That's not going to work and you know it, Willow. Besides, do you really want to pretend we didn't..."

"Nope. We're not going there. This whole shit show is weird enough as it is. And you're not making it any easier by bringing it up or saying random things or being nice to me and then turning around and being a dickhead. So, just stop. You don't have to worry about me. I'll be out of here soon." My heart cracks, but it doesn't make any sense. I shouldn't be sad I'm leaving.

"You're not going to listen to that asshole, are you?" Hawk asks from right behind me. I flinch and my back brushes his chest. There isn't enough space between me and the washer to put distance between us, but I'm not sure I want to.

"Not your problem. This isn't how one-night stands usually work, is it?" I whisper.

"Only one of us brought up a one-night stand, Willow. Now, tell me when you plan on leaving and why?"

I spin around as best I can with the small space he's left between us. His green eyes set my body on fire, flames licking over my nerves, and I struggle to tap down the desire.

The washer stops me from retreating, the cold metal digging into my back. He leans forward, invading my space. I open my mouth, but snap it shut when my hands brush his stomach as I twist them together.

"Answer the question," he growls, leaning his hands on either side, caging me in.

"I don't have a plan. I'm kind of a shit show. Besides, it's not your problem," I mumble.

His eyes dip, following the path of my tongue while I lick my lips.

"Ask me again."

I clear my throat, peering to the side. His eyes are too much, too captivating. They suck me in and drown my body in heat I can't afford to feel. I'm not asking him again if he wants me to stay. I'm not ready for the answer. I shouldn't want him either way. I want him to want me to stay, preferably in his bed, but I'm not ready for any other answer. I don't even know if I'm ready for *that* one either.

"I'd rather not."

"I'm going to answer anyway." He pulls in a deep breath, his abs brushing against my fingers again. "I'd rather you didn't leave."

"Why not?" I raise an eyebrow, meeting his eyes.

He hangs his head. We're so close his hair tickles my forehead, making me shiver. "You're not safe anywhere else."

"That's not your concern."

"Could be."

Part of me wants to run away—away from this conversation, this situation, this man. My feet are bolted to the floor though.

I'm so sick of doing the right thing, whatever that means. I don't like who I am, though. Who I am on the inside doesn't match who I present to the world. I never feel like I can be myself, always afraid they won't like who I actually am. Although, most people don't seem to like me regardless, so maybe I should say fuck it and stop trying to please everyone around me.

"This is getting out of hand," I whisper.

"Not nearly enough."

Hawk presses his body into mine, dipping his head and my limbs start to tremble. He freezes a hairsbreadth away from my lips. I waver as our breaths mingle, a shiver rolling through me. I catch his grin a half a second before his mouth is on mine.

Our kisses before were a whirlwind of lust and desire, pulling us down into oblivion. This is something else—something more. This is a soft flow of a creek, bubbling over rocks. It's a small glow of a campfire late at night. It's a firefly flickering through a soft, summer night.

His lips glide over mine, tongue caressing my lips, an invitation instead of a demand. He swallows my gasp as his hand skates along my hip up to the hem of my shirt, and his tongue caresses mine before retreating. I run my fingernails across his stomach, making his muscles jump. Pulling back slightly, he ghosts his lips across my cheek.

"Tell me what you want," he murmurs in my ear, a shiver of desire coursing through me.

"Uh..." I can't form words, not with him so close, filling my pores with fire, my nose with his scent, my mind with images of what he's done to my body.

He chuckles. "Tell me what you *don't* want then."

"I don't want to leave," I whisper before I can change my mind.

I close my eyes, holding my breath. The last thing I want him to do is walk away at this point. I'm throwing all my eggs in this basket. I'm done fighting and it hasn't even been a long journey.

For some reason, we were thrown together and I want something...normal. I don't know if this is normal, to want someone so badly I can feel it in every breath I take, every brush of skin, every passing glance. Even when he's pissing me off, he's turning me on.

No, this isn't normal. I'm not blind, thinking this is my happily ever after. I don't think I'll get that. I can't imagine it. Hawk is probably as close as I'll ever get and if I don't put myself out there, I'll never know what could have been.

"Tell me you want this," he breathes into my skin, sending a shudder through me.

My chest tightens. "I want you."

He groans, arms banding around me, fingers digging into my flesh. His mouth finds mine and we come together in a clash. I thought it would be different, that time and our differences would diminish the need to devour each other, but it's just as explosive as before.

I give up trying to analyze every touch, every sound rumbling through his chest, and just let go. He bends, fitting his fingers into the crease of my ass before picking me up. Clinging to his shoulders, I wrap my legs around his waist, grinding my core into his stomach. It's not enough. I expect him to set me on the washer, but instead he spins us around, pulling his mouth from mine to duck his head into my neck, nibbling on the soft skin. His stubble scrapes across my flesh, probably leaving red splotches behind, but I'm beyond caring.

As he walks us out the back door, I bury my head in his neck, sinking my teeth into his skin. Another groan reverberates from him and his steps falter. I run them along his collarbone, a sound of protest falling from my lips when his shirt stops me. We're wearing way too many clothes for what I want to do with him.

We're halfway across the yard before the fog of desire lifts enough for me to realize where we are. I squeal, hiding my face against his neck. A chuckle rumbles in his chest.

"Why the hell are we outside?" I hiss and his arms tighten around me.

"I'm not fucking you in Helms's house."

My body bounces as he bounds up the stairs of Mac's childhood home. I peek over his shoulder as my eyes adjust to the muted light within the house. It's a mess of rooms half torn apart. The layout is almost identical to the place next door, minus the debris.

Striding through the kitchen, I see how much work needs to be done still. I don't know how I'll be able to stay here if the rest of the rooms are like this. We reach the stairs and I bite his shoulder again, making him stumble.

"Knock it off, *mo dóchais,* or I'm going to drop you." He's trying to sound stern, but his voice is breathless. I shimmy up to nibble on his earlobe and his throat bobs as he digs his fingers into my ass.

Once we reach the top he swings to the right, carrying me into a large bedroom. I whip my head around, but the space is almost bare, with only a king bed taking up the far wall. He drops me onto the fluffy comforter and I crawl backwards to lean against the headboard.

"If we're going to do this, then you need to be all in," he says, staring at his feet.

"What does all in mean?"

"I don't understand fully what's happening, but if we take this further, I'm not going in for one night. I'm not going in for a fling. You need to understand, if we do this, you're mine."

Chapter Thirteen

Hawk

Willow's face is swathed in shock. Then it smooths out as she stares over my shoulder. I rock back, shoving my hands in my pockets and resign myself to waiting until she processes what I've said.

I don't understand the pull she has on me, but I'm done fighting it. I've been in constant distress since the moment she walked into Trigger's. There's no reason I should be this invested in Willow, only knowing her two days. I should want to steer clear of her, but I can't deny I want her. And I'm going to keep her.

Her face morphs again and she crinkles her nose, making me freeze. My muscles tense and my stomach drops. Our short history hasn't been the smoothest, and it's entirely possible she only wants a distraction from her problems.

I lean back, ready to run for the door. This is why I never put myself out there. The rejection is too much, too hard, too terrifying. I wasn't lying when I told Mac all those months ago she had something special. The jealousy churning in my gut at their connection— their love—is overwhelming. Willow's body jerks forward, eyes finding mine when I step back.

"I can't, but it's not you," she says, brows pulling together.

"Okay," I murmur, taking another step back, the need to rush from the room overtaking my senses. I wipe my hand down my face, trying to erase all emotion. She scrambles toward me, frantic.

"I swear it's not a line. You know how Joseph is. I can't stay. You said you don't want a fling. Okay, I get that, but I can't stay here. He'll never let me go. I'm not the one you want to keep," she rushes out as if I'll stop listening halfway through if she doesn't. Tears fill her eyes, threatening to cascade down her flushed face.

"You feel this too, right?" I ask, narrowing my eyes.

She nods, angrily swiping away the wetness coating her cheeks. I curl my hands into fists though my palms itch to reach for her. The ache in my chest spasms, making my heart stutter.

"I'm sorry," she whispers, sliding off the bed to stumble to the attached bathroom.

I don't understand why she thinks she can run from me. Hell, there isn't even a door on the bathroom yet. She stutters to a stop, head swinging around the small space. Her shoulders bunch and she tips her head back, a soft "fuck" falling from her lips, and I smirk.

She thought she could hide from me again, but I'm not about to walk away this time. I'm prepared to take on Judge Merrick. He's long overdue for a beating. Who better to deliver it than me? He ruined my life. From Willow's comments, he's done the same to her. I won't let that stand.

Willow glances over her shoulder before whipping back around when she spies me still here. She rips open the shower door and I cringe, praying it doesn't fall off the hinges. I'm not sure it's hung right and the last thing I want it to do is shatter around her.

Stepping through, she pulls the door closed behind her and the frosted glass warps her silhouette. I can just make out enough to see her sliding down the wall.

Shaking my head, I wonder how long I'll be able to resist going after her. I count to five before I lose the fight, stalking into the room and then pull the door open.

Her legs are splayed out in front of her, fingers twisting in her lap. She peeks up, tears still shining in her bright eyes, a look of misery stamped on her face. Stepping inside, I shut the door behind me and slide down the opposite wall.

Why the hell didn't I put a bench in here? She tucks her legs to the side and I smother a grin. Her feet don't even reach the wall next to me, yet my knees are sticking up, not able to fully stretch out.

"You should probably go," she says after a couple minutes of staring at the glass.

"Nope."

"What do you mean 'nope'? You told me what you wanted. I can't give it to you. So, we should go our separate ways."

She bites her lip, the move drawing my eye to the plumpness. I wish we could skip this part and get back to devouring each other. Her insecurities need to be dealt with though, or we'll never move on. They'll crop up, over and over, and she'll never let them go, clinging to the doubt like a life jacket filled with lead.

"You want this, don't you?" I raise an eyebrow when she doesn't answer. "You don't want to live under his thumb, do you?"

"No," she murmurs. "No, I don't."

"Then don't. Willow, I won't force you, but you know you belong here. It feels right. You can't deny that."

"I don't know that I belong here," she mumbles.

"Liar. You feel this, but that's beside the point. I think we've established you're a grown-ass woman, so why are you letting him make decisions for what you do with your life?"

"I have three thousand, one hundred, and twenty-three dollars to my name. Do you think that'll be enough? Do you think someone would hire me, a twenty-seven-year-old woman with no experience? Or should I live off the generosity of my friend? Perhaps I should trap you into taking care of me." She scoffs. "Not everything is black and white, Hawk."

I drop my hand to her ankle, brushing my thumb across her silky skin. Goosebumps run up her leg, disappearing under her shorts. Another pang shoots through my chest. I'll do whatever it takes to get her to take a chance on me. I may have waffled before. I may have said shit I shouldn't have, but I'll do whatever it takes to make it up to her. Fighting this feeling inside me isn't an option anymore.

"You don't have to do it alone. Doesn't mean you're taking advantage of anyone. This is what we do. We help people," I murmur, eyes fixed on my fingers circling her ankle.

"I thought you guys were an MC," she snorts.

She's trying to appear unaffected, but I notice the shiver coursing through her body when I sweep my thumb along the arch of her foot.

"I told you before, we're not that scary." I smirk, peering from under my lashes.

She scoffs, but I catch the vulnerability in her eyes as I run my fingers up her calf. Once I reach the back of her knee she twitches away from my touch. Gripping her leg, I raise my eyes to her face. She's fixated on my hand, lips slightly parted, and my cock hardens.

She clears her throat once, then again. "I can't promise I'll stay."

"I'm not looking for promises. By the time you think of running, I'll have already caught you."

I smirk as her mouth drops open. Willow is too easy to rile up, but I'm not complaining. It only makes things more fun. This space might be too small for what I want to do with her, but I can't wait any longer.

Gripping her leg tighter, I pull her toward me. As her knees bend, she lets out a squeak and her hands fall back, wide eyes finding mine as I grin.

"Got you," I murmur, running my hand to her thigh.

I watch her throat bob, lust filling her gaze when my finger traces the hem of her shorts. Another flush flows from her chest to her face, making her freckles stand out. Tugging her again so her hip is pressed against mine, she leans into my leg, fingers toying with the seam of my jeans. She's not even grazing my skin, but my leg still twitches, right along with my cock. It's only been two days since I've been inside of her and yet I'm craving her again.

"I should tell you..." she whispers, gasping when I move my hand between her legs.

I walk my fingers up her thigh, forcing her knees apart. Delving my fingers under the hem of her shorts I stop, waiting for her to continue. As I knead her flesh, I soak in the soft rasp falling from her lips.

"Later."

I lean forward, bringing my face close to hers. Wrapping my free hand around her neck to yank her closer, I capture her lips. This may not be the frenzied fuck we had before, but it doesn't diminish the fire burning between us.

Her mouth parts and our tongues duel, the taste of her overpowering my senses. I cup her pussy, heat already gathering between her legs, sending a tremor through her. Pulling back, I watch her lids flutter open, swollen lips still parted.

"There isn't enough room to fuck you in the shower like I want."

I release her before pushing to my feet. Holding out my hand, I wait as she studies it before reaching for me. I fold my fingers over hers, a pulse racing up my arm at her touch before tugging her to the bedroom. Pulling her in front of me, I trap her between my body and the bed and she ducks her head to my chest, hiding her face from me. I tip her chin up until our eyes meet.

"Sorry," she mutters, eyes darting away from mine.

"If you don't want to do this, Willow, tell me now." I wrap an arm around her waist, holding her loosely. The last thing I want her to think is I'm trapping her into something she doesn't want or isn't ready for.

"Oh, I want to fuck you." She claps a hand over her mouth and tips her head back. "Shit. Sorry. That was weird."

I chuckle before ducking down to run my lips along the column of her throat.

"The feeling is mutual," I murmur into her skin. "I'm going to tell you exactly what to do and you'll be a good girl and listen. Understood?"

Willow shivers, grabbing fistfuls of my shirt as her nails dig into my skin and I swallow the groan threatening to escape me.

"Tell me what you want," I whisper.

She rests her head against my chest again and my heart spasms. Propping my chin on her head, I hope I didn't freak her out.

"I want to be free." Her voice is muffled, but I catch the quaver in her tone.

"Free from what?"

"Inhibitions."

I pull in another deep breath. "Then lay on the bed, legs hanging off the side."

I drop my hands from her body and start counting. I get to ten before she's crawling onto the mattress, exactly how I want her. Willow stares at the ceiling, biting her bottom lip. Leaning over her, I tug the flesh from between her teeth with my thumb and her eyes meet mine.

"No hiding," I command.

She wants to be free from inhibitions and I want to be in control. We're a perfect match. Dropping to my knees between her legs dangling off the side, I run my fingertip along her arch, up her calf, all the way to the button on her shorts. I glance up and find her staring at the ceiling again. Grabbing a pillow and I tuck it under her head and she shoots me a small smile, then gasps when my hand cups her between her legs.

I sink to my knees again, releasing the button on her shorts and she lifts her hips while I yank the fabric from her. I didn't get to spend nearly enough time with my face buried between her legs the last time. I can't wait to have her thighs squeezing my head while she comes on my face.

My mouth waters, just remembering her taste on my tongue. Her legs are already shaking and all I've done is skim my hands along her silky skin. Pushing her legs apart, a whimper echoes through the room and her fingers curl into the comforter as I grin.

Leaning forward, I graze my nose along her thigh before sinking my teeth into her flesh. She squeaks, her fist flying to her mouth to smother the sound.

Once I reach her pussy, I swallow a groan when I find her already soaked. She might be shy, but her body doesn't lie. She wants this as much as I do. I'll work on getting her to stay once I've fucked her into complete blissfulness. I told her I was going to destroy her for any other man and I plan to follow through on that promise.

Trailing my fingers to her pussy, I spread her wider before I plunge my tongue into her core. She shudders, moaning around the fist still jammed between her lips. Her essence explodes across my taste buds and I swirl around her clit, noting every twitch and whimper she makes.

I plan on spending many hours on my knees, consuming her. Sucking her clit in my mouth while I push a finger into her, I glance up, finding her eyes have fallen shut. I grunt, releasing the small bud and shove another finger in, making her pussy clench.

"I said no hiding. Eyes on me while I'm making you come, *mo dóchais*," I growl. Her cheeks flush while I curl my fingers and she gasps. "Say you understand."

She nods, but I raise an eyebrow, flicking my thumb across her clit, making her gasp again.

"I understand."

"Good girl."

I bury my face again, plunging my fingers faster until her feet fly up, settling on my shoulders. I swirl my tongue around her clit and her pussy clings around my fingers. Glancing at her face, I find her eyes fixed on me. Then her legs clamp around my ears as she sails over the edge, pussy spasming as she moans.

I keep going until her legs fall to the side, feet sliding off my shoulders. Leaning back on my heels, I pull my fingers from her. She's panting, desperately trying to catch her breath, but her eyes are still on me. I smirk when she shudders again.

"That was..." Her eyes bounce away and she tucks her knees together.

Frowning, I wait for her to finish, but she just stares at the ceiling. I push to my feet before leaning over her. I'm not even touching her, but another tremor rolls through her body. I trail my fingers along her jaw until she looks at me.

"I thought I said no hiding?"

"You're for real, aren't you?" she asks, tilting her head, pressing her face into my palm.

"Oh, I am very real."

She smiles, huffing out a laugh. "I mean, you really want this, don't you?"

"Willow, this may shock you, but I'm pretty sure I've never wanted anyone as much as I want you."

She slowly nods, eyes fixated over my shoulder. She's lost in some process I don't understand, but I wait. I feel like I've been waiting for her my entire life, which is insane. I'm not going to call it love, but I need her, desperately. It's a need deep in my bones I can no longer ignore.

"I never thought I'd be here. Is that weird?" she asks, vulnerability flashing in her eyes when she meets my gaze.

"You just hadn't met me yet." I grin as she rolls her eyes. She grabs a fistful of my shirt before yanking me close, our lips almost touching.

"Fuck me now, please."

I groan, wrapping my hand behind her neck and capturing her lips with mine. Her essence still dances on my tongue and I hope she can taste how amazing she tastes. Parting her lips, she sighs as her body relaxes into the comforter. Her hand mirrors mine to wrap around the back of my neck, clinging to me.

Willow clearly isn't comfortable being the center of my attention. Or maybe she's just not used to someone worshiping her. I pull my mouth away before resting my forehead against hers.

"Wait," I pant. I'm pressed into her now, lying on top of her and her body tenses. I drop to my forearm, caging her in as she tries to roll from under me.

"What are you doing?" she whispers, turning her head away.

I run my nose along her jaw before answering. "What are your inhibitions? What's holding you back from letting go?"

She huffs as she shuffles her legs, working to close them, but I settle my body into her more. She can fight this all she wants, but she's going to tell me what's blocking her from enjoying herself. What's the point of overloading her body with bliss if I have to drag her there? The least I can do is help her overcome whatever reservations she's harboring.

"Tell me," I demand before grazing my teeth along the tendon in her neck. She shivers, wiggling again, making my cock twitch.

"I feel like you're a lot more experienced than me," she mutters.

"So? I like to fuck, Willow, but I'm not out here blasting through woman all the time."

She snorts, turning her face back. "Blasting through women?"

I smirk. "Seemed like a lot to say, 'I like to fuck, but I'm not fucking lately.'"

"That's a lot of fucks."

"Tell me what's really wrong and I'll reward you by making you come again."

Chapter Fourteen

Willow

My mouth drops open, mind racing to find an excuse. I snap it shut as Hawk grins before swooping down to press his lips to mine. My mind blanks when he licks along the seam of my lips, and I can't help but fall apart under his onslaught. I wish I could live in this bubble instead of deciphering why I'm so nervous every time his eyes alight on my body.

Pulling back, he leaves us both gasping for breath. He raises an eyebrow, chest still pushing into me with each breath, like he's challenging me to deny I want another orgasm. He knows exactly what he's doing, dangling the carrot in front of me.

"Fine," I snarl, suddenly pissed. "I'm embarrassed."

He rears back, eyes filling with wariness. He tucks his chin to his chest, hiding his face from me. I freeze, wondering if I should explain or stay quiet. Usually, I babble until someone tells me I'm annoying and to shut the fuck up.

I learned early on once Mom married Joseph to keep quiet. My ex confirmed what I suspected all along. People don't want to hear what I have to say. I don't spout my opinions or contribute to the conversation because it's not worth it. Mac is the only one who's ever shown interest in my opinions, which is fine with me. Hawk is just confirming what I already know.

"Sorry. You don't have to stay," I murmur, swallowing down the hurt in my voice. I push against him, but he's like a brick wall, a weight holding me in place to witness another death of what I really want.

His head snaps up. "Why do you keep trying to give me an out? If I wanted to leave, I'd already be gone. Tell me why you're embarrassed."

My chest tightens, lungs seizing. I can't figure out if he's pissed or something else. His voice is hard, leaving little room for argument. Again, I rack my brain for an explanation. I've never had to have this conversation before. Now I'm embarrassed that I'm embarrassed.

"I don't want you staying to spare my feelings, first of all. Second of all, I'm embarrassed because I'm lying here with no fucking pants on and you're fully clothed. I'm embarrassed because it's the middle of the day and we've known each other for two fucking days and at some point, you're going to figure out I'm not all that amazing. I'd rather you walk away now rather than later when I'm invested and you break my goddamn heart. I'm embarrassed because I know I'm not that good at this shit, so, yeah, I'm giving you an out. You should fucking take it."

I'm wheezing, some emotion I don't want to name swirling through me. All I know is I'm either going to scream or cry and I don't want to cry in front of him.

When the hell did this become so fucking complicated? I shouldn't even care if he walks away, but I do. I really fucking do. He asked me if I felt it before, the connection between us, and I didn't want to admit it out loud. I want to believe he wants me for me and not a fuck buddy. I never thought I'd have someone who knew who my stepfather was and would still want just me. Not what I could help him get. Not for a status I could afford him. Not for bragging rights that they banged the judge's stepdaughter.

Why I feel like I could have that with this man is beyond me. It doesn't make any sense. I want to let go and just trust that things will work out, but history has proven that won't happen. Time and time again, I've noticed that people are more likely to walk away than stick around, so I'm not holding my breath that Hawk will be any different.

"Willow." He rests his forehead on mine and whispers my name again, eyes falling closed. It doesn't seem like he's going to take me up on my offer to run as far from me as possible. I don't know whether to be relieved or terrified. Maybe both.

"Are you just going to keep saying my name or..."

"*Mo dóchais,* I don't even know where to start. Would it make you feel better if I took off my pants?" He grins, making me huff.

I don't understand the different versions of this man. He's controlling, and an asshole, and protective, and funny. He's hot and cold, never fully committing to anything. How can I trust what he's saying now?

"I'd rather you get off so I can put my shorts back on," I snarl.

He lowers his hips, jeans pressing into my skin, reminding me how naked I am. I wiggle, pushing my feet into his legs to slip from beneath him, but he cups my face, the grin dropping from his lips. His thumb brushes over my mouth and I swallow hard.

As much as I want to run or push him away, I can't deny I want him. I want to bask in the feelings he brings out of me when he sends me hurtling over the edge into oblivion. I want to seize whatever he's offering and hoard it within my heart. Staring in his eyes, I realize I'm too late. I am totally fucked when it comes to this man.

"I'm ignoring all that shit you spouted about how long we've known each other and how you see yourself. Given enough time, I can fix those things. What do you think you're not good at?" His voice is a barely a whisper, ghosting across my lips.

I bite the inside of my cheek. I can't look him in the eye anymore so I stare at his forehead until I force out the words.

"Boarding the beef bus." I wait, but he doesn't respond. "Churning butter. Planting the parsnips. Bedroom rodeo." He still doesn't say anything. "Exploring the hidden valley? Dammit. I'm not that good at sex. Okay?"

His body starts to shake, amusement dancing in his green eyes, his grin firmly back in place.

"How many more ways do you have to say 'fucking'?"

I huff. "A fair few. It's hard enough to talk about it. But if I say 'christening the yak' people laugh. Most of the time they look at me weird when I say things, so if I make it funny, then I don't make a fool of myself for no reason."

I freeze, staring at his shoulder. I've gotten so used to the way I approach people, I never realized how horrible it is. I hide behind being an odd duck so if someone actually thinks I'm strange, then I won't be hurt, since that's what I presented to them in the first place. I won't care if they walk away.

I've spent my whole life presenting what other people want to see that I don't know if this is really me or not. Shit. I don't have the time or energy to cultivate an entirely new personality. I like this version of me, so I probably won't mess with it, but I should stop lying to myself.

"I like weird," he whispers.

"What?"

My eyes snap back to his. I was so lost in my own thoughts, I'm two steps behind now. He chuckles, the sound reverberating through my body.

"I said, I like weird. There's nothing wrong with weird. I don't know who told you you're not good at boinking, but from experience"—he raises an eyebrow, smirking—"I have no complaints."

"I'd like that other orgasm now, please." I tip my chin up, hoping I'm not fucking this up.

You still have someone following you. I shake away the thought.

I'll worry about what could happen later. Whoever is stalking me is only after *me* anyways. If I have to leave Synd, leave Hawk, then so be it, but I doubt he'll be caught in the crossfire. It's much more likely this thing between us will fizzle out long before I'm ever forced back to Rima.

A pang shoots through my chest at the thought of leaving. I'll cross that bridge when I come to it. There's no reason to think my admirer will come busting through the door and kidnap me. I'm going to concentrate on the very real hunk of man meat currently grinding his jeans-covered cock into me.

"You just need to relax," he murmurs, pressing his lips to my jaw. "Let me take control." Another kiss. "Let yourself feel how your body responds to me."

He scrapes his teeth across my throat and I can't help the shiver that courses through me. Hawk can have all the control he wants if he keeps doing these *things* to my body.

He wraps his arm around my waist, the other gripping the back of my neck before rolling us until I'm on top. He drops his hands before tucking them behind his head. I don't know what the hell he thinks is going to happen, but I'm going to keep my cheek pressed to his chest. Cold air from the vent gusts across my very bare lady bits and I yelp, jerking against him. Hawk's warm hands envelop my thighs, holding me still.

"Don't hide your pretty pussy. You're going to do what I say, remember? I'm in control."

"If you're in control, then why am I on top?" I ask, voice muffled by his shirt while another shudder rolls through me.

"Sit up, *mo dóchais*."

I shift, slowly pushing up until I'm straddling him. He runs his hands up and down my thighs, eyes traveling from my face all the way down. I don't miss that he didn't answer my question, but even in this position I obeyed him without a second thought. I realize I need him to tell me what to do. He might be precisely what I need. Then I can let go.

He's still staring at my body, fingering the hem of my shirt. Glancing down, I notice my hooha is on display for him. Whipping my head up, I find his eyes on mine.

"Take this off," he grunts, tugging on the bottom of my shirt.

I bite my lip as he smirks, a challenge in his eyes. Gripping the hem, I tug it over my head slowly. I'm sure he thinks I'm trying to be seductive, but instead I'm wondering if I can force myself to keep going. My hands are trembling, and I can't look him in the eye as his fingers skims along my skin, following the fabric along my sides. Goosebumps chase behind and I'm not sure how long I'll last.

Once he reaches the edges of my bra, I'm close to panting. He's not even doing anything, but the anticipation is overwhelming. Whipping my shirt over my head, I toss it behind me. Hawk's finger tucks underneath my bra until he reaches the clasp in between my breasts. I'm mesmerized as he toys with it, but then he drags his fingertip to my stomach, straight down, disappearing into the curls between my legs.

I flinch when he hits my clit and his stomach jumps beneath me. He tunnels as deep as he can between my folds before dragging his finger back. The tip is glistening with my arousal and my breath stalls as I stare at it.

"Open," Hawk says gruffly.

I part my lips, a thrill vibrating in my chest and shooting straight between my legs. He slips his wet finger into my mouth and I close my lips around it. I don't know if it's the wantonness or if I actually enjoy it, but the flare of desire and satisfaction bursting in his eyes is enough to make it worth it. He drags it out and I nip at the tip, forcing a grunt from him.

"Fuck, Willow. Thought you said you weren't good at this?"

His lips pull into a smile and a flush heats my cheeks. I duck my head, but he captures my chin, forcing my eyes to his. He slowly shakes his head, reminding me—no hiding.

Closing my eyes, I slowly pull in a calming breath. I don't want my nerves to get the better of me. My eyes fly open when he flicks the clasp of my bra. It stays put though.

"Off. Now."

I'm no longer striving for seduction. I scramble to unhook it, but it catches twice before slipping free, the sides hanging open. I expect his eyes to dart down, but they stay fixed on my face.

I reach for the straps, but he shakes his head again, so I drop my hands back to his shirt. Swallowing, anticipation burning its way through me, I wait for his next command. That's what these are. I expected him to act like he did the first time, but instead he's made this some type of game. I can't say I'm disappointed. It's like he knows exactly what I need to let go and he's handing it to me without reservation, solidifying the connection between us.

"Are you still thinking about how you're the only one naked?" he asks, skimming his hands over my skin before they circle my waist, his thumbs rubbing along my hip bones.

"I wasn't, but now I am."

He smirks. "But you let go of your inhibitions, focused on the thrill of following my commands. I don't think you're embarrassed at all."

I snort. "Sure, go ahead and tell me how I feel. See how far *that* gets you."

"Oh, *mo dóchais*, I would never, but I still don't think you're embarrassed. I just don't think anyone found what makes you become a puddle underneath them. They didn't know how to handle someone like you."

He sits up to wrap an arm around my back, leaning into me as his lips ghost across mine. "No one ever told you how utterly delectable you were. How amazing it is to watch you fall apart. How delicious you taste. How incredibly intoxicating it is to be deep inside you, bringing you over the edge again and again."

I gasp, body vibrating by the time he's finished. He's right. Every other experience I've had involved men who took what they wanted with little regard to how I felt. No one made me feel sexy or wanted. No one made it their mission to make me come or find out what I wanted in the bedroom. I'm still riding the waves his words have caused when he pulls back.

Yanking his shirt over his head, he reveals his tanned chest, covered in swirls of ink. I trace one from his shoulder, to his heart, and it disappears beneath his waistband.

He lies back, settling his hands on my hips again before he drags me onto his abdomen. I'm sure he can feel the wetness from my pussy. He reaches behind me, digging his fingernails into my ass before he's attacking his buttons. His hips kick up and I let out a squeak, falling forward. I catch myself, planting my hands next to his head. Honestly, I almost smacked him in the face, but he only grins as he kicks his pants off before falling back.

"Get up here." He tugs on my hips.

"What?"

"Up, on my face. Now." He tugs again.

"I'm not sitting on your face," I say before huffing out a laugh.

"Oh, yes. You are."

We stare at each other for a good thirty seconds, my breaths coming shorter the longer we're locked together in a battle of wills. He can't honestly expect me to sit on him. The logistics of something like this is baffling. Most of the time I'm too short to accomplish any type of crazy positions. In fact, my feet are going numb from them being tucked under my thighs.

Licking my lips, I shuffle up. I shoot him a look when he grins. It's awkward lifting my knees over his shoulders. When his arms wind around my thighs, warm hands gripping me and opening my legs more.

I expect him to wait, since he's been slowly building me higher with each command, but instead he drags me down, burying his face between my folds. I fall forward as he devours me, legs already shaking. His nose grinds into my clit as his tongue pushes into my core. This whole thing is probably tame compared to what others do, but this is mind-blowing to me. He sucks on my clit and I'm done, whimpering as my body shudders through the explosions flying around my body. I try to push up, but collapse back onto his face. I'm sure I'm suffocating him, but his grip tightens, fingers digging into my flesh.

Finally, he releases me, stroking my skin and sending shocks through me. I push forward and fall onto my stomach while I gasp for breath. I can still feel my core clenching around nothing. Hawk shifts behind me, but I don't have the energy to even move my head, much less roll onto my back. I gasp again when his fingers push into me. He leans over my body, chest brushing against my back before he whispers in my ear. I can't concentrate on the words as he pumps his fingers in and out, prolonging the pleasure rolling through my body.

"Do you wish my cock was deep inside your pussy, giving you something to cling to? Do you want me to fuck you into the mattress?" he murmurs and I can feel the flood his words cause. "Oh, you like that, don't you? You like hearing all the dirty things I'm going to do to you." When I don't answer he presses his thumb to my clit making me gasp. "Use your words, Willow."

"I like it," I wheeze. I'm not going to be able to walk if he keeps this up.

He tsks, as if my answer isn't enough. Even with everything we've done and all he's said, I'm still holding back. I wish I could let go and tell him exactly how he makes me feel. I wish I could tell him I want to worship his cock.

Shit. That might be too far, but it's only in my mind, so he'll never need to know how much I want to drop to my knees for him. I probably would fuck it up, but at least I'd try.

"So many possibilities, but I can't wait to be inside of you. It's been too long," he growls. "Hands behind your back."

I rush to comply, smacking my hip in my haste. He chuckles as he slides the straps of my bra to my elbows. My hands press together and he holds my wrists lightly in his grip.

Hawk moves my legs further apart and his cock presses into me slowly until he's fully seated. I moan into the mattress, satisfaction flooding my veins. His hand tangles with my hair, forcing my head to the side as he leans down.

"I told you not to hide, Willow. That includes whatever sounds fall from that sweet little mouth of yours or I'll make you choke on my cock," he growls, pushing me into the mattress more. "Too far?"

"No," I gasp. An involuntary shudder runs through me and I spasm around his cock, forcing a grunt from him. He pulls back slowly, then punches his hips forward, impaling me again.

"You can do better than that. Tell me what you want," he groans, repeating the move.

I moan at the feeling of him filling me up. When he does it again, I swear he's slowing on purpose, waiting for me to answer. I've made it clear I need him to control things, even if I am self-conscious about it.

"Fuck me harder." My eyes roll into the back of my head when he slams into my core once more, the words falling from my lips before I can overthink them. "Faster."

"Shit," he grunts, then rears upright, releasing my wrists before digging his fingers into my ass and surging into me hard and fast.

I stop silencing the desperate noises escaping me, letting them echo around the room. They mix with Hawk's low moans. My orgasm lingers on the edge of my consciousness. With every thrust I push back, trying to take him deeper.

Then he hooks his fingers under my hips and yanks me to my knees, ass in the air and face still buried in the mattress. The new angle sparks a flame inside and I can practically taste bliss dancing on the tip of my tongue. When Hawk's fingers find my clit, I explode, sobbing as I spasm around his cock.

He doesn't give me any time to recover, still pounding into me, fingers circling my clit. I don't know if one orgasm rolls into another one or if it's the same one from before, but I'm wheezing by the time he groans my name, lingering in me as he twitches. He's gripping me so tightly, I'm sure I'll have bruises on my hips tomorrow, but the thought only sends another shudder through my body. This is what I needed—the space to let go.

Several minutes of gasping later, I'm practically purring when he lowers me, before slipping from my folds. Collapsing next to me, one hand lingering on my flesh, he skims his fingers up and down my back, sending tiny shock waves through me. I hum, so completely in this blissful bubble my lids flutter closed.

Hawk's sharp intake of breath has my eyes flying open. Peering at him, I expect the same contentedness to be etched on his face, but instead he's staring down his body with a look of horror.

He rubs his hands over his face before muttering, "Shit."

Chapter Fifteen

Hawk

I fucked up. Leaping off the bed, I race for the bathroom and my mind scrambles, trying to figure out how to fix this. Once inside, I grab a tissue and clean myself off, as if that'll make it better. I can't believe I fucked up so badly. I was so caught up in Willow, in her body, in her essence, I completely fucked up.

"Shit," I mutter again. "Goddamn fucking mistake."

A soft gasp has my head whipping up. I catch sight of Willow's blond hair swinging around. Great. Now, I fucked up royally. I charge after her, catching her around the waist, and I press her back to my chest. She's clutching her shirt, hiding her trembling body.

"Let me go, Hawk," she mutters, her voice wavering as she tries to hold back tears.

"I didn't mean you," I whisper into her hair, the strands tickling my cheeks.

"It's fine. You don't need to say anything. I get it."

With every word she utters there's another stab in my chest. I loosen my hold just slightly, but she huffs when she still can't pull out of my arms. I don't want to hold her hostage, but I'm sure she'll run if I let her go.

"You don't get it. I didn't mean you were a mistake. We didn't use protection."

She stops trying to wiggle away, every muscle pressed to me tensing. Then she relaxes in my hold, sinking into my body and I breathe a sigh of relief. Tugging her shirt from her slackened hands, I drop it on the floor before spinning her around. She ducks her head to my chest, hiding again.

"I'm sorry," she breathes. "I wasn't trying to..."

I wait, but she shakes her head, body still shaking. "Wasn't trying to what? Trap me?"

Willow's head whips up, blue eyes wide. She pushes against my chest and this time I drop my arms. She scoops up her shirt, holding it in front of her like a battered piece of armor. Her cheeks flush a pretty pink, but the fight in her eyes has me holding back my grin.

"I'm on birth control. So, you won't have to worry about anything. And I haven't...well, I'm clean. That's all you need to know." She grabs my pants and chucks them at my chest. I let them fall to the floor while she huffs. "You don't have to believe me, but I am."

She plants her fists on her hips, glaring. Her gaze snaps down, realizing she's naked and crosses her arms, trying to keep the fierce look on her face. Her cheeks redden and I follow the blush down to the tops of her tits.

"You're pretty sexy when you're all worked up." I smirk at her squawk of outrage. Catching her wrist as she stomps past, I swing her around to face me. "I wasn't worried about you trapping me, Willow. Do I wish we would have talked about it? Yeah. Will we figure shit out regardless? Yeah. It wasn't your fault and I'm not blaming you. I was pissed at myself. You wormed your way into my head and I lost the ability to think about other shit."

I reel her in, and my muscles ease when she comes willingly. Her arms circle my waist, nails digging into my skin. "Are you sure?"

"More than sure. Now, go take a shower," I say, stepping back. I smack her ass when she doesn't move quick enough, making her yelp.

When the shower door closes, I lace my fingers behind my head, tipping my gaze up to the ceiling and blowing out a long breath. I don't like lying to her, but she wouldn't understand. My first thought when I realized I wasn't wearing a condom was that she did it on purpose. By the time I was off the bed though, I had already dismissed the idea.

Willow may be a lot of things, but a conniving bitch isn't one of them. No, she's not trying to trap me with a pregnancy, but she is hiding something. It's more than the threat from Merrick. It's more than the need for a break from her life. Something else is chasing her. And I need to find out what—or who.

I grab my pants and pull them on. I'm not going to get to the bottom of things standing around naked. I sure as hell can't fuck it out of her, although that's exactly what I want to do.

I don't bother with a shirt as I pull my phone from my jeans pocket, seeing three missed calls from Ren King. I pull up his text and I swear he's ready to crawl through the phone and strangle me. I glance at Willow in the shower. Her silhouette dances against the glass, highlighting her soft curves. I pivot to walk out, but spin back.

"Willow," I call, watching as she wipes her face and turns to the door. "I have to make a call. I'll be downstairs."

I wait until she waves before I leave, calling Ren along the way.

"What's so fucking important, King?" I snarl.

"I would tell you to try again, Hawk, but I'm too busy to deal with your attitude. We have some activity happening in your territory. Or rather, by your territory," he says over the clicking of his keyboard.

My heart jumps and I clear my throat before answering. "What kind of activity? Night Slayers? Guild?"

"Doesn't look like it. Nemesis says it seems to be just one vehicle, but it sticks out like a sore thumb. If she caught it among the fleet of cars we drive around, it's weird. It's a shiny. Very richy-rich kind of car."

I shake my head, looking around the dismantled main floor. Half the walls are down to the studs, the living room demolished, and the kitchen is only slightly bearable. There's no way Willow can stay here. I need to figure out a way to get her to come stay at my place. Helms probably thinks I'm going to stay at his house with Willow. I'm going to do everything in my power to keep her as close as possible, ideally in my bed. I jolt, remembering I'm still on a call.

"I fail to see how some rich asshole driving around is classified as 'activity.' Seems like somebody joyriding around, wanting to check out the wrong side of the tracks."

He snorts. "Do you think I'd be calling your bitch ass if he wasn't acting suspicious? Just keep an eye out. I believe it might have to do with your new guest. Seems like you're getting quite a few of those lately. I'd rather not deal with the fallout if another shit show goes down in Reaper territory. Shit needs to settle down or I'm going to have a fucking heart attack at thirty."

"You're being dramatic, but I'll put out the word. Don't worry about who we have in our territory. We take care of our shit," I snarl.

"Like you took care of the Night Slayers alone? Or how you took care of rebuilding your section of the city? Get your shit together, Hawk. Don't let pride stop you from asking for help."

He hangs up before I can respond. Ren may come across as a quiet asshole, but he's more perceptive than he lets on. Somehow the dynamics between our families changed when the Guild tried to move in. Things solidified more when the Night Slayers came to bring us down.

Ren isn't wrong. We need a break. We need time to regroup and rebuild. At some point we're going to hit a breaking point. I hope whatever is coming for Willow doesn't boil over and sweep us away.

"Is everything okay?" Willow's soft voice floats from the stairs and I spin. There's something different about her. She's changed clothes, but it's something else. I can't put my finger on it. She raises an eyebrow and I realize I'm staring.

"Everything is fine. I need you to pack up your shit though." I drop my gaze to my phone, texting Helms an update.

"Oh, okay. I'll go...do that now."

"Don't take too long." A text pings and Doc's message comes up.

Her footsteps fade, but it's not until the back door clicks shut and Doc's reply comes through that I register what just happened. I forgot she had her stuff at Helms's house. I may not have taken Ren's warning seriously, but I'm still not going to let Willow out of my sight until she tells me what the hell is going on.

The way she reacts to seemingly nothing isn't someone who just needs a break or had a fight with her stepfather.

My stomach flips as I pound out the door. Scanning the yard, I can't find her. I swear she sprinted as soon as she got out of the house. I don't want to be a stalker, but I need to keep her in sight. My heart is already trying to leap from my chest as it is.

I slam into the back door when it doesn't open. The handle doesn't move and I can't see Willow through the window. I have no idea where the hell she went. Racing to the front, the pain in my chest rises, almost suffocating me. I almost miss the flower petals scattered across the front porch, but they're everywhere. Helms isn't the gardening type. I have no idea where they came from, but I barely slow as the dry petals crunch under my bare feet.

The knob, warm from the heat of the summer sun, doesn't budge, and I slam my fist against the wood. Bellowing Willow's name, I hammer on the door again, cursing myself for not getting her number. I punch my fist into the door, but it still doesn't give. I'm ten seconds away from breaking the goddamn window when the door pops open, revealing Willow's startled face.

"What the hell are you doing?" I bark, bracing my hands on my knees and panting. I can't pull enough air into my lungs. I swear this woman took ten years off my life with the stunt she pulled. I doubt it'll be the last time she almost gives me a heart attack.

"I was packing. Are you okay? Sit down before you pass out," she says, her hand landing on my shoulder to guide me to the bench Helms installed for Mac.

My stomach rolls when the bench swings back. I forgot it was on a track and I feel like I'm falling. Willow's hand shoots out to grab the wood, halting the motion.

Latching onto her wrist, I yank her down to my lap, sending it rocking again. I pull her close, cupping her face with my hands. A glimpse of her blue eyes widening is all I see before I crush my lips to hers and swallow her gasp.

I breathe in her essence, letting the taste of her seep into every pore of my being and calm my racing heart. She tastes like sunshine and innocence, though she's anything but. The things she's let me do to her body...my heart starts pounding again at the thought of her under me, moaning my name. I pull back, opening my eyes, but hers are still closed, lips slightly parted and swollen from my kiss.

"Willow, don't lock me out," I wheeze, trying to catch my breath.

Her lids flutter open. "I didn't think you'd follow me. I didn't want anyone breaking in. I only have a couple things left."

She leans back, but I latch onto her waist, holding her in place. I can't let her go yet. The panic from a minute ago is still exploding inside me. Having her in my arms is the only thing relaxing my muscles bit by bit.

"Did you need anything else?" she whispers, staring at my chest.

She's twisting her fingers in her lap, pulling at the skin on her knuckles. The flush is back, making her freckles stand out. I brush a finger over her nose, sending a shiver through her body. I don't know why she's trying to get away. Is it the bullshit someone fed her or something else?

"Let's go get you packed," I say, releasing her.

Willow scrambles off my lap, tripping as she stumbles through the door and I catch her around the waist. She huffs before tugging from my grasp. I have no idea why she's acting like this, but after the rollercoaster today has been, I'm not going to push her. She's working shit out in her mind. I can be patient while she decides when to talk to me about it.

I can't be patient when it comes to the threat circling her though. Sooner rather than later I'll have to force the truth from her, and she'll have to make the decision if she's going to fold or become one of the shadows she's run to.

Chapter Sixteen

Willow

Peeking over my shoulder, I whip back around when my feet trip on the step. Hawk reaches for me again, but I right myself before dashing up the stairs. I don't know what he thinks I'm going to do—probably steal something on my way out. Hawk is back to bouncing between sweet lover and raging asshole.

I can't deny he helped heal something I didn't even know was wounded. I've spent a long time assuming I was the problem when it came to men. The glimmer of hope he dangled in front of me was so enticing I seized it with both hands.

Then he turned around and told me to pack my shit. I would have locked the door anyway, but I can't deny I was trying to keep him out. I didn't think he'd freak out like he did. Then he was yelling and then kissing and now I don't know what to think.

Still told you to pack up and leave. The voice in my head is a bitch and sounds like my stepfather. I hate that his voice lives in my brain. I wish I could banish him from my thoughts, but he's always there, waiting for a moment of weakness.

When I finally opened up to Mac, she would counter everything he said and for a while, her voice drowned his out, but it's been so long since I've been able to have a meaningful conversation with her, he's seeping back in. I hate not knowing what to do. I've spent so long making decisions based on what others' reactions will be, I forgot I have my own opinions.

I shouldn't have to pack up and leave. In fact, Mac told me to stay put. I assume her words come from Ryker's orders, and since Ryker outranks Hawk...I spin at the top of the stairs, forcing Hawk to stumble back a step. Planting my fists on my hips, I glare.

"Fuck you," I snarl.

Shit. I meant to say more and now he's staring at me like I've lost my mind. "I mean—no. You know what? I stand by that. Fuck you. I was told I can stay here, so that's what I'm going to do. I get you're the second person in charge or whatever, but Mac told me I was more than welcome to stay for as long as I'd like."

"Well, Mac isn't here right now. She fucked off to Rima and left your ass here, making you mine to deal with."

"Hardly. If you have a problem with me, take it up with Mac. I wouldn't advise that though. She can be quite the bitch when you piss her off."

I lift my chin and cross my arms. Hopefully he thinks it's because I'm pissed off and not because I'm trembling. I'm blushing and trying to hide the fact I'm out of breath, both from bounding up the stairs and from telling him off. He could very well throw my ass out the door and I couldn't do anything to stop him.

Hawk opens his mouth, but then glances behind him. I should stomp off, maybe lock myself in the bedroom, but I'm not sure my legs will hold me. My knees are locked as it is. When he swings back to face me, he's glaring.

"At what point did you decide I was throwing your ass out?"

"You told me to pack my shit," I say with as much vitriol as I can muster, but doubt is worming its way in.

"I also said you were mine to protect. I can't very well do that in a half-finished house that doesn't have fucking doors, much less locks, Willow," he growls.

"My stuff isn't *at* the Raines' house. It's here. So, why would I have to pack, huh?" I raise an eyebrow.

He throws up his hands, a cry of frustration echoing down the hall and I hastily step back. "For fuck's sake, Willow. I'm taking you to my house!"

I stare over his shoulder at nothing. I didn't think he'd do that. It didn't even cross my mind he would want me at his place. My last boyfriend never invited me to his townhouse. I kept pushing the issue until he told me to stop being annoying.

When I ran into his mother at a benefit, she was cold, and I finally understood. I wasn't good enough for their precious son. Although, looking back, he wasn't good enough for me. He was a prick, to be honest. I shouldn't have clung to the relationship as long as I did, but we started dating right before Mac disappeared and I was lonely. It's the only reason I can think of why I put up with his asinine company for five months.

"Oh," I breathe, dropping my arms. "I didn't realize. I apologize."

I snap back to reality when his warm hands fall on my shoulders. I flinch, but try to cover the move with a small smile. His bright eyes, lined with pity, burn into mine and I step back. His hands fall to his sides as he watches me.

"At some point we're going to have to figure out why you get all formal when you think you've messed up," he says, pushing past me to step into the bedroom.

Standing in the doorway, I track his movements around the room. I don't know what he's searching for as he looks in the closet and flings open drawers. The only thing I have to pack is my charger and book sitting on the nightstand. I didn't take anything out of my bags, unsure of how long I'd be staying.

"This all you have?" Hawk asks, pointing to my luggage and I nod. "Where's the rest of your shit?"

"This is what I packed. I don't know what you're looking for," I say as he peers into the attached bathroom.

"We'll have to get the rest of your shit from Rima soon then." He grabs the duffel bags, slinging them both over his shoulder.

"That's my decision to make, Hawk. I've lived with a domineering asshole for long enough. I'm not going to let you start bossing me around just because we slept together."

My stomach is doing gymnastics, but a thrill rolls through me. I've spent too long letting other people walk all over me, telling me what to do, where to go, and what to wear. I'm done. Fear has held me back for far too long.

He raises an eyebrow before dropping the bags at his feet. Stepping over them, he boxes me in against the wall, pressing his hips into me. I should ignore the fact he's hard, but a shiver runs through me. He rests his forearms on either side of my head and leans down, brushing his nose along my jaw and I swallow the gasp wanting to leap from my lips.

"Do you know how sexy you are when you're putting me in my place, *mo dóchais*? You blush such a pretty pink. Fire burns in your eyes and I want to leap straight into the flames. See what you do to me?" he asks, pressing harder into me.

"I wasn't..."

"But if you think for one minute I'm going to let you walk back into that shithole and put yourself in danger, then I haven't made myself very clear. You're mine: to fuck, to keep, to protect. Remember that next time you want to tell me you're going to run headlong into harm's way. You'll force me to do something drastic."

"Like what?" I whisper.

"Like kill a judge. I'm very good at making people disappear, but I'd rather not deal with the cleanup." He grabs my chin, forcing me to meet his eyes. "I'll make this very clear for you, Willow, I have no intention of letting you go. You're exactly what I've been searching for my entire goddamn life. I'll fight anyone to keep you by my side. Eventually, you'll see how much you belong with me. Until then, don't do anything stupid—like run. You'll only force me to chase you and drag you back to my side, where you belong."

His words mirror Joseph so closely, my mind spins until I realize how different they make me feel. Joseph controlled me for himself, but Hawk's words make me feel safe. Even when he was upset, I never worried he'd withhold his protection.

Releasing me, he spins to grab the bags before marching out the door, grabbing my wrist as he passes. I don't know when we went from fighting and pissed at each other over a one-night stand to him declaring himself to me, but I can't deny the way he makes me feel. I may not be convinced I'm destined to be with Hawk, but he's certainly making me feel wanted. It's been a while since I've felt confident in any decision I've made. Hawk's words are sneaking their way into my heart, but it's too soon to be anything other than in lust with him.

I tug my wrist from his grasp when we reach the bottom of the stairs. "Do not haul me down the stairs. You can go all controlling alphahole in the bedroom, but I'm not going to allow you to drag me around like I'm incapable of walking on my own."

My words peter out when he opens the door and I see the yellow rose petals scattered across the porch. Hawk glances back, studying my face.

Was all this here before and I just didn't notice? How did I not notice?

"Willow? What's wrong?" Hawk's low voice floats through the ringing in my ears. I try to wipe my face of all emotion, but he narrows his eyes.

"Nothing. I just didn't notice this before. Do you think someone dropped them off?" It's a dumb question, since who the hell would leave petals instead of a whole flower, but it's out before I can take it back.

"Don't lie to me, Willow. You were talking about flowers earlier, so these aren't the same ones. Clearly, there's something wrong, so tell me. Stop hiding shit from me."

I roll my eyes. "We've known each other for like fourteen seconds. Slow your roll, dude. I'm not going to spill my entire life story to you. Now, are we going or what?"

Something flashes in his eyes, but I can't decipher it before it disappears. "Okay, but you're going to have to tell me eventually. Preferably before I take a bullet for you."

I shove past him, kicking the petals aside. "It's not that extreme. Geesh, stop being a drama queen," I snap, voice cracking along with my heart.

Hawk grabs my waist and hauls me against him. His hand snakes up, tangling with the hair cascading down my back. Tugging, he tips my head back until he can seal his lips to mine. Forcing my lips apart, he devours me and I meet him every step of the way.

Every time he kisses me, consumes me, I give in a little more. He's breaking down my walls, or rather, building something up inside me. He pulls away, scraping his teeth over my jaw.

"Keep being a brat and see where it gets you, *mo dóchais*."

He releases me abruptly before grabbing my hand and pulling me toward his bike. I glance back one last time at the roses. Maybe going to Hawk's place won't be such a bad idea after all. I freeze though, tugging from his grasp before grabbing my phone from my back pocket.

"Hawk, can someone track me on this thing? I mean, even with my location off?" I unlock it, staring down at the background of Mac and me.

"Yes. You think Merrick is tracking you?"

I pause, staring at Mac's frozen eyes, dancing with laughter. I wish we could go back to then—before she got hurt, before Joseph took notice of me, before someone started following me, leaving me trinkets and flowers and carving messages into my car, before my life started to fall apart. It hits me that Mac wouldn't have found her way back to Ryker then. I'd never wish to go back to that time just to make my life easier.

"Maybe. How do I get rid of it?" I look up at him, towering over me, but I don't feel small. I feel safe, which freaks me out.

He takes the phone and tosses it on the ground, grinding the screen beneath his boot. My mouth drops open, ready to cuss him out. That's my only lifeline to Mac. I don't care if Joseph can reach me, although I probably should. He could make my life infinitely harder if he wanted to. Hawk scoops up the shattered remains of my phone and tucks it into the side pocket of my duffel bag before continuing on to his bike.

"What'd you do that for? Now I don't have a phone," I squawk.

"I'll get you a new one. Besides, you're going to be living in my back pocket for the foreseeable future. You won't need a phone."

I'm definitely going to need to get my shit together and figure out how the hell I'm going to keep all my secrets from the surly man stomping away from me. Fuck me sideways and twice on Sundays. This is not going to be easy.

Chapter Seventeen

Hawk

I thought last night would be more of what Willow called sexy, fun times, but instead it consisted of me sitting on the back porch dealing with a bunch of bullshit with the MC. The Reapers run themselves for the most part. The guys know their roles and what they need to do, but with Helms off gallivanting all over the state, they're on my shit more than normal.

By the time I got back inside, Willow was fast asleep on the couch, book on the floor and a half-eaten piece of cake on the coffee table. She barely stirred when I gathered her in my arms and brought her to my bed. I don't know what I did to deserve her trust, but she cuddled up, draping herself over me and fell into a deep sleep. My muscles relaxed one by one, easing her more into me, and I slept through the night for the first time in years.

Now, I'm wide awake at six in the morning, her warm body pressed against me and her leg tucked between mine. My arm curls around her and I hug her tightly, until there's no room left between us. I'd be happy to wake up like this every morning. I should get up and start something, but I bury my nose in her hair instead, breathing in the floral scent of her shampoo.

Of course, my phone starts to rattle across the nightstand just then. I snatch it up, trying not to jostle her. Ren's name flashes across the screen and I answer it before sliding out from under her. I close the door to the attached bathroom before I say anything.

"King, do you have what I need?"

"Good morning, Hawk. I trust you slept well." Ren's deep voice, tinged with annoyance, rolls over the line. I can hear Sam laughing in the background before it's abruptly cut off with the click of a door.

"Are we really going through pleasantries, King? Seems a little pointless." I roll my eyes. I wonder if I can get away with pissing while on the phone.

"Sam has pointed out I might need to improve the way I speak with others. Humor me."

"Fine. I slept...well. This is fucking weird. We don't talk like this. Just stop."

"If she asks, tell her I tried. I have a new phone for your special friend. I also thought I'd tell you that shiny is still lurking around. We've got some fancy cars, but this one takes the cake. I still don't know what he's doing and Nemesis can't get a read on him. Any new developments on your end?"

"We have a few shipments going off the grid, but it's coming from Byrns's side. Has anyone dropped by to check on Mason? He wasn't looking so good the last time I saw him. We need to make sure Victor doesn't try to start shit again."

The last thing we need is Mason Byrns going off the deep end and Victor taking over. Again. The last time was a disaster, and I didn't even have to interact with him that much. Dealing with the Guild was bad enough. The Night Slayers put us even further in the ground. If something else is coming at us, we need to be prepared.

I crack the door to spy on Willow's still sleeping form. We're fucked if Victor takes over and whatever she's running from catches up to us. She's not prepared to fight her battles alone.

"Sam is dealing with him for the most part. She says he's getting better, but at some point, we'll all have to meet. With Helms still in Rima, you'll have to attend in his place. Sam is also bugging me to tell you to bring Willow by. She wants another friend, as if you're going to gift wrap your woman or some shit," he scoffs.

The more I interact with Ren, the less he acts like a robot. Working together to drive out the Guild changed something between our families. Helms seems to think we need to get back to how things were when they were kids. I wasn't a part of the MC back then, still holed up in the shithole that is Rima, but it sounds like they were very different.

"I need to run the meeting tonight. I sure as hell won't be bringing Willow to that, so I'll drop her off beforehand. Ask Sam to teach her some shit," I say.

"What the hell does that mean? What's Sam supposed to be teaching her?"

"I don't know. How to throw a punch or some shit. Sam knows how to defend herself, right? Willow knows absolutely nothing. Plus, she's hiding something. Maybe Sam can get it out of her."

I would teach her myself, but I haven't had any actual training. Mason seems like the kind of brother who would teach his little sister how to kill a man six ways to Sunday. I learned by getting my ass beat in a back alley.

"She's not an informant for you, Hawk," he growls. "You'll just have to go the regular route and gain her trust. Prove you'll protect her when shit goes down and she'll sing like a canary for you. I'm assuming you're no longer dealing with a one-night stand, so start acting like a fucking boyfriend instead of a fuckboy."

He hangs up before I can correct him. Fucking Alex King has been running his mouth, probably telling Shane, Ren, and Samantha everything. Ever since Sam jumped the river to live with the Kings, they've been nosier than usual. Alex has made it his life's mission to bring our families together.

I shoot a text to Alex, telling him he's an asshole before I take care of business and then start the shower. I should have taken one last night, but exhaustion had set in.

I'm halfway through my shower when my phone starts ringing again. It doesn't stop the entire time I'm rinsing or drying off. Byrns's name pops up again and I tuck it between my ear and shoulder to wrap the towel around my waist.

"What do you need, Byrns?"

"Well, good fucking morning to you too, asshole. Too busy seducing someone for pleasantries perhaps?" Mason chuckles. At least he doesn't sound like he's talking around a mouthful of gravel today.

"Why the fuck would you think that?"

"You sound weird. Whatever. Since Helms isn't going to be back for a while, we need to meet and go over the distribution shit I was telling you about. The mayor has been up my ass for the last two days wondering why there's empty box trucks littered on the side of the road, lining your territory."

"Most of them are from construction. We did blow up half our territory two months ago. Tank said there are some shipments going missing. They're supposed to be coming from the east side. I mentioned it to Ren, so I'm sure he'll obsess over it until he finds some answers. I also need some residential contractors. Ours are shit and I'm pretty sure Alex is going to float the ones he recommended."

"That guy has a sadistic streak. Although, I would pay cash money to see him beat Victor to a pulp. I hear the results were epic." He chuckles. He sounds better than he has in months, more like himself.

"I saw Victor at the last meeting before we took out the Guild. I wish I could have seen him when his nose was freshly broken. Little bitch was annoying as shit when he got shot."

"So, we going to talk about the woman you have holed up there?"

I sober, swallowing hard before I respond. "No. She's not your concern."

"Easy, Hawk. I'm not going to swoop in and steal her. She seemed pretty attached to you anyway. Sam told me there was something going on there, but she wouldn't elaborate." He laughs again and the knot in my throat eases.

"You couldn't steal her even if you tried, asshole. I didn't realize the mafia was such a cesspool for gossips."

"Apparently, we used to gossip a lot. I've been digging into some of the history. This shit is insane. The way the city is laid out, our houses, even the protocols from before, it's all scattered around. I might need to ask Ren's hacker for some help."

He sounds energized. I knew Helms was worried, but apparently giving him a purpose was the key to pulling him out of whatever hole he was in.

"You're going to pay for it, so be prepared. I gotta go. I need to deal with the shit here. Let me know when you want to meet. I'll be in the city later today if that works for you." I can tell he's no longer listening when he murmurs something before hanging up.

Willow yawns in the doorway, blonde hair a riot around her head. Her eyes are slits and I swear she's still half asleep. She shuffles in before wrapping her arms around my waist and laying her head on my chest. The tension riding me eases and I tug her closer, settling my hands on her lower back.

I kiss her head before saying, "It's early. You should go back to bed."

"You weren't there and I got cold. Plus, I don't normally sleep in," she says, yawning again. "Did you say you're going into the city?"

"We're going, but not until later. I have some things I need to take care of around here first. I'm going to drop you off at the Kings' place before the meeting tonight. Sam wants to meet you." I kiss the top of her head again, but she leans back.

"Who's Sam?" She's awake now as she scrunches her nose.

"She's...well, it's a little complicated. Has Mac told you anything about how things are structured around here?" The last thing I want to do is explain the politics of Synd to her.

"I mean, she said powerful people run the city and the Reapers are a small part of that. Wait, she mentioned Sam." She shakes her head before laying it back on my bare chest. "Did she mean powerful, like they're rich, or something else?"

I hesitate for too long and she leans back again. I don't know whether I should tell her the Kings and Byrns are mafia families. I trust her to keep it quiet, but her stepfather *is* a judge. I have no idea what kind of tactics he'll employ to extract information from her. Until she's set on staying here with me, I can't take the risk.

"They're rich and powerful, but they're good people. Sam is, uhh, with all the Kings." I smirk when she pops her eyebrow up. "She doesn't discriminate against multiple partners, if you catch my drift."

"That sounds...exhausting. Can you imagine dealing with that many dicks? Not to mention that many male egos? No thank you. You're enough to handle," she mutters, pulling from my arms.

She spins to the sink and I step into her body, cupping her ass and digging my fingers into the crease while she splashes water on her face. She glares at my reflection as droplets roll down her cheeks. I lean in, keeping my eyes on hers to whisper in her ear.

"That sounds like you're willing to stay and handle me, *mo dóchais*. I'm not sure you're ready for the game you're playing."

I smirk as her eyes widen and her ass clenches under my palms. When I dig my fingers in further, she jerks forward, smacking her knee into the vanity. She yelps and bends down to rub it, exposing more of her delicious skin as the t-shirt I gave her rides up. Tracing her red thong, I hook the fabric with my finger, yanking it to expose more of her flesh. She glances back and I grin, grabbing a handful of her ass and kneading.

"Don't think you can distract me with your dick. I distinctly remember you not answering the question of what kind of shit the Kings are in to," she says, straightening and the shirt falls.

I wrap my arms around her waist and nuzzle my face into the warm skin of her neck.

"Don't worry about it," I mutter before nipping my way to her jaw.

"You realize they'll probably assume you've already told me and I'll find out anyway. I'd rather not be walking in blind."

I meet her eyes in the mirror. "They're mafia. There's only a ten percent chance they'll kill you for knowing though."

I smirk at her withering look. There are a thousand things I need to do today, but the urge to carry her back to my bed and have a very special breakfast is too strong to resist.

Tucking my arm under her legs, I swing her up, and my towel drops from my hips. She laughs as I toss her on the bed. Bracing on her elbows she eyes me, a smile playing on her lips. Our rocky start would be enough to deter others, but I'm a persistent motherfucker. Something buried deep inside me knew before I was willing to acknowledge it that she is exactly what I'm looking for.

"We should get dressed," she says as she fingers the hem of her shirt, forcing it higher, exposing more silky skin. "We hardly have the time for whatever it is that's brewing in your mind. Plus, I'm hungry."

"Funny. So am I."

I drop to my knees beside the bed before encircling her ankles to yank her closer to the edge. The move causes her to fall back, her shirt bunching under her arms. Skimming my hands up her skin I grasp her tits, pinching her nipples as I bask in the gasps falling from her lips. I toy with the edges of her thong, barely covering her pussy before grabbing the fabric and tearing it from her body. I toss the remnants on her tits as she gapes at me.

"You ripped my panties!"

I chuckle. "Sure did. If you don't want to lose any more, don't wear them."

I spread her knees wider finding her already soaked and pulsing. Her whimper echoes through the room when I brush my fingers along her legs. I catch her gaze one last time before I bury my face into her pussy, groaning when the taste of her dances across my tongue. I could spend every day savoring her and it still wouldn't be enough. I already know I'm fucked when it comes to her body. I crave her. I want to possess every inch of her.

I don't have it in me today to go slowly as I devour her. I'm too hungry and impatient. I need to be inside her again, but not before she comes on my face. I push two fingers in, sucking her clit in my mouth, swirling and licking. Her fingers dig into my hair, yanking hard and then she's clenching around my fingers, a low moan leaving her. I linger, easing her through her orgasm. She's still shuddering as I pull back, her hands falling from my hair as her glazed eyes find mine.

"Such a good girl, keeping your eyes on me while I make you come," I murmur, stroking inside her. Her pussy spasms again at my words and I can't hold back my grin. Running my hand up her leg while I pull my fingers out, I lean over her. She's panting, that pretty flush painting her skin. A tremor runs through her and her eyes widen when I run my fingers, still wet from her pussy, down to her ass.

"Have you let anyone in here?" I ask, circling the tight hole.

"No," she breathes.

Her face is wary, but her body is shaking with anticipation when I press the tip of my finger inside. She can't hold back the soft moan, and I cover her mouth with mine to swallow the sound. I won't be able to take her there today but getting her ready for me later will be fun. I crook my finger inside her ass and another moan sounds in the back of her throat. She yanks her mouth away, gasping for breath.

"I...I need..." she stutters.

I grab my cock, lining myself up with her drenched pussy. Surging into her, I tip my head back and groan when her heat envelops me. I grit my teeth when I bottom out, resting my forehead on hers.

"That what you needed?"

She whimpers as she nods her head, squirming beneath me and my finger almost slips out and I press it in further. I expect her to pull away, but instead she meets me, pushing forward.

Her pussy clings to my cock and when I twist my finger, the move sends her flying over the edge again. I wasn't expecting her to come so quickly and her orgasm takes us both off guard.

Groaning, I pull both my finger and cock from her and then slam back into her as she spasms around me. Grabbing her hips, I pull her ass higher, and the new angle has my eyes rolling to the back of my head.

"You're going to ruin me, *mo dóchais*," I grunt as I thrust into her again—over and over as her needy moans swirl around us.

"Only fair," she gasps, latching onto my wrists, meeting my every thrust.

Grabbing her leg, I force it up so her ankle rests on my shoulder. I'm so deep inside her, I don't know where I end and she begins. I'm teetering on the edge already and my stomach tightens.

"One more, Willow. Give me one more," I say through gritted teeth.

Her hand falls to her clit and I almost explode, watching her fingers circle the small nub. We're both gasping and I won't make it much longer.

Reaching up to roll her nipple between my fingers, pinching, and she explodes around me, pussy pulsing in time with my thrusts. Once more I surge into her, sailing over the edge myself. My groans mingle with her cries and it might be the most perfect symphony of sounds I've ever heard.

When I've come back to my body, her pussy clings to my cock, and I lower her leg gently before covering my body with hers. I roll us until we're on our sides and I brush her hair away from her face. Her half-lidded gaze finds mine and she smiles.

She sighs, eyes falling closed. "This is exactly what I was looking for."

Chapter Eighteen

Willow

Hawk said the Kings lived in a house, but this is a legit mansion. It spans half a freaking block for fuck's sake, surrounded by forest with an honest-to-goodness guard shack at the entrance. I glare at his back through the helmet as we circle a huge fountain, featuring a mermaid with water spilling from her mouth.

When he finally parks beside the wide stairs leading up to the huge double doors, my stomach rolls. I'm sure my muscles would be tense if they weren't jelly from our escapades this morning after his shower. And again at lunch when he laid me on the kitchen island for "lunch," the remnants of our actual meal crashing to the floor. The mess was ridiculous, but I wasn't complaining. The more he fucks me, the more confident I become.

I never thought I'd be with someone who makes me crave his touch, but here I am. The memories of what he's put my body through is enough to send a thrill through me, and I swear I'm wet again. I'm going to have to get more panties if he keeps this up. When Hawk brought up going commando as I pulled a new pair from my bag, I scoffed. There's no way I'm going to walk around with a permanent wet spot. The last thing I need is people thinking I peed my pants.

Hawk catches me quickly when I stumble getting off, as if he anticipated my inevitable fall. I don't have it in me to tell him I didn't trip because I'm clumsy but because he fucked my muscles into a state of limpness I'm not sure

I'll recover from. He'll laugh and try to bake the potato on his bike in full view of anyone looking out of the eighty-seven bazillion windows staring down at us.

He beats me to the clip on the helmet, deftly undoing it and pulling the cover off. My staticky hair swirls around my head, reminding me of Medusa. A pang of disappointment hits me when he turns away and lopes up the stairs, not checking to see if I follow.

The nerves hit me again as the door opens, revealing a woman slightly taller than my own five feet. She grins at Hawk and my nerves turn to envy, but I push it down. I'm sure this woman is Samantha. Her head whips around and her deep auburn hair tied up in a ponytail smacks Hawk in the chest.

I can barely make out his grin as he lifts his hand to whoever is tucked away in the shadows behind Sam. I didn't realize they were on such good terms. They're friends, which puts me firmly on the outside, yet again.

Sam's dark eyes find mine, and I swallow when she smirks. Lifting my hand, I give her a small wave, but my feet refuse to move. Even when Hawk skirts around the woman's body and disappears from view, I can't move. He forgot about me. An old ache settles in my chest as she bounds down the stairs, skidding to a stop in front of me.

"You must be Willow. I'm Sam. Mac and I are friends, so she can vouch for me that I'm not going to conk you over the head and send you floating." She grins and I try to keep my face as neutral as possible.

"I don't know what floating means, but thanks, I think," I say, twisting my fingers. When her eyes drop down, I wrap them around my waist.

The last thing I need is to paint a picture of being a fish out of water. I'm used to being around rich people. These people are definitely loaded, but they're obviously on a different level than Joseph.

The problem is they're all friends. Mac and Sam have been thick as thieves since Mac came back to Synd, according to Mac. I push the resentment down with the envy boiling in my gut.

"River running through the city. Floating bodies down said river." She waves away her words. "Don't worry about it. Why are you standing out here instead of coming inside with Hawk?"

"Oh, I was just admiring the"—my brain scrambles. Shit, I used to be good at this—"the architecture."

I gesture to the house behind her, and she tilts her head, eyeing me. I didn't think Hawk was serious when he said these people were a part of the mafia. Living with Joseph has taught me about the corruption at the top, but the fact they're actually running things is bonkers. I can't wrap my mind around it. Mac being involved in an MC was hard enough to come to grips with. My entire outlook on the world changed when she came into my life.

Sam glances behind her at the still-open door. "What's up with you and Hawk?"

My lungs seize, wondering what the hell I'm supposed to say. Hawk might have said he wants me to stay and he's well equipped to take my body to heights I've never seen before, but that doesn't mean he actually means it. Plenty of people in my life say one thing and do another. I can't even count the number of times someone's walked away from me right when I need them the most.

Hawk may have walked away just now, but at least he didn't leave me on the side of the road.

I thought it was a fluke the first time *that* happened, but after the third time, I figured the problem was me and not them. I jerk my head up, realizing I haven't answered and Sam's eyebrows have progressively risen higher the longer the silence stretches on.

"Oh, he's being forced to keep an eye on me while Mac and Ryker are in Rima." I laugh softly, but she doesn't look convinced.

"Sure, and was that before or after you picked him up at Trigger's?" She smirks.

"How many people know about that?" I tip my head back, bracing my hands on my back and stretching. I'll have to come clean to Mac if others are talking.

"I mean, my guys know because Alex can't keep a secret from me, but he's not out spouting it to random people. I'm pretty sure Mason knows, but I don't know how. And Mac doesn't know yet, because I texted her yesterday and she didn't mention it. And you know she would say something, if only so I could work some magic and get you two together. So, do you want to go inside? Or are you going to wait out here until he notices you're gone?"

"I'm sorry. You shouldn't have to hang out with me just because I don't have anywhere else to go." My cheeks flush, and I clear my throat, forging on. "I don't have a phone, so can you call me a car? I can wait at the end of the driveway if it's a problem."

This whole trip was a mistake. I know Sam is trying to be nice, probably for Mac's sake, but she shouldn't have to babysit me because Hawk can't. I hate that I'm trapped in this situation. I probably blew the whole flower thing out of proportion anyway. Other than a few scattered petals, there's no reason to think he followed me here. It's more likely those flowers were left for Mac.

"You are a whole other type of thing, huh?"

"I don't know what that means, but okay. I just don't want to impose."

"And you're just going to flit off into the setting sun, leaving Hawk behind to wonder if you've been kidnapped or something?"

"I thought you could tell him I was going...back. I told him he didn't need to bring me here. He's afraid Mac will kick his ass if he leaves me alone. Again, I didn't mean to impose."

"Oh, I see. No one told you. Wow, what a bunch of a-holes." She shakes her head. "Listen, I get it. The last thing you want to do is hang out with a bunch of people you don't know, thinking they're only doing it because someone called in a favor. No one likes to be the tag-a-long when they weren't invited. You don't have to worry though. I wanted to meet you, but Alex said you were too busy getting railed and I should give it a little time." She laughs as I choke, bracing my hands on my knees.

"What the hell are you two doing?" A man's voice rings out and I straighten, trying to not look like I'm about to lose it.

He's imposing, lording over us from the top of the stairs. He looks like he could smoosh my head with one hand. I'm more convinced than ever Hawk wasn't lying about the mafia thing after seeing this guy. Tattoos are inked along his crossed arms and his eyes are a piercing blue. I'd hate to have his attention solely on me. I might piss my pants.

"We're having a conversation," Sam sneers, wrinkling her nose. "That's Shane by the way."

"Why the hell are you doing it in the middle of the driveway?"

"Because then I don't have to listen to you bitch about the towels not being soft enough, asshat," she calls, smiling as he scowls.

"They didn't use the right shit. That's a reason to complain, Princess. Now, get your ass in here. We need to figure out dinner."

He turns and makes it one step before Sam is yelling, "Hey, shithead. How about saying hello to our guest?"

He pivots, focusing his gaze on me, and it's so much worse than I imagined. "Hello, Willow. It's nice to meet you. Please get your ass in the house before we all starve to death."

He marches back inside, not bothering to close the door behind him, convinced we'll be on his heels. I start forward, but Sam's hand whips out, stopping me in my tracks. She shakes her head, eyes trained on the open door. I don't know what we're waiting for and I'm not sure whose orders I'm supposed to follow. As intimidating as Shane is, there's an edge to Sam I'm not sure I want to cross.

"We're going to wait out here for just a bit," Sam says, relaxing her grip on me.

"What are we waiting for exactly?"

"For them to pull their heads out of their asses. Shane's being a little bitch to me. Hawk is being a dick to you. I'd disappear, just to teach Shane a lesson, but honestly, I am getting hungry and I don't have enough snacks to sustain us. So, you wanna talk about Hawk? I'm no Mac, but I can listen while you bitch about him." She smirks, plopping down on the bottom step.

Sinking next to her, I wrap my arms around my legs. "We had a thing, then it was weird, and now it's whatever."

She shoots me a look I'm not sure I want to decipher. "So, are you going to stick around then? Or do you have shit you need to get back to in Rima?"

"Staying would be...hard. There are some loose ends I'd need to tie up if I wanted to move here. Besides, I'm not sure people will want me to stay after a while. Hawk and I haven't known each other that long. I'm sure feelings will change."

"Yours or his?" She settles her chin in her hand. "I get the feeling Hawk isn't the type of guy to go half in to a situation. If he says he wants you, I'd believe him until he gives you a reason not to."

"Like leaving me standing in the driveway of a random person's house without a backward glance?" I smile ruefully.

"Eeegh, yeah. Just like that. Well, men are assholes, we don't need them."

Someone clears their throat from behind and we spin around. Another ridiculously hot man is standing there with short-cropped hair and steel gray eyes. He skips down the stairs and holds out a phone to me. I take it, since I have no idea what else to do.

"Thanks?"

"This is Ren." Sam jumps up, wrapping her arms around his waist.

"That's for you. It's untraceable, so you won't have to worry anymore," Ren says, his gravelly voice devoid of emotion.

"Oh, thank you. What do I owe you?" I stand before patting my pockets, knowing I don't have any cash on me. In fact, the only thing I do have is some lip balm in my pocket.

"Don't worry about it. Let's go inside. I'm sure Shane's head is about to explode by now, so hopefully he's learned his lesson, though I'm not holding my breath." Sam skips up the stairs, disappearing inside and leaving me alone with another intimidating man staring at me.

"Hawk is concerned for your safety, Willow. I'm sure you understand what that means for us."

He follows Sam into the house and I'm left stranded halfway up the steps, having no clue what the hell he's talking about.

Chapter Nineteen

Hawk

"**A**lex, I don't know what you want me to do. I'm not a mechanic. I don't know what the hell is wrong with your car," I growl.

He's been ignoring what I've been saying for the last ten minutes and it's starting to piss me off. I'm still stuck under the hood of a car he "found."

My palms itch and my muscles cramp the more I think about leaving Willow alone with Sam. I'm sure she's fine, but having her out of my sight sets me on edge.

"Hawk, are you eating with us or do you have to leave?" Shane barks from the doorway.

"I have to get going. I have some things to do before the meeting," I say, wiping my hands on a rag. "Alex, call a damn mechanic. Or junk it. Not worth it."

"But I saved her! I must revive my baby." Alex claps me on the shoulder as he passes. "I'll call a guy though."

"Your woman was trying to skip out, by the way. Might want to reign her in or I'll be dealing with another frantic phone call to save your asses. I don't think I can handle another fucking crisis. I'd like a break where I can raise Emma and fight with Sam, so if you could deal with whatever bullshit is happening between you two, that'd be great," Shane growls.

I follow them inside, wondering when the hell I fell into this group. I barely paid attention to what was going on in Synd, much less who was running shit before. Helms dealt with the mafia the most and even then he almost never worked with them until the Guild forced us. We've been living in our own little bubble.

Now, relationships are changing and I'm not sure how to deal with it. The Reapers may have saved me, but it still took me a while to trust my brothers in the MC. Expanding that circle is frustrating and anxiety-inducing.

When we reach the kitchen, Sam is chattering away at the table while Willow looks lost. I want to pull her up and confront her about trying to run, but I'm not about to make a scene in front of the Kings. I'm sure Alex blabbed to everyone.

Ren catches my eye and gestures to the backyard. The last thing I want to do is chit-chat, but at least he won't make me look at another engine. And he'll get to the point.

"Hawk, I gave Willow a new phone. I already programmed our numbers into it. Please let her know if she needs anything she can text me. Also, Nemesis informed me that the Aston Martin we've been tracking has been in your territory fourteen times over the past three days. I believe he is looking for someone or more likely, found her. Has Willow mentioned anything about someone following her?"

"Willow's stepfather is Judge Joseph Merrick, if that means anything to you, and he's a class-A prick. I wouldn't put it past him to send someone to drag her ass home. She's hiding something though and she won't tell me what. I'd put money on it being the judge."

I glance back at Willow. A small smile plays on her face, but whenever Sam's attention wanders, her face falls. She glances my way but ducks her head quickly. I don't know what the hell happened between leaving my house and arriving here, but she's acting like we're strangers. I wonder if she thinks we're good at fucking and not much else yet. I watched Ryker and Mac dance around each other for months and I'm not about to fall into the same trap they did.

"You'll need to get her to open up to you then. We can't make any moves against him or the judge if we don't have a reason. There's always the possibility Aston Martin guy is an innocent bystander. I'd rather not make that mistake again. Nemesis tore me a new one when she found out we fucked that up last time. Plus, I have Mason on my ass about upgrading the system on his house. Someone keeps tripping the sensors over there and he can't figure out what or who it is," Ren says, eyes fixed on his tablet.

"Didn't you guys have that problem when the Guild was terrorizing everyone?"

"Yes, and I never found them. Shane was convinced it was Sam, but it continued to happen even after she came home. Then it just stopped. Apparently, they've moved on to Byrns's place. Start talking to your woman. She might be in trouble and I'm sure you'd like to keep her safe."

My woman.

Ren walks back inside, leaving me in the fading rays of the late summer sun. Every time I come here, I'm surprised at how quiet it is, though it's technically in the city. The forest surrounds the edges of the property, insulating them in a bubble within society. I'm used to the crickets singing through the air, but I always expect the city to encroach on their space.

I pull in a deep breath, the smell of fresh cut grass filling my nose. Ren's words sent a thrill through me when he called her mine. Quickly, though, it was replaced with cold fear seeping into my veins. I can't keep her safe if she doesn't tell me what the hell is going on.

"Hawk?" Willow's soft voice drifts over me, easing the tension in my muscles.

I hold my hand behind me until I feel hers slip into mine before tugging her to my side. She tries to pull away, but I grip her tighter, staring out into the slowly darkening forest.

"Shane said you were going to run," I murmur and she tenses.

"I wasn't running. I told Sam she didn't have to babysit me, that's all. I'm surprised you noticed I was gone." Bitterness seeps into her tone, and I glance down at her.

"Sam wanted to talk to you. I thought it would be easier for you to get to know her without a bunch of guys hanging around. And she's not babysitting you. We've established you're a grown ass woman who doesn't need someone watching her. But you do need to be protected, Willow. I need you to tell me what you're running from other than the judge." I watch her until she ducks her head, hiding her face.

"Things are complicated, but I didn't run to Synd. I don't have a rival MC after me. I've heard whispers of the Guild in Rima, but there's no evidence of that. They wouldn't bother with me anyway. All my problems are personal and won't affect the Reapers. Or these people. So, just leave it."

"It'll affect me," I murmur, tucking my arm around her waist and pulling her close.

"How do you figure?" Willow crosses her arms, like she's afraid to touch me.

I drop a kiss on the top of her head. "Because it affects you. You don't want to stay here with Sam, do you?"

She shakes her head, her knuckles turning white as she squeezes her arms.

"Okay, then let's get going. I'll reschedule with Mason, maybe for when Sam can meet us there so you two can hang out."

I drop my arm, grabbing for her hand again.

"What about the meeting? I'm not allowed in there, am I?" Her eyes finally find mine and they're lined with concern, but also relief.

"I'm acting president while Helms is away. I can do whatever the fuck I want."

Walking into headquarters with Willow is one of the hardest things I've ever had to do and with the way I grew up, that's saying something. I didn't think it would be that big of a deal, but as soon as we slipped through the back doors, every eye in the room swung toward us and the conversations died a slow death. Willow froze, that flush I love so much splashing across her face. I had to practically drag her to a chair off to the side at the front.

I didn't want to stick her in the back with a bunch of guys eyeing her, but I might have fucked up putting her center stage. Her knuckles are red from all the pinching she's doing. Doc posted up next to her and has been glaring at everyone who looks their way.

I wish I could have postponed this whole thing, but there are four shipments coming in this week and Tank has been on my ass about getting them all sorted. I glance at Willow again and her wide eyes meet mine. I need to wrap this up before someone goes off the rails or she pukes all over the floor.

"Anything else?" I bellow over the chatter that's started up again.

When Helms runs these things, no one starts randomly talking, but they push the limits with me. I could say something, make an example out of someone, but the thought makes me feel like a teacher scolding an unruly class.

"Are we just bringing anyone into the meetings now? Can I bring my hooker next time?" Rooster sneers, leaning back in his chair with crossed arms.

His gaze zeroes in on Willow and regret slams through me that Helms didn't pull the trigger months ago when he had his gun pressed to Rooster's head. He's let himself go the last couple of years, not caring whether he can do his job or not. His drinking is out of control, giving him a splotchy complexion and a nasty temper.

"You're on thin ice as it is, Rooster. You really want to push me?" My calm tone doesn't match the emotions grappling inside me.

"What are *you* going to do?" He smirks and I return it with one of my own.

I could strip him right here. It's been a long time coming, and not just because of how he's been treating the women. I cock my head, staring at him until he glances away, a flush crawling up his neck.

From the corner of my eye, I see Tank lean forward, ready to go at my say-so. I'd rather not float the cocksucker without Helms's approval, but I doubt Rooster would be missed. He's a remnant of the Reapers when Dain Helms, Ryker's dad, was in charge. He's part of the generation falling in between the old club and the new and he never made the transition with the rest of them. Personally, I think he wanted more power and Helms said no, but I've never asked.

"Anyone else?" I ask, raising an eyebrow as I scan the crowd. Some duck their heads, others openly glare at Rooster, but a few are eyeing Willow. I mark them before moving on.

When no one answers, I bellow, "Veiled in shadows."

"Chased by darkness," they rumble back.

The sound of almost a hundred chairs scraping across the tiles sets my teeth on edge. Willow is still frozen in the chair, lips barely moving as she whispers something to Doc. He nods as I approach and I tip my chin, pulling Willow to her feet.

She stumbles, but I steady her before tugging her toward the back door. I trust Doc to stop anyone who tries to follow us. The cooling summer humidity flows over me and I let out a deep breath. I never like running meetings, but having Willow there made it infinitely harder.

"That was interesting. I didn't realize you guys had, like, businesses and stuff," Willow says as I lace our fingers together and start toward Helms's backyard. I parked my bike there, instead of at headquarters, if only so I wouldn't have to deal with everyone else both before and after.

"Technically, we are a business, even if most of those businesses are shady. We're not trying to bring the city down though. If we manage shit, then it doesn't get out of control. We handle the supply and demand and fewer people get hurt."

I pull her to a stop, scanning the tree line, but there's nothing other than crickets and a soft breeze through the leaves marring the night under the rumble of a hundred bikes on their way home. Their departure is muted by the buildings, but I could have sworn I heard a branch snap at the edge of the forest.

"What's up with that thing you did at the end?" Willow's voice calls my attention back and I shove away the paranoia riding me.

"That's our motto for the club. Seems weird to say it at the end of every meeting, especially since it's not like it rhymes or anything. When I asked about it, Helms said it was a habit leftover from his dad's time."

"Would you change it if you could?"

I glance at her, but she's staring at the ground. I'd think she was hiding again, but I actually think she's trying not to trip in the dark. The thought makes me grin.

"No reason to change a motto. It fits us, but I wouldn't say it at every meeting if I didn't have to. Seems like the words would be more powerful if we weren't spouting them all the time."

We skirt the back porch, heading for my bike when I catch a flash of something swaying off the handlebar. Willow gasps as she rips her hand from mine and races forward. I snatch her around the waist before she can reach what I see now is a silver locket. A soft cry leaves her as her body curls, my arm the only thing holding her upright. She flings a hand out, swiping at the air to retrieve it, but she's too far away.

"Willow, stop."

I haul her back and she spins, sobbing into my chest. I have no idea what's going on, but she falls apart in my arms as I rub her back, glancing around. The last of the bikes are fading into the night, cicadas taking over the quiet. Everyone else is locked up tight in their homes.

As her tears ease, she hiccups and then holds her breath, trying to pull away, but I clutch her to me. I can't tell if she's frightened or upset. She seems to be teetering between both.

Tucking her arm between us, she wipes her face. Her body trembles even as she pulls herself back together. I'm convinced this present is tied to what she's running from. I can't let her keep putting me off.

"Willow, tell me what's going on," I murmur into her hair, resting my forehead against the strands.

"I'm sorry," she whispers.

"I don't need your apologies. I need explanations. You have to tell me what the hell is going on." I don't mean for it to come out as harshly as it does, but I have to know.

"That necklace was my mother's." She hiccups again. "It's been missing for three months."

Glancing at the silver locket swaying in the slight breeze and reflecting the light from the streetlamp with each pass, I tense. Whoever left this didn't return it out of the kindness of their heart. They did it to scare Willow. I need more information, but not here.

Scanning the trees, I remember the snap of a branch that echoed through the night as we walked here. It was normal before, but now it seems like an omen. I have to get her home before they come back. The hair on the back of my neck stands at attention and I peer behind me, trying to penetrate the darkness.

"We need to go, Willow. Get on the bike," I command, guiding her forward.

She reaches for the necklace, but I get there first, tucking it into my pocket. The last thing I want is for it to get lost again.

When she steps forward, her legs give out, and I scoop her up. On the seat is a pink and white flower. I don't know what kind it is, but she's shaking again. I sweep it away before placing her on the seat and her body curls before I can slip in front of her. I skim my hand up and down her back, waiting until her body stops shivering.

"A peony," she whispers, eyeing the flower.

"He obsessed with flowers or something?"

"It means anger," she murmurs, sitting up, and I settle in front of her. Willow's trembling arms wrap around my waist, one of her hands curling on my belt to steady herself as I crush the petals under my boot.

It's not until we're pulling onto the street and she tucks her face against my back that I realize she's not wearing a helmet. I slow, intent on pulling to the side when a small light glows from the trees, like a phone lighting up. I gun it and Willow's arms flex.

I circle the territory three times, looking for headlights trailing us. When I'm finally convinced there's no one else on the road, I pull into my driveway, parking in the back before twisting around to grab Willow and set her on her feet next to me.

Willow doesn't move, so I scoop her up again to carry her inside. The house is dark and she tucks closer to me as we approach the living room. I doubt she'll allow me to put her down now, so I plop on the couch with her on my lap.

Pulling out the necklace, I drop it in her waiting hand and she turns it over slowly, brushing her thumb over the engraving on the front.

"What flower is that?" I murmur, laying my cheek on her head.

"A hyacinth." She brushes her thumb over it again before popping it open. I expect a picture or a message inside, but it's empty.

"Was it always empty? Where did you lose it?"

Her body tenses. "I didn't lose it. I left it in my bedroom and then it was gone. I almost never wore it, because I was afraid it would break. My mother gave it to me before she died. I never had anything to put inside though."

"Do you think the judge left it for you?"

He clearly knows where she is. And he wants her back in Rima for whatever reason, based on the call I overheard. I wouldn't put it past him to use scare tactics to make her fall in line. She's silent so long, turning the locket over in her hands, I'm sure she won't answer when she lets out a humorless laugh.

"It wasn't Joseph. He's not subtle. This is someone else," she murmurs quietly.

"Who is it then?"

"I don't know."

I set her next to me before tipping my head against the back of the couch. I catch her small sniff at me distancing myself, but I can't keep going around and around with her. She needs to tell me or...I don't even know what I'll do. I'll never send her back. I refuse to let her go.

"We can't keep doing this, Willow. You need to tell me who left that on my bike. Now." I cross my arms if only to stop myself from reaching for her again.

"I told you. I don't know."

I shoot up, striding for the kitchen. Yanking open the fridge, I stare blankly at the emptiness inside as if something will magically appear to calm my ass down. There isn't anything that'll make this better, other than maybe sinking into her body, but even fucking her will only delay these feelings rolling through me.

I slam the door shut, spinning around to lean against the counter. Moonlight streaming through the window silhouettes Willow's frame in the doorway and a tear flows down her cheek.

"Hawk, I'm not trying to keep things from you. I honestly don't know who's been doing this."

"Doing what?" I track the emotions flitting across her face, trying to gauge if she's keeping more shit from me.

"It started with flowers. And then it moved on to small trinkets. I went to Joseph, and he said it wasn't a big deal and I should accept the fact that people would try to get to him through me. So, I just threw them away. Then things were moved in my room. When my things started going missing, I didn't notice at first. I thought the stress was making me forgetful."

Willow stares at her feet as she runs the chain through her fingers and a tear splashes on her hand.

"Someone was following me. There were...pictures left on my car. At one point one of my tires was flat, but I don't know if they had anything to do with it. It could be a coincidence."

"It wasn't," I grunt and her head pops up, eyes finding mine. They're swimming with wariness. "What else?"

"Right before I came here, I went on a date. Joseph insisted, seeing as how he's somebody's son or whatever. Sometimes it's just easier to go along with him instead of fighting. When I came out of the restaurant someone had carved something in the hood of my car. It freaked me out enough that I ran from Rima that night. I thought if I left for a while, let things cool down, he would leave me alone. He would find something else to fixate on."

"That's not how stalkers work, Willow."

She tips her head back. "I'm not convinced it's a stalker."

"Oh, it's a fucking stalker, *mo dóchais*. And they've followed you right to us."

Twenty

Willow

Hawk's words pierce into my already battered body. He's right. I led my stalker straight to them. Deep down, I knew. I was lying to myself every time I dismissed the signs. I never wanted to label him a stalker, since it felt like I was overreacting. I didn't have anyone to turn to, other than Joseph, and I'm not surprised he brushed off my concerns. The one person I mentioned anything to said I should feel flattered. At some point I have to take responsibility for my own role in this.

"I'm sorry," I whisper.

I don't know what else to say. There's nothing else to do but try to fix what I've done. This is why I told Hawk I wouldn't be able to stay. I blamed Joseph, but in reality, this situation isn't something I can bring on someone else. No one is going to save me. I need to save myself.

When Hawk doesn't say anything, merely staring at his feet, I step back. My feet whisper across the hardwood, until I reach the stairs. Ten seconds pass and he's still frozen in whatever mental war he's immersed in.

The locket digs into my palm, reminding me of why I need to leave. My mother never left, always thinking she could build a better life for us with more money. She lied to me, telling me she was in love, but looking back as an adult, I realize how terrible our lives were before Joseph came waltzing in. We weren't in a position to turn him down. She never saw that I would have stayed in that tiny apartment, living off noodles and bread because there was safety in that space. That security eroded bit by bit when Joseph stepped into our lives.

I fly up the stairs, tripping on the last stair and my knee slams to the floor, a soft cry leaving me. Tears spring to my eyes as I breathe through the throbbing pain. Holding my breath, I let it out in a whoosh and crawl to my feet when I realize I'm waiting for Hawk to come for me.

Glancing over the railing, my muscles tense when I find him still frozen in the kitchen. Of course he isn't coming. He told me he wanted to keep me, but he didn't grasp who I was, or what I was facing, where I needed to be. Hell, I don't even know where I need to be, but it isn't here.

I don't bother to close the door when I step into his bedroom. Like when I was staying at Mac's, I haven't unpacked. Most of my things are still stuffed away in duffel bags. I pull the phone Ren gave me from my pocket, hoping I can call a car. I haven't even put anything on it. I stuff it back in my pocket as the purr of an engine filters through the pounding in my ears.

Peeking around the corner, I track Hawk as he lumbers to the front door. As he pulls it open, the urge to stop him almost brings me to my knees. My entire body flinches when he steps outside and then my feet are moving before I can consciously make the decision.

Skipping the last three steps, my bare feet slap against the hardwood and Hawk twists, confusion etched on his face. As I glance over his shoulder, all I can make out is a sleek black car rolling past and then the window slowly descends. My legs give out as the sound of a gunshot ricochets into the quiet night, Hawk's face filling with horror and my hearing switches back on.

"Run," Hawk snaps.

His eyes are manic as his body falls, his head bouncing against the door frame on the way down. Tires screech and the car shoots forward, leaving something fluttering to the ground in its wake. I crawl to Hawk's side, shaking his arm. His body rolls, a dark splash of red bleeding into the fabric by his shoulder. My brain screams for me to do something, drowning out any logic.

"Pressure," I breathe.

I gather the hem of his shirt, pressing on where I think the wound is, and a soft grunt is forced from him. A sob leaves me when I spot the lump forming on his temple.

I reach for my pocket, but freeze when I see my trembling hand swathed in bright red. My breath comes in short gasps and I shake my head as I pull my phone out.

Headlights cut across my vision, blinding me and my phone slips from my grasp, clattering across the porch. Lifting my hand to flag them down, my heart stops as the same car barrels toward us.

"Hawk, they're coming back," I sob, tucking my hands under his arms, but he's too heavy.

His eyes open, revealing slits of green. "Run."

Ignoring his words, I tuck my hands under his arms, and brace my feet, heaving his body back toward the safety of the house. The soles of my feet slip and I land on my ass, but I scramble up again, intent on getting him inside.

Digging my heels in, a bloody trail smears across the porch as I fight for purchase. Hawk's eyes turn glassy, even as he groans my name, but I refuse to leave him. Whoever shot him isn't after me. I won't abandon him.

I'm wheezing by the time I drag his body over the threshold. When his hips clear the door, he passes out and I grit my teeth. The car flies past when I finally get him inside, bullets hitting the porch, inches from his legs.

I throw myself over his prone body, covering as much of him as possible. Whoever they are, they don't stop, screeching through the street as porch lights pop on, piercing the darkness in front of the houses. Someone returns fire, but the car speeds away.

I cup Hawk's face, leaning over him, screaming his name again and again, praying he didn't pay the price for my mistakes. He doesn't wake.

Jerking upright, I whip my head back and forth before settling my eyes on Hawk tucked in his bed, sheet pulled up to his waist. Guilt settles in my bones, but I try to push it away when I find his eyes open and fixed on me.

"Why..." He clears his throat, turning his gaze to the ceiling.

"I wanted to make sure you woke up. Ink was here, but he had to go take care of something. I called Mac but she didn't pick up. I didn't want to leave a message though. I think someone called Ryker." I'm rambling so I press my lips together to stop more words from bubbling out.

"I'm awake now."

"Yeah. Okay. I'm going to go then. You should rest." Shuffling to my feet, I will him to look at me, but instead he scans the space, throat bobbing as he swallows.

"You leaving?" he asks and I try to not let the sob caught in my throat out.

"I just wanted to make sure you didn't...well..."

"You're leaving Synd, aren't you?" he sneers, accusation clear in his voice.

I lace my fingers together, pinching the skin on my knuckles, but I curl them around my waist when he notices. It's an old habit I thought I'd done away with, but the last few months have brought out all sorts of things I thought I'd dealt with. I open my mouth, but snap it shut, not sure how he'll react.

"I already planned to—before. You were right. I shouldn't have brought my problems here. I didn't think I was dragging anyone else into this, especially not you. I didn't realize how far he'd go," I whisper, if only so he won't hear how close I am to tears. Even if my stalker wasn't the one who shot Hawk, this was a wake-up call I wish we could have avoided.

"He'll kill you."

I freeze, staring at the far wall. He doesn't have to remind me. I know what I'm walking into. My stalker might not kill me, but whatever he does I'll probably wish I was dead. A tear slips down my cheek. I wish I could hide it from him. I won't use my tears to garner pity. We both know what I'm walking back into.

"I know," I murmur.

"Why leave then?"

His choice of words doesn't escape me. He might not like it, but he agrees that I no longer belong here, no matter what he said before. I don't blame him for making promises. He didn't have all the facts. He didn't realize how hard it would be to keep me. I've already gotten him shot, I won't get him killed too.

Ink said he'd be fine, it would be barely an annoyance in a couple days, but still. He shouldn't be hurt because of me. My heart aches though, wondering where we could have gone if my life wasn't such a disaster. I tried to deny it, but he was exactly what I was looking for. Willingly leaving it all behind, some place I finally feel like I could belong—is tearing my heart from my chest. It'll stay here, long after I leave. Pushing him over the edge is the only way to end this without guilt riding him once I'm gone.

I let out a scornful laugh, meeting his eye again. "You can't be serious. You were fucking shot. You can't think I'd stay here after watching you bleed all over me, knowing it could happen again at any moment. I won't let you pay for my sins, Hawk, and certainly not with your blood. No, I'll take my chances back in Rima, or wherever I end up."

"Wherever you end up?" He raises an eyebrow.

"I might just see how far the cash I have can take me. I can figure out what to do from there."

"Seems like you've got it all figured out then, don't you?"

I swipe at the tear rolling down my face, scrubbing away the anger bubbling inside. Why I thought this was a good idea is beyond me. I should have slipped out after Ink saw him. I should have hitched a ride with Mac when she left. I shouldn't have come at all. I can't bring myself to regret it though. Hawk may deserve someone who doesn't have the baggage I do, but he's the one I'll compare everyone else to from now on. And I'll never find someone like him, if I even live that long.

"I'm sorry you got hurt." It's the only thing I can think of. I don't expect a response, since he's said enough already.

"Because of you," he says, glaring at the ceiling.

My heart shatters, but I gather the armor I have to put on when dealing with Joseph. Most of his words no longer touch me. Hawk's still worm their way through, but I won't show him how much he's hurting me.

I need to get out of here. I need to figure out what I'm going to do. I need to do what's best for him, even if it's not me.

Slipping out the door, I shut it softly behind me. I grab the bags sitting right outside just as the lock on the front door clicks. Fading more into the shadows of the hallway, I hold my breath, letting it out in a whoosh when Doc comes strolling through. I haven't been here long enough to really know these people, but Doc's been nice. He intimidated the hell out of me when he plopped down in the chair next to me at the meeting. But he was kind and listened whenever I spoke, which is rare.

Mostly people ignore me or talk over me. I'm so used to it, I've started pausing when I think I'm talking too much, giving them the pass, which is fucked up. I shouldn't care about taking up space.

I wait until Doc is halfway up the stairs before I give him a small smile. He eyes the bags in my arms before his eyebrow ticks up.

"Going somewhere?" His soft voice soothes some of the tension riding me.

"Yeah, I'm going to go...seems like the right choice," I murmur, glancing at the closed door.

He nods, following my gaze. "Hawk know you're leaving or are you slipping out without a word?"

I swallow the bubble of laughter. Wouldn't it be ironic if I left without so much as a note just like he did that first night?

"He knows. He's not very happy with me right now and I don't blame him. He should be angry. Not much more I can do than leave. Things will settle down once I'm gone. Thanks for all your help. You were really nice to me and you didn't have to be."

"Did he actually tell you to leave or is that what you think he wants?"

I snort. I don't want to dissect Hawk's words with Doc. "He made it clear. Things will go back to normal for you guys and I won't be in the way anymore. I'm sorry about all this."

I skirt around him, which isn't easy with his size. He's over a foot taller than me and almost as wide as the stairs, but he lets me pass. I tense when his feet shift, but force myself to plod down the rest of the steps. The front door springs open again and I jump back, bringing the bags in front of me, as if they'll protect me from attack. Ink barrels through, a scowl firmly in place and I tense.

"Blue is outside, Willow. He can take you wherever you wanna go." He glares at me before stomping up the stairs, almost knocking Doc over in the process. I don't know how he figured out I was leaving, but the packed bags might have given it away.

A heavy breath whooshes from me when I spot a car idling at the curb. The last thing I want to do is get on the back of a bike. Not only is there nothing between me and someone who wants to shoot me, but it would feel weird riding with anyone other than Hawk. When that happened, I have no idea.

I tense again when I spot the puffs of rhododendrons littering the curb. Everyone else is tucked in bed. I'm sure none of them even know the Reapers VP was shot, and I'm the one who caused it. The telltale evidence of my mistakes is scattered upon the pavement. I shake my head as my heart cracks.

"You're making a mistake, Willow." Doc's voice floats down the stairs. I don't bother to turn.

"Maybe, but I won't stay where I'm"—I scramble for something else to say other than tell him I'm not wanted here—"putting others at risk."

My flip-flops scrape across the threshold as I pull the door closed behind me. The click reverberates in my chest, feeling like a finality I'm not sure I'm ready for.

Twenty One

Hawk

The pain radiating through my shoulder is excruciating. I've been shot before, but it didn't feel like this. Lifting my left arm is impossible. Opening my eyes when my bedroom door flies open is hard, as if rocks sit on my lids.

Memories skip around my brain as Ink paces to the bathroom. I must have passed out at some point, since I don't remember anyone carrying me to bed and there's no way Willow could manage that. The moon filtering through the window catches on Ink's tattoos as he stomps to my side.

"You know, this would be a lot easier if you assholes would stop getting fucking shot," he grumbles, poking at my shoulder, sending white hot pain radiating down my arm, and I grit my teeth.

"Didn't really ask for it, dumbass. I'll try to step out of the way next time."

Doc slams the door open and the sound reverberates through my skull, making me wince. He huffs and I wonder how many times I'm going to get my ass chewed for something I had no control over. I guess I could have had more sense and not opened the fucking door, but I won't admit that to them.

"What the fuck are you doing?" Doc growls, crossing his arms.

"I'm planning a goddamn vacation. What the hell does it look like I'm doing?"

"Thought you were intent on keeping her? Now you're just done?"

Ink mumbles under his breath, ripping off the bandage from my wound and I swallow hard when the burn sets in. I swear he took off some skin with the tape.

"What the hell are you talking about?"

"Willow, fucker. She's gone," Doc bellows.

I rear back against the pillows and Ink straightens, turning wide eyes to Doc. I don't know if I've ever heard him raise his voice. I got used to the fact he was unflappable. Apparently, all it took was me fucking up my life with a woman to bring out his rage.

"She's probably going to Helms's. She's not going to leave Synd in the middle of the night."

I didn't handle this situation with her the right way, but I need more time to process. I knew she was hiding something, but a stalker wasn't what I imagined. Then minutes later I was shot with no warning. This whole thing is a shit show, and now I have to deal with the fallout.

"Blue is driving her to the train station as we speak."

Doc's words take a good thirty seconds to filter through my brain. Once they do though, I bolt upright, groaning when the move sends more pain shimmering through me. Panting, I wait for my vision to clear before I swing my legs over the side.

"What the fuck are you doing? Get your ass back in bed," Ink snaps, but I reach for my pants.

"You can't go after her, Hawk. You can't even ride. I'll call Blue, have him bring her back." Doc's voice mellows and he slips from the room.

Ink points to the bed and I collapse back, gulping down deep breaths. "I didn't think she'd actually leave. I thought I'd have time to stop her."

"Word of advice, Hawk. Don't wait until the right time. Even when you're pissed. She seems like the kind of girl you'll need to be super fucking literal with."

He pulls out more supplies, getting ready to put another bandage on my wound. For how small the hole is, I'm surprised it hurts as much as it does.

"Why's that?" I wheeze.

"I don't think Willow has been told point blank what she's worth. If she's significant to you, tell her and follow through on that shit." He presses a little harder on the tape.

"When did you become a fucking therapist? Thought that was Doc's role?"

"Don't be an asshole, Hawk," Doc says from the doorway. "Blue is bringing her back. She fell asleep on the way there anyway, so she might not even notice he didn't take her to the train station. Might freak her out when she wakes up next to you though. Oh, and Blue said she was sobbing most of the way until she conked out."

Ink marches out ten minutes later, still grumbling under his breath. Doc is posted in my door frame, arms crossed and scowling. I close my eyes, not willing to face the accusation on his face, no matter how right he is.

I fucked up when I reacted the way I did. Eventually, we would have gotten on the same page. We would have talked, figured shit out, and I could have protected her. Instead, I let her walk away thinking I was pissed.

I don't know how to protect her from him. I can fight her stepfather. I can go up against another MC. Hell, I can fight the whole fucking world if need be. But going up against someone I can't find? A faceless enemy? I don't know how to save her from that. I'm not a fucking detective. I don't have the skills to find this guy and end him.

The exhaustion has me swimming in that gray area between waking and sleeping. My eyes pop open when a warm body presses against me. Blue gives me a sad smile as he draws the covers over Willow.

I swallow around the sudden thickness in my throat when she sighs, cuddling closer. Tucking an arm around her, I hold her close as my eyes fall closed. I expect the darkness to pull me under, but I end up counting her breaths deep into the night.

I'm ripped from my dreams filled with blood and heartache as Willow pulls from my grasp. I tug her back and she squeaks. My brain is still scrambling from the scenes floating in my head. I can't tell reality from dreams and it's messing with me. Willow is the only thing grounding me, and I can't force my fingers from her skin. Closing my eyes again, I breathe in the scent of her wafting over me.

She relaxes into me, but when I ease my hold, she tries to slip away again, so I tighten my grip. She mumbles under her breath and I realize she thinks I'm still sleeping. My mouth twitches, but I bite back the grin wanting to break free. The memories from last night crash into me then. Willow's stalker shooting me should be the worst of them, but in reality, it's the fact she tried to run. And I fucking let her.

When she tries to roll, I can't keep silent. "Stop it, Willow. It's too early to get up."

"Of course, you're fucking awake. Let me go, Hawk. I need to pee."

"Fine, but then come back to bed." I yawn, squeezing her hip one more time before letting her go.

She scampers from under the covers straight for the bathroom, slamming the door behind her. A grin blooms across my face as she turns on the faucet to cover the sound. She's in there so long, I start to drift off again.

Inching the door open, she tiptoes across the hardwood. My eyes are slits and I wait until her hand is easing down the handle of the bedroom door before I say anything.

"Going somewhere?"

She freezes, glancing over her shoulder. "I need to find my bags?"

"Was that a question or an answer, Willow? Because it sounded like a question. And why would you need your bags? Planning on running again?"

I feel ridiculous having this conversation while lying down, but I don't know how painful it'll be to move and I'd rather not have that override the discussion we need to have. She drops her hand and spins to lean against the door.

"It was an answer. There are clothes in my bag. And I didn't run before. You made it clear I should leave. We both know it's the right decision. I don't even know how I made it back here. Blue said he was taking me to the train station and suddenly I was waking up here. It's not my fault," she says and I can't help the grin spreading across my face. "What the hell are you smiling about?"

"You're exquisite when you're all fired up. Actually, you're hot all the time, but you're especially sexy when you get all heated. Come back to bed and let me show you how much I love when you get all feisty."

Her mouth drops open. "What the fuck, Hawk. You can't fix all our problems with your dick."

"Don't see why not." I grin at her withering look. "I can't chase you right now, *mo dóchais*, so you really need to come back to bed."

I flip the covers back and pat the space next to me. She stares at the spot, gears grinding in her brain. I don't have the option to rush her, not that I would.

She's right, we need to discuss things my cock won't fix, but I need her next to me when we do. Even having her across the room is making my palms sweat. I wish I could throw her over my shoulder and keep her safe in my bed, no matter how impossible that is. I'll need to clue the rest of the guys in, but I won't do it until we've talked.

She slowly shuffles to the other side of the bed. She doesn't crawl in though, like I want her too, but at least she's closer.

"Blue can take me to the train station now. As much as I'd like one last...well, it wouldn't be a good idea." She tucks her lip between her teeth and my cock hardens.

"Didn't mean for you to leave, Willow. I thought I made myself clear before. You're mine. Do you honestly think I'd let you go just because I got shot?" I growl.

She snorts. "Oh, you're insane. I see. That makes a lot more sense."

"Not insane. I just know what I want and I want you. Listen, you threw me off-balance. Then you started talking about leaving and I was pissed." I grab her hand to stop her from twisting her fingers together. I hate that she's nervous with me. I don't want her to doubt me just because shit went a little sideways.

"Pissed at me," she whispers, her eyes filling with tears.

"Maybe. More at whatever made you think I wouldn't want you anymore just because of this shit. You're worth everything, Willow."

Twenty Two

Willow

Hawk squeezes my hand, shocking me back to reality. I've been lost in my head, in my emotions, for far too long. I want to crawl in next to him and let him do whatever he wants to do to my body, but it won't solve the problems I'm facing. It'll make me feel better, but then I'll be right back where we started.

"What should I do about him?" I murmur.

"Try again." His husky voice flows over me, easing the weariness in my bones.

I feel like I've lived a lifetime since last night. The moment he said I led my problems right to the Reapers, I checked out. I don't know if I can handle anyone else getting hurt because of me. I'll be responsible if someone dies. I swallow a sob, but I can't stop the tears running down my face and splashing onto our linked fingers when the image of my hands covered in his blood flits across my mind.

"I can't ask you to take this on, Hawk. I didn't think he'd follow me here. I didn't think he'd hurt someone because of me. I don't have any more solutions." I try to tug my hand away, but he grips me tighter before pulling me closer to the bed—closer to him.

"You're not responsible for his choices, *mo dóchais*. You don't need to fight this alone. You don't need all the answers. We'll figure it out together. I hear that's a thing we're supposed to do."

Peering at his face, I swipe at the tears with my free hand. He gives me a half smile, tugging on my hand again and I tumble onto the bed practically face-planting onto his cock. I catch myself at the last second, but my shin scrapes against the bed frame and I let out a yelp.

"Shit. Sorry." Hawk reaches for me, knocking the arm holding me up and then I actually do faceplant into his crotch.

Great, now it looks like I'm trying to mouth holster his yogurt cannon. He busts out laughing, his entire body shaking, which doesn't make anything better. I'm almost positive this situation couldn't get any worse when footsteps pound up the stairs and the bedroom door swings open, slamming against the wall in the process. I tip my chin up, since I can't get my arms under me, and see Ink frozen in the doorway.

"Uh, I c-can..." he stutters before spinning around but he doesn't leave. Then he's throwing his hands up as if he's warding off evil spirits or something. More footsteps pound up the stairs and I swear I'm going to burst into flames since my face is burning with embarrassment. Hawk isn't helping, seeing how he's laughing so hard he's no longer producing sounds other than the occasional groan.

Finally, I have the good sense to roll and my head settles on his trembling thighs. I throw an arm over my reddened face. I fall to my side and curl into a ball before grabbing the edge of the comforter and yanking it over my head. My legs are still exposed, but at least I'm wearing leggings.

"Not helping," Hawk wheezes, fits of laughter still bubbling from him.

I swear the other two are giggling, but I'm not going to uncover myself to check. This is more embarrassing than when my mom caught me making out with a boy when I was thirteen. Or the time someone I *thought* was my friend set me up on a fake date. Or the time...shit. I have too many embarrassing moments to choose from. All those were because of someone else's choices though. They didn't really have anything to do with me.

I fling the covers back before sitting up, twisting until I'm facing the two bikers in the doorway. Neither of them face us and their heads are bowed, but I'm convinced they're laughing at me. I paste on a smile before pushing off the bed.

"Ink, you should check his shoulder. Doc, I don't know why you're here, but if you don't have anything to do, you should make him some breakfast."

I plant my fists on my hips, glaring at their backs. Ink glances over his shoulder, his eyes bouncing around as if he'll encounter something scandalous. I roll my eyes before meeting his and they widen. I'm sure my face is bright red and I look like I'm about to jump out the window, but I'm done feeling embarrassment over the slightest thing.

"Well?" I ask, tapping my foot and Doc takes off for the stairs. Before long, the clang of pans and cupboards float up to us. Ink is still hovering in the doorway, refusing to turn.

"Just get in here, Ink, before she drags you. She's small, but certainly knows how to..."

"Do not finish that sentence." I scowl as Hawk smothers his grin behind his hand. "Ink, move. I'll get out of your way."

I shuffle back, but Hawk's hand shoots out, snatching my wrist. Ink glances between us as he drops his bag on the bed. I tug once more but there's no give, and I huff before settling on the bed next to him, leaning against the headboard. Ink tucks an arm under Hawk's shoulders and props him upright, leaving Hawk panting.

"Does it hurt?" I murmur, eyes fixed on his face. His hand slides down and he laces our fingers together, warmth seeping into my palm.

"Nope." His eyes are pinched though, and I swear he's grinding his teeth.

"Don't fucking lie," Ink says, scowling as he rips off the bandage.

The hole is a lot smaller than I expected. Then again, I've never seen a bullet wound, so what would I know? Ink pokes and prods at it, and I can't look away.

Guilt crashes into me, swirling in my gut. I'd probably throw up if I had anything in my stomach. I turn away, not able to face what I did to him. Rays of sunlight stream through the curtains, and I watch the beams dance across the wood as I strive to calm my racing heart.

Hawk's voice whispers across the shell of my ear. "It wasn't your fault. Don't fall down that hole or I'll be forced to crawl down and haul your ass back up to reality. As much as I'd like to chase after you, I'd rather end up with you underneath me, begging me to let you come."

Ink makes a choking noise, then starts mumbling under his breath. I can't make out his words, but I'm pretty sure he's cussing us out for being dirty. My face heats again and I think about scolding Hawk, but I'd be wasting my breath. Instead, I dig my elbow into his side, forcing a grunt from him. He buries his nose into my hair and tucks me closer to his side.

"Don't be like that, *mo dóchais*. You know you love the thought of me chasing you."

"Would you two knock it the fuck off?" Ink rips off another strip of tape and pushes it against Hawk's skin. He throws the roll in his bag and snaps it shut before storming from the room.

"I think you pissed him off," I whisper, flinching when the front door slams shut.

Hawk slides down until he's settled on his back, the sheet barely covering his lower half. I trace the various tattoos dotting his chest and he shivers.

I should stop. I should continue our conversation from before. I should do a shit ton of things other than scrape my nail over his nipple. He cracks a lid, a smirk creeping onto his face while he eyes me.

"Keep that up and we'll be late for breakfast," he murmurs. His thumb brushes over the arch of my foot and I shiver.

"You fuckers better be dressed," Doc yells from the kitchen.

I leap off the bed, smacking Hawk's arm along the way. "Put some pants on before he gets mad. Do you need help?"

He groans as he rolls. "Only if you're helping by taking those leggings off and sitting on my face."

Rolling my eyes, I pace from the room in search of my bags. I don't know what Blue did with them. I'm not sure what Doc's doing, but he's got an apron on and pot holders on his hands. Where he got the apron, I have no idea and my bags are still nowhere to be found.

I'm about to call out to Doc when Hawk's arms wrap around my waist, pulling me against his warm and very naked chest. He molds his body to mine and rests his chin on my shoulder. He's probably hunched over with the height difference.

"I'm surprised you're able to stay upright with a bullet in your shoulder." I mean it to come out light and airy, but my voice catches at the end and he squeezes.

"Ink took the bullet out, so there's just a hole left. No big deal. Besides, who says I'm not using you to stay on my feet?"

I can feel the pull of his smile against my neck as he drops a kiss on my skin. The sinking feeling in my stomach returns. The way he's acting is completely different from what he was projecting last night. I don't know which version of Hawk to believe. I want the one holding me, whispering dirty words, and making me feel safe to be real. I rarely get what I want though. Then again, I've never demanded anything in my life. I've always gone along with what everyone else wants, thinking they'd accept me then.

"What's going on inside that pretty little head of yours, *mo dóchais*?" he murmurs.

"I was just wondering how long this version of you is going to stick around this time."

My heart pounds in my chest and I'm pretty sure if I move I'm going to puke over the banister, but at least I said the words.

"I'm not perfect, Willow. I'm going to fuck up. I wasn't very clear with my shit last night. Ink and Doc already busted my ass for it. I'm pretty sure I've got a slew of texts from Helms telling me the same if they said anything to him about us," he says, rubbing his nose up my jaw before nipping my lobe.

"They shouldn't have done that." My voice is breathless, giving away what he's putting my body through. I still feel like I want to puke.

Sighing, he tucks his chin on top of my head. "Needed to be said. We're going to have to figure out a plan, Willow. I need to loop the others in. As much as you don't want it to, this will affect the MC. We can't ignore that, regardless of how much you might want to."

I pull away, leaning on the banister. It gives a little and I jerk back, slamming into his chest. He catches me, gripping my hips and I close my eyes, banishing the dizziness invading my head. I don't know what just happened, but the vertigo almost tipped me over the railing. His hand slides around my waist, pulling me back toward the bedroom.

"Doc, get lost," Hawk yells over my head.

Doc whips around, still swathed in an apron with steam wafting around him. He scowls, dropping the mitts before ripping the apron over his head. Hawk kicks the door shut before Doc makes it to the front door, but the echo of him slamming it after him rings through the house two seconds later.

"Hawk, what are you doing?" My voice is breathless, heat already pooling between my legs. "You should be resting or at least eating something."

He chuckles, his breath ghosting across the shell of my ear, making me shiver. "Oh, I'm definitely hungry, *mo dóchais*."

"You've already used that line."

As soon as the words are out, I trip over his feet, sending us both tumbling backwards. An oof followed by a groan rumbles from him when we hit the bed. I roll to the side, settling on my stomach and hide my face in the fluff of the comforter. The bed is shaking and I should check on him, but I can't bring myself to lift my face.

Last night was another rollercoaster of emotion, and my brain is mush. I spent most of the ride to the train station that wasn't actually a ride to the train station, mourning a relationship that isn't even a relationship. At least, it's not like any relationship I've ever been in. Then again, none of them felt real. This does. Somehow Hawk has become more vital to me in a week than any other man I've been with, no matter how long the relationship lasted.

Hawk's leg brushes against my arm and I peek out as he pulls himself up and settles against the headboard. His head tips back and I bury my face again, arms tucked to my sides and legs dangling off the bed. I could slither right off the edge and crawl out, but not before he'd notice.

"Willow," he grunts, his voice laced with pain.

I scramble up before crawling to his side, settling on my knees. He rolls his head toward me, grinning. Of course, he's not fucking hurt. Here I am thinking I injured him and he wouldn't be able to use his arm for the rest of his life, and he's smiling, like he doesn't have a fucking care in the world.

I push back, but he catches my hips before I get far. Hauling me up, he plops me on his lap. Straddling his gray sweatpants and staring at the tattoos swirling across his chest, I cross my arms, determined not to look at him. He rocks me back and forth, and I swallow a moan when his cock hits just the right spot. How I'm still wet after his ridiculousness is beyond me. It's like he has a pheromone keyed to my body.

"You're hurt, Hawk," I say, even as my hands drop to his chest and I dig my nails into his skin. I rock my hips in time with him and he tips his head back, slits of green fixed on my face.

"That's why you're going to ride me, Willow. It's the least you can do after I've been shot."

I catch his smirk right before my vision is obscured by the fabric of my shirt. Lifting my hands, I let him peel it the rest of the way off. My hands drop to his shoulders as I give him a small smile. His hands glide up my sides, his thumbs stopping right under my breasts, brushing my skin. I jerk back when the front door slams again and my eyes find his.

"Hawk, you'd better get down here."

Twenty Three

Hawk

Fucking flowers. What is it with this guy and his obsession with flowers? Scattered across the road in front of my house are petals and bunches of at least five different plants. I have no idea what the point is other than scaring the shit out of Willow. She's huddled on the front steps, arms wrapped around her knees as she scans the carnage around us.

"Hawk," Doc grunts and I turn.

He points a thumb over his shoulder as he starts for the back. I meet Ink's eyes and he nods, shuffling closer to the porch. Bikes rumble in the distance, coming closer every minute. I'm sure Doc called some people to clean this shit up. Part of me wants them to leave it, if only to send the message to Willow's stalker that we don't give a shit. I'd rather wipe away the haunted shimmer in her eyes though.

I wish I could go back to yesterday—rewind time and tie her to my bed. I'd do it now if I thought it would help. The only thing I can do is eliminate the threat and hope we make it out on the other side.

A curse falls from my lips when I make it around to the back. Both tires on my bike are in ribbons. How the hell someone got back here and cut them without anyone seeing is unfathomable. Rage rolls through me, and I run a shaky hand through my hair. Doc blocks my view, waiting until I catch his eye.

"There's more, but I don't want you to lose it."

I want to break his fucking face for being so calm, but it won't help release the anger seeping into every pore. I take a deep breath before nodding, but he still doesn't move.

"I'm fine. Show me."

He nods, eyes fixed over my shoulder, and I spin. For fuck's sake, this asshole spray-painted my house. Over and over, in oozing, bloodred paint is a message just for me.

SHES MINE

"Asshole thinks he's going to scare you away," Doc sneers, stepping next to me to survey the wreckage.

"Fucker doesn't know who he's dealing with."

"One last thing, and this one might actually piss you off."

He pivots back to my bike and points at the chrome, marred now with scratches. My body starts vibrating, a wave of rage crashing into me again. It's not the ruination of my bike so much as the message he's sending.

"Does that say 'whore'?" Willow whispers from behind me.

I spin, catching her around the waist before hauling her into my arms. If I can get her away fast enough, we can outrun the words cutting into her. I pound up the back steps in time with her racing heart and Willow clings to me as we make it inside. I set her on the kitchen island and plant my hands beside her hips.

Her face might be calm, but the rapidly beating pulse in her neck gives her away. I whip my head to the side when Doc steps through inside and I narrow my eyes. He backs away slowly, shutting the door gently behind him.

"We need to clean up," she murmurs, staring over my shoulder.

I tip her chin until her eyes meet mine. I expect fear—instead they're blank, looking but not really seeing.

"Doc will take care of it. It'll be gone by the time we go back out there."

"Your bike...I'll pay for the repairs. I..." Her eyes fall closed.

"Willow, look at me. I don't give a flying fuck about my bike. I don't want to upset you more, but you need to tell me what he's done. Everything."

She whimpers, dropping her head to my shoulder. Stepping closer, I tuck my arms around her and press my body into hers. She's shivering, muscles locked, and her fingers dig into my sides as she pulls in deep shuddering breaths. Her voice is muffled when she finally starts, and I tip my head to hear her words.

"You know about the stuff in the beginning, but when my things started going missing, it included my underwear. I was driving a car, but Joseph said I wasn't allowed to use it anymore. The next day, the brakes were cut and there was a tracker on the car. He carved 'whore' onto the hood of the car I was driving when I went on that date. I left that night. That's why Joseph is pissed. He thinks I cut the brakes and vandalized his shit and I'm blaming it on some ghost that doesn't exist for attention."

"When did it start?"

"I don't know. I mean, I had a flat tire a couple months ago, but who knows if that was him or not. It might have been a coincidence. It's never consistent. There's no rhyme or reason to any of this. I feel like I'm being followed all the time. I never know what's going to happen next. I thought coming here, he would give up. I thought he would move on, but all I've done is pull everyone else into this."

The back door flies open and Doc stomps in. His footsteps slow until he leans against the counter next to us. He crosses his arms and stares at his feet. When Willow lifts her head, eyes clearer than before, he clears his throat.

"Who could this guy be, Willow?" he asks curtly.

"I don't know."

"Yes, you do. You may not know who it is, but you know who it *could* be. So, start naming names."

She shakes her head, resting her head on my shoulder again. "The most obvious person would be Joseph, but it doesn't make sense. Maybe someone who has a vendetta against him. I guess it could be an ex."

My arms tighten around her when she mentions her previous boyfriends. We've both been with others, but I don't like hearing about it.

"Any particular ex who seems like they didn't want to let you go?"

Doc's voice brings me back. I need to focus on the problem at hand, instead of who she let into her bed before me.

"No. Most of them were only to appease Joseph or who I thought I should be with. None of them mattered." She ducks her head before continuing, "I mean, I went on a date the night I left, but it was only one and it never went further than dinner. I haven't even had a boyfriend for like six months."

"You think that guy could be salty about breaking up?"

She's shaking her head before he's finished. "He's the one who helped me after I had a flat tire. He was, I don't know, nice. We just didn't click. The breakup was mutual. It was right around the time Mac disappeared."

"Does he have any connection to the MCs around there? Or maybe some connection to the judge?"

"No, I met him at a bookstore."

Doc's eyes meet mine and he tips an eyebrow up. I don't know why he's fixated on this one guy. Doc's instincts aren't usually wrong, but this isn't adding up. One random dude she went out with doesn't point to someone turning into a stalker. I'm not an expert, but I've never seen anything like this before.

"Hawk, it's time to call Prez. The rest of the club needs to be looped in. We can't wait until this spills over into Reapers' business. Neither of us wants another Night Slayer or Guild situation."

I nod, tightening my arms around Willow and dropping a kiss on top of her head. Sliding my hands under her thighs, I gather her up. I'm hoping I can get her to go back to sleep before I deal with all the bullshit we're suddenly in the middle of. I make it all the way upstairs before she lifts her head from where it's tucked against my neck. At least her body isn't shaking and her tears have stopped.

Setting her on the bed, I have an irrational urge to snatch her back, keeping her as close to me as possible. She unravels herself from my body, and I step away instead, shaking out my hands to shed the itching in my palms.

"I'm going to call Mac. You shouldn't have to tell Ryker about this. I can tell both of them." She runs her trembling hands through her light hair. "We need to revisit the other thing."

"What other thing?" I grunt, though I have a feeling I know where she's going with this.

"Maybe I should...go."

"Why?"

"Why? You can't be serious? Let's see, should we go just with the big things? You were shot. Your house is vandalized. Oh, and your bike is ruined. There are people I've never met cleaning up my mess. Your entire life is being consumed by this situation. I don't expect you to do all this. I understand you're concerned for me, but the only thing I'm contributing to your life is more misery. That's not healthy." She pulls her lip between her teeth, worrying the flesh while she scrubs her hands up and down her legs.

"Concerned for you? I think I've made it pretty clear you're mine, Willow. Mine to protect. Mine to keep. Mine to possess in every fucking way you'll let me. I'm not going to let you go merely because some asshole thinks he can scare me away. I'm more than concerned for you. I fucking care about you. I'm going to keep telling you how worthy you are until you believe the words, but I won't accept you thinking you're only spreading misery. I've never felt more complete than when I'm with you. This isn't normal, but that doesn't mean it's unhealthy."

I'm panting by the time I finish my tirade. I don't know how much clearer I can be. She isn't a fling and she certainly isn't a job I need to get through. She's more and I've known it since the moment I rode away from that motel room. I just hadn't accepted it yet. I'm not letting her walk away merely because she thinks she's burdening the MC—burdening me.

"I don't know how I can help though. I don't know what I'm adding to this."

"You're adding to me. You're making my life worth living."

"How?" she asks, her piercing eyes challenging me.

I open my mouth, but snap it shut when no words come out. Other than the dips and heat of her body, I don't know much about her. It's merely a feeling deep within my bones, telling me she's the one I've been searching for. How am I supposed to explain that feeling if it's not sinking into her pores and settling into her body like it is me?

"See? We don't have anything other than we're exceptionally good at cleaning the cobwebs from the womb room. That's not a relation..." She sucks in a deep breath, eyes bouncing away.

"You're hiding again," I growl. "I told you not to do that. Relationship isn't a dirty word. I can't explain what I feel for you, but that doesn't mean it isn't there, Willow."

She throws her hands up, scoffing. "That's not an answer, Hawk. We've known each other for like a week. We should still be doing dinner dates and getting nervous when we text each other. You're talking about keeping me and fighting my battles, and I don't know what to do with that. You can't tell me anything you actually like about me. Whatever this thing between us is can't be based on a one-night stand."

"Why the hell not? Who says we have to do things that way? Who made up the rules and said we're not allowed to fall fast? No one, because they're not living our lives. They're not us. If it feels right, why are you fighting it?"

My fingers tingle and hopelessness fills my veins. I'm losing something I feel like I never truly had with every word she utters.

She shoots off the bed and starts pacing. She's muttering, but I only catch the end, I'm so wrapped up in the inevitable loss of her. "...completely missed the point."

I grab her arms, backing her into the wall, a gasp falling from her lips as I cage her trembling body with my hands above her head. Her bright blue eyes find mine, surprise and a tinge of desire in them. I tuck my chin to my chest before I act on that lust. I can't keep trying to convince her she belongs with me by using my cock.

"You want to know what I like about you? You're loyal. Even when you didn't understand how shit worked in our world, no one would ever think you'd try to turn on us. You're strong." She scoffs, but I lean in until she meets my gaze. "Even in the face of Merrick's wrath, you never gave in to him. You're independent. Even though it was terrifying, you still left. You had no idea what you'd find here or whether you were allowed and you did it anyway. I love how you fight with me, challenge me whenever you think I'm fucking things up. You're confident. Hell, you picked me up in a goddamn biker bar. You had no idea who I was, but you went after what you wanted. I could keep going, if that list isn't enough for you." I'm panting again, praying she finally understands why I'm so drawn to her.

"I...I d-don't..." she stutters, lips falling open.

"You don't believe me? Or you don't know how to accept that maybe you're not the mess everyone has convinced you to believe?"

"Oh," she breathes, eyes fixated on my shoulder.

We stay like that for so long, I wonder if she'll snap out of whatever process she's embroiled in and come back to me on her own. It hits me, no matter what she says or does, I'll wait as long as she needs. I'm sure everyone around us will question how I could fall for her so fast, but I don't give a flying fuck. As long as she's by my side, I'll take whatever shit-talking the others throw at me.

"I didn't see it. I wanted to be like Mac. She's so—" She puffs out a breath. "She's all those things you described and I thought I wasn't because I'm not like her. I've hid behind being proper for so long, I don't know if I know who I am anymore."

"Were you hiding or were you surviving?" I whisper, tucking her hair behind her ear before skimming my hand down her side.

"Surviving. You're right. I'm all those things. And I'm pretty fucking amazing." Her voice wavers, but determination shines from her eyes and I grin.

"Fuck right you are, *mo dóchais.*"

She stands on her toes, winding her hand around my neck to pull my mouth to hers. It's not passionate or wild, like we have been. This feels like a sealing of fate—a mutual understanding that we're in this together and we're beyond the insecurities chasing us. We'll face them together.

Her feet slap down again as she pulls away, leaning her head against the wall. "I have a question though."

"What's that?" I murmur into her skin as I bury my face in her neck, then nip at the pulse pounding there.

Her voice is strained, but clear. "What's your real name?"

I lurch back and my arm falls from the wall along with my hand from her body. Her gaze widens at my sudden movements, but I don't have it in me to reassure her.

No one has asked me my name in years. Helms asked when I first showed up and I shrugged. He told me to pick one and I did. He never asked again. No one has. They all accepted me for who I was, not what name I gave them. I made Hawk my own, shaped the persona to who I wanted to be. Some fear it and others revere it, but they all respect me.

"My name is Hawk."

Her face falls for a split second before she wipes the devastation away and replaces it with a carefully blank look. I fucking hate it. I imagine this is the face she shows the judge. This is the one she wears when she's forced to mingle with the elite of Rima, never fully immersing herself in their ranks. An ache shoots through my chest when she nods, steps away, and starts for the door. I catch her hand, but she doesn't turn.

"It's fine. I shouldn't have asked," she murmurs, trying to tug from my grasp.

Stepping behind her, the hitch in her breath resonates through me. I lean until my breath skitters across the shell of her ear. I can't give her much, but I can give her this.

"Hunter Shea."

Twenty Four

Willow

Three days is not enough to ease the tension swirling around us. I thought watching Hawk get shot would be the worst part, but the waiting is torture.

I never did get to have the conversation with Mac. Apparently, they went into lockdown, so Hawk is still dealing with the MC plus all my shit too. The circles under his eyes darken more with every passing day. I keep asking what I can do, but he puts me off every time. I don't blame him. It's not like I have a hidden set of badass skills to tap into. The only thing I can do is not get in the way.

I've taken to hiding in his room whenever someone stops by, but inevitably Doc or Ink come and drag me out. Hawk insists I be a part of the conversations, but I don't know what he's expecting from me.

A pounding on the door stabs into my thoughts. The stool I'm posted up on tips, taking me with it, and I crash to the ground, clipping my elbow on the counter along the way. The bowl of cereal I was eating seems to fall in slow motion and I kick my foot out, hoping it won't shatter on the hardwood.

I yelp when it hits my toe, but at least it doesn't break. Milk splashes across me, the floor, and the island. I watch in horror as the handle jiggles on the front door and then twists. Slowly it swings open, revealing Sam's concerned face. She's clutching a knife in her hands, but tucks it away when she spots me.

"What the hell happened?" she asks.

I spy Alex's grinning face right before she kicks the door shut. I swear that man is always smiling. Freaks me out, but he seems like a nice guy, if one could call someone in the mafia nice.

"I'm a little jumpy," I mutter, righting the stool before scooping up the bowl. Hawk will be home soon and I'd rather he didn't walk in on this mess.

"Got that. You realize there's like fourteen bikers milling about, right? No one is going to be able to sneak up on you. And your stalker certainly wouldn't knock." She bounces around the small space, checking in cupboards and behind doors before she finally hops onto the counter.

"Logic doesn't exist for me. I'm living a nightmare with no way to wake up and I dragged everyone else into it with me, so excuse me if I'm not the cool cucumber you're used to." I duck down, mopping up the milk and it hits me how snarky I sound. I take a deep breath and pop back up. "Sorry. I shouldn't take any of this out on you. You didn't do anything wrong. What can I do for you?"

She waves away my words and I spot a baggie in her hand. She grins and throws a handful of trail mix in her mouth. I don't know if I would call it trail mix though, since it seems like there's only chocolate and pretzels in the bag. Sam holds it out, jiggling it as she quirks an eyebrow, but I shake my head.

"You say sorry a lot, don't you?"

"Why do you think that?" I ask, throwing the sodden towel in the sink and grabbing another.

"Just seems like a thing with you, like someone told you being agreeable is the way to go, but forgot to mention it also makes you a fucking doormat. You shouldn't apologize for existing." She says it so matter-of-factly, as if it's common sense, but I'm pretty sure she just blew up my world.

"I never thought of it that way," I mutter, slowly wiping the evidence of my anxiety away.

That's what this mess is—a visual representation of how my world was blown to smithereens and I'm left cleaning up the mess.

"It's not a bad thing to be loud, ya know. Or to piss people off. I do it all the time and only a handful have tried to kill me over it." Sam grins, as if that's an entirely normal statement to make.

"My mother always told people I was a good kid because I was quiet. Once I got older and she died, I figured out pretty quickly the people in my world don't want someone who speaks their mind. They want...something else. Something I don't think I am. Not that I wanted to be one of them, but it was easier to just do what they wanted. Not many options when you're stuck somewhere."

"Well, you're here now, so you can be whoever you want to be. Pretty fucking amaze-balls if you ask me." She grins again. "Hawk wants me to teach you how to defend yourself."

She hops off the counter, tossing the empty bag in the trash before planting her hands on her hips to look me up and down. I glance at my outfit of jean shorts and a tank top, then at her decked out in gym clothes. I don't have anything like she's wearing. I do in Rima, but going for a jog wasn't at the top of my list when I was throwing shit in a bag.

"I'll need to change," I murmur as the stickiness of the milk seeps into my shorts.

She waves me on and I rush upstairs, clomping back down five minutes later. Leggings and a tank top are the best I can do. I'll just have to make it work. Sam is back on the counter, scrolling through her phone.

She hops down, saying, "You're short, which is totally awesome. Helps slipping out of people's arms since there's not as much to grab on to. Then again, it also means you might not have enough strength behind your hits, so we'll have to work on techniques that'll play up your strengths. Let's go to the backyard and we'll figure shit out."

Sam walks off, intent on the back door. I should finish cleaning up this mess. It'll be sticky if I leave it, but Sam doesn't seem like the kind of woman who would wait. In fact, I'm pretty sure she'd tell me to make Hawk clean it up instead.

The summer sun is blinding when I step outside. Hawk's small house doesn't have a lot of windows, making the interior dark. I don't notice until how bright it is until I go outside, which hasn't been the top of my list lately.

Glancing around, my breath hitches and my heart races, until my mind registers the men sitting on the back deck are Alex and Ren. Alex ignores me, engrossed in whatever he's saying, but Ren nods and his lips twitch.

I look to Sam, who's pacing the backyard, staring at the ground before meeting Ren's eyes again, and I give him a small wave. These men are a different type of intimidating than what I'm used to. I never know how to act around them, though they've been perfectly nice to me.

"You coming?" Sam yells, giving me a look, and I scramble down the steps.

Missing the last one, I stumble a bit, but catch myself before I can plow face first into the ground. Sam's mouth hangs open, before looking helplessly at her guys.

"Sorry. This might not be the best idea. I'm not exactly coordinated."

She snaps her mouth shut and shakes her head. "If I can teach a gangly teenager to throw a punch, I can totally teach you. Plus, adrenaline will work in your favor. You're nervous, but if you're in the middle of shit, you won't have time to be anything other than a badass. We just need to get your muscles to remember the moves. You'll fuck up, but as long as you're still fighting, you have a chance. It's when you give up that they win."

The next two hours are brutal. I swear she's trying to turn my bones into jelly. Bruises pepper my limbs and there's no doubt I'll feel this tomorrow. How Sam keeps going with only a little break here and there is beyond me. I think I'm going to pass out any second, but she still pushes onward.

I swear there's more people milling about, but every time I look, Sam kicks me or slams her hand into my side, forcing me to concentrate.

Sam wraps an arm around my throat and squeezes, cutting off my air. My brain scrambles, Sam's lessons jumbling together, and I can't remember how to get out of this. Black spots blur my vision and I'm seconds from passing out when her grip eases just the slightest bit.

"Better remember quick or you'll be out and Hawk will bleed out on the floor. You'll come to, only to see his glassy eyes staring back from his lifeless body." Her words grind into me, stabbing at my heart before settling into my bones.

She's been egging me on for the better part of an hour, upping the ante each time. Every other time I've burst into tears, fear flooding all my senses, and I shut down.

Her voice doesn't sound like hers this time, though. It sounds like Joseph threatening Hawk, the man who somehow snuck in and became vital to me. Tears still flood my eyes, but rage drowns out everything else. I don't think about what I'm doing, barely registering my elbow slamming back or my fists flying.

Suddenly I'm panting, standing over Sam's body lying on the grass. Sound rushes back in and the fog I was under clears.

"Shit, I am so..."

"Don't you dare," she wheezes, clutching her stomach as she grins up at me. "That was perfect. But now I really do need a break."

Her hand wraps in mine and I haul her up, muscles screaming in protest. I was right, I'm going to be jelly tomorrow. Maybe I can get away with staying in bed all day. Or just sitting in the shower, since Hawk doesn't have a bathtub. I won't be able to move if I lie down.

I follow behind her, finally taking in the audience we've somehow attracted. Sam flushes, but I'm not sure if it's from the training or embarrassment. My own cheeks redden and I duck my head. Of course, that means I slam right into someone and my head pops up, the apology on the tip of my tongue.

"Oh," is all I get out before Hawk's arm wraps around my waist and his mouth slams into mine.

Someone whistles as he bends me back, keeping a firm grip on me while devouring my mouth as the rest of the world fades away. I didn't even know he was here, so absorbed in what Sam was trying to teach me. He rights me, pulling his mouth from mine, and his breath whispers across my ear.

"You have no idea how fucking beautiful you look. If all these people weren't around, I'd fuck you right here in the yard. Fuck, I might do it anyway." His hoarse voice rumbles through me and I shiver, heat pooling between my legs. "You like that, don't you? Thinking of me sinking into that sweet pussy of yours without a care of who's watching."

I shake my head, because I don't know if I would actually like that, or if I just like the *idea* of it. I doubt Hawk would do it. He's said several times over my orgasms belong to him, so I'm convinced he's trying to rile me up.

A thought flits across my mind to mess with him, test how far he'll go, but I'm not brave enough to go that far. Knowing my luck, Hawk would call my bluff and I'd be naked in front of all these people I don't know. A shiver spins through me at the thought, and I catch his smirk as he pulls back.

"Stop eye-fucking each other," Shane grumbles from the deck.

I didn't even notice him standing there. I also failed to see the others who are now disappearing around the house, leaving only Doc and the Kings. Doc motions to Hawk and he drops a kiss on my head before following the large man around the corner.

Swallowing a groan, I start up the stairs, my knees refusing to bend all the way. I end up hobbling to the top before collapsing into a chair next to Sam. She rolls her head towards me and grins. I don't have the energy to return it.

Alex tosses a water bottle to me and I track it as the plastic bounces off my knee and rolls under the table. I lift my eyes and his widen before glancing at Sam. She giggles and I finally crack a smile. Shane mumbles under his breath, snatching the water up. He even opens the bottle before passing it to me. I down half of it before Sam's hand shoots out, stopping me from finishing the whole thing.

"You'll puke if you do that. Go slow." Sam pulls out another baggie from somewhere, filled with dessert.

"You'll puke if you eat all those brownies too, Princess," Shane grunts as he leans against the house, crossing his arms. She shoots him a cheeky grin before stuffing an entire piece in her mouth.

"Thanks for helping me, Sam. I really appreciate you doing this. I'm sure you had other things to do today."

"Don't do that," she mutters, her eyes falling closed as she tips her head back against the chair.

"Do what?"

"You're feeling guilty that I came over here and you're trying to tell me how grateful you are, even though I just kicked your ass into the ground."

"I seem to remember *your* ass being on the ground last," I mutter.

There's a beat of silence and then they all burst into laughter. Even Ren chuckles. I don't think I've seen him smile before, much less laugh.

Peeking at Sam, she wipes her eyes before saying, "I'm so proud of you."

"King," Hawk calls and the three of them sober, whipping their heads toward him.

His tone is worrying and I don't want to acknowledge it. If I ignore him, nothing more will go wrong. I can live in this bubble of random happiness where Sam teaches me how to kick ass and Hawk whispers dirty words in my ear. People laugh and no one is in danger or hurt or shot. Nothing gets vandalized or broken. For a few precious hours, no one is stalking me.

Sam might have used the fear of my stalker hurting Hawk, but learning something new, training my muscles to react differently, and focusing on making myself a weapon overrode everything else.

The three men, who I still can't see as part of some gang, hustle over to him. Shane lingers behind before snatching Sam's hand and pulling her along. She shoots me a sympathetic smile over her shoulder as Doc drops into her vacated chair.

"You did good out there. Always good to have a little surprise in your back pocket they're not expecting," he says, eyes trained on the group. They're too far away to hear anything, but Hawk catches my eye before concentrating on whatever Ren is showing him on his tablet.

"What happened?" I murmur, still watching them.

"I'm sure Hawk will fill you in. The Kings will help. Ren knows how to find people who don't want to be found. And if he can't, I'm sure his hacker can."

"Hacker?"

He waves away my question. "Nothing to worry about. We'll get this sorted out before long. Your tail is escalating, which doesn't seem like a good thing but actually is. This is about the time they slip up. I don't want you to worry, but don't do anything stupid."

"Were you a detective or something? Is that how you know so much about this sort of thing?"

His eyes take on a faraway look as his face blanks. A lot of the members get this way when I ask questions, as if they're not used to people being interested in their lives. No one's told me to stop though. I figure they'll tell me to fuck off if they don't want me asking. Not so long ago, I would have assumed they were annoyed and kept my mouth shut.

"No, I wasn't a detective, but I used to work with"—he clears his throat—"all sorts of people. I learned a lot."

"I'm sorry you're having to deal with this," I murmur.

"Don't worry about it. We take care of our own." Doc pushes to his feet before going to join the others.

I watch them for a while before his words sink in. They may take care of their own, but I'm not entirely sure if they'll include me in that group once shit really hits the fan.

Twenty Five

Hawk

Willow tries to slip from my arms before I've opened my eyes, and I squeeze her hip, keeping her close. Her breath puffs across my skin as she brushes her finger over my chest. She's taken to tracing my tattoos. Some have faded to gray, but most are a stark contrast on my skin—a map of my life, painted across my skin. I rarely pay attention to them anymore, but they fascinate her.

I imagined Willow would demand to know what the hell was going on yesterday afternoon, but when the Kings finally left, she disappeared inside, retreating to the shower when I tried to talk to her. Once she finally came out of hiding, she withdrew into her book, mostly ignoring all my attempts at conversation. I let her be, not wanting to push more on her.

The stress was clear on her face, and I couldn't bring myself to add to it. The sigh she let out when I carried her to bed after she fell asleep on the couch echoed in my ears long after I left. I wanted to climb in next to her, but instead I stayed up late into the night, planning with Doc and Ink. I wanted to deal with things within the MC, but the Kings had other plans, texting me into the early hours of the morning. I swear none of them sleep.

I grab my phone, barely glancing at the screen. It was after three when I settled next to Willow, and I'm still waking up to dozens of texts from each of them. Byrns joined the mix somewhere around five, it seems, throwing out suggestions. It feels like a repeat of the Guild. I want to tell them to fuck off and let me handle things, but I know I'm in over my head.

"Stop trying to get away. Told you I wasn't letting you go," I mumble when she tries to slide from under the covers.

"I have to pee. I'll be back," she whispers, wiggling her ass to squirm away and my cock responds, probably tenting the sheets.

"Promise?" Even I can hear the vulnerability in my voice, but I'm too exhausted to try to cover it.

She's become vital to me in a way I can't describe. The more time we spend together, the longer she stays in my arms, the stronger the connection between us becomes. I hope she can feel it too, or I'll have a helluva time convincing her to stay with me. This whole shit show is going to take a deep nosedive before we come out the other side, hopefully unscathed.

"Promise, promise," she murmurs.

I let her go, watching through slitted eyes as she tip-toes to the bathroom. She doesn't latch the door all the way or turn the faucet on this time, and a grin blooms across my face as my eyes fall closed again.

Minutes later her warm body slides next to me, cuddling into my side, and I wrap my arm around her. Skimming my fingers over her soft skin, I savor every dip and curve. I've memorized every inch of her body, lapped up every sound that falls from her lips, and learned all her hidden desires and still, it's not enough. I don't want to pop this bubble, but once I get up I'll be too busy, and Willow will avoid talking as long as possible if I let her.

"Don't run away." I tighten my grip as she rears back. "We need to talk about yesterday."

"No, we don't," she says, trying to wiggle from my grasp.

"Yes, we do. You need to know what's going on. I'm not going to keep you in the dark just because you don't want to face shit."

"I'm not hiding," she whines and I scoff. "I just wanted to be normal for a little while."

"Willow, nothing in our world is normal. Better get used to that."

She stiffens, causing my heart to clench. She might have agreed to stay while we're dealing with her stalker, but we haven't talked about afterward. Not really. I've made it clear I'm all in, but I'm pretty sure she thinks I'm going to change my mind. She's still trying to give me an out. I wanted her from the moment I spotted her, and the feeling of completeness has only strengthened since.

"Fine. Tell me what happened, since you're so insistent on bursting my bubble."

I smile, though nothing about this is funny. The longer she spends here, the more her sass seeps out and I can't say I'm upset about it. I feel like I'm getting the real Willow—the one who's been shut down and buried—every time her control snaps.

"When most of us were busy witnessing you put Sam on her ass, headquarters was plastered with pictures."

She tilts her head up, confusion swimming in her eyes. "Like actual pictures?"

"Polaroids. They were scattered across the front lot. Unfortunately, no one saw anything and the cameras aren't working. So, we're dealing with someone who knows how to hack into the system and disable them. Anyone you know who could do that?"

"No, but most of the people I know are rich. They'd just hire someone to do it for them. Hell, even Joseph could do that. Do you think it's him?"

Some of the tension eases from her body at the thought. Why she's not as concerned about him versus it being someone else is ridiculous, but I keep the thought to myself. If it makes her feel better imagining it's her stepfather messing with her, I'm not going to dissuade her. We'll have that conversation later. I know how dangerous he is in the courtroom, but how much of that translates to the outside world is something I haven't figured out yet.

"I don't know, but it doesn't really matter. Clearly, we're dealing with someone who has a lot of money or has done this shit before. Either way it's not good. There's more." I wait until she nods. "The pictures are of you."

Her eyes take on that distant look she gets so often when she's lost in thought. I don't want to show her, but she needs to know how serious this is, so I plow ahead.

"Several of them were disfigured. I think a couple had blood on them, though we're not sure. I'm sorry, Willow, but—" I scrub my hand down my face before continuing. "—some of them were of us."

"What do you mean, us? Like, he's following us when we go places and taking pictures?"

An ache in my chest stabs into me and I duck my head, soaking up the warmth from her body pressed against mine.

"Pictures of us at the motel and when we were together at the Raines house. And the time on the back porch."

She stills, her face falling. "You mean when we were..."

Her body starts to shake as her eyes slam shut. Her body bucks, but when I don't release her, she curls into herself. Her hands slap over her ears and she gags. I turn, tucking her close to my chest. I'm waiting for the tears, but none come.

There are few times in my life I've truly felt helpless. Seeing her lose herself because of what this fucker has done is both terrifying and paralyzing. There's nothing I can do for her other than hold her and whisper into her hair, hoping the words reach through the terror. She's unraveling in my arms and I don't know what to do. She lets out a stuttering wail and my heart cracks.

"Willow," I grunt, cupping her face and forcing her head up. "Look at me. Now." Her eyes flutter open, abject terror drowning out the whites in her eyes. "I will not let him take you. I will erase him from this world and make sure he never hurts you again."

"B-but h-he...he took—"

"I know. I know what he took. He will never take anything from you again. His final breath will be mine and I'll feast on it as it leaves his body."

She freezes, head still tucked against me and I worry I've gone too far. I won't take it back though. I will do whatever it takes to keep her safe and it won't be quick or painless for him. He's taken too much to afford him anything but a slow, torturous death.

"You'd do that for me?" Her small voice whispers against my skin and I shiver.

"I'd do anything for you, Willow. Including ripping his spine from his body and using it as a jump rope."

She snorts, glittering blue eyes finally peeking up at me. "A human spine isn't long enough to be a jump rope. You might be able to strangle him with it though."

I swoop down, kissing her soundly before pulling back and grinning. "Been thinking about how many ways you've learned how to kill a man, have you?"

The corner of her mouth pulls up. "Sam might be rubbing off on me a little. She told me to stop apologizing for existing."

Her voice is a whisper now, as if the thought never occurred to her that she didn't have to stifle herself for others. The ache in my chest pulses.

"She's right."

I roll us so she's straddling me, her warm center settling on my rapidly hardening cock. Her hands fall to my chest as that small smile makes another appearance. I use my grip on her hips to rub her along my length, forcing a gasp from her lips. Digging her nails into my skin, she leaves neat little half-moon indents behind.

Brushing her fingers over them, she says, "Sorry."

I grind her harder into me and her eyes fly to mine. "Thought you weren't going to apologize?"

"But I hurt you," she cries, all while her eyes roll back in her head when I angle her body to rub her clit along my cock.

"Maybe I like the bite of pain you inflict on me. Ever think of that?"

Raising an eyebrow, I smirk when she looks at me again. Her hands slam back onto my chest and her blond hair falls around us as she leans over my body, a curtain shutting off the outside world, leaving just us in this bubble of pleasure and pain.

"We might need to"—she gasps as I reach up and pinch her nipple—"dammit, Hawk. I'm trying to be sexy."

"You don't need to try, Willow. It just comes naturally for you." I pinch her other nipple and she shudders, head dipping. "I'm sure you'd love to explore how far you can push me before I snap, but you'll have to be patient."

"Patient?" she gasps, her forehead resting on my chest, and her puffs of breath flutter across my skin.

I flip us so she's on her back, a squeal escaping her as I capture her wrists and force them above her head. Her shirt rides up, exposing her red thong.

"Thought I told you not to wear these anymore," I growl, fingering the seam along her center. She squirms, chasing my fingers as I trail them along her inner thigh.

"I'm not going commando just so you can dip the wick whenever you want."

Her sass is back, but her voice is still breathless. Her panting causes her tits to heave up with every breath, and her nipples beg for my mouth through the fabric. I can't resist.

I lower my mouth to one, nibbling on it through the shirt and I swear her entire body turns to jelly, ripe for whatever pleasure I want to inflict on her. The thoughts of everything I could do to her flood my brain and I groan. She bucks, shoving her tits in my face, and I pull back, denying what she's silently begging for.

"Stop squirming or I'll tie you to the bed and leave you aching for my cock," I growl.

"You wouldn't."

She glares, daring me to try, but there's a gleam in her eyes that sets my blood on fire. I smirk as I cup her pussy, warmth flooding her and my cock twitches at the image forming in my mind.

"Oh, I most certainly would."

She bucks again, a smirk gracing her lips as she does. I sink my body onto hers, holding her in place. Keeping hold of her wrists as I dig under the mattress, I free the padded cuff attached to the hidden restraint system. As they dangle from my fingers, her eyes widen before she licks her lips.

Circling the cuff around her wrist, I secure it slowly, giving her plenty of time to pull away. When I slip the other cuff from under the bed, her hand whips up, and she sets it within the fabric.

"So eager to be at my mercy," I murmur into her skin before biting her neck and then sucking the soft flesh into my mouth. I pull back, surveying the mark I've left, and hunger surges through me.

Willow's hips kick up, rubbing against me, seeking any friction she can find. As I slide to my knees, she whines, her bottom lip popping out.

Shaking my head, I lean to grab the remaining cuffs tucked by my foot board.

Her eyes widen and her mouth falls open when I capture her ankle before sliding the cuff around one and then the other, tightening them until she's secure.

I stand, surveying her body, spread-eagle on the bed. She's still clothed though, and that's a problem. I run a finger along the arch of her foot, eyes fixed on her toes as they curl.

"Hawk," Willow whimpers when I yank each of the straps. She can't move at all, and I grin.

"Couple things, Willow, and these are very important, so listen closely. You'll be able to remove these yourself if need be. They're made specifically for this type of thing." Her eyes widen and she nods, finally understanding how serious I am. "I want you to want this, so if you don't feel comfortable, we should stop now."

"I'm good," she mutters, and I shake my head, reaching for her ankle, but she jerks, though she can't move more than an inch.

"I'm good isn't good enough, Willow." I reach for her ankle again and she tries to kick me. I roll my eyes.

"I get it. Don't you dare fucking stop. I want this, but I've never done it before, so I'm a little overwhelmed at how much this is actually"—she swallows hard—"turning me on. Keep going."

She tips her head up and I wait a beat, searching her face for any hesitation. When I'm finally satisfied, I brush the back of my hand up her calf and she shivers.

"You need a word."

"What word?"

"Any word you choose. You say the word and we're done." I think she's ready for this, but what she's ready for and what she's ready to admit are two entirely different things.

"Oh, okay. Any word?" she asks and I nod. "Kumquat."

She says it with such confidence, glee dancing in her eyes, I can't help but bark out a laugh. She's pretty fucking smug and pride surges through me.

Weeks ago, she never would have done this. She may have wanted to, but she never would have admitted it. I wonder how many other fantasies she harbors, fearing the backlash if she voices them out loud. If I can convince her to stay, I'll have years to explore all the kinks she is hiding.

"One last thing," I murmur, wrapping my hand around her calf and squeezing. From this angle, I can see her pussy clench through the lacy red fabric of her thong and a thrill races down my spine before sinking into my cock.

I don't know how long I'll last with her spread out like a fucking feast for me. Her eyes track me as I make my way over to the nightstand to pull out a scrap of fabric, dangling it from my fingertips.

"You want to blindfold me?" she squeaks even as her body flushes with desire.

"I'll let you come all over my cock if you do."

Twenty Six

Willow

The urge to give in is suffocating. I've never been blindfolded before. Hawk has put in place every conceivable safeguard though, most of which I never would have thought of until I was too far in.

I never imagined I'd be in a position where I would trust someone enough to tie me to a goddamn bed. Yet here I am, spread out like Thanksgiving dinner, ready for him to devour. The farther he goes, the wetter I get, and he's barely touched me yet, other than grinding his cock into me. The anticipation alone is enough to make me come.

Wiggling my fingers, I test the cuffs. There's enough give I can reach the strap to release them and some of the tension eases from me. Hawk stares, waiting for my response.

He does that a lot, letting me work through whatever thoughts trip through my mind. He never rushes me to tell him what I'm thinking or to make a decision. I didn't realize it was something I craved until he handed it over on a silver platter.

The question isn't whether I'll wear a blindfold and let him tease me while I'm tied up. Ultimately, it's, do I trust him enough to keep me safe while I'm unable to move? Unable to see? My heart is screaming yes, but it's too aligned with my pussy right now. They're in cahoots, trying to push me into this because it'll feel amazing. Trying to separate the rational part of my brain from the horny part is harder than I thought, and I close my eyes.

"Question," I whisper, not sure I trust my voice not to shake. "What if I want to do it, but once I'm doing it, I no longer want to do it, but I don't want to stop, I just want to change. Like if you put the blindfold on and then I get all weird about it and I want it off, but I don't want to stop doing...stuff."

I peek at him and he's smiling. It isn't a grin or a smirk, but a soft smile gracing his lips. He leans over the bed, resting his elbows next to me, and he settles his mouth on mine, kissing me slowly, coaxing my lips apart and sweeping his tongue in. It's sensual and sweet.

Most of the time we're tearing our clothes off, sometimes literally. This is a slow unraveling of my senses and some emotion I'm not ready to name settles in my soul. My body melts when he leans back, brushing my hair from my face.

"I told you before, you're in control. Always. Just say"—he grins—"kumquat and I stop. If you want to keep going after that, you just have to say so."

"Awesome sauce," I mumble and then a chuckle leaves me. "I mean, okay. Yeah. Let's do that. Blindfold it is."

"You sure?"

"Yes."

I'm not ready to tell him how many fantasies just like this I've had over the years. A dozen more have risen to the surface in the short time we've been together. One day, I might have the confidence to tell him, but not today. At this point, I'm content letting him lead. He seems to thrive off calling the shots.

I track his hands as he lifts the blindfold and gestures for me to lift my head. He slips it over my hair. His glittering green eyes are the last thing I see before the fabric descends, plunging me into darkness. There's a ringing in my ears and his fingers brush over my cheek and then my jaw.

"Such a good girl," he whispers in my ear, the rasp in his voice giving away how affected he is seeing me like this.

A surge of confidence rolls through me, and I finally comprehend what he meant when he said I held power over him as he bent me over the railing of the back porch last week, uttering the words with a stifled moan. He was deep inside me, about to fall over the edge after making me see stars more times than I could count. I didn't understand what he meant then, but I do now.

The bed heaves as he pushes off, but after that I have no idea where he goes. His bare feet make no sound across the hardwoods and for a split second I panic, tension seizing my muscles as I wonder if he's left me here.

Forcing them to relax one by one, I uncurl my fingers and take a deep breath. His hand at my hip makes me jump and I swallow the giggle floating in my chest.

"I've got you, *mo dóchais*. I won't leave you." His words loosen the vise in my chest and I shiver, focusing on his hand kneading my flesh.

Hawk's thumb rubs along the seam of my thong, sending goosebumps skittering along my stomach. Squirming, I try to force his fingers under the elastic as heat floods my core. I'm sure I've soaked through another pair. He's probably right. I should stop wearing anything to bed, but it still feels weird to not have anything on when I crawl between the sheets each night.

"You can choose the easy way or the hard way, Willow. Are you going to be good for me and stop squirming, or do I need to take drastic measures?"

I snort, since I don't know how much more drastic we can get. "I'm blindfolded and tied to a bed, Hawk. You made me pick a safe word. Don't know how much more drastic you can be."

He chuckles darkly and a shiver runs through me. "Oh, you have no idea how far I can go, *mo dóchais*, but I look forward to seeing how much you can take."

My lashes brush against the fabric as my eyes widen. Releasing the tension, I give myself over to the sensation of his hand still stroking my flesh. He's getting nearer to my clit with each pass and I jerk my hips toward him, impatience flooding my body. I just want him to touch me. Hell, I want him to make me come, but he's dragging this out. I don't know how much more I can take without a little relief.

"Hard way it is," he murmurs and his hand leaves me. Whipping my head from one side to the other, I search for any indication of where he's gone. My stomach tightens and my arms shake. I realize I'm pulling on the straps and I ease up. Wrapping my fingers around them, I grip them tightly.

Suddenly, his fingers brush against the top seam of my thong before the fabric is torn from my body. There's a bite of pain when it doesn't give all the way, and the elastic digs into the crease of my thigh. I tip my head back, and a gasp falls from my lips. I still can't see anything, but I no longer care. He grabs the hem of the shirt I'm wearing, his shirt, and rips it too. The remnants of fabric flutter to my sides, tickling my skin as a breeze washes over my suddenly exposed body.

I don't need my eyes to tell me he's perusing me from head to toe. Not only does he do it every time he gets me naked, but I can feel the burn of his eyes on me. Another shudder racks my body.

His hands settle on my knees, squeezing before they skim up my thighs and then he tucks a finger under the elastic still wrapped around one leg. When he snaps it, I yelp at the sting, but my pussy clenches at the same time. He chuckles, repeating the move, and I kick my hips up again. When he gathers the elastic again, I tense, waiting for the snap and pain, but he shimmies it down my thigh until I slides off my foot, probably dangling on the restraints.

Hawk goes silent, and when I'm sure I'm going to lose my mind, he pinches both of my nipples, rolling them between his thumb and finger. An unbidden moan erupts from my throat before I can stop it and he hums his approval. I'm pretty sure I've soaked the sheets under me at this point.

There's a thud by my feet and I pick my head up, grinding my teeth when only blackness meets my eyes. How I forgot I'm wearing a blindfold is beyond me.

Hawk's teeth sink into my inner thigh and my head falls back again. I wiggle down as far as I can when he blows on my pussy and then bites my other thigh. He's not even holding me down and still I'm vibrating with need. I'm so close to pleading with him to put me out of my misery when his tongue spears into my core.

I whimper as he slowly licks, swirling around my center before retreating again. When he sinks a finger into my pussy, my eyes roll back into my skull. I rock as much as I can in the restraints, as he drags it in and out before he circles my clit with his tongue. My legs are already shaking and I grip the straps harder, nails biting into my palms.

Just as I'm about to fall over the edge into ecstasy he stops. Only the tip of his finger remains and I huff, trying to peek from under the blindfold. My orgasm flees and I drop my head back with a thump.

Hawk sinks his finger back into me, curling it when he's deep inside and I squirm again. Forcing myself to stop, I let him build me back up slowly as he sucks my clit back in his mouth and I cry out at the sensations erupting within me. A desperation overcomes me when he adds another finger and I rock my hips in time with his thrusts. Building me up, he creates a frenzy and then freezes again when I'm seconds away from coming. A frustrated groan erupts from my throat and I pull in a deep breath filled with the scent of fresh linen and my own arousal to calm my racing heart.

"What the fuck are you doing?" I huff.

He chuckles, his breath ghosting along my skin as he runs his tongue along the crease of my leg, making it shake. "This is called edging, Willow. You want to be a brat, I'm going to make you pay for it."

"Edging?" I pant.

"Bring you right to the edge, but never over." He presses a kiss to one thigh and then the other. "Do you want me to stop?"

"Didn't say kumquat, did I?" I moan as he sinks his teeth into my flesh.

Hawk chuckles, flicking his tongue against my clit.

"Then you'll take your punishment for not listening."

He doesn't give me a chance to respond before he's burying his fingers inside me again, faster and harder than before. My legs tremble and I swear if he doesn't let me come this time, I might burst into tears.

Every nerve on my body is on fire, begging for release. I've never been so close to the edge and been denied at every turn. The fact I can't even glare at him adds another layer of frustration on top of it all. When he stops a third time, a sob breaks free.

"Please, Hawk." I'm beyond demanding release and fall straight into plead-ing.

"What do you want, Willow? Tell me what you want," he murmurs, his mouth still wrapped around my clit. The vibrations of his voice streak through me, sending a pulse straight to my core and I squeeze his fingers, still stroking inside me.

"I want to fucking come," I howl, all my inhibitions leaving me in the face of being denied an orgasm.

"Do you think you've earned it?"

"Yes," I hiss.

When he sucks my clit into his mouth again, I moan. Whirling his tongue around, he pumps his fingers faster. My body is so close to the edge it only takes seconds before I'm teetering, convinced he's going to send me over the edge.

When he pulls away, tears form in my eyes, soaking the fabric covering my face. My hips move of their own volition and needy sounds I've never heard before fall from my lips. My blood roars in my ears, blocking out any other sound he might be making. When he lies next to me, his skin pressing against my side, I surge toward him, yanking at the straps preventing me from rolling.

"Shh," he murmurs as his hand stroking my heated flesh.

"Please don't leave me like this," I whimper as I tuck my head to my shoulder.

Hawk cups my face and kisses me lightly. "I would never."

He kisses me again, before lying back, his hand resuming its journey across my flesh. His fingers dip down, stroking my soaked pussy before circling my clit, over and over. When he rubs two fingers along the sides of the bud, my blood sparks. He builds me up again, and I tense, almost losing the flame surging through me.

He thrusts two fingers into my pussy as his thumb rubs my clit and I explode, stars bursting behind my eyes. I'm sobbing again, but this time in relief as my body shakes. Hawk whispers words between pressing kisses to my chest, but I can't make them out over the hum of pleasure in my ears.

I barely register him moving, pulling his fingers from me. Incoherent noises echo through the room when the warmth from his body retreats.

Just when I'm sure he'll pull the blindfold from me, his hands grip my hips and he surges forward, his cock filling me in one stroke. I gasp as my head thumps back and I arch my back.

Another orgasm crashes into me. He rolls his hips, circling my clit with his fingers as I pulse around his cock. I've gotten used to coming multiple times now, but I've never fallen over the edge with one thrust.

Before I've stopped shaking, he starts moving. Slamming into me, harder and faster with every thrust. The bed scrapes across the floor. Reaching up, my nails scratch against the headboard until I finally find the rail and wrap my hands around it. My hips can barely meet him as he buries himself into me. His hands latch onto my sides, forcing my back off the bed, and my heels dig into the mattress. I wail Hawk's name as another orgasm flames through me, setting every nerve in my body alight. He never slows, and one orgasm rolls into another one as he douses my body in pleasure.

I'm panting, pleading with him now. I don't even know if I'm begging for him to cease or never stop. My mind floats along a sea of complete rapture, waves of bliss lapping at my body.

"Once more, *mo dóchais*."

Another orgasm slams into me. A weightlessness invades me and my hands fall from the headboard. He surges into me once more before he erupts, groaning my name as he does.

My body quivers as I spasm uncontrollably around him and he collapses, barely catching himself from crushing me. My wrists are freed and though my arms are jelly, I cling to his shoulders while he peppers my chest, running his mouth over every inch he can reach. He's still buried deep inside me and I clench around him again, forcing a grunt from his throat.

Sounds rush back in, and I can finally hear the words he's whispering into my flushed skin.

"So fucking beautiful. Fucking perfect."

I brush my palms over him as my heart slows and contentedness fills me.

"Never letting you go. Not in a million fucking years. Nothing will take you from me."

I'm still riding the high of pleasure he's put me through when his warmth leaves me and I whine, still swathed in darkness. My ankles are freed and then the blindfold is pulled from my head.

He tosses it aside as he slides next to me, tucking my body into his as his hands run over my skin. Ripples of pleasure course through me as he murmurs into my hair. I hum as my eyes fall shut and sleep overtakes me.

Twenty Seven

Hawk

Slamming the phone on the counter, I curse Helms under my breath. Willow, who's camped on the couch with her book, glances over her shoulder and lifts an eyebrow. I shake my head and spin around to grab a glass. There's no point in explaining why I'm frustrated. I've complained enough over the past week about Helms going off the grid. She doesn't need to hear it again.

My eyes glaze over as I fill the glass and the image of Willow barely a week ago, blindfolded and tied up, completely at my mercy, flashes through my mind. I bought the restraints on a whim, never thinking I'd have the chance to use them. They've been tucked away under my mattress for a year until last week.

I jolt back to the present when the water splashes over the rim, soaking my hand. I jab at the handle before tipping the glass.

"Are you okay?" Willow's soft voice floats over me.

"I'm fine," I snap, shaking the water from my hand.

"You're not, but okay."

Glancing over my shoulder, I track her as she shuffles back to the couch. She rocks on her heels, peering around the room before scooping up her book and then skirting around the couch.

I open my mouth as she passes me on her way to the back porch, but my phone rings and I snatch it up as Willow freezes before pivoting to make her way upstairs. I wait until I hear the click of the bedroom door before I answer without looking, convinced it's Helms.

Heavy breathing ripples in my ear and I pull the phone away. *Unknown number* flashes across the screen before it goes dark.

"Who is this?" I ask, but the only answer is more heavy breathing. "I'm not playing this game. Who the fuck is this?"

I put it on speaker and pull up another app Ren installed last week. I never thought I'd need it, but now I'm grateful he did. A low chuckle rings out and a chill skitters down my spine. I connect to Ren, blowing out a breath when it flicks to green as he joins, listening in. I'm convinced this is Willow's stalker. It could be Helms though, being held, Mac abused and broken somewhere. There's so many people still out there, waiting for us to fall.

"Is there a purpose to this call? If you're going for fear, you're falling flat."

"Be careful. I might just up the ante."

His voice grates against my nerves, like gravel grinding in my ears. I can't even tell how old he is, his tone is so low and gravelly. The line crackles and my eyes shoot to the screen. Everything looks normal and the call is still connected.

Bare feet shuffle behind me, and I throw up my hand without looking. Peering over my shoulder, I spot Willow halfway down the stairs, frozen. I shake my head, trying to shoo her back upstairs, but she doesn't move.

"Not much farther you can go without exposing yourself. By then it'll be too late. Best walk away now before I put a bullet in your head," I say, eyes fixed on Willow's face.

The color bleeds from her face, and her knuckles whiten as they grip the banister. Tipping my chin, I gesture for her to retreat up the stairs into the safety of the bedroom, far away from his words, but she still doesn't move.

He snorts, the most human sound he's made so far. "Remind me of that when you're bleeding out on the floor at my feet. Don't worry, I'll let her see your glassy eyes staring back from your lifeless body before I take her away."

Willow stifles a sob and rage burns in my gut. My finger hovers over the screen, trembling with the effort to not hang up.

The front door flies open, and Doc grabs the wood before it can slam against the wall. He eases it closed before walking to the bottom of the stairs and watching Willow. She slumps down, wrapping her arms around her legs and resting her cheek on her knee to watch me through the slats.

"I'll be coming to collect what's mine soon," he sneers.

The call disconnects and the app turns red. Ren's text comes moments later telling me to send him the data and my thoughts jumble, trying to remember what I'm supposed to do.

"Hawk," Doc says, voice low and concerned.

His eyes are focused on Willow, who has a blank look on her face again. I wave him away before sending the info to Ren. Doc backs up as I approach, and I nod my head toward the door. He scowls before stomping out.

"Willow," I murmur, reaching for her, but I pull my hand back and tuck it into my pocket. "Remember what I said."

Her eyes focus on me, but there's still a faraway look swimming in them. "Sam said the same thing when she was teaching me."

"Which part?"

I rub my forehead before pinching my nose. I can't imagine what Sam said that could be remotely close to what that asshole parroted. He wasn't exactly encouraging.

Willow stares at the door, pursing her lips before saying, "She was trying to make me mad. Or at least push me enough so I wouldn't break down when it counted. She told me I'd be passed out and you would be bleeding out on the floor. The whole bit about your glassy eyes and all that...yeah. It was almost word for word."

"I'll talk to Ren about it," I murmur, reaching for her again.

She startles when I wrap my fingers around her wrist. Her eyes meet mine when I tug gently, and she tumbles into my arms. No tears wrack her body this time, but her limbs snake around me, clinging to me as she ducks her face into my neck. I hold her, wishing I could wipe these moments from her memories.

Would I erase them if she would forget me too? I shake my head, not willing to entertain a hypothetical question that would never be possible in the first place.

My phone blares into the silence, and she tenses before unraveling her limbs. I hold her closer, grabbing onto her thigh to tuck her leg around my waist again. The obnoxious ringtone sounds again and she huffs, trying to drop to her feet, but I dig my fingers into her ass and bound up the stairs.

"Hawk, what are you doing? That's probably someone important. What if it's him again?" Her voice is muffled by my skin.

"I don't give a fuck who it is."

I walk through my bedroom and straight to the bathroom. Hopefully the hot water will burn away the anxiety within her, restoring order to her world. I haven't found much else that eases her muscles and calms her down other than this or distracting her with orgasms.

Leaning into the shower, I twist the knob, still holding her body to mine. Finally, I drop her to her feet and yank the tank top over her head, leaving her in jean shorts and a bra. I pop the button on her shorts and she looks down, watching as I shimmy them over her hips. When they hit the floor, she looks back at me, but my gaze is fixed on her bare pussy.

My heart races, and I'm pretty sure my brain short circuits. "You're not wearing any underwear."

Willow bends, her face blocking my view, and she raises an eyebrow. "You did inform me I shouldn't. I'm running out of panties since you keep ripping them off me."

"Good," I growl, desire swooping through me, making my heart race and my cock swell.

She rolls her eyes as she steps out of her shorts and spins. I pinch the clip on her bra and it pops open, one of the straps falling off her shoulder.

"I'm perfectly capable of getting undressed myself, thank you very much."

I smirk as I grip her hips and shuffle us back until her chest is pressed against the warm glass. Sweeping her hair over her bare shoulder, I reveal the smooth skin on her neck before dipping my head.

Running my lips across her flushed skin, I breathe deeply, her scent filling me. The longer she's with me, the more intoxicating she becomes. I don't know what it is about her, but she's my person. The one I've been searching for without even knowing it. She waltzed into my life and drew me in—captured me so completely I'll never get enough. Even that first night, I knew she was different from the rest. I've never walked away and regretted it before, but with her it was a visceral reaction. My body knew long before my mind did how much I needed her.

"Hawk, we should deal with things," she says while grinding her ass into me. Her hands splay across the glass and she rests her forehead against the shower.

"I am dealing with things, starting with this sopping wet pussy."

I cup her, drawing a finger through her folds as I grin into her skin. She's soaked already. All for me. Her breath stutters when I sink my finger into her core before dragging it out slowly and circling her clit. Her head thumps against the glass and a moan leaves her. Pushing two fingers into her pussy, I wrap my arm around her waist.

"Open the door, Willow."

It takes a few seconds for her to comply, but I'm sure her brain is already mush. Steam billows out when she finally does and I pick her up, fingers still deep inside her.

I'm careful as I step into the shower. The last thing I want is to end up on my ass from slipping on the wet tiles. The shower isn't big, but I've been dying to fuck her in here, and I won't let the size of the space stop me.

"Hawk," she whines when I set her down to press her into the foggy glass. "We can't do this in the water."

"Why not?" I pump my fingers once, twice, before pressing on her clit again, making her spasm.

"I-I-" she stutters, and her head thumps against my chest as she tips her head back. "I'm too short. The only way you'd be able to wet the willy is from the shower."

"That sounds like a challenge," I murmur and roll her nipple between my fingers, watching as it hardens under my touch.

"You're still fully clothed!"

I snort, releasing her nipple and fumble with my belt. I don't care that my shirt is plastered to me or that I'll have to peel my jeans off later. I don't need to be naked to fuck her.

I slip my fingers from her and a muffled groan fills the space, echoing around us. Shoving them down enough for my cock to spring free, I squeeze my cock. The idea of fucking her just like this is intoxicating, but she's right. It wouldn't work with our height difference. Doesn't mean I have to give up on my fantasy though. She slips when I haul her around to face me. I grip her hip, righting her as her wide eyes find mine.

"See? This is not going to work," she huffs as the steam billows around her.

Her eyes dip down before she wraps her hand around my cock and squeezes. The glass rattles when I slam my hand against it, and I tip my head back and groan. She strokes a couple times, squeezing the base each time, and my breath stalls in my chest.

Panting, I drop my gaze, watching as she keeps going, too slow to get me anywhere, but just enough to drive me insane. I thrust into her fist, but then she freezes. Water splashes over my shoulder as I glance at her, and she slowly shakes her head before she starts stroking me again and I shudder. I've always been the one in control in the bedroom, but the dominance in her eyes is breathtaking.

"You're going to have to go faster if you want me to come for you, Willow," I groan, unable to stop my hips from jerking forward.

"Who says I'm going to let you come?"

My cock jerks in her grasp and my nostrils flare as my mind blanks. Gritting my teeth as my muscles tense, fireworks explode in my brain. I don't know why I was chosen for this woman, but I refuse to fight it. She's ensnared me within her grasp and I'll willingly fall at her feet.

"Willow, you have no idea what you're doing to me."

Her giggle catches me off guard as she squeezes again. "I've got a pretty good idea."

Suddenly, she sinks to her knees, the warm water splashing against my back and peppering her flushed skin. I'm convinced I've never seen such a beautiful sight as she guides my cock to her mouth, but I'm proven wrong. I can't pull my eyes away, even when she swirls her tongue over the tip. Moans echo over the spray of the water and it takes me a minute to realize they're coming from me. Her eyes fall closed as she sucks harder, pulling my cock further into her mouth. My knees threaten to give out from under me when she swallows.

She's teasing me, her hand chasing her mouth as she moves deeper. Her pink lips wrap around the tip and she twists her hand at the base of my cock and I see stars. Thrusting back into her warmth causes her to gag as I hit the back of her throat. Tears mix with the water streaming down her face and I try to pull back, but she tightens her grip. Her tear-filled eyes find mine and the image is burned in my brain.

Burying my hand into her hair, I hold her head in place as I bury my cock in her mouth over and over. She gags again, but urges me on. My balls tighten and I'm seconds away from coming down her throat when I tighten my grip on her hair and pull from the warmth. As much as I want to, I can't explode without her coming first. When she strokes me, I wrap my fingers around her wrist and pull her upright.

Thankfully, she releases my cock and I pull in a deep breath, holding it until I'm certain I won't tip over the edge the next time she touches me. Her lower lip juts out and I wrap my hand around her throat, pushing her back into the glass. My grip is loose, but she shudders and her hand circles my wrist, forcing my fingers to contract. My head swims as a heady feeling floods my senses.

"We'll talk about *that*"—I flex my hand again—"later. Right now, though, you're going to touch yourself until you're a puddle on the floor at my feet."

Willow's eyes flutter closed as her body trembles in my hold, but she doesn't move.

Leaning in, I nip at her damp skin and she tips her head to give me more access. My fingers retreat from her throat, tangling with hers, and I guide her hand down her body. She gasps when our hands brush over her nipple and I pause, wondering how far I can push her before she stops me. Her head thuds back, rattling the glass and the door pops open. The cool air blasts in and she squeals. Laughing, I grab the door and shut it.

"That was fucking cold," she whines.

She curls her body into mine, her hand still enclosed in mine. Looking up, a smile blooms across her face and she steals my breath. Her face softens and I swoop down, capturing her mouth with mine.

Gliding my tongue over hers, I deepen the kiss, putting all the emotions boiling up in me into it. She smiles against my lips as she wraps her hand around my cock again, forcing a grunt from me. I nip at her bottom lip as I pull back.

"Naughty girl," I growl, yanking her hand away and guiding her fingers between her legs.

The water is cooling off now, and I reach back to turn it off. She takes advantage of my distraction to reach for my cock again, so I lean back against the opposite wall.

Wrapping my fist around myself, I stroke myself once before tipping my chin at her. She ducks her head, but her eyes are still fixed on me stroking my cock. Three pumps later and her fingers trail down her flushed skin, chasing the water droplets tumbling toward her pussy. I track them until they disappear between her legs.

"Spread your legs, *mo dóchais*. Let me see you touch that pretty little pussy of mine."

She stops, head snapping up and her eyebrow rises slowly. "Yours?"

I smirk. "Oh yes, Willow. That pussy belongs to me. Your orgasms belong to me. Every shudder, every spasm, all mine."

Her feet slide apart and desire fills her eyes. I start pumping again as I fixate on her fingers circling her clit. She tilts back, leaning against the glass as she quickens her movements. I work myself faster, squeezing and twisting at the base.

I can tell she's getting closer as her lips part, tongue darting out before disappearing. The sight hits me hard and fast, remembering her tongue lapping at my cock, and I move before I've registered what I'm doing. I yank her hand away, latching onto her hips, and pick her up.

Willow's damp skin collides with the wall and the door pops open again, but I leave it this time. Her legs snake around my waist, and I plunge into her dripping pussy. Her gasp is cut off by her head thumping against the wall.

I don't give her time to do anything other than grip my shoulders before I'm pounding into her, basking in the completeness that flashes through me every time I'm deep inside her.

It doesn't take long before she's spasming around me and I grit my teeth against the sensation. I could let go, fill her up, but I won't. She clings to me while her pussy pulses, moaning into my neck. Her teeth sink into my flesh and I thrust into her, slowly dragging out, just to hammer into her again. Every time I bury my cock in her core, she gasps and her pussy flutters.

"Rub your clit, Willow. You owe me another one," I say through clenched teeth.

She doesn't hesitate now, her hand stealing between our bodies and a whimper falls from her lips as she delves between her legs. Her pussy tightens and her legs tremble as she hurtles over the edge of oblivion. I surge into her once more and then explode, following her into ecstasy with a low groan.

Sliding down the wall, I slip from her warmth, settling her on my lap as we catch our breath. I hold her close, melding our bodies and sealing our lips together. Pulling back, she cuddles into my chest, and I skim my hands along her skin, savoring this stolen moment amid the turmoil invading our peace.

Twenty Eight

Willow

A week after Hawk's conversation with my stalker, I find myself nervously glancing around the Flaming Skillet. I peek at Hawk in the booth across from me. He's still scanning the area, as if my stalker will randomly walk up and steal me away. It's the first time we've been out of the house in almost a week.

"Hawk, let me pay for it," I whisper, leaning over the table.

Mia wipes down the booth behind him and catches my eye, giving me a look. I subtly shake my head. I don't know what happened, but she's decided we're a team, and she's ready to go balls to the walls for me. She practically cussed Hawk out when he ordered for me. I asked Hawk what the hell was up with her, but he just shrugged.

"Seriously, tell me how much it was," I mumble, tracking Mia's walk back to the kitchen.

"Drop it, Willow. I'm not letting you pay for my bike," he mutters.

He still won't look at me. In fact, all day he's been avoiding me. Either he's pissed his bike cost so much to fix or something else is going on and he's mad at me for something. Ever since his bike was dropped off this morning, I've been trying to talk to him and it's like he's on another planet. The last few days have been a slow descent into this.

Leaning back against the leather seat, I gaze out the window. Once again, the parking lot is almost empty. It's a little out of the way, but the food is good. I wonder how they're able to stay in business if no one ever comes here. Then again, I've only been here once, so what do I know?

"Are you going to ignore me the entire time?" I ask, some of my exasperation bleeding into my tone. I pull out my book, laying it on the table.

"I'm not ignoring you. I'm here, aren't I?"

His head is turned, watching the people behind him. I think he might have left me at his house if he could have gotten away with it. When I suggested I hang out with Doc instead, Hawk ripped him a new one, as if *Doc* was the one who wanted me to stay behind.

I don't understand what the point was of me coming along. At least if I was at his house, I could read in peace. I feel like an obligation. The last couple days has been devoid of everything—conversation, explanations, and even sex. As if he's second-guessing helping me at all.

I pick up my book and find my place as the words swim in my vision. When I blink, a tear drops on the page, bleeding into the ink. Peeking at Hawk, I make sure he's not looking before I swipe at my face. Of course he's not, and I scrub the other eye before focusing on the book.

I open my mouth, intent on bringing up again my leaving to put us both out of our misery when Mia drops a plate in front of Hawk. He grunts as the porcelain clatters across the table and then glares at her.

I kick him under the table, but he catches my foot, squeezing my ankle before dropping it. He never looked at me once during the whole incident, and now he's shoveling food in his mouth.

I smile in thanks at Mia when she gently places my plate down. It's perfect this time—even the toast is exactly how I like it. She glares at Hawk before she turns to me, leaning her hip against the table and smiles.

"Whatcha reading?" She wiggles her fingers, and I place the book in her waiting hands. Flipping it over, she starts reading the back.

"Can we help you, Mia?" Hawk asks before shoving another bite in his mouth, eyes fixed on his plate.

"As if I'm bothering you." She rolls her eyes. "At least I'm paying attention to her. You're being an asshole. Willow, you wanna come hang out at the counter? Ingrid and I will take care of you up there."

Peeking around her, I spot one of the servers from the first time I was here. Pink streaks her hair now, and I smile as she wiggles her fingers at me. Mia reaches for my plate and Hawk's hand shoots out, fingers wrapping around her wrist. She tugs and he waits until she lets go of the food before releasing her. Dropping my book on the table, she crinkles her nose.

"Give me that book when you're done, yeah?" she asks before flouncing away. She posts up at the counter, eyes fixed on us. The other woman slips into the kitchen, combat boots stomping as she disappears from view.

Staring at the corn beef hash, still hot and perfectly made, I realize I can't bring myself to eat. The longer we sit here, the more I'm reminded that he's pissed. It's been a hot minute since I've felt the urge to run, but I can't take him ignoring me.

I knew this would happen. It always does, though there's usually more of a warning. The pull back is normally slow and subtle. I hate the feelings creeping up, suffocating me until I'm struggling for air. I should have known it wouldn't last, that my issues were too much to handle. A stalker isn't something most people want to deal with, and I can't blame him for his reaction.

"You were going to go with her, weren't you?" His hostile tone pulls me from my thoughts.

"Maybe if you let me-—"

"Fucking hell, Willow. Not this again."

He tosses his phone on the table and then wraps his hands around the back of his neck, tipping his head back. I didn't even notice he had his phone out.

My brain shuts down, irrational thoughts of what I can do to make this better racing around, bumping into each other and a wave of dizziness hits me. Something in my head clicks and I rear back, anger burning away the devastation swirling through me.

I open my mouth when the blare of a ringtone pierces the space between us. I huff, looking out the window again. Half the time we start a conversation these days, he gets a call. I can't be upset since he's dealing with so much, but it's annoying. I came here for a break. Now I need a break from my break.

Although, if I'm being honest, I didn't come for just a break. I was scared and had nowhere else to go. The idea of skipping the city to some small ass town hours away from both Synd and Rima floats by, dissolving into mist as the phone rings again.

"Answer the damn phone, Willow," Hawk growls, grabbing his own.

I jolt, ramming my elbow into the table before fishing out the phone Ren gave me. Sam's name flashes across the screen, but I really don't want to answer. She'll know something is wrong and ask what's going on and then she'll want to yell at Hawk, or she'll sic one of her boyfriends on him and then he'll blame me. She'll keep calling if I don't answer though, so I swipe at the screen.

"Not smart, sweetie," Sam says in a singsong voice.

"What's not?" I ask, pushing my plate away. Hawk glances at it, scowling before focusing on his screen.

"Oh. Ooh, okay. So, your voice sounds like you're ten seconds away from breaking shit, which I fully approve of if it's Hawk's face, since I'm assuming he's the one who pissed you off. Next time, answer the first time I call though, so I don't worry about you."

"Worry about me?"

For some reason, the idea that she remembers enough to check on me is throwing me off. No one has ever cared enough to worry about me, other than Mac. And she's been dealing with so much the last year, I'm sure I'm an afterthought in the grand scheme of her world. I can't blame her for that.

"Duh. We're friends, that means I worry about you when you go off the grid. Now, tell me what's going on with Hawk, because I'm assuming it's him you're upset with. Wait, are you home?"

She's talking a mile a minute, the laughter of her guys reverberating in the background. I don't bother correcting her that this isn't home. I don't really have a home, which makes my emotions dip again.

"Not right now. Everything is fine. We're at the"—Hawk cuts his hand across his neck, glaring—"we're eating."

"He told you not to tell me, as if it's hard to guess where you're at. Whatever. Tell him he's a little bitch. We need to do another training session. Five times isn't enough to make that much of a difference."

I hum, buying time to come up with an excuse. The last few times she's come by, Hawk disappears and won't tell me where he went. At the rate we're going, I'll be long gone and all her time and training will have been a waste.

"Maybe another day," I hedge, stealing a glance at Hawk, who's staring out the window, arms crossed, and plate cleaned. "Listen, I have to go, but I'll text you later."

"Don't hold it in. Don't let him get away with shit. Call me later or you'll force me to come over and make sure you're standing up for yourself." Sam laughs and I nervously join in.

I wait until she hangs up before slipping my phone into my pocket. Sliding out of the booth, I dig around for the cash I grabbed before we left. Mia appears from nowhere, grabs the money, and shoves the bills into my bra.

"Make him," she mutters, before grabbing our plates and retreating again.

Hawk scowls, throwing some cash on the table and marches out, not even waiting for me. There's no hand holding this time, no running into mafia leaders, and no butterflies. They've fled now that he's no longer interested in whatever we were.

My heart skips and my stomach tightens when I finally acknowledge his lackluster enthusiasm. He kept asking me why I wouldn't call this a relationship, why I wouldn't commit to staying after things were dealt with. I didn't have the heart to tell him I knew this was coming.

Following after him, he's already throwing his leg over his bike, shoving the helmet in my direction. Déjà vu hits me and I shove the plastic cover on quickly.

I'm half expecting him to drive in circles, like he did the night after we met. He waits for me though, and I try to keep a little space between our bodies but end up sliding forward anyway.

He grunts when I wrap my arms around him and then we're flying down the road. Ten minutes later, we cross the line into Reaper territory. It's subtle, but I spot the members tucked away in the shadows of Trigger's. A lot of the buildings are half-burnt.

Usually, there are crews working on them, trying to rebuild, but it's Saturday, so there's no construction work, but a lot more people. Several guys wave to Hawk, but he doesn't acknowledge them. I expect him to go back to his house, but he pulls into headquarters.

I've barely got my feet under me and he's already striding for the open doors. My fingers slip as I try to unclip the helmet. For some reason, I haven't been able to figure out how it works yet. Hawk has been taking it off for me, but as he disappears into the shadowed interior, I doubt he's going to come to my rescue this time.

"Need some help?"

I spin as Doc walks up. He doesn't wait for me to respond before he snaps the clip and the straps fall away from my face. Yanking it off, I set it on the seat before shaking my hair out. Strands are sticking to my neck and I pull my hair back, throwing it up in a ponytail.

"Thanks. What's up?"

I clip the helmet to Hawk's bike, shuffling back so I don't knock it over. It's brand new now, since he had it fixed. It was one of the first thing Hawk got upset at me about. I want to pay for the repairs, but clearly he doesn't want me to, or maybe he just thinks he shouldn't make me.

Doc gestures me forward, but I plant my feet, refusing to follow Hawk like a lost puppy. Doc's eyebrows disappear under his hair before he nods.

"I needed to talk to Hawk about re-siding the Raines house. Did something happen? You seem a little on edge."

"Nope. Everything's fine. I mean, other than the mess following me around. Is there anything I can do? I feel like I'm just sitting around mooching off the MC." I force out a laugh, but Doc tilts his head, eyeing me.

He grabs my arm, tugging me toward the doors. He's not holding me tightly. I could break free, but I go along with it, letting him yank me along. It hits me how sick I am of being dragged around everywhere with no one caring what I want. It's happened all my life and I'm at my wit's end about it.

We're halfway through the space when I get enough confidence to act on my thoughts. Twisting my arm, I wrest it from his grip. Doc stutters to a stop, looking back at me, but my eyes are fixed on Hawk at the front, deep in conversation with someone I don't recognize. Doc looks from me to him before leaning to block my view.

"Start talking."

I tilt my chin, glaring up at him. "I don't have to tell you shit. I'm not going to let you yank me around, thinking you're in charge of me or something. Just leave me the fuck alone."

My heart is pounding and I'm pretty sure I'm about to pass out, but at least I stood up for myself. All my limbs are trembling, waiting for the backlash. I may not be able to feel my fingers anymore, but I did it. Doc probably doesn't deserve what I'm throwing at him, but he's the straw and all that.

Doc's arms drop and I jerk back, swallowing hard. My cheeks burn as his face softens and he holds up his hands. I'm not afraid of him, but for some reason, he's acting like I'm a frightened doe about to bolt for the trees.

"I'm not going to hurt you, Willow. No one here is going to hurt you. You know that, right?"

"I'm well aware of that. Please leave me be." The surge of courage is draining away. I need to get out of here before I cave.

"I can't do that, Willow."

I bristle, narrowing my eyes. "Why do you keep saying my name? I get you're some big hot shot in the Reapers, but I'm not part of the MC. Someone is trying to get your attention."

I gesture behind him and he glances over his shoulder. With his attention elsewhere, I pivot, taking measured steps for the door. I'm almost free when Ink walks through.

I swear, I can't catch a break. I skirt around him as Doc's shout rings out behind me. As soon as I'm in the summer sun, I take off for Mac's old house.

Is it smart to run off when I'm actively being stalked? No, no it isn't. Am I too far gone to turn back now? Yes. I'm so tired of how my life has turned out. I'm tired of being this timid person. I'm tired of constantly relying on others. I'm just fucking tired.

Hawk's roar echoes across the parking lot, and my feet falter, but I keep running. I'm panting by the time I reach Ryker's front porch, collapsing when I hit the door. Even with Sam's training, I can't make it to Mac's old childhood home.

It's not until I stop that I realize tears are streaming down my cheeks. I wrap my arms around my knees and bury my face in my arms. Humidity squeezes my lungs, though the hot summer sun is blocked by low hanging clouds. I can't pull in a full breath.

I can't do this anymore.

Twenty Nine

Hawk

"What the hell do you mean, she ran from you?" I grunt at Doc while chasing after Willow.

She disappeared around the fence, and I don't have eyes on her anymore. There aren't many places she can hide, but the idea that he's watching, waiting for her to slip away from me so he can grab her, sends me spiraling.

It doesn't matter if Doc thinks he won't kill her. Her stalker will break her beyond repair, and I won't be able to put the pieces of her back together. She'll never be the same. I'll have lost her before I ever fully had her.

"I fucked up," Doc pants, keeping pace with me instead of running ahead. "I don't think it matters though."

"What the hell do you mean?"

As we round the fence separating the properties, I spot her curled up on Helms's front porch. I slow, throwing an arm out to stop Doc from rushing her. I can tell from here her entire body is trembling. Eyes fixed on her, I slow to a stop.

"She had that look in her eye. The one Mac would get before she spiraled. I don't know what the hell is going on between you two, but you'd better figure your shit out. You're going to lose her before you ever really had her."

With those dire words ringing in my ears, he stomps back to headquarters, leaving me to deal with the mess I've made. They mirrored my own thoughts a little too closely for me to ignore.

I could bound up the stairs and shake her, ask her what the hell she was thinking. I could go in, guns blazing, and make her face everything she's hiding from. Instead, I end up sliding down next to her, resting my arms on my knees. We sit like that for several minutes until she sniffs, wiping her eyes.

"What were you thinking, Willow?" I breathe, too drained to even be upset anymore. The longer this goes on, the less we find, the more I feel like I'm failing her.

"Are you talking to me now? I didn't think that was in the cards for today," she says bitterly.

"Willow, I have been talking to you. Shit is stressful right now. You're going to have to give me a break," I huff, thumping my head against the wood.

"Yeah, okay." She ducks her head again, dismissing me.

"That's it? You're not going to explain why the hell you yelled at Doc and then ran away? Or why you're crying on Helms's front porch?"

I shouldn't take my shit out on her. It's not her fault everything is falling apart around me. Taking over for Helms is harder than I thought it would be. The last couple of months were a grind, but at least he was here to bitch to. With him and Mac fucking off to Rima, it's all on me. Doc has been on my ass about sharing the load, but he's already dealing with keeping the members in line. Everyone is overloaded.

Willow's stalker has been silent since his weak ass attempt to scare her. I doubt he was trying to get under my skin. No, he was banking on us being together. It was a direct shot straight at her. I wish I could have hung up on him, but Ren insisted Nemesis could find him if we used the app. Every time I talk to him, he's a little more pissed off they can't find this asshole.

"What's the point? You're either going to ignore it or yell at me, so I'm done." When her muffled reply filters through the million other things I'm dealing with, all my muscles lock up.

"Done, huh? So, that's it? Shit isn't going your way, so you're just going to bail?" I push to my feet, knowing I'm fucking up even as I do. "Guess I shouldn't be surprised."

I wait for her to move, say something, anything to defend herself, but she's frozen, face hidden from view.

Scoffing, I turn to catch Ink watching by the fence. He'll keep an eye on her while she has her little temper tantrum. I make it one step before I'm flying through the air. Stumbling, my arms flail on the way down and then I'm sprawled in the dirt. I push from my hands and knees to my feet, not bothering with the dust covering me now and spin to glare at Willow.

Horror flees from her face when our eyes meet, and she crosses her arms, jutting her chin out as she narrows her eyes, daring me to say something. I snap my mouth shut.

Ink barks out a laugh, but when I look, he's halfway across the parking lot. He shoos away the others milling around outside toward the doors of headquarters. Fucker left me to deal with this on my own. Even I know I'm being a whiny little bitch, but I'm wound so tight I don't know how to deal with it all.

"What the fuck was that, Willow?"

"You're pretty smart. Figure it the fuck out."

She smirks, even while her skin flushes a delicious pink. I may be stressed and pissed, but she still takes my breath away. She still feels like mine, no matter how upset she is.

Grinning, I swagger back to her. She's barely taller than me now, planted at the top of the stairs, but I still have to tip my head a little to look her in the eye. Her body sways the closer I get, and I want to reach for her, snatch her up, and fuck the anxiety out of us both. I doubt that strategy will work this time.

"What the hell are you smirking at?" she asks before pressing her lips together.

"Told you once before, Willow, you're hot when you put me in my place." I push up the first step and her eyes widen.

"I'm not in the mood for your bullshit, Hawk."

Shaking my head, I slowly take another step. "Doesn't make you any less sexy."

A frown graces her face, grooves appearing between her eyes. "You really want me to push you down the stairs again, don't you?"

"If it'll make you feel better, go right ahead." I spread my arms wide, heart skipping when she purses her lips. I don't want to end up on the ground again, but if it's what she needs, I'll gladly offer myself up.

Her face falls along with her arms. "I'd rather you just tell me what's going on. I understand this isn't what you signed up for—all this drama, so if you're having second thoughts, I'd like to know now."

My pulse quickens and the urge to grab her and tuck her away somewhere safe floods my senses. Flexing my hands, I fight the battle inside me.

It's the same response she has every time, and I don't know how to combat it anymore. The more I tell her I want her with me, the further away she drifts, assuming I'm going to kick her out when I'm done. I don't know whether to be hurt or pissed she thinks I'm capable of being that much of an asshole.

"How many times do I have to tell you I want you with me? How many times do I have to claim you before you'll admit you're mine? How many times do I have to fight for you against yourself? Tell me how much longer I have to do this. Tell me how many more times we need to go through this."

"So you can figure out if I'm worth it?" Tears fill her eyes, even as her lip curls.

Taking another step, I force her back as I reach the top and cup her face, resting my forehead against hers. Her entire body trembles with the effort of keeping her emotions in check.

"Oh, *mo dóchais.* I don't care if I have to keep reminding you for the rest of our lives. I'll do it every fucking day, if that's what it takes," I murmur before pressing my lips to hers.

She shudders as her fingers twist in my shirt, pulling me closer. I tilt my head to deepen the kiss, but then she shoves me back and I stumble, almost tumbling down the stairs again.

"Just...stay over there," she says, nostrils flaring as she turns, running her hands through her hair.

I track her as she paces back and forth before leaning against the door. I wait as she stares at my feet, a myriad of emotions chasing each other across her face.

When I can't take it anymore, I glance away. I don't know what the hell is going through her mind. The look in her eyes suggests she's still thinking of leaving. Other than telling her, I don't know how to get through to her that I'm not going anywhere, no matter what happens.

Her soft voice pulls my eyes back to her. "You keep saying I should stay, but then you treat me like I'm a nuisance. I understand things change, and you might feel like you're stuck with me, at least for the foreseeable future."

"A lot of shit is going on, Willow. Not everything has to do with you, but you're not a nuisance. Nothing has changed on my end. I don't understand where this is coming from, other than you wanting to pay for shit you shouldn't have to."

Her head thumps against the wood and our eyes meet. "I've done this before, Hawk. I understand how it works. I would appreciate if you tell me you're not in this and we can go from there. It doesn't mean I'm going to leave, since he's still out there, but we should talk about where *we* go from here."

"Understand how what works?" I growl, stepping closer and her throat bobs.

"You jumped into this, said some things you might not feel anymore, and now you're pulling away. It happens enough that I'm used to it."

"So that's what I'm up against? Every other asshole you've dated telling you that you weren't worth it? What was their excuse other than being complete dumbasses?"

She purses her lips, confusion twisting her face. "This isn't about them. It's about how you've been treating me the longer we're together."

"But you assumed I was out. You figured this is what everyone else does, so I must do it too." The more she reveals, the more my chest tightens.

"I tried to talk to you."

"No, you kept trying to pay me for shit. As if I wanted your fucking money. Then you stopped talking."

"What's the point of talking if you're not listening," she cries, throwing up her hands.

I glance around, but the road is empty. Ink herded everyone inside headquarters, so the parking lot is clear. Biting the inside of my cheek, I scan the abandoned house across the street. I didn't realize how exposed we are, shouting at each other on the president's front porch.

Willow mumbles something, but with my focus on the hiding spots I'm suddenly aware of, I don't catch it. The urge to throw her over my shoulder and run itches between my shoulder blades, and I shake my hands out.

"We need to go," I murmur, still scanning the area.

"I told you before, Hawk, you can't solve all our problems with your dick," she snarls.

I'd throw a witty comeback at her, but I'm too amped up. I can't shake the feeling that something is coming straight for us, and I've ignored the signs until now. There's nothing around us other than the summer sun filtering through the trees, a light breeze holding the suggestion of fall, but when a cloud covers the sun, casting the world in shadows, a shiver runs down my spine.

"Willow, we can finish this later, but for now, we need to go."

Her reply is cut off by an explosion splitting the air, cleaving the silence in two. Instinctively, I duck, throwing myself toward her. Our bodies collide and we slide down together, me covering as much of her as I can.

"Get off. Hawk! Get off!"

She pushes against me, her shrill cries piercing through the roaring in my ears. Shoving myself up, I grab her arms to haul her next to me. Dozens of members are streaming from headquarters, eyes fixed behind the building. I race down the stairs, rounding Helms's house and freeze. It's been less than twenty seconds, but smoke already overtakes the sky. The last licks of flames from the explosion float away on the wind, leaving a glow in its wake.

"Hawk, it's coming from..."

"I know."

Bikes roar to life around us, drowning out whatever Willow was going to say. I'm torn between racing to my house, saving what I can, and staying with Willow.

It's a trap, I can feel it in my bones. Even if I can't save my own place, I need to stop the fire from spreading to my neighbors. Doc's voice rings out over the chaos, telling me to move my ass, but I still can't, as the smoke casts a shadow over the day.

"Hawk, go. You need to go." Willow tugs on my arm, her voice becoming frantic. "I'll go to headquarters. Just go."

I relent, kissing her hard before I take off for the clubhouse where I'm parked. Her footsteps chase mine. I fire up my bike, waiting until her blonde hair disappears through the doors before I ride away, hoping I won't regret leaving her behind.

Thirty

Willow

I thought headquarters would be chaos, but the building is empty. My heart is still racing from both the conversation with Hawk and the explosion that lit up the sky minutes ago.

Wandering through the space, I skirt around the tables and chairs scattered about. An abandoned card game is on one, the remnants of a meal on another. It almost feels like everything stopped, leaving behind scraps of the MC frozen in time. I've only been here twice, both when the space was brimming with tattooed members and filled with the cacophony of voices. The silence invading the room feels heavy and ominous.

Sucking in a breath to fill my lungs, they stall halfway, sending me into a coughing fit. Hawk wouldn't want me going toward the explosion, but he probably won't be happy I'm here alone, either.

Rubbing my palms against my jeans, I try to erase the evidence of my uneasiness. I'm used to being alone, but this is excessive. Whipping around when the front doors slam shut, cutting off the sunlight, I'm dowsed in shadows. A shiver runs up my spine as I pull my phone from my pocket.

It takes me three times to unlock the screen, but I'm finally able to pull up Sam's name. Bouncing from one foot to the other, I wait for it to connect until a buzzing sound fills my ear. I yank it away, peering at the screen as it goes black. When I unlock it again and try to call her, it won't connect at all. Glancing at the ceiling, I wonder if the concrete blocks are the problem.

I make it two steps, intent on the front doors, when a bang comes from behind me, and I spin toward the noise. Opening my mouth, I snap it shut when a thud reverberates through the room. I won't be one of those stupid girls who gets killed because she didn't know when to keep her damn mouth shut.

Shuffling sideways toward the hall I glance at the screen and with trembling fingers type out a message. I quickly stow my phone in my pocket when I hear the scuff of a shoe across the tiles.

"Don't make me chase you, little Willow," a deep voice rumbles from the darkness. It tickles the back of my mind, screaming at me to remember.

I start moving again, as if he won't see me if I creep along. My fingers ache, they're clutching my phone so tightly. I'm almost there when the whisper of a shoe on the floor sends me dashing for the safety of the hallway. I don't dare look back, afraid of what I'll see.

Black spots dance in my vision as I spot the door a mere ten feet away. I stumble, crashing to my knees, and pain radiates through my body. Pushing to my feet, I hold back the sob threatening to escape. I can't hear him over the thrashing of my heartbeat in my ears.

The knob is cool under my touch, but when I twist it, nothing happens. I slam it into the wood while tears stream down my face, and I clutch my throbbing shoulder. It still doesn't give, and I frantically scan the darkened hallway for another exit. There, in the very back, is an outline of what looks like a panel, though there's no handle.

Abandoning the door, I race toward the dark when thick arms wrap around my body, hauling me clean off my feet. The arm around my chest tightens, squeezing the air from my lungs as the hand on my hip grips me painfully.

I kick backward, Sam's lessons taking flight in the wake of my panic. We practiced this. She taught me how to escape and yet I can't make my body move.

My muscles lock as his teeth sink into my neck, biting deep. A shudder of revulsion shoots through me, and I can't stop myself from gagging. Shoving me forward, he traps my body between his own and the wall.

His hot breath skims across my ear and I freeze. "I told you not to run, little Willow. I'll always catch you. Now, if I let you go, will you scamper away, forcing me to find you again? I like a good chase, but I'm not sure you remember who you belong to. Don't worry, I'll remind you."

He lowers me to my feet, and my knees almost give out. I catch myself as he releases me, though my hands have gone numb. Panting, I rest my forehead against the wall, knowing what I'll find when I turn.

It's finally clicked where I've heard his voice before, but my mind won't accept it yet. I dismissed him. I didn't think he was capable of something like this. He was a blip on the radar months ago. He never gave off creepy vibes. He was the nice guy, for fuck's sake.

"Come on, little Willow. Don't hide from me," he murmurs, running his fingers through my hair.

Nausea coils in my stomach and I swallow down the bile. Curling my body to the side, I strive to maintain the small space between us as I face him. I'm met with a man with a crazed look in his eyes, though with his mop of light brown hair falling over his face, he's exactly how I remember. When we first met, I told him it gave him a boyish look.

He flashes the lopsided grin he did back then. By normal standards, he seems like an average rich man, with slacks that probably cost a fortune and a button-down shirt. It seems strange to label him as average, but I've seen this exact version of man time after time at countless parties.

He straightens his cuff, the meager light shimmering off a watch that probably costs more than Hawk's bike. When he tilts his head, a wave of panic floods me and I shove it deep. I'll never survive if I freak out.

"What do you want, Thomas?" I cringe when my voice shakes.

The surge of confidence I felt when confronting Hawk fled in the wake of Thomas's appearance. Digging my nails into my palms, I use the edge of pain to center myself. I won't make it far if I run, but I might be able to lead us out of this tight space enough to make an escape.

"Did I not make myself clear? I'm here to collect what's mine, little Willow."

The smile he tosses my way would be charming in any other circumstance. In fact, that smile was the reason I agreed to go out with him in the first place. The only reason I broke things off was there was no connection. It was supposed to be mutual. Apparently, I should have listened to my gut more. I clench my jaw, hoping it hides the tremble that's overcome me.

"I don't belong to you, Thomas. I never did and never will."

He laughs long and low, eyes fixed on me. "Time to go."

He sweeps his hand out, ushering me back toward the open room, but my feet refuse to move. I shake my head and his eyes harden the slightest, reflecting some of the mania he has locked inside. Thomas's eyebrows disappear under the hair falling over his forehead, but still, I can't force myself forward.

At some point, I'll push him too far and he'll lash out, just like he did before. It hits me then, that this man was the one who terrorized me, scattered pictures of me for everyone to see.

"You shot him," I whisper.

I didn't mean to say it out loud, but I couldn't hold the words back if I tried. Tipping my chin up, I meet his gaze. Rage flares in his dark eyes, flaming out as he smiles.

"Necessary to get your attention. You ran from me. You hid from me. I was content to play the game for a while, but I won't tolerate you breaking the rules," he says.

"I didn't realize there were rules," I murmur.

"Of course there are fucking rules," he shouts as his hand slams against the wall beside my head. I flinch and he rears back, straightening his cuffs again as he throws his shoulders back. "We need to go. Wouldn't want to run into anyone on the way out."

He gives me a look as he pats his pocket. I have no idea what the gesture means, since he doesn't seem to have a gun, but I'm not willing to risk anyone else getting hurt because of me. I shuffle to the side and when he doesn't stop me, I skip forward.

Wrapping his hand around my arm, he yanks me back to his body and my head swims. Passing out at his feet would be the worst possible outcome. Shaking my head, I try to clear the spots from my vision as he pulls me along.

I trip over my own feet and his hand tightens before yanking me upright. I swallow the cry of pain. The bruises he's creating will piss me off later, but I can't worry about it now. The fuzziness invading my head is more concerning.

When we reach the main area, I twist away from his grasp and sprint for the front doors. I expect him to tackle me long before I reach freedom, but my fingers are brushing the handle when he sweeps his arm around my waist again, dragging me away from the salvation inches from my hands.

My sobs fill the air as I claw at his arm and his hand circles my throat, squeezing until I choke on my tears. Teetering between terror and rationality isn't helping. I'm kicking myself for refusing Sam's extra training.

"I wanted to do this the easy way, but it seems as if you've spent too much time with *him,*" he snarls as he tosses me to the ground.

Pain engulfs my body when I hit the tiles. The snap in my wrist is the least of my worries, but there's a stinging sensation zinging through my arm. I need to get up. I need to run. I need to escape. My arm collapses beneath me and I crash to the floor face first.

"Fuck," I wheeze, breathing through the pain.

"I didn't want to punish you, but you leave me no choice, little Willow."

My head burns as his fingers twist through my hair before dragging me along. A shrill cry falls from my lips and my eyes tear up as my useless wrist connects with the ground. His other hand grips my throat again, cutting off the little air I'm able to pull in.

I thought I'd have enough time to escape, but the more pain he inflicts, the more I wonder if I'll die here, trapped within the Reapers' headquarters. I wonder if Hawk will burn it to the ground when he finds my body.

Guess he'll be the one to see my lifeless eyes staring back at him. The thought has another sob coursing through me.

Thomas marches us toward the back door, the muted light casting the corners in shadows. I doubt there will be any place to hide once we're outside, but it might be my only shot at freedom.

A heaviness invades my limbs the further he shoves me. My eyes catch on the banner hanging over the top of the double doors, the Reapers logo staring back at me. I stutter to a stop, almost tumbling to my knees when he slams his hand between my shoulder blades.

Thomas's hand curls around my upper arm, as if he could foresee my plan to bolt. I slow, allowing his body to become flush with mine before I slam my elbow as hard as I can into his stomach. A low groan rumbles around us as he bends, but he doesn't release me. The groan turns into a chuckle as he pulls me against him again.

"That wasn't very nice. How about I make this easier for you." He throws me against the wall, my injured shoulder colliding with the brick, leaving me breathless. With no time to recover, he spins me around to face him, trapping me again.

"You already know what I'm capable of. I'm sure I don't need to explain who is responsible for the little detonation. Wouldn't it be upsetting if there was another one? What a shame if your toy was caught in the blast this time."

Numbness sweeps through me, and I swear my vision darkens. I was so focused on getting away from him, I forgot about the danger Hawk is facing. Of course, this crazed man is responsible for the fire Hawk ran to. It shouldn't be surprising Thomas has a back-up plan to manipulate me.

It's finally starting to sink in that the Thomas standing in front of me is the same person who's been stalking me for months. The fact he knows how important Hawk is to me is disturbing, and a shiver rolls through me. I'd never risk Hawk's life, so I nod as I swallow around the knot in my throat.

"That's what I thought." He smiles, sweeping his hand between us to usher me outside, as if we're out for a nice stroll instead of in the middle of a kidnapping.

The humidity smacks me in the face when I push the door open, the setting sun plunging the world into what should be a balmy night. I kept asking Hawk if we could have a fire, but it never happened.

The tendrils of danger snaked through our lives so completely, all our plans were drowned in the wake of terror flowing within us. Tonight would be the perfect night to sit, basking in the peace we found in each other. Despair engulfs me when I realize we'll never get that moment.

Our fight seems silly now, insignificant in the wake of everything crashing down around us. Maybe we would have worked it out. Maybe he would have fucked the insecurities out of me. Maybe things would be different.

"Don't look so sad, little Willow. This is how it should be. You with me, submitting as you should. I'll forgive you for your previous missteps, but we'll need to address this fascination you have with the criminal."

Glancing behind, I strain to see Ryker's backyard, and I silently beg someone to appear. Thomas's hand falls heavily on my shoulder, forcibly guiding me around the other side of the building, where his Aston Martin is tucked away in the shade of a tree. It's the same one Hawk said Ren and his hacker kept spotting in the area.

As we approach the back, I twist from his hold, dropping my phone into the gap by the window, praying he doesn't notice. Thomas shoves me into the car, and my elbow connects with the metal, instantly going numb, but at least he didn't notice what I did. Rubbing my arm, I turn and glare, but he just smiles.

I expect him to shove me in the trunk or tie me up in the backseat after his manhandling, but he opens the passenger door. I fall into the low seat, barely sweeping my foot inside before he closes it, the lock snapping as it latches.

As he rounds the hood, I brush my fingers over the armrest, searching for the button. The leather is cool and smooth beneath my fingertips. My eyes dart down, the ache in my chest throbbing when I see there's nothing there. No buttons, no knobs, no handle. I jump when his door slams shut and I whip my head to the side.

He brushes his fingers over my cheek and I flinch back. "You're so pale. Such a good thing I got to you when I did. Wouldn't want you to get sick, would we?"

His tone is soft, almost calming, but the edge of contempt creeps in. I stare out the windshield as he pulls away, bumping over a gravel road behind headquarters.

My teeth clack together when he hits a rut, and I paw at the seatbelt. I didn't want to put it on before, hoping I could tuck and roll when he wasn't paying attention, but I might not make it if we're taking a path through the goddamn woods.

He wrenches the wheel to the side, and the car bottoms out along the curb when it hits the pavement. He guns it down the quiet side street. Everyone has probably raced to the trap Thomas set, leaving me on my own. He whips around another corner, hardly slowing.

The further we travel from headquarters, the more my head clears—fog burned away as the sun flashes across the windshield. I glance in the side mirror and watch as Reaper territory fades in the distance, leaving the last of my hope to disappear with it.

Thirty One

Hawk

"**I** don't fucking care if he doesn't want to come. Our fucking world is on fire. You tell him I'll personally put a goddamn bullet in his head if he doesn't get them out here now."

I stop myself at the last second from chucking my phone into the burning inferno in front of me. We've had to move back twice now as it spreads. I glance at my place, two houses away.

When I raced over, I assumed it was my own home being destroyed, but instead it was the neighbor. I found the family standing on the front lawn, their smallest boy sobbing. The relief that swept through me was quickly followed by guilt swirling in my stomach.

My phone vibrates and I answer, barely catching Shane's name on the screen. "What the fuck is going on, King? I can't fucking deal with Hendricks. He's refusing to send a firetruck down here and my fucking territory is on fire."

"I've already spoken with him. He'll be replaced by morning," Shane grunts before his voice becomes muffled. "Sam won't shut the fuck up, so tell me you've got eyes on your woman."

"She's at headquarters with..."

I scan the area, searching for whoever isn't here. Whipping my head back and forth, I see Doc and Ink, soot-covered and striving to fight the flames. Tank is surrounded by other members, dousing the house between mine and the one on fire. Blue and Tiny are posted on each end of the street, directing members and the others who live in Reaper territory on where to go. Sirens finally blare through the city, though they sound like they're still miles away.

"Hawk? Where is Willow?"

My heart skips a beat, torn between staying where I am to lead the men around me, and finding Willow. I should stay here. If Helms was here, I would have never left her, but I'm in charge. The blast already took out the house behind this one and if someone doesn't get here soon, we're fucking screwed. The entire block will go up in flames.

We're still rebuilding our territory. Shane has been on our ass about dealing with the shit here, but I'm only one person. Willow swooped into my life and turned it upside down. Hunting down her stalker has taken all my time. And now I don't know if she's safe. Now I've failed twice over.

"She's at headquarters. I don't know who's there with her though." Even I can hear the anxiety in my voice. "Fuck!"

"We're almost there. Go. I'll deal with the fire."

I'm still torn, striving to convince myself she's fine. The pull between doing my job, taking care of the family who took me in when I didn't have anything to offer, and racing for Willow, *mo dóchais*—my hope—is gut-wrenching. I can't force the words out, I'm so paralyzed.

"Hawk, get your shit together," Ren barks. Shane must have passed the phone to him. "Go fucking get her. Now."

"I need to—"

"You don't need to do anything other than make sure Willow is okay. You won't be any good to them if you're worried about her. Bring her with you when you come back." He clears his throat, lowering his voice. "Besides, Sam will probably throw you in the fire if you don't."

"I'll be back. Don't let my fucking house burn." I hang up before snagging one of the prospects who's covered in sweat. "Tell Doc I'll be back."

He nods and then I sprint across the street. Finding my bike in the sea of others parked along the street would take longer than just running the few blocks back to headquarters.

Crashing through yards, I vault over at least three fences before stumbling onto the main road. I can just make out Helms's front porch and I push myself harder. Swiping away the sweat rolling down my face, I strain to find Willow's figure.

Dust kicks up behind me when my feet hit the parking lot. I slam through the double doors, the heavy metal rattling against the wall, echoing into the dark space. With the sun setting, light dances over the tiles from the high windows. Long shadows in the corner of the room mingle with the silence permeating the space.

I keep expecting to glimpse Willow's blonde hair streaming behind her as she swings around the corner, but the space is devoid of life. Most of the main room is visible from where I'm standing, and half-played card games and leftover meals are all that remains after the explosion blasted into our world.

Pivoting, I resist the urge to sprint, and I wrap my hand around the doorknob leading into Helms's office. It doesn't move and I pound on the door.

"Willow, it's me. Open up," I shout before pressing my ear to the wood, holding my breath while I struggle to hear anything on the other side.

The numbness flows from my fingertips to my palms the longer I wait. When I'm certain she's not inside, I stride for the hidden entrance tucked away at the end of the dark hallway. The edges are barely visible as I pry it off. I didn't even know about this place until Helms shoved Mac down here for her safety a couple months ago. I'm about to punch in the code when it hits me that Willow wouldn't be able to get past the keypad. I abandon it, not bothering to replace the panel.

By the time I'm back outside, I'm sprinting. Helms's house is locked up tight, but the Raines' house isn't. I didn't have time to fix the back door. I pound up the back porch and then jiggle the handle until it gives. I don't bother to shout this time. I already know she's not here. I can feel it in my bones.

Thirty seconds later, my feet are planted in the backyard as I scan the tree line. I doubt Willow would take her chances in there. She always thought there were ghosts living in the shadows of the forest.

The sun is setting faster now and I won't be able to search for long if I go into the trees. Then I'd lose the light for searching around here. Making my way around the back of headquarters, I pull out my phone.

"Alex, is she there?" The desperation in my voice makes me wince.

"No, why would she be...Did you fucking lose her?"

"She's not here. I'm checking around the building now, but I haven't found her yet."

"You have got to be fucking kidding me. You fucking dumbass. Why the hell would you leave her alone?"

He yells something else, but I've already pulled the phone away. I don't need him adding to my problems, as if I don't know how badly I fucked up.

I assumed someone would stay behind. I assumed she'd be safer here. I assumed a fuck ton of things I was wrong about. I promised to keep her safe and then turned around and left her. Sagging against the building, I let the roaring in my ears drown out Alex's voice. She's not fucking here.

She's not here.

I slide to the ground, resting my arms on my knees and my head sags. I left her and she's gone. He was probably waiting for me to leave—snatched her from right under my nose. I was so focused on my goddamn house I failed to see the threat until it was too late.

There's no telling where he took her. I wouldn't even know where to start. She's vanished as quickly as she appeared in my life. My chest seizes and I end up on my hands and knees, heaving into the gravel.

"Get the fuck up." A low voice flows over me, but I gag again. "You're not going to help her by rolling around in the dirt. Get. Up. Now."

I push to my knees, rubbing my hands down my face and swallowing hard, hoping I don't puke all over myself. Shane towers over me, the sun casting his face in shadows. He looks every inch the mafia leader.

I don't have the energy to fight him, but I can't bring myself to move either. I stare at him, not bothering to school my face. I don't fucking care anymore.

He crouches, lacing his fingers together, and his eyes meet mine. "I know. I felt the exact same fucking way when Sam was taken. It was like someone turned off the sun and plunged my entire world into darkness. The pull between tearing the world apart to find her and doing my duty to the family was excruciating. Nothing felt right until I admitted I loved her. I couldn't live without her. And I'd do anything to get her back. I remembered that even though the sun disappeared, the shadows are a far better friend."

"I don't know where to start," I whisper, hanging my head.

"You start by getting the fuck up. Unless you don't love her. Unless she really was just a fling. Unless you don't care if she lives or dies. Then by all means, keep kneeling in the dirt."

He gestures to me before pushing to his feet. He makes it five feet before I'm scrambling after him. I still don't know where to start, but he's right.

"King." I wait until he swings around. "I don't know where to start."

He nods, spinning back before walking away. I jog after him, pulling up Helms's name. The rest of my messages sit unread, but I send him another one anyway. He said he wouldn't be able to respond, but on the off-chance he sees, I have to let him know what the hell is going on. I wouldn't be surprised if he demotes me after the shit show I've landed us in. Mac would normally rally for me, but since I lost her best friend, I'm pretty sure she'll kill me instead. I wouldn't even fight her.

"You think he'll kill her?" Shane asks, sending another bolt through my chest.

"No," I wheeze. "He's obsessed with her. Thinks she's his."

"Is she?"

"Fuck no. She's mine. I'll rip him to shreds with my bare hands for touching her. He'll beg me to end his existence. And I'll feast on his pleas for mercy. Then I'll let Willow take over and decide his fate," I snarl. A fire ignites inside me, burning away the numbness still clinging to my body.

He nods sharply as we round the corner, and I spy Ren leaning against the front doors, fingers flying across his tablet. Shane keeps walking, but I stop in front of Ren, waiting for him to acknowledge my existence. The longer I wait, the more my nerves fray. I'm about to rip his head off when he swings his tablet around.

"I don't understand what the fuck that is, Ren. Where the hell is she?"

"I don't know. Nemesis is looking for his car, but this"—he points to a dot on the map—"is Willow's phone. I'm assuming it was tossed, since it's not moving and still in Reaper territory, but I'll check it out."

I'm already moving, but my feet can't figure out which way to go. Willow's phone is several blocks away, but my bike is in the opposite direction. I stumble when I can't decide and then Ren is in front of me. He shoves a set of keys in my hand as he points over my shoulder. His fancy-ass car is parked at the far end of the lot.

Sliding into the driver's seat, I'm already cursing. I haven't driven a car in almost a year, since the Guild picked the wrong city to fuck with. It's weird to be behind the wheel instead of riding a bike. The car jumps forward as I readjust to using pedals, but then I'm speeding down the road.

Pulling up to the block Willow's phone pinged from, I hop out. I already knew she wouldn't be here. Walking one side of the street and then the other, I search the ground. *It has to be here.*

Ten minutes later, I'm still searching, my muscles twitching the longer it takes. I'm about to give up when I grab something poking from a bush nestled against a fence.

The screen is cracked, but it still turns on. I don't know how to get anything off it, so I need to get it back to Ren. I gave up trying to figure out how to do whatever he does. Plus, I'm not sure there's anything he'll be able to find that would point to where she's at anyway.

As I slide into the seat, her phone vibrates and absently I glance down. There's a text message thread pulled up—mine and hers.

Im sorry Hunter.

Thirty Two

Willow

I've almost puked seven times. The first was when Thomas dangled a strip of fabric in front of me, telling me to put it on. It's like every fantasy I lived with Hawk is being twisted and destroyed.

I've lost track of how long we've been driving. I tried to count the turns, but I wasn't made for this. I never thought I'd be in the position to pull a Sherlock Holmes.

The scratchy black fabric darkens my surroundings as the sun sets, and no matter how much I squint, I can't make out where we are. The seatbelt cuts into me when he slams on the brakes and kills the engine. I reach for the blindfold but freeze when the cool metal of a barrel is pressed against my temple. Thomas's fingers grip my hand and lower it to my lap.

"Leave it. I like seeing you entirely at my mercy," he breathes before his tongue licks up my jaw and he nips at the fabric. "Stay."

My skin crawls as he guides me from the car, and my shins crash into a set of stairs. A muffled yelp leaves me as he yanks me up them. When the door slams behind me, it feels like a death toll ringing through my body.

Thomas slides the fabric from my face, and I blink the spots from my eyes. I'm paralyzed by the thought that I'll never leave this rundown house. The paint is peeling and the entire place stinks, the floral scent barely covering the moldiness.

Flowers cover almost every surface. Everything from white roses to red tulips. The bleeding hearts are what set my heart racing though. They are all renditions of love, spilling across the floor like blood from an open wound.

I lean away from his hands, but his arm circles my waist, propelling me forward. The entire place is devoid of life and furniture. Our footsteps are muffled by the pea green shag carpet running through the entire space, even the kitchen. There's a door with a keypad tucked away in the hallway leading to the living room, and when he pushes me toward it, I balk.

Digging my heels into the carpet, I end up sliding, leaning into his body. He'll put me down there, lock me up, and I'll never see the light of day again. He'll hide me away and break me down and nothing will be the same.

I want to believe Hawk will look for me, but when I'm nowhere to be found, he'll give up. I don't blame him. I'll fade away from his thoughts, only a what-if that occasionally crosses his mind.

The keypad lights up when he presses a thumb to it, and he swings the door open. "Down the stairs, little Willow. Use the rail. We wouldn't want you to tumble, would we?"

He steps back and I spin around, intent on making one last break for it, but his phone is in his hand, and he raises his eyebrows. Wiggling it back and forth, he dares me to move. He'll catch me long before I reach freedom anyway. I won't risk Hawk's life for the wisp of a possibility. I slowly spin, creaking my way down the stairs.

"It's not much, but once you're done acting out, we'll see about moving you to more comfortable quarters. I realize you're used to more luxurious lodgings, but until I'm certain I've wiped his touch from your body, you'll have to settle for this."

He sweeps his hand out, as if he's presenting something more than a dirty mattress on the floor and a toilet in the corner. One single stem of red salvia rests on the mattress. I tuck my arms around my waist, digging my fingers into my skin, hoping the pain will distract me and keep the hysteria at bay. The last thing I want to do is show weakness, but I'm close to breaking down.

Thomas brushes my hair behind my ear before bounding up the stairs, leaving me standing alone under a single light bulb. The ping of water dripping into the drain in the middle of the floor grates on my nerves already.

I don't know how long I stare at the wall, waiting for a portal to magically appear and whisk me away from this nightmare. I thought the minute the door shut and the lock beeped, I would break down. Instead, a numbness spreads through me and my mind empties. I count to a hundred before starting over, trying to center myself again.

You'll fuck up, but as long as you're still fighting, you have a chance. It's when you give up that they win.

Sam's words filter through the dull roar rushing through my mind. I unlock my muscles one by one before straightening my shoulders.

I fucked up, giving Thomas all the control. I gave in so easily, assuming I had no options, forgetting I'm more than I once was. I'm stronger than when I was in Rima, when I first met Thomas.

Flinging the mattress up, I shove it to the side. There's nothing underneath, but I search along the wall, kicking the mattress back in place when I'm sure there's nothing more to find. Everything feels slightly damp when my hand brushes against the stone and I can't suppress the shudder of revulsion that runs through me.

Peering at the walls, I find them weeping, leaving a rusty taste in the air that hits the back of my throat. I give the toilet a wide berth, the stench of urine overpowering my senses, but I'll be forced to search it later if I can't find anything else.

When I get to the stairs, I spot the camera by the corner of the door, pointing directly at me. My body sways without thought before I force my feet back. I want to rip it from the wall, maybe beat Thomas with it the next time he comes through the door. Instead, I flip it the bird, hoping he's watching.

Glancing behind, I examine the window. Even if it wasn't in the direct sight of the camera, I still wouldn't be able to get out that way. I'm too short to reach it and it's tiny and barred.

I flip off the camera one more time before I move under the stairs. There's a panel tucked away in the shadows, three screws fastening it to the wall.

Prying the unsecured side back, I spot pipes inside. The metal rattles back into place as I resume my search for any way out or a weapon to use to overpower him.

Sam may have given me a little training, but I'll feel better if I have something to defend myself with. Other than ripping the back of the toilet off, there doesn't seem to be anything I can use in here.

Sinking down onto the edge of the mattress, I swallow hard, forcing down the nausea. My eyes keep going back to the panel under the stairs. I'm not street smart like Mac or as skilled as Sam, but I can figure shit out. It might take me longer than other people, but there's something here. I just need to find it.

I glance at the ceiling, then close my eyes. Finally, the shuffle of Thomas's footsteps reaches me. He may be here, but he's not about to bust through the door at least.

Scrambling up, I shudder when my hand hits the mattress. It's damp, like everything else down here. I can't tell if my jeans are cold or wet, but I push the thought from my mind so I don't puke.

I thought it would be hard to pry the panel off, but it bends. My wrist screams in pain when I brace it against the metal and I bite my lip to keep my scream locked inside. A coppery tang explodes across my tongue and a whimper leaves me.

I cradle my hand to my chest, peeking inside, and spot various pipes. There's no way I could pry most of them off without tools, and if I had tools, I'd just use a wrench to smash his fucking head in.

Reaching inside the dark, I pull my hand back quickly. It's insane to think being kidnapped doesn't send me into a downward spiral, but reaching into a dark space might.

I brace myself, reaching in again as my breaths come faster and my stomach turns. I feel around until my fingers brush something that clangs against the other pipes, and I stop, straining for any sign he heard.

Wrapping my hand around the cool metal, I pull it out and the pipes reverberate through the wall. I hold my breath, waiting for the pounding of Thomas's footsteps, but it whooshes from me when nothing happens.

There's nothing I can do about the panel, and I hope he won't notice, since it's under the stairs. I shuffle back to the mattress, cringing as I sit. I crush the flower under my heel, leaving a smear of red in its wake.

The section of pipe I have is only about seven inches long, one end threaded, but the other is sharp. Rubbing my thumb over a jagged section, I yelp as a blood seeps through the wound and a single drop lands on the floor, mingling with the stain of the flower.

The door swings open, slamming against the wall before Thomas's footsteps stomp down the stairs. By the time he's at the bottom, I've backed against the far wall. I tuck the pipe behind my leg, trembling as I lean back. I don't know if it's from my nerves or the ick factor from the wetness seeping into my clothes. Probably both.

"We'll need to address your timidness, little Willow," he murmurs, placing a plate filled with apple slices next to the mattress. "Come eat."

"I'm not hungry," I say, sliding along the wall to position myself closer to the stairs, but he matches my steps, blocking my escape.

"You'll eat because I'm telling you to. And while you do, I'll tell you how things are going to be from now on." His lip curls when he spots the petals crushed on the floor.

I have no desire to listen to him babble on. I'm slightly terrified he's poisoned the apples, mirroring a sick and twisted fairy tale. It'd be par for the course for him, seizing anything he can and distorting it for his own perverted pleasure.

I'm sure he doesn't want to talk about why he thinks I belong to him. This isn't a silly movie where the villain reveals his master plan and all the reasons he's done things, giving me the perfect opportunity to be saved. I doubt anyone is coming to save me anyway.

The pipe slips through my sweaty hands and I grip it tighter. I'm pretty sure my lungs are going to collapse as my heart tries to squeeze between my ribs. I don't need someone to save me. I can save myself. At least I hope I can. I'd rather he kill me than live under his psychotic control for fuck knows how long, losing pieces of myself bit by bit. Even if Hawk miraculously found me, I'd be a shell of myself. I can't let that happen.

He stalks toward me. "I'm done with this attitude. You've spent too long with the biker. I don't want to beat it out of you, but I will. Now, get over here and eat."

I wait for him to grab me, but he just stands there, tracking me with hooded brown eyes. It hits me he's past the point of forcing me now that I'm here. I'm already in his grasp, so the chase is over. He wants me to submit.

I sidestep him to make my way past, and he pivots with me. I don't want to have him at my back, but it's the only way to put some space between us. His hand brushes my hip as I pass and I force myself to not shy away from his touch.

"That's a good girl."

He barely has the words out when I spin, whipping my hand up and stabbing toward his throat. He jerks back, but the pipe still grazes his skin. A snarl bursts from him as ruby red blood splatters across his collar and then he lunges for me, but I dance back just like Sam taught me. Thomas reaches for me and I slash the pipe through the air, forcing him back.

I have about seventeen seconds of lessons in how to stab someone, but I feel like I'm holding my own. My muscles relax, adrenaline pulsing through me as whatever training has seeped into my body takes over.

"If you wanted to play, little Willow, you just had to ask," he says, smirking.

He weaves back and forth, blood lust flashing in his eyes. A chill runs down my spine and I bend my knees, hoping to draw him in. I can't overpower him and I lost the element of surprise, but at least I kept hold of my weapon.

Jabbing at his hand as he reaches for me, he grins crazily. He's feeding off this, just like he did when he was toying with me at headquarters. I straighten, pressing my lips into a thin line as I drop my hands to my sides. The fire in his eyes flickers out and his grin drops, deep grooves appearing on his forehead.

He tilts his head, which almost makes him look like a lost puppy. It's the same look he gave me when I told him we should just be friends. Guilt turned my stomach then, forcing me to wonder if I was making a mistake. He never seemed like anything other than a lost rich boy who didn't understand how normal people lived.

Now, I can see the edge of madness around the corners of his mouth, the jerkiness of his gait, and the frenzied flare of his nostrils. I should have seen it before, but I was so blinded by how down-to-earth he appeared compared to all the other toxic rich boys who pretended to be men, I missed it.

"I'm sorry," I whisper so he doesn't hear the disgust in my voice.

"Oh, little Willow."

I can't help but stagger back as he reaches for me. Tripping over the plate, the apples scatter, leaving slippery landmines in my path. Jumping over the mess, I take off for the stairs.

Time slows as my foot slides on a lone slice, squishing under my shoe. My ankle rolls, and my body crashes to the concrete, my injured shoulder taking the brunt of the fall. The pipe skitters away against the concrete, my only hope trailing in its wake.

Even with the air forced from my lungs, I push to my hands and knees, intent on crawling as far as I can before he catches me. Thomas's hands grip my waist and he hauls me to my feet. One arm circles my throat and my lungs seize.

He squeezes, cutting off my air, and I dig my nails into his skin. My mind blanks as I kick my feet, even though I know it won't help. Sam's voice is screaming in my head, telling me to get my shit together. But I blacked out when I flipped Sam. I don't remember how to do it. The panic overrides everything else.

I slam my eyes shut as my toes scrape across the concrete and Hawk's face flashes in my mind, green eyes sparkling. There's a softness in his face I've only seen when he looks at me.

I curl my body as much as Thomas's arm allows, despair engulfing the terror. My vision blurs as tears stream down my face. I didn't even realize I was crying.

Black spots dance in front of me and I pull in the tiniest of breaths, but it's not enough to stop the room from spinning.

"I could end you now. Don't make me do it. I have so many plans for you. For us," he grunts, cutting off the last of my air supply.

I couldn't answer, even if I wanted to, but his words trigger something inside. Pulling my knees up, I kick forward until my feet touch the ground. Thomas cusses as his grip loosens a little and I suck in a breath.

Grabbing onto his arm, I bend, arching my back and using his momentum to throw him over my body. His head makes a sickening crunch when he hits the floor and I wince. His groans echo through the room and I scramble for the broken pipe. My stomach coils tighter when I slam to my knees next to his head and I spot blood already pooling underneath him.

I scoot back, far enough away that he can't grab me again, all while clutching my makeshift weapon. I don't think I can go through with killing him unless he forces my hand. I'm sure everyone else I've surrounded myself with the last few weeks wouldn't hesitate, but I've never been in a situation like this before. There haven't been many times in my life where I've had to defend myself, much less kill someone.

Staring at the blood slowly inching toward my knees, I pull in deep breaths to calm my still racing heart. The adrenaline from moments ago ebbs from my body, leaving an ache in its wake. I won't be able to fight him if he wakes up. My wrist is throbbing and pain shoots through my shoulder every time I move. I may not want to finish Thomas off, but I don't have to save him either.

Heaving to my feet, I wince as I pass his twitching body to scramble up the stairs. The handle twists, but the door doesn't budge, no matter how hard I shove into it. My heart starts racing again when the keypad above the handle flashes red. I'm kicking myself for not noticing it earlier. There aren't any buttons, only a fingerprint scanner mirroring the other side.

Racing back down the stairs, I crash into the wall at the bottom, body protesting. I skid to a stop close to Thomas's side. His chest is still rising, but his eyes are closed.

I tap my foot against his thigh, searching for a phone or key, but his pockets seem to be empty. He'll probably wake up if I roll him over, and I don't want to see the back of his head, but I'm out of options. His hair is a little longer now, so maybe it will cover the wound and I won't puke on him. I wouldn't care, but if I'm stuck down here, I'd rather not sit in the smell for fuck knows how long.

Placing the pipe next to me, I tuck my hands under him, grunting as I try to roll his body. He barely moves, so I lean over him, glancing at his face before I yank on his clothes, pulling him toward me, and a moan leaves him. I scurry out of the way, panting, eyes fixed on his face. A line forms between his eyes, but they still stay closed.

Rounding his body, I poke my toe at his back pocket and my heart sinks. I don't know what to do other than force my way out the window, but even if it wasn't so small and high, I doubt I'd get past the bars.

I grab the pipe and wander back to the stairs to stare at the camera, my limbs hanging limply at my sides. I'm drained and out of options.

Sam would have already found a way out. Mac would have been waiting at the door for him to come in. All the men I've encountered never would have gone with him in the first place. Hell, I'm sure Sam and Mac wouldn't have either. It wasn't the best decision, but I was blindsided. I'd rather die than live in a world without Hawk.

"Holy shit," I whisper, blankly staring at the stairs.

Thomas groans and I whip around. When he pushes to his hands and knees, I unlock my muscles before rushing up the stairs. I might be able to trick him into opening the door. I don't know what I'll do once I get out, but maybe I can lock him in the basement instead.

The stairs creak with his heavy steps and I lean back against the wood, watching his slow progress. He doesn't look like a lost puppy or an arrogant rich boy now. He looks unhinged and very pissed off.

"I thought you could be redeemed, Willow," he says. His words slur and blood trickles along his neck, seeping into his collar.

"Open the door, Thomas."

He shakes his head slowly, a manic grin stretching across his face. I don't know how he recovered so quickly. He should still be passed out on the floor, bleeding, and suffering. Dying. I could kick him down the stairs, hope the fall would take him out. Knowing my luck, he'd grab my leg and take me down with him or I'd trip and break my neck. The worst would be if he survived.

When he reaches for me though, I can't help myself. I kick out, the sole of my shoe hitting him square in the chest, and a muffled cry leaves him along with the air in his lungs.

Tripping backwards, he scrambles to catch himself, but his hand slips from the banister and his weight sends him tumbling. Shrinking into a crouch, I force myself to stay by the door. The good girl I was taught to be is screaming in my head to grab him, save him—to not sink into the shadows.

I straighten as he hits the bottom before I slowly descend, gripping the pipe tighter. His arm hangs at an unnatural angle, one leg trapped beneath his body, and the closer I come, the more fear laces his eyes.

"You should be scared. You should feel every ounce of fear I did. I could end you right here. Or maybe I'll just watch as the light leaves your eyes and relish the end of your miserable existence."

I reach the bottom and I can't pull my eyes away from his. Scraping my thumb over the jagged piece of pipe, I welcome the pain. It centers me, focusing my mind on what I have to do.

He chokes out a laugh, blood dribbling from the corner of his mouth. "You're not going to"—he coughs, blood splattering down his chin—"do anything."

Tilting my head, I wonder how in the hell I ever let him manipulate me. I brace my feet and lean down to see whether or not he'll grab me. He doesn't look like he'll last long, but then again, I thought I knocked him out before and he came back. I feel like no matter what I've done to get away from him, he comes back twice as hard. He doesn't reach for me, but he does grin.

"You're going to be a good..."

I swing my arm around, stabbing the pipe toward the side of his neck. The jagged edge scrapes across his skin, leaving angry red streaks in its wake.

I hesitated. I thought I could end him, that I could take back the control he stole from me, even while I was battered and bruised at his hands. At the last second though, I pulled back, not sure what the act would do to me. Since I came to the Reapers, I've been dancing with the shadows, never fully giving in to their allure.

Thomas slides to the side, tilting his head to expose more of his flesh. "Need some help?"

I rear back before shoving the pipe as far into his neck as possible, embracing the shadows I've become.

I expect blood to douse me, but instead it trickles out in a thin line. I should take the pipe out, make death arrive faster, but I leave it in. The stairs catch my heels and I stumble back, crashing onto the wood. The air whooshes from my lungs and I press a hand to my chest, my eyes transfixed on the red staining his skin, soaking into his shirt. His hands paw at the metal sticking out of his throat, and I wince when he hits it.

I thought he'd die instantly. I never imagined I'd have to sit here and watch him succumb to the wounds I inflicted. Lifting my hand to brush the strands from my face, I rear back. Turning both palms up, I find his blood marking them, cutting into the deep groves and gathering under my nails.

The sounds of Thomas's life bleeding out in front of me are drowned out by my harsh gasps. I scrub my hands against my jeans, but it doesn't stop the panic from rising in my throat. The harder I try to erase the evidence of what I've done, the more it seeps into my soul.

Tears blur my vision and I finally meet Thomas's glassy eyes. His hands have fallen to his sides and the blood has slowed. The tang of copper hits the back of my throat and I gag. Swallowing hard, I force the nausea down.

When I grab the banister, I can barely feel the sticky wood beneath my fingers. It's like the layer of blood coating my hands is creating a barrier, which only makes me freak out more.

Staggering over Thomas's leg, I crash to my knees, a sob escaping me, and before I know it, I'm curled in a ball, feet from his lifeless body. Hawk's face floats in front of my closed lids and Sam screams in my head to get up, but I need this. Deep down I recognize the need to process everything I've been through—everything I've done. I bite my arm, screaming into my skin until I'm hoarse.

Thirty Three

Hawk

"How the fuck would I know where she is? I've been searching for almost four hours and she's nowhere to be found. Why hasn't your hacker found the fucking car, King?" I yell into the phone. I've been pacing the parking lot of headquarters for the last fifteen minutes, waiting for the others to come back.

"I haven't been able to get a hold of Nemesis for several hours. I don't know why she isn't answering." He sounds worried, but him losing his hacker is the least of my problems.

"What the hell am I supposed to do, then? Ren, I have to find her." The sharp pain in my chest stabs, leaving an echo of pain in its wake. I push my fist against the spot, hoping I'm not about to have a heart attack.

"We're doing everything we can, Hawk. I realize that's not what you want to hear, but there's not much more we can do. We've got guys out looking for the car. I'm searching the cameras. What else would you like me to look into?"

I search the streets as if she'll walk out of the darkness, unbroken and free. They stay quiet though, the crickets singing into the night while the clouds cast shadows over the full moon.

I've scoured the entirety of Reaper territory, pulling every last member from whatever job they were on to help, but we're still coming up empty-handed. With every minute that passes, a little more of my hope ebbs away. The despair

I felt before Shane knocked some sense into me is slowly creeping back in, whispering all the horrors Willow could be going through.

"I need to find her. I need to save her," I say as the rumble of bikes splits through the night. For a while after we defeated the Night Slayers, the sound of dozens of bikes sent my heart racing. The more time passed, the less anxious I got, but it's back in full force.

"I'll do what I can."

He hangs up before I can say anything more. I didn't have more to give him anyway. A numbness spreads through my fingers and I slip my phone in my pocket before I drop it. Doc pulls into the parking lot, stopping next to my bike.

"Anything?" I call out as soon as the engine dies.

"You think I would leave her behind if I'd found her?" he says, running his hands through his short hair.

I scowl, pulling my phone out again. I text Helms and my eyes glaze as I see all the others I've sent that sit unread. It's been over a week since I've heard from him.

"Where haven't we looked? She has to be somewhere," I grunt, searching the streets again.

"You think he took her back to Rima?" He retreats, holding his hands up when I snarl at him.

"She's still in Synd."

Maybe I'll believe the words if I say them enough. I can't go running off to Rima, no matter how strong the pull is to find her. The connection I felt weeks ago is wrapped around my heart, tightening with every heartbeat, as if the further she gets from me the closer it is to snapping. It's not unbearable yet, but soon I won't be able to breathe through the pain.

"We've been all over the city. The Kings have men out looking for her and the car. We focused on the east side of the river, since Byrns isn't answering. We've put everything else on hold, Hawk. I don't know how much longer some of the members will go along with this. At what point are you going to call it?"

"What about Reaper territory? Her phone was here, maybe she is too." I'm grasping at straws, but I'll exhaust every avenue I have before I give up.

"It's likely she put her phone on the car and it came off while they were driving away. Or she may have dropped it out the taillight if she was in the trunk." His words send rage coursing through me. "It's possible though."

"What's possible?" The roaring in my ears is making my brain fuzzy, unable to remember what I just said.

"She could still be here. It would make sense why we can't find his car, since we don't have cameras in the residential areas." He swings around, staring at the dark houses. "We'll need to..."

I bolt for my bike, leaving Doc shouting behind me. I'm not waiting around for him to catch up. He'll make his own decisions. I haven't had to take over for Helms often. Since he fucked off to Rima, I've realized I'm not great at delegating. Most of the time they can manage themselves, but I should work on it for times like these. Hopefully, Helms won't have more shit dropped in his lap and I'll never have to do this again.

I don't even know if this is something I should ask the guys to deal with anyway. Willow isn't Reapers' business. She's mine and I'll do whatever it takes to find her, including using my position in the MC.

Two hours later the adrenaline has ebbed away, dissipating with the exhaust trailing behind me. I feel like I've been searching for days. He's disappeared with the setting sun, hiding within the shadows and taking Willow with him. This asshole must have someone helping him. My hope is slowly dwindling, along with the check-ins from the guys. Doc is the only one texting me anymore.

I glance at his latest text: *nothing on the west side.* Letting out a string of curses, I glance around the dark street. I started where I found Willow's phone, branching out and searching for anything out of place. Looking for his car is useless. We haven't been able to track it anyway, so I assume he switched to something a little less conspicuous.

I've been in and out of charred houses and warehouses, abandoned after the Night Slayers came through. Trying to get crews out to demolish and rebuild them is hard with so much damage.

Grabbing the back of my neck, I turn a slow circle in the middle of the street, praying for some type of sign. I've been up and down the blocks all over the east side and at this point I'm going to need her to jump in front of me, flapping her arms like a duck for me to figure out where she is.

My phone buzzes, but I don't bother to pull it out. There isn't anyone on the streets this late. Even the rumble of bikes has faded away. Most of the members went off to their various jobs or home hours ago. Doc is the only one still out looking, but even he's lagging. Alex texted, told me they're still out. I've ignored them all, too consumed by the need to find Willow. My phone buzzes again and I huff, finally pulling it from my pocket.

"Hawk, she's not on this side. I took to knocking on doors, asking if they've seen anything. We've got some pissed off families, but I don't know where else to look. Anything on your side?" Doc says, exhaustion lacing his tone.

"Go home, Doc," I say, scanning the dark neighborhood.

"What are you going to do?"

"I don't know. You might need to take over for a while. I just need..." I don't know how to finish my sentence.

There's nothing left in me. I thought Judge Merrick handing down my sentence and damning me was the worst I would go through. I thought leaving Rima was the hardest thing I'd ever do. I thought starting over again and again was hard. This overshadows everything else.

"Hawk, admit it."

"Admit what?"

Barely paying attention to him, I start walking. I need to find her. I need to save her. She is mine and I told her I'd protect her, but I'm failing. On every level, I've failed her.

At this point, I wouldn't blame her if thought I wasn't coming. Even if I find her, tear her from his grasp, she won't want to stay. She'll never trust me again.

My heart cracks, knowing in my bones she deserves so much more than I can offer.

"Damn, you really are fucked, aren't you? You love her. You'll find her. Other than Prez, I don't think I've seen someone as messed up as you are over her."

"I can't—" My legs give out and I fall to my knees "—it doesn't matter. Just do what you need to do."

I hang up before I lose it completely. My phone clatters across the concrete and it buzzes, lighting up the night. My hands are shaking but I can't feel them. Time slows as spots dance in front of my eyes. I try to breathe, but it's like the air has been sucked from my world and lightheadedness overtakes me.

A low purr of a car pierces the silence, and I shake my head, bracing my hands on the ground. Heaving up, I stumble before I find my feet. I don't bother to grab my phone, leaving it buzzing on the ground.

I race toward the sound of the engine gunning it through the night, ducking through yards and behind buildings. The chances of it being Willow's stalker are slim, but I won't let the only lead I've come across pass me by. I stop on another street, spinning around as the sound fades. I take off again, straining to hear anything over the pounding in my heart and my panting.

I spend the next ten minutes racing back and forth, searching driveways and back alleys, and coming up empty. The last of my hope dies as I trudge back to my bike. I swear it takes another ten minutes to find it, since I ran all over the east side of our territory. My still rattling phone guides me long before I see my ride parked along the side of an abandoned house. Snatching it up, I roll my shoulders before answering.

"What?" The dejection in my voice rings through the night, but I'm beyond caring. Doc's heard worse, I'm sure.

"Don't get your hopes up, but I have a lead."

"Start talking. Now."

"Ren has been trying to call you, but when you didn't answer, he called me. He spotted a shiny crossing into our territory less than an hour ago. It's not the same one, but suspicious."

"Where?" My heart is pounding again, fire licking through my veins as he rattles off an address nearby.

"Hawk, don't go in without me. We don't know what the hell he's doing to her."

I hang up, glancing between my bike and my destination. I abandon my ride and take off. I understand why Doc wants me to wait, but each passing second she's in that psychopath's hands is another opportunity for her to slip further from me. I'll spend a lifetime righting every wrong, stitching her back together, if only she'll let me.

Thirty Four

Willow

I don't know how long I'm on the floor, screaming out the pain radiating through me, but my eyes are gritty and the air burns my throat. The moon tracks across the small window, almost done with its journey through the night.

My muscles protest when I try to push to my feet. I end up on my ass, cringing when I feel how damp my clothes are. The smell of urine has lessened, but I'm pretty sure it's seeped into my clothes and my skin. I can barely smell it now I've been wallowing in the filth for so long.

I spend the next hour pacing around the room, skirting Thomas and the toilet. I'm about to piss my pants, but I can't bring myself to use it. My legs are so short, I won't be able to hover and I refuse to touch the seat.

"I could just piss on you, couldn't I? You wouldn't mind," I mutter as I pass close to Thomas's cooled body. When I turn away, something moves from the corner of my eye and I jump.

"Fuck," I wheeze. A manic laugh bubbling up as I press a hand to my chest when I see it's my own shadow.

The beep from the keypad reverberates through the room. It wasn't as loud before, but I think my hearing is amplified from being in this deadened space for hours.

My feet ghost over the concrete and I duck under the stairs. When I crouch, my arm scrapes along the bent metal panel, leaving a gash in its wake.

Blood weeps from my skin and tears well in my eyes. I wipe them away as footsteps rattle the wood above me.

Fancy leather shoes appear between the slats, and I track their descent. I can't see more than their feet and some gray slacks. They pause before Thomas's prone body and a heavy sigh bounces through the space.

My eyes catch on the copper pipe sticking from Thomas's neck. I should have removed it—kept it with me in case someone else came. I assumed Thomas was working alone in his crazed obsession. There are so many things I could have done differently so I wouldn't be in this position, and now I have to live with the consequences.

"Get out here, Willow," a familiar voice growls and the blood in my veins ice over. "Don't make me drag your whore ass out of there."

Unfolding my limbs, I keep close to the stairs as I stand. When my stepfather turns to me, I infuse every molecule with the remaining strength in my body, straightening my spine and throwing my shoulders back. I'm sure it doesn't do much to make me more intimidating, but at least it helps my confidence.

I don't know if I could overpower him, like I did Thomas, but that was more luck than any skill on my part. Using the training Sam taught me ended in disaster.

He sneers, scanning me up and down. Joseph hasn't changed in the slightest since I saw him six weeks ago. His carefully coifed salt and pepper hair is gelled like the perfect politician he pretends to be.

He lectured me more than once, stating judges held more power than anyone else in the political sphere, so he could call himself whatever the hell he wanted—do whatever he wanted. Even standing in a dirty basement, he's dressed like he's going to court in a suit that probably costs more than the house we're standing in.

Tucking his hands in his pockets, he rocks back on his heels. "You've caused a lot of problems for me, Willow. I never understood why you couldn't just fall in line. I'd blame your mother, but she's not here. So, I'll have to blame you, won't I?"

"How did you get in?" It's a stupid question, but I'm afraid if I ask any of the others swirling around my head, I'll start screaming and never stop.

He chuckles, the persona he shows the world shining through. Glancing around the room, he wrinkles his nose when he spots the toilet and I inch closer to the bottom of the stairs. I need a weapon, but I'll have to get him back through the door first.

"Now that you've fucked up the plan, I'll have to enact the backup. I'm disappointed in you, though. We'll have to talk about how you'll be conducting yourself in the future. Although, perhaps I should just leave you down here. It might be a while before someone finds your body, which would take care of the problem."

"I have no idea what you're talking about," I murmur.

"Of course you don't. You didn't need to know. Westerfield wasn't supposed to go off the rails, but once he became obsessed, there was no stopping him. That boy had too much money and not enough smarts."

It's a phrase he's said so often I barely register it anymore. Too much money and not enough smarts is how he describes the juveniles coming through his courtroom.

I shuffle another foot to the left, fixing my stare on him. Several feet sit between us, but he could reach me long before I get to the pipe. He's at least eight inches taller than me, and his long legs would eat up the space. I've been riding the anxiety train for so long, my heart might give out any second, but at least this rollercoaster will be over then.

"Why do you care? I don't understand why you can't just let me go."

He throws his head back, laughing, but there's nothing funny about my question. Maybe he thrives on the control, like Thomas, but it seems like there's something more at play here. He tucks his head to his chest before lifting his ice-blue eyes to mine.

"I'm not entirely sure you'd understand the nuances that come with everything. I also don't know how you were taken in by this biker gang. Would you care to explain how the Reapers ensnared you? You're not exactly their type.

Though I'm sure they'll take anyone who's willing to spread their legs," he sneers, his lip curling as he eyes me.

"I'd rather not. Did you let Thomas into my room?"

He raises an eyebrow. "Look at you, clever girl."

"What's the motivation? Power? Did Thomas promise to help you on your path to greatness?"

He waves away my sarcastic words, pulling his phone from his pocket, and my eyes home in on it. I renew my efforts to reach the weapon now that I have a way to contact the outside world.

I don't know Hawk's number, but I memorized Mac's. She hasn't been answering my texts and she told me not to call the police, but I might not have a choice. I'd rather take my chances with them than die in this basement. I'm getting ahead of myself anyway. At this point, Joseph is still standing between me and freedom.

"I am more than capable of acquiring power for myself, as you have seen. However, the capital to obtain said power is...steep."

I freeze, swinging confused eyes to him. "What does *that* fucking mean?"

"Language," he snarls before his face smooths and he tilts his head. "I'm sure you can figure it out."

I don't have any money. Sure, Thomas has old money, but in order for me to have any impact on that, I'd have to...

"You wanted me to marry him?"

"That would be useful. What else am I going to use you for? The life insurance payout isn't enough to sustain my plans. Now you've forced me to find someone else who can handle dealing with you, though you'll need to cease your whorish ways. Pity you're still useful and I can't abandon you down here. Let's go."

I jump when he reaches for me and my back slams into the wooden stairs. A nail digs into my back and I gasp as it pierces my skin. There's a ripping sound as I pull away.

I'm going to be a ball of hurt if I live until tomorrow. I want to make him drag me away, but I'd rather save the little energy I have left to escape when we're back in the outside world.

Shaking his head, he pivots, expecting me to comply, like always. I wait until he's halfway up the stairs before I follow. I hold my breath as I skirt Thomas's body. There's some smell coming from him and I'd rather not have his stench stuck in my nose.

"Keep up, Willow. I've already wasted enough time driving all the way from Rima. I don't want to lose any more of my night."

His body covers the pin pad as he presses his thumb to it and the door pops open. I shy away, expecting light to flood the stairwell, but darkness meets us.

I almost ripped the pipe from Thomas's neck as I passed but thought better of it. His head probably would have fallen off in the process and then I'd have nightmares for the rest of my life. I'll probably have them anyway.

A calmness spreads through me when I step over the threshold. For some reason, Joseph doesn't scare me. I should be worried he'll somehow drag me back to Rima and marry me off. Instead, I'm disgusted. I'm not the same woman I was before. I'm stronger and capable of standing up for myself. Now that I'm out of the basement, he no longer has the control.

Once we reach the carpeted kitchen, I stop, putting the cracked breakfast bar between us. Peering over his shoulder, he does a double-take before pivoting to march back, rage rippling over his face.

I brace myself for more screaming and demands, but he slams his hands on the counter, making the tiles rattle. One plummets to the ground, bouncing across the puke green carpet. He pulls in deep breaths, eyeing me. When I can't take it anymore, I clear my throat.

"I'm not going anywhere with you, Joseph. You can go back to Rima, but I'll be staying here," I state as calmly as I can.

My heart races, my muscles tremble, and nausea crawls up my throat. I learned long ago not to defy my stepfather. He never attacked me, but his violent displays never needed to leave bruises. I barely flinch when he slams his fists on the counter again. Usually, I would scramble to obey him, just wanting everything to stop. I refuse to be that compliant little mouse any longer. His nostrils flare when I stare back, forcing a blank expression on my face.

"Don't force my hand," he growls, and I tip my chin up.

"You can leave." I should yell or scream or run, but I'm torn between the rush of confidence and the utter terror flooding my system.

"This ends now." He reaches across the counter and I stumble back, tripping over my feet before I crash to the ground.

I crab walk until I'm flush with the cupboards as all the courage drains from my body. He grins when he sees me frozen, yet I still can't move. There's a ringing in my ears and I press my hands to them, drowning out the voice screaming at me to run.

He takes two steps and then jerks, a surprised look splashing across his face. I grind the heels of my hands into my ears, thumping my head against the wood, hoping it will all stop.

His body tilts to the side, his hands grasping at the counter before sliding out of view. I shake my head violently, black spots bursting across my vision. I swear my eyeballs are shaking. There's no air left in the room.

I barely register my body sliding to the side, Joseph's blue eyes piercing into mine as he lays there, gasping. They're the last thing I see before everything goes dark.

Thirty Five

Hawk

"She's been out for an hour, Ink. What the hell is wrong with her?" I yell, slamming my fist into the wall. He doesn't even flinch as he scowls in my direction.

"We don't know what she went through. There's only a few injuries on her. If you're so fucking worried, take her to the goddamn hospital."

He slams out the front door of my house, and I kick it closed after him. Doc opens his mouth and I bare my teeth, stomping past him up to my bedroom. Sam sways as she glances over her shoulder, hand clasped in Willow's. Dark rings circle her eyes and her hair is a riot around her head.

"When did you show up?" I snap as I march around the bed and collapse into the chair I hauled up here.

A cool breeze dusts across my neck and I huff out a laugh. Of course she came through the fucking window.

Now that I've been paying attention, I realize Sam is a lot more talented than she presents to the public. Between her ability to fight and sneak into places she shouldn't, I've figured out I'd rather stay on her good side. I'd hate to wake up to her standing over me.

"When you were downstairs bickering with Ink. She hasn't woken up yet?" Her shoulders slump and I swear her cheeks are sunken in.

"No. Ink said she should be okay though. What the fuck is wrong with you?" I need to focus on something other than counting Willow's breaths. I can't fix her problems yet. Since Sam is the only one willing to put up with me, I'll concentrate on her issues instead.

"It's been a weird couple of weeks. Fuck, it's been a crazy year. It didn't use to be this hard, right?" She raises her eyes to mine, their usual brightness faded to a muddy brown.

"Guess we were due for some shit."

"Didn't think it would be this hard though. I feel like I'm being punished," she whispers, as if I won't hear her if she says it quietly.

"What would you be punished for?"

She huffs out a laugh. "That sounds dirty, but I'm too tired to make a joke."

"What are you being punished for, Sam?"

"What if"—she clears her throat as she tucks her hand in the pocket of her hoodie—"if I'm the reason shit has been going bonkers?"

"How the hell would you be responsible for all this?"

It's ridiculous to even think, but trauma makes people react in strange ways. Doc told me that years ago and for some reason, it stuck.

She snorts, shaking her head and pushing Willow's hair from her forehead. Willow twitches and I tuck her other hand in mine. Her head tilts toward me and my heart cracks a little more. By the time this is over, all I'll be able to offer her are the shards of my heart, hoping she'll help me put them back together.

"I'm not. I know I'm not. Weird, though, how as soon as I wanted something more, the world was set on fire. I thought it was done, that we'd dealt with all the bullshit and I could finally be happy. And then Mac came and I gained a friend, but then those bikers came and we almost lost her. Now this? Makes me wonder if I would have stayed in my lane..." She snorts. "It's stupid. I know."

I gently brush my thumb over the back of Willow's hand. Sam's right, it's stupid. None of this is our fault. We went so many years building our separate empires, coexisting with minimal issues, we forgot what it's like to go through shit. Others probably deal with these types of things all the time, from the beginning, but we lucked out somehow. Now we're paying our dues.

"When was the last time you slept, Sam?" I murmur, eyes fixed on Willow's face.

"I dunno."

She sways again before sinking onto the bed. She looks like she's about to pass out. I don't know if I want to make the call to one of the Kings that she keeled over in my bedroom.

"You should go home. I'll let you know when she wakes up. She'll probably want to see you..." *before she leaves.*

Hell, she might want to go stay with Sam while she recovers. I left Judge Merrick unconscious among the tulips and bleeding hearts, his blood dyeing the petals a deeper red. Doc will take care of him. I wasn't about to deal with him while Willow was hurt. I carried her for blocks before Blue finally showed up.

"Don't do it, Hawk," she warns, letting go of Willow's hand.

"Don't do what?"

"Don't fuck this up. I can tell you're going to anyway, but don't fuck this up with her."

She's gone by the time I look up, the door shutting softly behind her. I spend the next seventeen minutes warring with myself on whether Willow will wake up or not—whether Sam is right or not—whether I could have done something more to get to her earlier.

Bruises grace her body, painting her skin in a myriad of dark colors. I find so many, I can't even count them. Her wrist and shoulder are both swollen and I swear there's a bite mark on her neck. At some point, she bit her lip. I cleaned the blood from her face, but it's still bruised and puffy.

Someone's footsteps pound up the stairs and I brace myself for the door to slam against the wall. It opens gently though, and Ink steps in, carrying his bag.

Dropping it on the floor, he rummages around in it, a scowl on his face. He mutters under his breath as he wraps her wrist. I ignore him until he starts to pull up her shirt, and I haul myself to my feet. Knocking his hand away, I bare my teeth.

"Knock it the fuck off, Hawk, or I'll throw your ass out."

"I'd like to see you try," I growl.

"Hawk," Doc says softly and I start. I didn't even see him come in, I was so focused on Willow. "We need to talk. Let Ink do his job."

I hesitate, peering down at Willow. Leaving her feels wrong. I trust Ink, but there's only so much I can handle after the night I've had.

"I'll take care of her. Go." Ink's voice is so low, I almost don't catch it.

I nod, leaning to brush a kiss on her forehead. I don't care what they think anymore. I'm not going to hold back.

Sam was right, I can't fuck this up. I'll have to fight for her and I'll do whatever it takes to keep her with me. I told her she was mine and I need to make good on my promises for as long as she'll let me. Glancing back once, I freeze as Ink lifts her shirt, exposing the bruises splattered across her ribs.

Doc shoves my shoulder, ushering me out the door before he cuts off my view of her. I shudder, shaking out my hands as I make my way down the stairs to the living room and collapse on the couch.

"What is it, Doc?" I can hear the exhaustion in my voice, and I scrub my hands down my face, trying to rid myself of all emotions.

"I heard from Helms. He's dealing with some shit, but he should be back in a couple days. Mac isn't happy about what happened, but I'm sure he'll be able to calm her down by the time they make it back. Merrick's body was gone. I doubt he had another accomplice waiting in the wings, which suggests he wasn't quite dead when you grabbed Willow. We got into the basement, which held one dead body. I'm guessing that was her stalker, but I don't know if Merrick killed him or if Willow did." he says, shooting me a look.

"Did you dispose of the stalker's body?"

"We floated him. What do you want to do about Merrick?"

"I don't know. I have a feeling he didn't broadcast he was coming to Synd, but I don't know if he'll run back there or keep trying to get to her. When Willow wakes up, I'll talk to her. We'll need to deal with the car." I tip my head back, staring at the ceiling. Everything is piling up again, and my chest tightens.

"Alex King is on it. He almost creamed his pants when he saw the Aston. And then almost cried when I told him to strip it."

"The money needs to go to Willow."

"We'll deal with that later. I need you to not check the fuck out, Hawk. At least until Prez is back. The guys are getting restless, and we don't want anyone questioning whether or not we can lead. This last year's been hard on us all, but we can't afford for you to fall apart. A lot of the members aren't happy. They don't understand why this shit keeps happening."

Running my hands through my hair, digging my nails into my scalp. "I couldn't just leave her."

"I didn't expect you to. A lot of them are jealous. Not a lot of people coming through our territory, butted up against the forest like we are. They want what you and Helms have."

"What do I have? What do I really have, Doc? Because from where I'm sitting, I've got an MC that's falling apart, a shit show within the territory, and a woman passed out upstairs who I don't even know will want to stay once she wakes up." My chest tightens when I finally admit my fears out loud.

"First of all, the MC isn't falling apart. The bridge is almost finished being repaired, the rebuild is coming along, and almost nothing was destroyed this time. I'd say that alone is a fucking miracle. Second, that woman adores you. If you don't see that, you're dumber than I thought. Maybe you don't deserve her then."

"Fuck you," I spit out, launching to my feet. I dig my nails into my palms, using the bite of pain to keep me from throwing him out the door.

He leans back in his chair, a gloating smirk dancing on his mouth. "That's better. Stop being a dumbass and go take care of your woman. I'll get the guys in line. Hell, maybe I'll let Tank run the meeting tomorrow. That would be entertaining."

The anger bleeds from my body and I collapse back on the couch, but the tension in my shoulders doesn't ease. Leaning forward, I rest my elbows on my knees, burying my face. Sparks of light dance behind my lids when I dig the heels of my hands in.

I should deal with everything myself, but I'm only one person. Helms makes it look easy, keeping everything together, dealing with these assholes, and still managing to spend time with Mac. I've been running things for less than three months, and I'm drowning. The weight of responsibility didn't settle on me slowly. It crashed into me, leaving me floundering to find my feet.

"I'm only going to tell you this once, Hawk. You're lucky you found someone who will have your back and fight for you. Don't be dumb and throw it away. It's not as common as you think," Doc says. His feet scuffle across the floor as Ink appears, and the door snicks shut behind them.

His words swirl through the air, flinging me back to the past, when I said almost the same thing to Mac. It was annoying to watch them struggle and fight against their feelings for so long when they were clearly made for each other.

Apparently, I'm an idiot too. It was harder than I realized to see the truth. I kept telling Willow she was meant to be mine, but I never fully believed she'd stay. I failed before I even started with her. Pushing myself up, I shake my hands out, then spin around when Ink comes down the stairs.

"Well?"

"She's fine. Still hasn't woken up and she'll need some time to recover, but she's fine. Don't push her. Wait for her to come to you." He starts for the door. He swings around, resting his hand on the knob. "Don't fuck this up, Hawk."

I bound up the stairs instead of answering, and the door clicks shut on his way out. Leaning my forehead against my bedroom door, I close my eyes. With my heart racing and my head swimming, I'm not ready to see her battered body yet. I can't walk in there unsure of what I'm going to do.

The terror I felt when she went missing sweeps through me. It never left, sitting in the back of my mind, waiting to strike. It gathers in my chest and slowly smothers my senses until my head pounds. The wood warps in front of me and I sway. A yelp pulls me from my spiral, yanking me from the edge of the void looming before me.

Rushing through the door, I scan the room. I shouldn't have left her alone. The sheets are a mess on the bed, the emptiness an extra layer upon the mattress. I let out a string of curses, rushing to the bathroom, but that's empty too.

I clench my jaw, keeping the anguish inside as I rush back in, only to freeze. Willow is tucked between the nightstand and bed, knees bent and hair blanketing her face. How she was able to hide herself away in that small space is beyond me.

Crouching in front of her, I brush my fingers over one of her arms, which are wrapped tightly around her legs. She jerks back, causing the lamp to rattle, and I yank my hand away.

"Willow," I murmur.

Her shoulders shake and her nails dig into her arms, knuckles white from the strain she's under. My chest hollows and I drop my head. I want to grab her, hold her, do something to pull her from whatever hell she's locked in, but I curl my hands into fists, fighting the urge. I don't know how to save her.

I should call Mac or Sam. They'd know how to help her. They'd fill in the gaps where I'm failing.

"I'm going to get help," I whisper before leaning back.

"Hawk?" Her voice is quiet, edged in tears. The vise around my heart squeezes tighter.

"I'm here, *mo dóchais*. I'm right here."

Thirty Six

Willow

I want to hide again, but Hawk's voice had too much in it. Too much emotion, too much devastation, too much helplessness. They echo in his eyes, and I'm falling into their depths instead of the blackness licking at the edge of my vision.

When I woke alone, I didn't know where I was. My brain blanked and panic drowned out the feeling of security. Low voices filtered up the stairs, worming into my mind and distorting everything around me. The pain radiating through my body wasn't enough to stop me from sliding off the bed and hiding in the only place I could reach without collapsing. I almost passed out when the door opened and heavy footsteps echoed through the space.

"I'm sorry," I whisper, ducking my head. I can't handle the accusation in his eyes.

"Willow."

That's all, just my name. I swallow the sob crawling up my throat. I don't know how long I was out, but the sunlight filtering through the window tells me it's been several hours at least. It blinded me at first, but I refuse to close my eyes. Every time I do, Thomas's lifeless body floats up from the recesses of my mind.

The numbness in my fingers spreads, but the essence of blood still clings to my palms. I'm not stupid. I did what I had to do to survive, and I don't regret killing him. The bastard deserved it for the pain he caused, but now I have to live with the consequences.

"Is Joseph dead?"

I need to know how much time I have to run if he's not. I heard the gunshot and saw him fall. But I've seen enough corruption in the world to know the real villains don't always stay down.

"Willow. Look at me."

Hawk's fingers wrap around my wrist and I jerk back, squeezing my legs as hard as I can. The bed frame digs into my leg and the ache spreads the longer I'm pressed against it. I wish I could burrow into the floor—straight to hell. At least the flames would burn away the ice in my veins.

I peek at him as he runs his fingers through his hair, the strands falling over his forehead as he looks toward the window. The locks brush the nape of his neck now, longer than it was when we met.

"You should get a haircut," I say, clamping my mouth shut as soon as the words escape.

He whips his head back, gaze finding mine. The corner of his mouth tips up as his eyes soften. There's still a speck of doubt in them. I won't ask. I won't be able to handle the answer now. I just need to know if my stepfather is dead. I can't ask more of Hawk.

"Willow, we need to get you back in bed," he murmurs, reaching slowly for me.

I shudder when his flesh meets mine. He slides his fingers down my arm, but when he reaches my hand, I yank it from his grasp.

"The blood," I gasp, scrubbing my hands down my legs.

"There's nothing there. I washed them."

He grabs my hands, but I rip them away, unable to stop the sensation of stickiness coating them.

"Willow."

The roaring in my ears drowns out whatever else he says. My vision blurs and when my tears fall, splashing onto my arms, crimson shimmering within the drops.

"Where's it coming from? Fuck, no. Make it stop," I cry, shaking the droplets from my skin.

"Willow, stop!"

Hawk hauls me from my hiding spot, tugging me into his arms until I'm smothered in his smoky scent. My breathing evens out and all the fight drains away.

Coughing around the gravel in my throat, Hawk tightens his grip and I sink into his body, his essence filling up my pores, chasing away the emptiness. I don't know how long he holds me, but the tears subside and my limbs feel heavy.

"I'm sorry," I say again, voice muffled by his shirt.

I'm curled in his lap and while I don't want to leave this bubble of safety, I'm sure he doesn't want to keep holding the pieces of me together. My fingers are cramped, curled in the fabric of his shirt, and my knuckles crack as I free them one by one. Leaning back, I try to scramble from his hold, but he doesn't release me.

"Hawk, let me go," I breathe, ducking my head. I push tiredly against his chest, but I'm not trying that hard. I want him to hold me, to make me feel safe, to want me.

He won't care that I killed Thomas. He might be upset I went with him in the first place, but Hawk would get over it. The accusation in his eyes though, shows me how much I've fucked up.

I should have gone back to Rima with Mac. Or ran somewhere else, anywhere else, when the signs first popped up that my stalker followed me. Since I've come here, I've seen how integral Hawk is to the Reapers. I've noticed how important the MC is to the city and how seamlessly they work together. They've been trying to rebuild after the Night Slayers swept through, decimating their territory, and then I came along and derailed all those plans.

"Don't, *mo dóchais*. Don't make me let you go yet," he whispers into my hair.

"I killed him." The confession slips out with no warning.

"I know."

"Is Joseph dead?" I didn't miss the fact he never answered me. My heart races and the crushing feeling in chest returns.

"No."

That one word rips through me, tearing away all sense of security. I push against him harder, kicking my feet out. He grabs for me again, but I wiggle free. I'm boxed in between his body and the frame with nowhere else to go, so I scramble across the bed, feet slapping against the hardwoods. Hawk's arm wraps around my waist before I can reach the door.

My brain fizzles out. Rationally, I realize I have nowhere else to run. My brain won't accept it though. I have to get away from here. I'll be damned if anyone else gets hurt because of me.

"Stop, Willow. It's okay. I won't let him hurt you. I know you don't believe me, but I swear I'll keep you safe."

His frantic voice barely registers over the blood coursing through my head. Slamming my hands over my ears, I curl my body until Hawk is the only thing keeping me upright. He stumbles backward, landing with a groan on the bed. He cradles my body, taking the brunt of the fall.

"I can't, Hawk. I can't," I sob, the adrenaline leaving me.

The ache in my bones is immediate, reminding me of all I've been through over the last twenty-four hours. I'm surprised I'm able to move with what Thomas put me through. The rollercoaster of emotions bouncing inside of me overwhelms my senses, deadening the outside world as his hands skim over me, sending a shiver down my spine.

"Willow, we don't have to talk about this now. I need you to heal. I need you to be okay. I can't lose you again. Please."

The darkness beckons from the edge of my vision, calling me to sink into its warm embrace. I don't fight it this time.

The shadows haunt me in my dreams. When I open my eyes, the moon filters through the curtains as the shadows chase me into reality.

Hawk's form propped against the wall, arms crossed and eyes shut tight, catches my eye. How he's able to sleep sitting up is beyond me. I watch as his chest rises and falls with each breath, but when he shifts, I freeze, waiting for him to wake.

He settles, and I force my muscles to unlock, easing into the softness of the pillow. I tense again when the door creaks open and close my eyes until they're slits. Ink slips inside, followed by Doc. I clear my throat and Ink rushes closer.

"You shouldn't be sleeping on your wrist like that," Ink says, reaching out a tattooed hand, and I brace myself for the pain. Instead, he cradles my arm gently, pulling it closer to inspect the bandages.

"It doesn't hurt. The scrape on my back is worse," I murmur, wiggling to ease the itching.

"Why don't you roll over and I'll put some medicine on it."

Rolling to my stomach, I stifle a whimper. He pushes my shirt up and a tremor runs through me. I don't understand how someone so large and intimidating can be so gentle. As he spreads a cooling liquid on the wound, I fix my eyes on Hawk's sleeping form, and the cream chases the sting away.

I wonder how long he stayed awake, waiting for me to lose my shit again. I thought he would have shot up the minute the front door opened, but he's still propped against the wall. Ink taps my shoulder and I roll back.

Doc crouches next to the bed, blocking my view. "Willow, can you think of any place Merrick would go?"

I turn my head away to hide the tears filling my eyes. I don't want to have this conversation. I don't want to think about Joseph being out there, waiting for me. I want to imagine he'll leave me alone. Normal people would run far away once they were shot. But Joseph is anything but normal.

I'm still reeling from the shock of his appearance. He wasn't the villain of my story. He wasn't the puppet master, pulling the strings. He was the annoying gnat, buzzing in the corners of my mind. An annoyance, but not a threat.

Even now, part of me still doesn't think he'll come for me. I'm too much work. I may have freaked out earlier, but I realize I'm in the safest place I could possibly be. Joseph wouldn't dare come here. He may have resources, but between the mafia leaders and the Reapers, he won't find any help in Synd.

"I don't know. Back to Rima," I murmur.

Ink unwraps my wrist, twisting it this way and that, but it doesn't hurt anymore. I thought it would be broken after everything I put it through. Glancing at his face as he works his way over my wounds, assessing each as he goes, I wonder how much they'll push me for information. I didn't think I had that many injuries, but the more he finds, the more I realize the situation I was in.

"We think he's still here. We tracked his car on the east side, but lost it in the shuffle of traffic. We'd rather not be ambushed, so anything you can tell us would help." Doc's words roll over me, and my brain runs riot over the safety I felt seconds ago.

I'm an idiot, thinking Judge Joseph fucking Merrick would leave me be. He doesn't know how to let go. His need for control and his actions in every facet of his life say otherwise. The fear he instilled in me for years swamps my senses, and I battle against the need to give up.

He would leave the Reapers alone if I went with him. He could take me back, force me to marry whoever he can manipulate, and I'll probably die in the process. I could run further from Rima, hoping he'd eventually leave me be. I could do what I should have months ago.

Turning my head, I find Hawk still propped against the wall, but his eyes are fixed on me now. His gaze is intense, burning into mine. If I left, he'd follow. If

I ran, he'd catch me. If I said anything other than I was his, he'd remind me how wrong I was. A shiver runs through me and his eyes darken.

"Get the fuck out," he growls, eyes still fixed on me.

Doc swings his head around and then they both run from the room, the door slamming behind them.

Hawk's moves border on predatory as he unfolds his limbs and stalks toward me. My body ignites, despite the bruises covering me. The aches and pains disappear in the wake of the desire whipping through me. I expect him to lie next to me, maybe hover over my body, but he drops to his knees next to the bed.

"What are you doing?" I whisper, tracking his gaze as his eyes travel up and down my body.

"Wondering why you're thinking about running."

My breath hitches, the desire fleeing. "I wasn't."

He ducks his chin and scrubs his hands over his face. "So, you're staying then?"

His voice is barely a whisper and I swallow hard. The about-face my emotions are taking sends a wave of dizziness through my head. I didn't think I'd have to worry about whether he wanted me to stay or not—whether he wanted me or not.

"I don't know what you want me to say."

I don't want to beg. I don't want to face the reality things might have gone too far, that the risk isn't worth the reward anymore.

Ink told me Hawk had the entire MC out looking for me. Their territory was hit because of me. Thomas may have been stalking me, but the Reapers were caught in the crossfire. Hell, Hawk was shot, all because I didn't take shit seriously. He might have protected me, but it might be time for me to protect him.

"I know I said you were mine. I told you I wouldn't let you go, but..." He ducks his head, but not before I catch the shame in his eyes.

Staring at the ceiling, I wait for him to damn me with his words. I choke back tears as a numbness steals through my body. My stomach cramps, and I roll away from him, hanging my head over the side and gag. All I end up doing is dry heaving until I curl into a ball.

Hawk's warm hand brushes the hair away from my face. He murmurs something, but the blood rushing past my ears silences him. I wretch again and I swear I'm going to throw up my lungs. My heart is trying to burst from my chest like an alien making its way into the world. Hysteria bubbles up in my throat. It would be just my luck to die from a broken heart instead of being thrown around like a rag doll.

Hawk's words filter through the fog floating in my head. "Willow, breathe. I've got you."

A frenzied giggle escapes, ending with a sob. "Don't. Please, don't."

I slide from his grasp, his touch sending licks of fiery pain through me, reminding me of what I'm no longer allowed to have. All the pain and suffering. All the terror and anxiety. I endured everything only to be brought down by him. The man I called a knight in shining armor. The one who convinced me I was more than what everyone told me I was. The man who taught me more in mere weeks about my own desires than I ever could have imagined.

The one who is trying to let me down gently, still striving to protect me—from myself, from the pain, from him.

I land on the dark hardwood, my arms quivering as they try to keep me from dissolving into a puddle on the floor. There's no use hiding the tears, the utter devastation flooding my body. He's already seen me at my worst.

I can't even blame him. I can't be upset he's choosing to protect the Reapers over me. They're his family—his salvation. Still, rage unfurls like a shadow inside me, binding with the regret coiling around my heart.

I heave my body up, swaying as I find my feet. Hawk reaches for me, but I step back, lifting my head to meet his gaze. His emerald eyes shimmer in the sunlight streaming from the window behind me, and my calculating thoughts stop in their tracks.

"Willow?"

Tilting my head, I search for something, anything, to say he'd choose me, but all I find is regret. I huff, tipping my head back and closing my eyes.

To be fair, I always thought it would come to this. I've never quite been good enough for someone to keep. I've always been the placeholder until someone better came along. But I *was* enough, they just couldn't see it.

Hawk saw my worth. At least, I thought he did.

"I'm fine," I say, meeting his eyes again. "I'd like to shower, if that's okay."

"We need to talk about this, Willow."

"I fail to see what more words will accomplish. Circumstances won't change just because we talk them to death."

He gives me a look I can't decipher, but I'm done caring. I'm done trying to figure out how to fit in. I'm done making decisions based on others and how it will make them see me. I'm done being a doormat.

A thud downstairs makes me jump and then I'm pressed into the corner. I don't remember moving. The low rumble of voices flows up the stairs. Hawk shakes his head before stalking to the door and then he's gone, slamming it behind him. The creak of the window snaps me out of my trance as Sam slips through, scanning the room.

"You know you can use the door, right?" I smirk when she snaps around, reaching for something at her back, probably a gun.

"Well, aren't you a sneaky little thing? You don't look like a zombie anymore. All better, then?" Sam grins, crossing her arms and leaning against the window frame.

"I'm fine."

That's my line from now on. I've buried the trauma of being kidnapped deep within, stacking the shame, insecurities, and heartache up and topping it off with a dollop of bitterness.

"Oh, so we're lying to ourselves now? Great. What are you going to do then? Merrick is still out there, probably waiting for you to do something stupid, like run. You're not going to be stupid, are you, Willow?" She cocks an eyebrow. A crash downstairs has us both turning, but I stay put while she moves to the door.

I use the distraction to search the room for my shoes, finding them thrown by my bags in the corner, clothes spilling from them. I never even got far enough to unpack. Not that I would have.

Hawk never told me to do anything with them. Our relationship wasn't one that included emptying drawers and making space in the closet. It was a whirlwind of emotions and promises that withered in the face of uncertainty.

"Sam." I wait until she turns back. "You wouldn't happen to have a weapon, would you?"

Shock flits across her face before it morphs into something else. Pride maybe.

"You want something easy to handle, or are you looking for something more up close and personal?"

"Both."

The numbness from earlier seeps further into me, freezing my heart and walling off my emotions. I'm not trained. A couple sessions with Sam don't count. I'm not stealthy, despite what Sam says, but I won't be hiding in the corner when I hunt my stepfather down.

The only way I'll be able to have any semblance of peace is to take out the threat. It might not work. Logically, I know I don't have enough skill to take him down by myself, but I can try. And if I'm no longer around, Joseph will leave the Reapers alone. He doesn't care about a biker gang in a different city. I'm all he wants. Why I'm his meal ticket to the top, I still don't fully understand. Not many things in our elitist world make sense.

"Alright. I've got knives and a gun. You need to promise me you're going there to actually kill him and not turn yourself over to him. That won't do anything other than cause more problems for everyone involved. Then I'll be forced to tell Mac and Hawk and Ryker and I'll get in trouble."

"I have every intention of giving him everything he deserves for all the years he was an asshole, but I have to do this alone, Sam. I can't have anyone fighting my battles for me. I spent too long giving in and then I let Hawk take on my problems. I need to do this." A sliver of doubt seeps through the haze and my stomach quivers.

She eyes me before nodding. "I won't say anything unless you to do something stupid. Don't try to stab him unless you need to. Shooting him from a distance is better. Oh, and don't forget to double tap—good advice for killing and fucking."

I huff out a laugh. "I'll keep that in mind."

"Don't fuck this up and make me regret it, Willow," she murmurs, handing me the weapons.

I don't have a reply.

Thirty Seven

Hawk

I slam the door behind Tank. He spent the last twenty minutes bitching about the shit going down with the contractors fixing the bridge. It's the least of my worries, especially with how I left things with Willow. I would've thrown him out, but I've been neglecting shit within the MC. The whole conversation devolved into him calling me out on shit.

Deliveries are being missed, renovations on businesses are being pushed, meetings are happening without the Reapers, not to mention members are getting pissed. I can't keep ignoring the things going on.

Willow is safe for now, and I won't be letting her out of my sight. I won't make the same mistakes twice. We'll deal with Merrick, and she'll be free to do whatever she wants.

My feet are dragging by the time I make it up the stairs. It's only midmorning, but sleeping on the floor for only a couple hours wasn't enough to make up for the intensity of last night. Steam wafts from the bathroom and the knot in my chest loosens the slightest bit. Her reactions earlier were night and day.

The panic attack came out of nowhere, at least for me. I couldn't seem to calm her, no matter what I did. I'm loathe to continue the conversation of her staying. The visceral reaction she had followed by the blankness on her face freaked me out. I'm almost glad Tank interrupted.

The bathroom door creaks as I push it open further and more steam wafts in my face, temporarily blinding me. I expect Willow's cloudy form to be under the spray, but instead I find a shadow tucked in the corner. My heart starts pounding again as I rip open the glass door. She doesn't look at me as she rocks, letting the water flow over her, plastering her hair to her face.

"Willow?" I murmur, crouching. She's folded into a tight ball, arms cinched around her bare legs. I want to pull her in my arms, but with how she reacted last time, I don't want to set her off again.

I clear my throat. "Willow."

She looks up, staring at me with blank eyes. I see the moment her mind clicks over, absorbing the fact I'm in front of her. She unfolds her limbs slowly before swiping the water from her face. There's an edge in her eyes that wasn't there before, but she blinks and it's gone, a small smile playing on her lips.

It doesn't feel real. It doesn't feel like her. Something's changed. Everything's changed. This right here is why I wanted to give her an out. I won't make her stay if it's not what she needs. I'd rather have her whole and healed, far away from me, rather than seize the pieces of her that are left.

"What do you need?" I ask, and she tilts her head.

"Your clothes are getting wet."

"I don't care. Tell me what you need."

She shakes her head, glancing away as she pressed her lips into a thin line. I wait another minute before pushing to my feet and closing the door behind me. I look back once before it snicks shut. Something in me breaks, and I double over, digging my fist into my chest.

Sliding down, I thump my head against the door, wishing I could rip the pain from me. It's everywhere though, seeping into every pore and infiltrating all my senses. I don't know how long I sit, straining to hear any movement from behind the wood. It's just the water hitting the glass, masking everything she might be feeling.

A buzzing in my pocket forces me back to reality. "What do you want, Byrns?"

"Don't be an asshole, Hawk. I'm doing you a fucking favor here," Mason says.

I wonder if I can get away with hanging up on him. "And?"

"You think I don't have anything better to do than hunt down rival MCs and dirty judges for you? You realize I've got a whole part of the city I'm keeping in check, right? But no, here I am, working with people I don't particularly like and calling in favors from others, and dealing with the bullshit you Reapers keep getting yourself mixed up with."

"Are you getting laid, Byrns?" I ask, pushing to my feet.

I strip off my wet shirt and pull on another one before stalking out the bedroom door. She'll probably be in there awhile, stitching herself back together. Or avoiding all the trauma left in the wake of facing her stalker. I haven't even asked her how he died—if she was forced to kill him.

"Fuck you," he grunts, a bell jingling on his end. I swear I caught someone's tinkling laugh before the sound cuts off.

I'm in the kitchen before I figure out how to respond. "Do you need a sticker for being such a good mafia boss?"

There's a clatter on the other end, and I can hear him cursing faintly. He must have thrown the phone down. Leaning against the counter, I chuckle as he rants and raves.

I sober when the shower upstairs shuts off and I tip my head back as if I can track her movements through the creaks in the wood. Eventually, the noises fade away. I hope she's sleeping.

"Are you done being a dick or should I call King instead? Have us play telephone and hope the information gets to you eventually."

"Calm your tits, Byrns. It hasn't been a stellar year for any of us. Tell me what you found."

"Your fancy-ass judge's car. Found it at a chop shop on the south end. Almost completely stripped. If he's moving, he's not using a shiny to do it anymore. I've got eyes at the train station, but nothing there. He might have gone back to Rima."

"He hasn't. Helms is there. Merrick hasn't been spotted in a couple days," I say, letting the frustration bleed into my voice.

"Is there uproar? I gather he's a big deal over there."

"His assistant let it slip to the media he was looking for Willow. Made it a huge sob story about how she was lured away or something. I'm sure he'd try to twist it against the Vipers, maybe bring us down in the process. Innocent little rich girl seduced by the dark side of the law, straight into the clutches of a biker gang," I scoff.

"What the fuck. You watch too many movies."

I chuckle. "Actually, that would be Willow's books."

"Whatever. You think he'd take the train?"

Doc walks through the front door without knocking, and I scowl. Fucker is getting way too comfortable waltzing into my house whenever the hell he pleases.

One look at his face says this isn't the right time. His dark brows are pulled low over his eyes, mouth set in a thin line. I can't imagine what more could possibly be wrong. He motions me to hurry up before collapsing on my couch.

"No, I don't. He's a rich prick. He'd throw his weight around or just buy another car. I'm surprised he got rid of his shiny as it is. He might be reaching out to others like him though—the commissioner, the police chief, hell even the mayor. He'll try to use them any way he can."

"He'll be in for a rude surprise then. Listen, I got some shit going down here I might need..." He cuts off, shouting something I can't make out, and the line goes dead.

I call him again, but it goes straight to voicemail. I send him a text before texting Sam to check it out. She responds with a ghost emoji—whatever the fuck that means. Mason Byrns might not be my responsibility, but the last thing we need is another crisis to deal with. It was bad enough when he fell into a coma for months. We can't afford to lose him. Plus, I actually like the fucker when he's not being a morose little bitch.

"What's your problem?" I drop on the couch next to Doc as he texts someone.

"Some shit is going down on the east side. Byrns doesn't seem to be dealing with it."

"I just talked to him. Seems like he's got a lot on his plate. We might need to loop the Kings in. Not much we can do unless something big goes down."

"Well, I'd rather not have more shit go wrong. We've dealt with enough. The Reapers need to regroup and rebuild."

I nod, tipping my head back against the couch. The exhaustion of running around our territory all night and then sleeping on the floor is catching up to me. All I want to do is slip into bed next to Willow and hold her as long as she'll let me. I probably won't have many more days with her before she leaves.

"You still moping?"

"Tank was here earlier, bitching about the construction on the bridge. Do I need to deal with that?"

"So, we're ignoring shit. Message received. I'll get Tank in line. He's just pissed 'cause of the shipments being fucked up again. I also think he got rejected when he tried to take someone to dinner. Not to mention all the shit going on with Willow. He's not happy we've been pulling resources for her. A lot of the guys aren't."

"Which we already talked about. Once I deal with Merrick, things will settle down."

"We might not have time for that, Hawk. We've been burning the candle at both ends and can't afford for you to chase after him. Your responsibilities are here."

I nod, not willing to fight with him on it. I'm capable of doing both. Things might be slipping through the cracks, but I don't have to choose. Not yet. I'll fight Willow's demons and keep the MC afloat until Helms can take the reins once more. He's better at leading anyway.

"Just a little longer," I murmur, pushing to my feet. "Then it'll be over."

A creak behind has me looking over my shoulder, but no one's there. It would be just my luck for Willow to stumble on our conversation, not understanding what's actually going on.

"Hawk, don't fuck this up. It's more than just you who's suffering here," Doc says, bringing my attention back to him.

"Why do I get the feeling you don't know what the hell you want me to do? This morning you were telling me to be there for Willow and not fuck things up with her, and now you're lecturing me on taking care of the MC. Which one is it? I can deal with everything, but not all at once and not by my-fucking-self."

Doc stands, eyeing me before glancing at his buzzing phone. "Shit changes. I'll help as much as I can, but I'm not built to lead."

"Neither am I," I shout, throwing my hands up.

He shakes his head. "Therein lies your problem, Hawk." He claps me on the shoulder before stalking out the door, phone already pressed to his ear.

I'm torn between getting shit done while Willow sleeps and curling up next to her, soaking in the fact she's alive. Trudging up the stairs, intent on at least checking on her, but when I push open the door, I find the bed empty and my heart skips. It doesn't take me long to check the room. The bathroom and closet are both empty.

Rushing out, I search the rest of the upstairs before moving to the main floor. The back door is still locked and there's no way she'd be able to slip out the front, not with Doc and me sitting in the living room the entire time.

I race back up the stairs, combing the room for evidence of a struggle. Her bags are still sitting on the dresser, stuffed full of her things. She never did unpack. The bottom two drawers are empty and waiting for her, but she never asked and I never offered. I wish I had now.

I spin, scanning the room, at a loss for where she could be, when I spot the window sitting wide open with something fluttering on the sill. My stomach turns the closer I get.

Ice fills my veins as I finger the scrap of fabric left behind. I'm not good at this type of shit, but somehow I know she went out the window. She ran, with nothing more than the clothes on her back.

Staring out at the charred wreckage of my neighbor's house, guilt stabs into me. There's still several hours of daylight left. I could go after her.

Before her stalker took her, she was worried about the effect her being here would have on the MC. After hearing our conversation, I'm sure she felt justified in leaving, assuming she was doing what was best for us. Instead, she left the remnants of my heart trailing in the wake of her flight.

Thirty Eight

Willow

I can barely make out Hawk's shadowed form in his second-story window. I wasn't going to stick around once I clambered out, but something kept me in the shade of the house across the street, waiting for him to appear. I knew he'd find out I was gone eventually.

It takes me much longer to realize what I'm waiting for. I hold my breath until he stalks away and still, I stay hidden, eyes fixed on the house where I spent the last few weeks.

After ten minutes, I realize he's not coming after me. My heart drops and fuzziness invades my head as I lean my forehead against the warm wood of the front porch.

I don't think anyone lives here anyway, so I could sit here until the sun sets. I won't though. A few minutes is all I need to process the emotions running rampant in my body.

"You'll be fine," I whisper, closing my eyes.

Pushing away, I wince at the burning scrape on my shin. I thought I could slip out the window as gracefully as Sam did. Instead I ended up almost falling to my death.

Thankfully, there was a thick sill for my feet to catch on. I landed on my tailbone instead of my feet, but at least I didn't break any bones. Sam wanted me to wait until nightfall. She said she'd help, but after hearing Hawk's conversation with Doc, I couldn't.

I couldn't pretend things were fine. I couldn't wait for Hawk to lie down next to me, knowing he wasn't invested anymore.

After the shower, I told myself I would finish the conversation he started. Hope bloomed inside, and I wondered if I misunderstood his words. He agreed with Doc though, and that told me how the rest of it would have gone. Hopefully, he won't feel so guilty now. If he had to let me down gently, I wouldn't have survived.

I still might not.

I slip deeper into the shadows cast by the sun, losing sight of Hawk's house. I honestly don't know if I'll see it again, much less the man within.

Doubling over at the thought, I lean against the house, struggling to catch my breath. I lock the misery deep within and my muscles ease one by one. Dashing across the street, I run away from the pain welling up within me, refusing to stay hidden.

Ducking between houses and hiding in backyards from the bikes streaking through the streets, I search for a way out. I'm not sure where the line is other than the one by Trigger's, and I can't go that way.

Even during the middle of the day, there will be members outside. Someone will recognize me and report back to Hawk, and this whole plan will go to shit. I'll breathe easier once I get out of Reaper territory.

I cross to another street and freeze. My heart races and I run my sweaty palms along my leggings. It's too hot for them, but the nights are getting cooler and I'd rather not be stuck outside, freezing my ass off. Spinning around, I try to place where the panic is coming from when I spot the run-down house down the block. It's only been a day or two since Hawk pulled me from the building, leaving Joseph behind. Time has bled together, jumbling up the days.

I don't remember Hawk rescuing me. The images of my short time there flash in my mind: my stepfather's rage-filled face screaming, Thomas's lifeless eyes, the apple slices scattered across a concrete floor, hyacinths and roses and tulips scattered over every surface, their cloying scent wafting through the air to suffocate me.

The road wavers as my vision blurs and I dash away, cutting through a yard filled with weeds and random tires. It takes me five minutes and three blocks of stumbling blindly around before I realize I'm headed back toward headquarters—back to him. I pivot, wondering if I should just abandon this whole thing.

I'm not even able to get out of the neighborhood on my own without freaking out. I have no training. I'm not a badass who goes out and kills people, regardless of whether or not they deserve it.

You killed Thomas.

Satisfaction flows through me and I shake out my hands, the weight of the gun tucked in the back of my pants comforting my frayed nerves. Sam showed me how to strap the leather holster to my arm for the knife. I don't know what it's called, but I hid it under my sleeve. Though I thought it would be cumbersome when I slipped out the window, it's a comfort knowing the weapons are there. I may not know how to use them well, but at least I have some way to defend myself. At least I'll have a way to stop Joseph if I find him.

"This is still a terrible idea," I mutter as I finally cross from Reaper territory and into the east side of the city.

I feel like an idiot for not noticing the red and black Reapers' colors plastered over the windows and hanging off fences along the border. We always passed by Trigger's bar when we came back. I didn't realize the whole line was sectioned off this way.

I spent so long trying to get away from Reaper territory, the sun sits low in the sky as I wander around. The buildings here are ominous and imposing. None of them seem like they're occupied. It feels darker, grungier, and more menacing. I've crossed some invisible line into another world. The lights from the city barely filter into this area and a chill snakes down my spine.

When I slide around the corner of a metal lean-to, my shoe hooks on a jagged piece sticking out. I trip and my hand slams into the side, metal reverberating into the ever-darkening night. Ducking, I whip my head back and forth, searching for ghosts in the night.

When none appear, I push to my feet slowly, careful not to catch the metal again. It's a lost cause though, since seconds later my knee smashes into the wall and a boom rings out. I wince, waiting until the noise fades away before I sneak around the corner.

"You shouldn't be out here, girly," a low voice echoes through the dark, and I squeak. A large hand wraps around my arm as I tumble backwards. "Easy there."

He sets me right and a streetlamp flares to life the next block over, revealing a stout man with a wild red beard covering most of his face. He plants his hands on thick hips and his bushy eyebrows pull low over his dark eyes as they sweep up and down before settling on my face. I don't know if I should run or shoot him or scream bloody murder.

"Looks like you've seen the wrong end of a fist there." He scowls and I clamp my hand over my forearm where the knife sits. His eyes track my movements and I drop my hand to my side.

"I'm sorry," I murmur, hoping he'll let me go.

"Just fucking great," he growls.

I take a step back, but a howl from behind makes me stutter to a stop and I almost end up on my ass. The ruddy man scowls again, leaning forward, as if he'll catch me before I fall. We're in the middle of the city, close to the river. There shouldn't be anything that *can* howl down here. After all I've been through, I wouldn't be surprised at this point if a wolf jumped right out of the dark, intent on devouring me in front of this man.

"I'm going to go," I say, sliding to the side.

He shakes his head, glancing behind him before pinning me in place with knowing eyes. "Won't end well. Why does this shit always happen to me?"

"I don't know what you're talking about."

"Where you come from?" He scans me, eyes snagging on the ribbon peeking from my pocket. Sam told me if I was insistent on going, I needed to keep it on me at all times. I didn't understand why, but when the man's eyes alight on it, he grunts.

"I should go," I whisper.

"You know the girly, huh?"

I freeze, not sure how to respond. I know next to no one here. He shakes his head, throwing up his hands and stalking back inside the shed. I can't tell if he lives here or if it's a workshop of some kind, but I take advantage of his disappearance and tiptoe past the door.

I hear the creak before his hand snatches my arm again, swinging me around. My lungs seize and I twist, pulling it free from his grip. I don't know where the move came from, but something clicked in my brain and my body took over.

"Ah, there's the girly comin' out."

"What the hell are you talking about?" I cry, spinning around instead of running away like a normal person. And then it clicks. "Are you talking about Sam?"

The corner of his mouth twitches, like he wants to smile but forgot over the years living in this forgotten place.

"She won't like you here. This is the Barrens. And you're an easy target."

"Oh, I just need to get to the train station," I say.

I shouldn't have told him where I planned on going. He nods though, pursing his lips. I'm probably going to get murdered and stuffed under the floorboards, but at least I tried.

"Let's go then." He sweeps his hand around, gesturing me away from the river.

I shouldn't let him lead me anywhere. I shouldn't walk with him at my back, but I've made so many mistakes since I came to Synd, I doubt one more will matter. I'm already convinced this will end with me dead, but I'm hoping I can take Joseph down with me. Still, I wait for him to make a move.

He scowls before stomping past, the darkness swallowing up his large frame. I hesitate as the streetlight dies. It's one thing to tell him where I'm going. It's another thing to follow a strange man who looks like he could pop my head like a melon down a dark alley. His grunt echoes through the night, and I rush to catch up.

After an hour my feet are killing me, and the plea to take a break dances on the tip of my tongue. He's plodding along at a steady pace, but my feet are lumpy sores, and all the aches and pains I was ignoring before have overwhelmed my system. I swear we're going in circles, but with the twists and turns here, I can't be for sure.

I open my mouth for the fifth time to beg for a break when he stops. I almost run into his back but catch myself at the last second. A shiver runs down my spine. I don't think he'd appreciate me plowing into him.

Peeking around his massive frame, I spot the train station several blocks ahead. I'm convince now that he took me the long way around. The light from up ahead is blinding after the darkness and I pull back, blinking rapidly to clear the spots from my vision.

"Here you are then. Don't do anything stupid, girly."

His gruff voice is jarring after so much silence. Even the traffic seems muted. I can't remember what day it is, but the train station is empty. I hear another howl from deep in the Barrens and glance over my shoulder.

When I turn back, he's gone. Spinning around twice, I strain to figure out where he slipped off to. I wouldn't think someone so bulky could be so silent.

I resign myself to waiting on a bench and watching the trains going by, but I only make it ten feet before I hear the low chuckle of my stepfather filtering from the shadows. I tense, slowly pivoting toward him. I can only see half his face, but it's sallow, eyes sunken in his head.

Maybe this won't be so hard after all.

Thunder rattles the metal shacks around us. The wind picks up as low clouds filter over the moon. It feels appropriate a storm would blow in as soon as I'm striving to end this chapter of my life once and for all.

Ice flows through my veins when he steps into the light. I assumed he would be rumpled and dirty, maybe bloody from getting shot. Instead, he's impeccably dressed in a three-piece suit. He looks like he's about to walk into the courtroom, damning young people to a life of hardship they don't deserve, all in the name of the power he craves so much. How my marrying someone will help him gain more than he already has doesn't make sense.

Tucking his hands in his pockets, I see what I missed before. His suit isn't tailored like I thought, hanging off his frame. His eyes are red-rimmed with bags under them. When he takes another step, his movements are jerky, as if he's not in full control of his limbs.

"Nice of you to come to me, Willow," he says, and I startle. His voice is off, tightened with pain.

"I'm not going with you, Joseph. I don't know why you thought I'd let you marry me off in the first place."

Now that I'm standing in front of him, I don't know if I can go through with my plan. Maybe I can convince him to go back to Rima. He can continue to sow seeds of discord and amass more power, and I can be free of him.

I don't know what I'll do once I can make my own decisions. Even if I could convince Hawk that Joseph has left for good, I doubt he'd believe me. Or maybe he wouldn't believe Joseph. Regardless, Hawk made his choices when he didn't come after me, when he didn't fight for me, when he chose to let me go.

"I've abandoned that plan, actually. I think it's time to deal with you once and for all."

He pulls a gun from behind his back, pointing it at me while he grins manically. I stutter back, but don't reach for my own weapon. I brace myself for the sharp report, the searing pain, the blackness—but nothing comes. He stands, gun shaking in his grasp, with that same crazed smile fixed on his face.

I pop my hand on my hip and raise an eyebrow, trying to channel Sam's cockiness, with a dash of Mac's confidence mixed in.

"Well? I don't see you doing anything. Are you going to shoot me or what?"

I'm beyond exhausted. I don't even know if I'd care if he shot me at this point. Joseph has finally pushed me to the edge, and I'm done catering to his bullshit. If he shoots me, so be it. I'll die knowing I stood up to him.

"No begging? That's a pity. Your mother begged so prettily when I ended her."

My chest seizes, and my breath stalls in my lungs. My head gets fuzzy, and I sway, denial sitting on the tip of my tongue, begging to refute the truth etched on his face. The numbness starts in my fingertips, traveling up my arms and shooting down my legs. The thundering of my heart roars in my ears and my entire body vibrates with the force.

"No," I whisper. "She died from cancer."

Something in my chest cracks alongside the lightning streaking the sky, his scornful laugh seeping into the night. He told me it was cancer. He said she kept it from me for months—for my sanity. She didn't want me to worry. It felt like one day she was there and the next she wasn't, and I was left with him.

There was no mourning. It was inappropriate to cry in front of the cameras. It was disrespectful to display any emotion in front of his colleagues. It was ridiculous I cared as much as I did. I shoved the grief down deep, only letting it out when I was alone, and even then I was afraid of getting caught with a tear-streaked face.

"Even *I* was impressed at how well you swallowed that lie. I didn't have to put in any effort. It's one of the few reasons I stopped myself from burying you too."

"But the doctors?" I stutter, confusion clouding my mind.

Joseph waves away my question, as if it's so inconsequential he won't even entertain it.

I don't know why I'm so shocked. I always knew what a despicable man he was. He never hid it at home, at least after he married Mom. He knew how to wear the mask in front of others so well though.

With the games he plays, the persona he puts forth, and the power he amasses, no one would have believed me had I told them what he's really like. I never bothered. I kept my head down, hoping one day I'd be free.

How he was able to fool actual medical professionals, though, is something I can't wrap my head around. One doctor even came to the house, explaining what happened, and offered me comfort when I broke down sobbing. I must have been too far gone to question whether he really was a doctor.

"Why?"

"When things no longer become useful, best to prune them. I don't expect you to understand. You never were very bright. I'm sure it'll bring you comfort in your final moments to know she put up a fight, even in her weakened state." He smirks at my noise of protest. "Though that may have been due to the strychnine."

The confusion must be written across my face, because he shakes his head.

"That's a drug, little Willow. A bad, bad drug."

I still don't know understand what strychnine is, but it's clear he was poisoning her. I didn't notice at first, but after the cobwebs of grief flee from my mind, I recognize the signs of what I thought was the cancer ravaging her body.

The tightness in her jaw and her rigid movements became more common, and fear joined the crazed look in her dull eyes. Clearly, I didn't understand what was going on at fifteen. I should have suspected Joseph was behind it all.

"Why don't we go someplace quieter, where no one will hear your death?"

Joseph gestures with the gun off where the man disappeared. I doubt Sam's friend stuck around, but now I wish I would have asked him to stay.

Taking two steps, I force myself to turn my back to him, and the barrel digs in a moment later, forcing me deeper into the shadows. The lights from the train station dim as we slip around the corner.

Spinning, I grab at his wrist, knocking his arm away. A gunshot ricochets off the buildings and my heart jumps into my throat. Joseph grunts, pushing into me, but I've already hooked my leg around his and I shove against his body.

He cries out as he falls, fingers scrambling for purchase on my shirt and I stumble, almost landing on top of him. The gun bounces from his grasp and my breath whooshes from me.

You'll never win if they get you on the ground, especially if they're not hurt. Sam's voice whispers through my mind.

I right myself, skipping several steps back to get out of his range, but I doubt I need to. Joseph is sprawled on the ground gulping down air like a fish out of water.

His body spasms, fingers scratching against the ground. As Joseph's brown eyes stare at the stars, I grab the gun tucked away in my waistband. Clearly, Joseph never thought I'd have a weapon. The fact it stayed put in the scuffle instead of slipping down my pants is a stroke of luck.

Something scuttles behind me and I whip around. I can't tell if the shadows are fog or people, and the gun hangs useless by my side. I'm terrified it's Sam or her friend who helped me and I'll accidentally shoot them.

When nothing emerges, I swing around and stumble backward as Joseph launches himself at me. My weapon flies from my grasp as he crashes into my body, and my head bounces against the concrete, stars erupting across my vision.

I suck in tiny breaths while a vise squeezes my lungs. Joseph's hands wrap around my throat, not that it matters, since I can't breathe anyway. Scratching at his arms, I try to yank his hands away, but there's no way I'll break free. I abandon my attempts, cringing as his spittle drips onto my face.

As my vision darkens, I drop my hands to my stomach and slip my hand up my sleeve, pulling the knife free from the sheath.

Slashing it upwards at Joseph's stomach, warm blood coats my hand as his grip slackens. Tumbling off me, he stumbles before falling on his ass, hands pressed against the wound. Red blooms between his fingers and I'm mesmerized by how real it looks. A nervous giggle bubbles from me and I shake my head before pushing to my feet.

Don't hesitate.

"I won't," I say under my breath. The only reason I've been able to survive as long as I have is because of Sam. I won't throw away my only opportunity.

There's a satisfying crunch as my heel sinks into Joseph's nose and his body tips back. Hands still pressed to his stomach, his head hits the ground again and blood trickles down his face. He coughs once, twice, before meeting my eyes.

Flipping the knife, I display the blade. I expect fear to dance in his blue eyes, but instead he grins manically, scarlet painting his teeth. His chuckle ends in a cough and he tips his head to the side, blood trickling from the corner of his mouth.

He turns back, arching his back. "You won't finish it. Be a good girl and call for help. I might even tell them to spare you if you beg."

His body blurs as rage sears through me, the voice in my head egging me on. He has no idea why those words are the worst thing to say to me.

I stomp on the hands clutched over his wound, and he wheezes. I do it again, if only to relieve the tension in my muscles, the ache in my heart, and the pounding in my ears. He grabs one of my ankles, but he's weak from blood loss.

I have no idea where Hawk shot him, but it must have affected his ability to fight back. All the better for me. Twisting my leg away from his hand, I drop to my knees next to him.

"You going to kill me, little Willow?"

"You killed my mother."

I stab down, shoving the blade as deep as I can into his chest. It doesn't go far, probably hitting a rib, and my hand slides down the handle from the force. Sam told me not to aim for the heart, that I'm not skilled enough to find the small space, but I try anyway. His fingers grasp feebly at my arms, staining my skin crimson.

"You killed my mother," I grunt.

Pulling the blade out, I slam it in higher as his blood-soaked hands slip from my wrists. I stab again, and the flesh finally gives way, as a crack of lightning bounces off the metal buildings, thunder crashing around us, muffling his gasping breaths.

"You killed my fucking mother, you fucking bastard!"

I wrench it out, blood splattering across my face with the force.

I slam the blade into his throat, digging it deep within his flesh, praying it's enough. Rage swirls around us as I grit my teeth. Joseph's glassy eyes blink slowly and his hands fall away.

I'm panting when I heave off his slackened body, the knife clutched tight in my fist. I stumble back, intent on witnessing every second of his death. His chest rises once more and then ceases as a single tear slips free from his lifeless eyes.

I wait for the hysteria, the breakdown, the guilt, but nothing comes except the cleansing release of rain from the sky, washing away the poison of his words. Tipping my head back, eyes falling closed, I scream, basking in the salvation I've found within the shadows.

Thirty Nine

Hawk

Swiping the rain from my face, I stare up at the King estate. The guards almost didn't let me through, but as soon as they saw the patches, they changed tunes pretty quickly.

Pounding on the door before bracing my hand on the wall, I hang my head. Water drips from the hair plastered to my head, but I don't bother with it anymore. The rain has been threatening for hours until a light mist started. I'm slowly drowning in the steady patter that's gradually washing away any hope I have of tracking Willow.

I kick the door, but the fight drains out of me. Too many hours and too much stress have overwhelmed my system. The door swings open, revealing Alex's laughing face. It quickly morphs to alarm before dissolving into concern.

"What the fuck, Hawk. Wait"—he holds his hand up—"let me guess. You lost your girl again and you need our help."

"I just need to talk to Sam," I say roughly, clearing my throat.

Bile builds and I swallow it down, making my stomach turn. The panic I've been fighting licks at my peripheral, but I blink it away.

"Uh..." He looks over his shoulder. The door shifts, almost closing, and he has a hurried conversation with someone. I don't even bother listening in. I don't fucking care. I only need Sam. Willow would come to her. She'd talk to Sam about getting out.

I spent the little time between when she left and when I finally made the call to Helms searching her things. Willow left all her money behind, so she'll need someone to help her get around. She's not in any condition to be wandering around Synd, especially in this weather.

The door swings open again, and Alex runs his fingers through his light hair. "She's not here, Hawk. What's wrong?"

"Nothing. Tell her to call me." I mutter, turning away.

I make it halfway down the staircase when the door slams shut. The rain is letting up, but it'll still be hard to search for Willow. Synd always felt small, mostly because we keep to Reaper territory, but tonight it feels massive. I snort as I pass the fountain.

"Can mermaids drown?" Alex claps me on the shoulder as he matches my pace.

"What do you need, Alex?"

A young guard ducks his head as we pass the shack before glancing behind him. I look at Alex, who smirks. I don't have time to figure out what the hell is going on there.

"Figured you could use some help," he says, loping along regardless of the rain. He doesn't even have a jacket on.

I eye him as we walk to my bike. I refuse to give him a ride, so I don't know what he thinks is going to happen. The back of my bike is reserved for Willow.

"Hawk?" Sam calls, stepping from the tree line bordering the road, her hair almost black and plastered to her head from the rain.

I stalk toward her, squeezing my hands into fists so I don't shake her. "Sam, have you heard from Willow?"

She tilts her head, looking me up and down. The ache in my chest tightens the longer she stares. The pain's been chasing me since I stood at my window. I don't even know how she got out in the condition she was in.

Sam knows something, I can see it in her eyes, but it'll do me no good to force her. I'm seriously considering begging at this point, but I don't know if that would work either.

"I may have helped her a little," she says, crossing her leather-encased arms.

"Want to elaborate?" I growl, stepping toward her, but Alex stops me with a hand on my arm.

"Easy there. Not Sam's fault Willow ran off. You can't tame the wild ones." His eyes widen when Sam cocks an eyebrow at him. "Not that we'd want to. We love them just the way they are."

She rolls her eyes. "She needs to do this on her own, Hawk. Sometimes you gotta let her make her own decisions."

"And sometimes she needs help fighting her demons, so tell me where the fuck she is."

Sam slides between Alex and me as his hands turn to fists by his sides. I don't know what set him off, but Sam's capable of taking care of herself. She rests a hand on his chest as he glares over her head. Murmuring something I can't hear over the thunder, he finally looks at her. I don't have time to wait for them to work their shit out.

I stalk toward my bike. I'll deal with shit on my own, like I have been since Helms fucked off to Rima. No one seems to think Willow is in danger, even after being kidnapped, and I don't understand why.

It was all hands on deck when Mac was threatened. The entire King operation ground to a standstill when they fucked off to find Sam. But when I need something, they don't care. I thought things were changing with how the factions of our city interacted, but I'm not on the same level as them. As VP I'm not important enough to help. That's just fine.

"Hawk."

Whipping my head up, I spot a car parked several feet from my bike, with Mason Byrns leaning against the grill, arms crossed over his suit.

Shaking the rain from my hair, I glance back at Sam and Alex, still engaged in a heated discussion. Stopping in front of the mafia leader, I cross my arms, ready to fight him too. The idea of dealing with more arrogant assholes grates on my nerves.

"What do you want, Byrns?" I match his stance, brows pulled low as the rain lets up.

"A lot of things, but I figured I'd help you with your issue first. I spoke with a contact in the Barrens—Mack.

"Mac?" I shake my head.

"You think Helms's woman is running around the Barrens? No, it's Sam's friend Mack, with a 'k'. Doesn't matter." He waves away my confusion. "He ran into someone who didn't fit. Figured out she belonged to Sam, but my sister wasn't answering her phone so he called me. Willow was at the train station, but she's not there anymore. Mack said she headed back into the Barrens...with someone else."

I'm already racing for my bike before he's finished. The Barrens aren't very wide, but they span almost the whole of the city. I hope she hasn't slipped too deep into them. I'll search the entire area if I need to.

I wish I could call Doc or Helms, or fucking anyone in the Reapers to help, but Doc made it clear where their focus lies. I can't even be angry about it. The Reapers are my family, but Willow is *mo dóchais*—my hope. Without her, I'll cease to exist.

I race away, heading for the river, leaving the cries of Sam and Alex in my wake.

The Barrens are darker than usual, the rain skewing the lines on the road and obliterating the view. I don't come down here often. In fact, I rarely leave Reaper territory. I know my way around, though. The engine of my bike still pierces through the drizzle. I'll have to abandon it before long and I'm not looking forward to it.

Riding straight to the train station, I park in the lot before sprinting for the shadows of the Barrens a couple blocks away. Most of the residents here will be tucked away in their makeshift houses, seeking shelter from the storm.

I race back and forth through the alleys, past abandoned buildings, looking for any sign of a struggle. I should be more vigilant, but I can't slow. The burning in my chest expands the further I go, and I wipe my face before rubbing at the ache.

Coming around a corner, I skid to a stop. Merrick's body lies in the middle of the street, arms splayed wide, and blood runs in rivulets toward the gutter. A street lamp flares to life, glinting off the blade of a knife and silhouetting Willow's form several feet away.

Water streams down her face as she tips her head toward the sky, the deluge creating a halo around her body, casting her as an avenging angel as blood drips from the tip of the dagger.

A noise escapes me and her eyes shoot to mine. I don't know what she sees, but a slow smirk eases across her face, sending a shiver down my spine.

This isn't the Willow I met at Trigger's, giggling and carefree. This isn't the woman afraid of her own sexuality. She's someone new, birthed from trauma and heartache—fueled by shadows and darkness, and utterly magnificent.

I search the street before stalking toward her. I don't know what I expected, but it wasn't for her to cock an eyebrow, waiting for me to reach her.

The dagger clatters to the ground when I haul her body into mine, mouth on hers before she can protest, drinking in everything she is. I came to save her and find she's saved herself just fine without me. Pride courses through me as I bend her over, snaking a hand into her hair and forcing her head back.

Ripping my mouth from hers, I nip at her bottom lip as she gasps before dragging my teeth over her pulse point. Sucking her skin in my mouth, I breathe in her unique scent, letting it settle into my senses to ease the lingering panic.

I pull her upright, keeping our bodies fused together and resting my forehead against hers. Her bright eyes are lined with desire, but there's still a flicker of shadows dancing in her eyes.

She sighs, resting her head on my chest. My heart still pounds, and I wonder if she can feel it. I should get her out of here, but I won't rush this. Once we move, the questions will come. We'll have to discuss everything that's happened. I'm not ready to face reality. Out there, beyond this bubble of contentment, I'll have to convince her to stay and I don't know how to do that yet. All I know is I can't live without her.

Forty

Willow

"Hi," I whisper, soaking in his warmth.

His brows pull low as he scans my face. "Are you hurt?"

"Not really."

There's a scrape on my leg from the window. Plus, I'm pretty sure my entire body is one big bruise. He's not talking about the aches and pains of falling out a window or rolling around in the mud. He wants to know about the blood. It's seeped into my clothes, but I can't tell where since I'm soaking wet.

"That's not an answer, Willow."

"We need to deal with"—I gesture behind him—"that."

"I'll handle it."

A sniff escapes me and I push from his arms. He shudders and tenses, as if he'll haul me back into his embrace, but he drops his hands to his sides, flexing his fingers over and over.

My skin flushes from both killing my stepfather and the desire Hawk drew to the surface. I can't handle the push and pull from him. I won't allow him to pick me up whenever he wants, shoving me aside when I'm no longer of use to him.

"Sorry," I murmur.

Blood is smeared across his chest, some bleeding into the patches sewn onto his leathers. Pain slices through me as I brush a finger across the threads spelling out his rank in the Reapers.

He wears his loyalty on his chest, like a badge of pride. I don't see how I could ever replace the Reapers, not that I'd want to. It was never about taking their place. I just wanted a seat at the table. I wanted to feel like I belonged.

"For what?"

I wave at his leathers. "The blood. I didn't think..."

I gaze into the darkness seeping from between the buildings. I don't know how to deal with this shit. I've never had to navigate the intricacies of a relationship after trauma. Every other ending was a slow death, silence filling the spaces in between.

I watch as he glances down, taking in the mess I've left in my wake. I should have stopped him. Him kissing me only muddies the waters more. Stepping around him, I swipe my hair from my face and he wraps his fingers around my arm.

"Are you okay?" he murmurs.

I tilt my head, eyeing him. Concern splashes across his face, swimming in his eyes, but that was never the problem. I never questioned whether he cared. My issue has always lain in whether I was too much. The upheaval I've caused within their ranks is too much for him to bear.

Now that Joseph is dead, my life can go back to normal. I won't have to constantly look over my shoulder, waiting for him to come back. Hell, I could pack up my things and go anywhere. I've never had the freedom to just leave. I huff out a laugh as I shake my head. Now that I can, I'd rather stay here.

"I'm fine." I tug, but he doesn't let go.

"No, you're not. Talk to me."

"Hawk, we don't have time. I'm fine. We need to get this cleaned up. I need a shower and to get my stuff. I appreciate you coming out here and finding me, but we don't have time to chitchat." I yank and he lets me go.

I stumble over the pavement toward Joseph's prone body and a noise filled with frustration follows me.

His low voice rumbles through the night as he calls for someone to deal with what I've left bleeding all over the ground. I spend the time searching for both our guns. It takes me much longer to find Joseph's, since I didn't see where it flew off to.

"Willow?" Hawk yells, his anxiety-riddled voice piercing the silence.

Heavy footfalls ring out before he skids around the corner. He's panting as he braces his hands on his knees. Then he's crushing me to his chest. There's no frantic kissing this time, but his heartbeat races in my ear and his hand cradles the back of my head. It takes me a minute, but it hits me he's vibrating, all his muscles trembling.

"Don't do that," he whispers into my hair.

"Huh?" My reply is muffled by his leathers, the distinct scent flooding my senses.

"Stop disappearing on me. I can't handle it. I've spent the last couple days having a series of heart attacks," he murmurs and my breath hitches.

Looping my arms around him, I press him closer, stealing what little comfort I can.

"Don't make me leave." The words slip out before I can stuff them back in.

Tears fall, tracking down my face, and I'm reminded of the blood splattered across my skin. It probably looks like I'm crying crimson, which will freak him out. I bite my lip to stop the chuckle from escaping. The agony wells up, battling with the hysteria.

"Oh, I should have pushed." He tucks me closer to him.

"I don't know what that means." I hiccup, trying to force the tears to stop.

"You didn't listen, *mo dóchais*." He shakes his head, pushing me back gently. "We have to get going. It's not good to hang around the Barrens, especially with a body."

Tucking me to his side, he leads me away, scooping up the dagger I dropped before continuing on. I pull up my sleeve and he slips the blade into the sheath. Fingers folding around mine, he tugs me toward the lights in the distance.

We weave in and out of alleys and I hope the rain has stopped for good now. Thunder rumbles in the distance as clouds hang low in the sky.

My feet are aching by the time we reach the edge of the Barrens and I'm lagging. Hawk glances back, following the connection of our hands before swinging me into his arms. I don't even bother protesting, opting to snuggle closer. I'm cold, so I'm going to soak in all the comfort I can, at least until we finally get wherever we're going.

"Did you mean it?" I ask, gripping his jacket as his bike comes into view.

"Mean what?"

I clamp my mouth shut when his phone buzzes. Tensing, I brace myself for him to put me down, but he keeps walking, gripping me tighter.

"Mean what, Willow?" he growls.

"Aren't you going to get that?"

"Nope. They can deal with their own shit. Now answer the question."

I huff, suddenly not wanting to have this conversation. We're too exposed out here, both covered in blood. There are things to deal with outside of our personal lives. The worst part is, I'm not ready for the answer. A flush crawls across my cheeks, and I wiggle until he puts me down next to his bike.

"We can talk about it later," I mutter, taking the helmet hanging off the side of his bike, but it's ripped from my hands.

"Now."

Looking down at the blood coating me, I grimace. The rain washed away some from my arms, leaving streaks of pink in its wake.

"I won't make you choose," I finally say, twisting my fingers together before wrapping them around my waist and squeezing.

My stomach tightens, and I really don't want to puke. I got through everything tonight without tossing my cookies, and I'll be damned if I do it now after the actual murdering is done.

Gagging, I double over, and Hawk rubs my back. I don't know if he's making it better or worse. I try to push him away, but he curls his body over mine, whispering words I can't hear.

Hawk's voice finally filters through as he says, "I've got you, Willow. Don't fall apart on me."

"He killed my mother," I choke out.

I stuff my fist in my mouth, screaming my anguish out around my hand. My cheeks are itchy as the tears track through the dried blood coating them.

"And you made him pay for those sins."

"It wasn't enough," I wheeze.

"It never is."

I let out a shuddering breath and my stomach rolls again. Hawk's hands cup my face, pulling me upright before brushing away my tears with his thumbs. A chill runs through me and I cling to him. I have to pull myself together.

"I don't regret it. He deserved everything he got," I snarl and pull away. "Can we go home?"

Exhaustion sets in. I'll be lucky if I don't keel over on the way there. I sway as he pushes the helmet on and helps me onto the bike. I wish I could lay my head against his back, but he'd never let me go without the protection. Looping my arms around him, I hook my fingers into his belt.

"Gonna have to hold on tighter than that, Willow. No scraping you off the road, remember?"

Forty One

Hawk

I refuse to drop Willow off at my house. I'm not entirely convinced she'll stay where I put her. Plus, I won't be able to function if she's not in sight. Doc's text message demands my presence at headquarters anyway.

I want to take her home and get her cleaned up, but there's little I can do about it. I expect the lot to be full for the meeting, but there's only a few bikes parked out front.

"Why are we here? And where is everyone?" Willow asks, sliding off the back. She hops a little before taking off the helmet, finally able to get it on her own.

"No idea. I expected more people to be here too."

A shriek rings out, and we spin toward the door. Mac pounds toward us, dark hair streaming behind her. I catch the look of horror on Willow's face before she's smothered by Mac. Beyond them, framing the doorway, is a glaring Helms. His eyes dart to our two women, still hugging, before meeting mine. He jerks his head, turning around to disappear inside. I hesitate, glancing at Willow as they have a hushed conversation.

"Go, Hawk," Mac says.

"Don't disappear." I don't know if I'm talking to Mac or Willow, but it applies to both of them.

"You don't give me orders. Besides, I think you've done enough," Mac sneers.

She wraps an arm around Willow's shoulders and leads her further away. Willow looks behind and mouths *sorry*.

"Get in here, Hawk," Doc says from the doorway and I follow him.

The entire inner circle is inside, lounging at a table in the middle. Helms is nowhere to be found. Doc points down the hall and I pivot toward the open office door.

When I enter, Helms's back is to me. Dropping into the seat across the desk, I wait until he swivels in his chair, arms crossed over his chest. I don't know where the hell he's been, but he doesn't look like he's slept in weeks, with bags under his eyes and his face pale as shit.

"What the fuck happened to you?" I grumble, crossing my own arms.

He rolls his eyes and I almost smile. The more time he spends with Mac, the more he picks up on her mannerisms. I'll never tell him though. I spent the last several months watching them fight each other and their feelings. I'm not about to insert myself into their relationship.

Mac's reaction to me tonight is telling, and my knee starts bouncing. I hold my breath as he eyes me. Rubbing a hand over my jaw, I try to remember how long ago I shaved.

"You want to tell me what's been happening here while we've been gone?" He raises an eyebrow and a throbbing pain shoots through my temples.

"I sent you texts. And I'm sure Doc filled you in. Not much else to say."

My stomach rolls and I wonder if I've just fucked myself. Helms holds my entire life in his hands. He could strip me of my colors, shoot my ass and float me—he could take everything from me, including Willow. She'll listen to Mac, who is clearly pissed at me. And Helms will listen to Mac. I'll lose everything in a matter of minutes. Yet here I am, mouthing off like I'm some kid who hasn't learned his place.

"Doesn't really tell the whole story, does it? I'm pretty sure you're keeping shit from me. I just want to make sure it's what I think it is."

He swipes his hand across the desk, though it's spotless. The prospects come in once a week and dust, but I don't know why. Helms rarely uses this space anyway.

"What exactly do you think I'm keeping from you?"

"Is this just a quick fuck kind of thing? 'Cause Kenzie won't appreciate that. I told her it was none of our business, but she's a little pissed Willow got hurt."

"You're right. It isn't any of your fucking business. Willow and I will deal with shit on our own without your meddling. Is that all?" I push to my feet.

He points at my vacated chair. "Sit your fucking ass down. I had to listen to Kenzie go on and on about how you weren't doing your job, so you're going to sit here and we're going to pretend I yelled at you and then we'll go find them."

"Fuck you," I snarl, and he cocks an eyebrow.

The leather squeaks as he leans back in his chair. "Hawk, sit down and start talking."

"Or what?"

I can't sit in this office any longer, waiting for Helms to stop spewing bullshit and make up his fucking mind. I need to talk to Willow. If he's going to strip me of my colors, so be it. I'll take Willow and we'll go somewhere else. Maybe we'll go back to Rima. A shudder runs through me at the thought.

Even though Merrick is dead, the possibility of going back to where I grew up doesn't sit well. My upbringing was hard and fast. It's probably changed in the last decade, but that doesn't mean I'm willing to relive the memories. We could go anywhere. I just have to convince Willow. And I can't do it from this office.

"How the hell am I supposed to know? Not like I'm going to shoot you. For fuck's sake, we're family, Hawk. I'm trying to figure out what the hell is going on between you two."

I sag, bracing my hands on the table and hanging my head. A chuckle starts low in my chest until I can't hold it back anymore. The last couple weeks have been a rollercoaster and everything is hitting me at once. The number of times I've thought I lost Willow over the last few days is more than anyone should have to endure. Lifting my head, I meet Helms's eyes and lose it again. The look of concern sinking into his face is warranted.

"Fuck," I wheeze. "It's not a fucking fling. Mac's pissed. She'll probably shoot me herself, but it'd be nice if she wouldn't do it in the same shoulder."

"What the fuck does that mean? Did you get yourself shot? Doc just said shit was going down but it wasn't that bad."

I plop down again, leaning back. Two minutes ago I wanted to rush out of here and bundle Willow on the back of my bike, riding as far away from here as possible.

"I sent you a fucking text. Where the hell were you?"

"Seems like there's a lot of shit I missed. We were searching for Dante. He's into some deep shit. We might have to go back," he says, taking his phone from his pocket, scowling at the screen.

"She killed Merrick tonight. I called in a clean-up, so that's taken care of, but I need to get back to her. We need to do this later." I push up again and stalk to the door.

"Hawk, don't tell Kenzie I said this, but don't let her dictate what you do," Helms mutters.

I rest my hand on the handle. "Mac's like a sister to me, but like hell is she going to get between us. Willow's fucking mine."

"Well, when she's yelling at you, remember she means well, but she has no say in your relationship."

"You think I don't fucking know that?" I say over my shoulder as I yank open the door.

I stop short when Mac blocks the way, eyes narrowed. My heart skips a beat when I don't see Willow, but then she leans around Mac's body and gives me a small smile. It hits me how different she looks. There's an edge of confidence in her eyes now. I skip my eyes back to Mac.

"Kenz, get the hell out of the way," Helms snaps. The chair squeaks as he collapses into it.

I push past her, snatching Willow's arm as I pass. We make it ten steps before she rips her arm away.

"Don't yank me around like an unruly child, Hawk. I'm capable of walking on my own," she snarls, stomping past me, drawing the attention of everyone else in the room. Blue and Tiny duck their heads, but the rest track Willow's progress out the door.

"Wouldn't let her run too far, Hawk. You don't have the stamina to catch her," Tank laughs, and the others join.

I flip them off as I chase after her. When I get outside, the parking lot is empty and my stomach drops. I sway as spots dance in my vision.

When they clear, I pound across the parking lot toward my bike, rocks skittering away into the dark. My boots skid as I stop next to my ride. I ran my ass all over the territory looking for her once before and I'll do it again, no matter what the guys say. Mac might hand my ass to me for losing sight of her again. Hell, she might do it regardless.

"Hawk," Willow's soft voice floats to me from the building and I whip around.

She's leaning against the building, hidden in the shadows. Dropping my head, I pull in deep breaths to stop from puking all over the chrome. When my fingers finally stop tingling, I walk over to her slowly.

She's crouched, arms around her legs, and the image of her tucked between my bed and nightstand flashes in my mind. I didn't know how to help her then. I didn't have enough time to figure it out. Crouching in front of her, I wait for her to meet my gaze.

"Willow," I whisper, lifting a hand, but I drop it when I remember how she freaked out last time.

"You're waffling," she says, her voice muffled by her arms.

"Can you look at me, *mo dóchais*?"

"No. You need to tell me what the hell is going on so I can make plans. I'm sick of wondering if you want me or not," she mutters, propping her chin on her knees.

"I know what you overheard, but that was Doc playing head games. Not me."

She snorts, rolling her eyes. "You said plenty on your own. I get that all this shit was hard on you. I didn't want to be a problem, but they seem to follow me.

So, if I've become too much and you're done, then say that. Don't try to let me down easy. I'm fucking sick of everyone handling me with kid gloves."

"Willow, I told you, you're mine. What else do you want from me?" I ask, exasperated.

I push to my feet and start pacing back and forth. Pent-up energy courses through my body, and I can't seem to shut it down. The things she heard, the way I've said things, is fucked up. I should have made it clear she was staying. Instead I tried to give her an out. I did exactly what she always tries to do—hide from the potential pain another can inflict.

I can feel her eyes on me, tracking my jerky movements. Glancing from the corner of my eye, her nostrils flare as her eyes narrow. She shoves off the ground and I stop, waiting for her to finally talk to me. Instead, she spins on her heel and storms away.

"Where the fuck are you going?" I yell after her.

She swings around, marching back to poke me in the chest. "You asshole. I'm not putting up with subpar anymore. I'm sick and tired of you not being clear. I've spent my whole goddamn life wondering what other people actually think of me or if anyone truly wants me for me. And then you blast into my life, claiming I'm yours and handing me all these promises and then turning around and acting like I'm disposable. Just like the rest of them. I'm fucking sick of it and I'm fucking done. Do you hear me? I'm fucking done."

She's screaming by the time the last of her words echo into the night. Gaping, I track the flush dusting her cheeks as tears fill her eyes. Her chest heaves with each breath and yet I'm frozen—struck by her beauty in a way I never thought possible. I wanted to keep her before, but now it feels as if fate was always on our side, throwing us together to lead straight to this moment.

I slam my mouth into hers, cutting off her gasp and drinking in her taste. She's sweet and salty and everything, all at once. She slides her hands up my chest before tangling with my hair. Easing back, gentling the kiss until our lips brush against each other and I sigh.

"Stay."

Forty Two

Willow

I push away from Hawk's arms, still panting. When his face falls, I dig my fingers into his shirt before yanking him into me and we stumble.

His hand at my back steadies us before his mouth is back on mine, stealing my breath. It doesn't escape me he never answered my questions. The adrenaline from earlier rushed my system, rearing its head and engulfing me.

He eases back, resting his forehead on mine. He's hunched, his body pressed into me, and my breath hitches. I want to live in this bubble, where nothing exists but his green eyes shining brightly in the night. I'll need an answer before long. Reality will shove its way back in, forcing him to make a decision he might not be ready for. I can't wait around though.

Someone clears their throat behind us and I jump back, slipping from his arms. When I spin around, I find Mac glaring at Hawk. Rolling my eyes, I cross my arms and lean against the wall.

I love her, but the tirade she went on after we stopped squealing was enough to make my skin itch. That might be from the dried blood coating me, though. I didn't think it was that bad, but her wince told me otherwise.

Mac's response to everything that's gone down was normal, but I'm not the same woman I was when I got here. Something's shifted and I don't want to go back to who I was. I never liked that version of myself anyway.

"If you're done sucking face, I need to talk to you, Willow." Mac plants her hands on her hips, still glaring at Hawk.

"I'll be right there," I say.

"I don't have all night," she says, the tapping of her foot echoing off the building.

"I don't live by your schedule, Mac. I've got a lot I need to deal with, and unfortunately, listening to you lecture me like an errant child is at the bottom of my list. The top of that list, if you're wondering, is a fucking shower. Don't know if you noticed, but I *am* covered in blood."

I don't know where the sass is coming from, but I wasn't lying when I told Hawk I was sick of people pushing me around. Mac may mean well, and her actions were justified when I was a naïve girl wandering into Viper territory, but I've changed. The sooner she figures that out, the easier this whole thing will be.

"You have got to be kidding me. Willow, we found you in the goddamn Barrens. Do you have any idea how terrible this could have turned out? You could have been hurt. You could have been *killed*," she hisses.

I spin, seething as I take in her crossed arms and narrowed eyes. "Mac, I love you dearly, but if you don't back the fuck off I'm going to—"

"Going to what? Willow, be real. You're not equipped for this life. I understand you've been dealing with all this shit, but your world is wildly different from ours. *You're* different."

I clear my throat. "You're right, Mac. I am different. I changed when you fucked off to Rima and left me to fend for myself. I won't apologize for doing what I needed to survive."

Tipping my chin up, we stare at each other. She grimaces and her foot starts tapping again.

"You've always wanted to"—she throws up her hands—"This world isn't a fucking vacation from your life, Willow! It's fucking hard. You assume you could survive here because, what, you got lucky when you stabbed someone? Because you slept with *him*?"

A snort echoes through the night, and I glance behind me as Mac groans. Only shadows dance around the lot, until a darker one steps forward, revealing Sam.

She moves silently, even over the gravel. I wish I had the skills she does. Hawk hinted at the fact her training went beyond the normal stuff, but I don't know what the normal stuff is. I wasn't about to ask. She scares me enough that I have a healthy amount of respect for her.

"Mac, stop being a bitch. Let them deal with their shit," Sam says, smirking as she leans against the building.

"Don't think I'm not pissed at you too, Sam. I know you're the one who gave her the weapons so she could gallivant around the goddamn city. She's lucky she came home with all her limbs, for fuck's sake. I went away for like a second and all my friends fell the fuck apart."

Mac pins Hawk in place with a glare when he tries to slip around her to avoid her wrath. Honestly, I wish I could escape too. Her words are cutting, regardless of where they're coming from. All I want is a shower and sleep. Everything else can wait. We can work out our shit and she'll see I've changed.

"And look at that, she's perfectly fucking fine. In fact, I'd say she's better than fine. Aren't you, Willow?"

I turn my wide eyes to Hawk, and he shakes his head. I have no idea what that means, but I'm pretty sure I'm on my own.

"I don't fucking care if she's fine. You were supposed to show her basic self-defense, but you turned around and gave her a gun. Hawk was supposed to keep her safe, but he went off and got her kidnapped—multiple times. What a fucking failure."

My blood boils and my hands tremble, but I can't keep the emotions blasting around inside my head.

"Shut the fuck up, Mac. Just fucking stop," I cry, clenching my hands into fists. "I'm not an invalid. It's no one's fault. If you want to blame someone, blame Thomas. Blame Joseph. They're the assholes in this, not those two." I sweep my hand around, gesturing to Hawk and Sam. "And quite frankly, I did a damn good job keeping myself safe. You can go around hollering about all the shit that went down, but I fucking took care of it. No one had to save me. No one had to step in. I didn't stand around and wait for anyone to fight my battles for me.

"I know you're not used to me being anything other than a meek little bitch who lets others walk the fuck all over her, but this is the best goddamn thing that's ever happened to me. So, if you don't like it, you can just fuck right off."

As soon as the words spill from me, I want to shove them back inside. I'm not mad at Mac. I get why she's protective, but in the last month I've grown. I'm not afraid. At least, I'm not afraid of who I am anymore.

I turn to Hawk, his face blurring as tears gather in my eyes, and I blink them away. His face softens before his lips pull up in a smirk.

"Why don't we talk about this in the morning, yeah? Little weird to be screaming at each other in the middle of the night in front of a biker clubhouse. I'm sure someone's going to start talking about how crazy we are and we'll have to engage in some light stabbing. Although, that might help," Sam laughs, tapping the flat side of her knife against her chin.

"Put the fucking dagger away, Sam. We're not stabbing anyone for being misogynistic," Mac says, but I catch the gleam in her eyes.

"I haven't had a lot of practice, but I'm already covered in blood so..."

Sam bursts out laughing, while Mac rolls her eyes, a grin breaking out on her face. Soon we're all manically laughing. Sam leans on the wall, doubled over as Mac clutches her stomach and gasps for breath, as Hawk looks on, horrified. I'm sure he thinks we've lost our marbles, but I can't stop.

Everything has piled on top of me and now that I feel safe—free—they're overwhelming my senses. When our laughter finally dies away, a strange silence takes over. We're still going to have to talk, but exhaustion is settling into my bones and I sway. Hawk is by my side in an instant, sliding his arm around my shoulders.

"You three can have your breakdown later. I'm taking her home now. She'll call you when she wants," Hawk says before scooping me up.

The protest dies in my throat when his warmth seeps into me. I didn't realize how cold I was. Mac looks like she's going to say something, but Sam smacks her arm and Mac's mouth snaps shut.

"I can walk," I mumble as my eyes fall closed.

"No. In fact, I'm not even taking you on my bike. You'll tip right off and I can't have that. We're going to the old Raines house."

"Are we okay?"

"We're fine," he grunts, and my stomach drops.

"That's not good," I mutter. "Put me down, Hawk."

His arms tighten around me, and a growl sounds in the back of his throat. "That's not what I meant. I'm pissed, but not at you. Right now, my focus is on getting you clean and in bed."

I snort. "I don't think now is the time to pierce the hogshead."

"Pierce the...what the fuck does that mean?"

I peek up at him, grinning. "It's Shakespeare. Although, I'm pretty sure it was more for virgins."

"So, definitely not you," he chuckles. My muscles relax and my stomach settles. There's something about the tilt of his lips and the light in his eyes, but I can't put my finger on it.

"I don't want to leave," I whisper.

Now that we're alone and all the fighting is behind us, I need to say it again. I need to keep saying it until he finally listens. I'll repeat it until I get the answer I need. The problem is, I don't know if I'll believe it even if he says the right thing. Maybe there aren't any magic words to make me trust what he's saying.

The blame doesn't lie with him. It's me, but I don't want to feel like this anymore. I don't want to keep wondering whether or not he wants me around. I don't want to live second-guessing everyone around me, including him.

"Willow, do you really think I would let you? If you leave, you take me with you. Whether you realize it or not."

I swallow hard, letting his words seep into me, warming me from the inside out.

"But what if..." I can't even get the words out. I'm sure Ryker is pissed. After all, I've disrupted his entire operation with all my baggage.

I expect Hawk to put me down when we reach the porch of Mac's old house, but he punches in some numbers on the new keypad set in the door and it swings open.

It's not until we're in the upstairs bathroom that he sets me on the counter. I track him as he starts the shower, the spray hitting the wall and filling the silence. Soon steam is floating around the room.

Glancing down, I take in the damage to my clothes. They're stiff and I'm sure I stink, but I've gotten used to the coppery smell.

Hawk plants his hands on the counter, boxing me in. "I told Helms I'd leave."

I whip my head up. "What? You can't leave. This is your home—your family."

I try to push past him, but he crowds me back. "Where are you going?"

"I'm going to talk to Ryker. He can't kick you out. That's not fair. I'll go and you can stay." My voice cracks and I blink back the tears.

Hawk ducks his head, burying his face in my neck. An arm circles around my back and he presses closer. Tipping my head back, I rest my hands on his shoulders, hoping my tears will dry up before he pulls away. The back and forth we've been through is eating away at my sanity, what little is left of it.

"It's not that serious, Willow. He's not stripping me. You don't have to go down there and beat him up."

"You asshole," I say, smacking his side.

"Willow, I just want you to know I'll follow you anywhere. If you go, I go. I don't want to leave the Reapers. You're right, they're my family, but you, you're my soul. I'd be a shell without you. Besides, if you run, I'll just catch you. I'll catch you every time. Every time you fall. Every time you run. Every time you stumble. I'll catch you." His lips brush my neck.

I roll my eyes, even while tears stream down my face. Those were the words I was looking for. The ones that shift something deep inside and everything snaps into place. It's more than just what he's said. They're merely the final piece slotting into place.

I've lived with this feeling for so long, I didn't see the state of constant fear I lived in. I thought it was normal. When all those doubts fell away, one by one,

I didn't know how to live. The persistent dread invaded every moment of my life until I thought it was how everyone felt. The freedom, though, is almost as suffocating. Now, some semblance of peace seeps deep into my heart.

I drop my head to his shoulder. "Doesn't seem like I'm bringing much to the table."

"*Mo dóchais*," he breathes. "My hope. My everything."

"Sorry, I don't know how to cope." I may have wanted him to make some grand declaration, but I never thought about the after.

"You don't have to say anything." He pulls back. "Let's get you cleaned up."

The pain in his eyes has me reaching for his hand before he can retreat too far. He doesn't turn though, just drops his head to his chest.

"Hey," I whisper and he turns, raising an eyebrow, masking the pain. "Come back here."

He turns hesitantly, and my heart squeezes. I wrap my arms around his neck until my face is pressed to his throat and I feel him swallow. Pulling back, I cup his cheeks, guiding his head down until our eyes meet.

"I love you, Hunter Shea."

Epilogue

Hawk

Three Weeks Later

"Come on, Willow. You have to keep up if we're not going to get caught," I whisper, glancing back as I hold out my hand.

Her fingers intertwine with mine and goosebumps run up my arm. Even three months after we had our one-night stand, my heart still flips every time she smiles at me. I doubt it'll ever stop. The looks the rest give us when we're together is getting annoying though. Last night I overheard Mac whispering something about a honeymoon phase. I flipped her off, but she only smirked, unfazed.

"Stop yanking me around, Hawk. You're going to pull my arm from my socket," she scolds, but laughter laces her tone.

Wrapping my arm around her shoulders, I duck into the woods surrounding the Byrns' estate. Willow's stealth skills aren't exactly top notch, but she is dressed in all black and is trying her best not to crash through the underbrush.

"They're going to catch us, aren't they?" Willow whispers sorrowfully when she trips over another branch.

"Don't worry. I took care of it," I say and pull her down onto a fallen log.

I can just make out a couple lights shining from the house. We have a perfect view of the driveway from here.

"What does that mean?" She turns to me with wide eyes, and I grin.

"I talked to Moss. I wasn't going to sneak onto Byrns's property with you otherwise. He said he wouldn't shoot us, but he's not going to cover for us if we get caught. Remember the alibi," I say, pulling my eyebrows low.

A giggle escapes her before she smothers it with her hand. "I'm not going to tell him you wanted to chase me around the woods, Hawk."

I yank her onto my lap so she's straddling me, my hands gripping her waist. Her breath hitches when I latch onto her earlobe.

"Do you like that, *mo dóchais?*" I whisper in her ear, and she shivers.

"We probably shouldn't be doing this here. Someone might find us." Her voice is breathless and she grinds her pussy into me, contradicting her words.

"I told you before, I don't care who hears us. As long as no one sees you come, they can listen to how I make your body sing all they want."

I'm inches from her mouth when a truck pulling a trailer rumbles up to the curb. She gives me a small smile as I sigh, and my heart skips. I stand, holding her to me.

"Hawk, put me down," she laughs while winding her arms around my neck.

"Nope. You're too loud. We gotta be sneaky," I whisper in her ear.

A couple Reapers pile out of the cab, most dressed in black, except one prospect, and I scowl. One simple fucking rule and he couldn't follow it. Of course, it's Nick. He's been riding a fine line since he walked into Trigger's all those months ago. Willow might not have been mine yet, but he's a cocky little shit, so I'm going to blame him for it anyway.

"Leave him be, Hawk," Willow murmurs.

"Fuck him. He keeps eyeing you like you're a snack he wants to devour. I'm about ready to float his ass," I grumble.

She sighs. "I am a snack, so that's understandable. Can't blame him for appreciating my sexiness."

I bury my face in her neck to smother my chuckle. The longer we're together, the more confident she is. I won't take the credit, but I love that she finally has the space to be herself.

"Hawk, where the fuck do you want this thing?" Tank grunts, gesturing to the golden hippo statue. It's been sitting in front of Trigger's for too long. Helms said take care of it, so here we are.

"We're putting it next to that plant. Far enough away he won't notice it when he steps out the door, but close enough it'll bug the piss out of him."

"Why not next to the fountain?"

"And have to pay for his car when he crashes into it? Abso-fucking-lutely not," I say.

Willow snorts as she unravels her limbs from me. Steadying her, I watch the guys unhook the straps from the hideous monstrosity. It seems larger than when it was sitting in front of the bar. The nose of the hippo is worn down from the dozens of hands rubbing it. The kids in the Reapers family loved climbing on it.

"Do you think we should have left it where it was?" I murmur to Willow.

She meets my gaze, eyes softening as she tucks her body close to mine. "I'm sure it'll come back to us. As long as Mason doesn't melt it down and make it into rings or something."

Raising an eyebrow, I smirk. "Funny."

The back of the house lights up and everyone freezes. Nick tumbles off the curb, slamming into the truck. Pinch slams his hand over Nick's mouth, cutting off his howl of pain. The hippo is half off the trailer, balanced precariously between four guys, and their muscles strain to keep it from crashing to the ground. The last thing we need is a headless hippo rolling down the street in front of the Byrns' mansion. The lights wink out and there's a collective sigh of relief. Willow sags against me, head thumping against my chest.

"Let's go." I wrap my arm around her waist, gripping her hip.

"This shit is heavy, Hawk. Why the hell didn't we get a forklift?" Nick spits out.

I catch Tank's eye, pushing Willow toward him gently. She glances back and I shake my head. Tank smirks, guiding her to the spot we've picked for the statue.

I stalk to Nick, who's leaning against the truck, and grab him by the throat. His head bounces against the metal and I squeeze, cutting off his protests.

"The only reason you're here is because you whined your way into coming. I'd think very carefully about your next moves, Nick. You've forgotten how easily we can make you disappear," I growl.

To his credit, he doesn't scramble to wretch my fingers away, but his hands curl into fists at his sides. Malice and hate bloom in his eyes, and I squeeze tighter until his breath is cut off and he finally moves. This has been coming for a long time. We've neglected the prospects while we dealt with the rest of the shit being thrown at us. I step closer and his fist swings toward me, but I block it, snarling in his face. Fear flashes in his eyes and satisfaction seeps through my body.

"Hawk?" Willow's soft voice cuts through the roaring in my ears.

Glancing toward her, I brace myself for the inevitable fear reflected on her face, only to be met with a small smile.

"Help," Nick wheezes, and I slam his head back without taking my eyes from hers.

"Seriously?" She gapes at him, planting her hands on her hips. "You're going to ask *me* for help when all you've ever done is be a dick to me? Absolutely not. I didn't come to help you. I came to tell Hawk he won't hear any complaints from me if he floats your ass."

She flounces away and pride rushes through me. Turning back to Nick, I paste a feral grin on my face. I'm not like Tank, dealing with prospects on a regular basis. I'm nowhere near as terrifying as Helms, whose position alone strikes fear in the hearts of those who cross him. I think they forget what I can do—the power I hold, and the extremes I'll go to when pushed.

Throwing him to the ground, I stare as he coughs, curling on his side. His face is flushed from the lack of oxygen. I close my eyes, nostrils flaring as I suck in a deep breath, reminding myself why it wouldn't be wise to shoot him in the head right here. Helms wouldn't care, but Byrns might.

I leave him writhing on the ground to go to Willow. This was supposed to be a fun prank, but of course, it was fucking ruined. Gathering her in my arms, I press my chest to her back and rest my chin on her head. She sighs, melting into me as we watch the guys struggle to position the statue.

"I'm sorry," I mutter before kissing her head.

"Don't be sorry. I'm still having fun."

Tank brushes past us, grumbling, and the rest file after him. Nick's curses are cut short and then the truck takes off for Reaper territory. The lights flash on at the front of the house and I snatch her hand, pulling her behind me as we run for the mouth of the driveway. Willow's giggles follow us through the night, and a grin spreads across my face.

We make it a block before Willow tugs back, panting. She's been training with Sam more since she killed the judge, but her stamina isn't enough to make a mad dash through the city just yet. Slowing, I pull her into the forest lining the street, and she wraps her arms around my waist, pressing her face into my back.

"You know, it's pretty dark out here," I say, latching on to her wrist.

"Are you afraid of the dark? Should I get my phone out, light the way for you?"

Her nails dig into my skin, grazing down until they settle on the waistband of my jeans. She's playing a dangerous game, getting me hard in the middle of the forest so close to Byrns's place. I don't know how far out his guards patrol. Anyone could stumble upon us, but the thought just sends a thrill through me.

"Wanna play, *mo dóchais*?" I ask, my voice husky with desire.

Tugging her hands away, I yank her in front of me, studying her face, the moonlight reflecting off her eyes. I've imagined this exact scenario and here it is, dropped right into my hands. We've whispered about this in the middle of the night, or when I teased about catching her, but we've never brushed so close to the actuality of it before.

"What did you have in mind?" She glances around, taking in the quiet night, the hum of traffic muted in the distance. Realization dawns and her face splits into a nervous grin.

"Nothing intense, just a little stroll in the woods. If you choose to run thou gh..." I smirk, waiting for her to decide.

"If I choose to run?" she asks, a breathlessness in her voice.

She shuffles back, fingers trailing along my stomach, and my muscles jump under her touch. I drop my other hand to her hip, lean down, and graze her neck with my teeth.

"Then I'll be forced to chase you."

She shudders, curling her body into mine. Skimming my palms along her back, I dip under the hemline of her shirt, tracing her skin, leaving goosebumps in my wake. When her body sways, I drop my hands, desire rushing through my veins before settling in my gut. Tracking her muscles bunching, I snatch her wrist.

"Remember, Willow," I warn, waiting until her eyes meet mine.

"Kumquat. I know." She tenses again as I drop her wrist, but she grabs my hand. "It'll be like we talked about, right?"

"It always is, *mo dóchais*. Always will be."

Tugging her toward me, I kiss her gently, sliding my hand into her hair. The last couple of weeks have been quiet, just like this kiss. The longer she's here, the further I fall. Gripping the strands tighter, and angling her head, I slate my mouth over hers. When I pull back, we're both panting.

"Run," I growl.

She takes off, giggling as she glances back before disappearing into the dark. Closing my eyes, I take steady, deep breaths to calm the adrenaline coursing through me. If we were in Reaper territory, I'd only give her a minute, but since we're in the middle of Synd, I give her two, since she's not familiar with the area. This time should be fun. The more we do this, the deeper we'll go, but I won't push her yet.

Checking my phone, I count down the last few seconds before grinning and slipping it back in my pocket. Willow knows she can't outrun me, even in the dark with a head start. She'll weave through the trees, thinking she can outsmart me. The only question is whether she went left or right.

I start off through the trees to the right, ducking under branches and over fallen logs. Stopping every once in a while, I listen for any signs of her. Less than five minutes later, I catch the first hint she's been this way. A branch snaps to my left, and I lick my lips in anticipation. The closer I get, the more my stomach tightens and my cock throbs. Her heavy panting is cut off abruptly, but I've already pinpointed the tree she's tucked behind.

The leaves haven't started to fall yet, so I only need to be mindful of stray twigs as I pick my way over the ground. Running my fingers through my hair, I realize my hands are trembling. Skirting around the tree, my fingers brush her shirt and she explodes, shrieking as she runs again. She's no longer giggling and skipping through the forest. I chuckle, letting her get ahead before I dash after her.

Wrapping an arm around her waist, I lift her off her feet and she lets out a sob, kicking as she tries to escape. Moving one hand to her throat, I squeeze until she quiets. Setting her gently on her feet, I force her toward a tree.

We're steps away when she twists from my hold, crashing to her knees and then scrambling to gain her feet. Pouncing, I land on top of her, careful not to crush her, and she squeals, bucking in her haste to get away. Fear weaves through the sounds she's making and my chest seizes.

Flipping her around, I snatch her wrists in one hand, holding them over her head. I study her face as she gasps underneath me, but she doesn't seem to be freaking out. Relief eases the panic rolling through me.

"Check," I wheeze, resting my forehead on hers, and she stills beneath me.

"Are you okay?" she whispers, as if I'm the one who needs comfort.

"Check," I grunt, not able to get anything else out.

"Green," she breathes.

A shudder goes through me, and I grind my cock into her. She bucks, struggling to free her wrists, but I tighten my grip. Flames lick through me, reigniting the desire. I could end things right here. I could haul her up and over my shoulder and carry her ass back to my bike. I enjoy fucking her in my bed. Actually, I enjoy fucking her everywhere. This may be a fantasy we've talked about, but it can wait. I loosen my hold on her and she freezes, gazing up at me.

"Let's go home," I murmur as she tilts her head.

She hums as I push up. Warily, she stands, dusting off her pants. When I peer over my shoulder at the dark night, a twig snaps behind and I whip back around, only to see Willow's light hair streaming behind her as she takes off.

A curse falls from my lips as I chase after her. She won't make it far, but I can use this time to get my blood pumping again. She ducks under a low-hanging branch and then disappears. Rough bark digs into my skin as I use the offshoot as leverage. A crack resounds through the air as the branch breaks free.

Throwing myself forward, I barely make it before the whole thing crashes to the ground where I stood. Wheezing, I peer around, trying to catch sight of where Willow went, but she's long gone.

"Fuck," I breathe, my heart beating from my chest for a whole other reason now.

This is possibly the worst chase ever. I scramble to my feet, leaning around a trunk and close my eyes. The sounds of the forest amplify, highlighting the crickets' song, the leaves rustling with the wind, and a lone owl calling for its mate. Over all that, another twig snaps to my right, and I stalk between the trees toward the noise.

"Oh, *mo dóchais.* You thought you could run from me," I say softly, skipping forward lightly.

Her trembling sigh floats on the wind from behind another fallen tree. A grin splashes across my face as I launch myself over, landing in front of her, and she shrieks, slipping on the dead leaves littering the ground as she scrambles to get away. Snatching her around the waist, I bury my face in her neck.

"Don't you remember? I'll always catch you. No matter how far you run, how hard you try, I'm always here."

My words are both a promise and a reminder. We might be playing a game, immersed in a scene, but I never want her to forget I'm right here, always ready to catch her should she stumble. She shudders, muscles easing for a second before she renews her efforts to escape.

I grunt when her elbow connects with my gut, loosening my hold just enough for her to break free. As her feet hit the fallen trunk, I reach for her, fingers brushing her shirt as she launches over to the other side. A growl rips from my chest as I leap after her.

Once more, my arms encircle her waist, and I twist as we tumble toward the forest floor, cushioning her body as we fall. She kicks, heels connecting with my shins and fingers gouging into my arm, never letting up. Wrapping my leg around hers, she bucks, reaching back to scratch my face, but she's too small. I roll until she's under me, wheezing.

Tugging her pants down, I get them to her hips before she stills. I freeze, waiting for her to tell me to stop, or at the very least, say it's too much, but she doesn't. With her arms trapped under her, she's at my mercy, and yet something's not right. I sit up, straddling her and glancing around the quiet woods. The normal night noises surround us and a sigh of relief flows from me.

"Hawk?" Willow asks, her voice still breathless.

Easing from her, I pick her up gingerly until her feet are under her. I avoid her eyes as I right her pants and then brush the dirt and leaves from her clothes. There are small rips in her shirt across her chest, and I finger one before gazing at her face.

"What's wrong?" Her small hand grazes my jaw, and I lean into her touch.

"I thought I wanted this, but it doesn't feel right," I murmur, pulling her close and tucking her head to my chest.

"Did I do something wrong?"

A snort leaves me. "No, *mo dóchais*. You didn't. But this isn't what I want. And you're doing this for me. Let's go home."

Stepping back, I hold out my hand and she slips hers into mine. We've barely breached the density of the woods, the trees hardly muffling the city sounds. When lights filter through the trees, she quickens her pace, and we emerge just half a block from where I parked my bike.

"You know, I wasn't going to say anything..."

I glance at her as we walk, but she doesn't continue. "Tell me."

"I think it would have been fine, but while I was running, I was having flashbacks. I don't think I'm ready for that sort of thing," she whispers, gesturing toward the forest to her right.

Tugging her to a stop, I force her to face me, cupping her cheeks. "Not okay, Willow. At no point are you to try to force yourself into a situation you're not comfortable with. Fuck, I knew something was wrong. This is why you have a safe word, so shit like this doesn't happen."

I drop my hands before grabbing her arm and stalking toward my bike, hauling her behind me. Glancing back, I catch the despair on her face and then I face forward again. Her sniffles catch up to me and I stop again, swinging around. Devastation—within her eyes, splashed across her face, and rolling down her body—is all I can see.

My heart aches as I pull her into my arms, but she doesn't melt like she usually does, and it's all my fault. I should have reacted better.

"Willow, look at me," I say, waiting until she tilts her head back to meet my eyes. "This isn't your fault."

"I'm sorry. I should have said something, or tried harder," she says, a sob catching in her throat as she buries her face in my chest.

"No. You don't need to try harder. I'm upset because you didn't tell me to stop. I knew something was wrong, but you didn't speak up. You need to trust me enough to know how to help you, and I can't do that if you don't talk to me."

Pulling in a deep breath, her muscles ease one at a time until she's putty in my arms. I skim my hands over her body, ducking my fingers under the hem of her shirt to trace along her waistline. When she shivers, I grin as I duck my head into her neck to breathe her in. Her flowery scent settles the last of my nerves.

"We might not be doing what we planned, but I still have a surprise for you," I murmur, nipping at her skin before lapping at the small hurt.

As her nails dig into my lower back, I grab her ass, fitting my fingers into the crease before picking her up to carry her the rest of the way to my bike. She giggles, trying to wrap her legs around mine, but her body slides down.

We're almost there when car headlights cut across the night, casting long shadows in front of us. I take off, Willow's yelp trailing behind us. I'm sure it's nothing, but I'd rather not get caught either by a bullet or by Mason Byrns.

After setting her down, I toss her helmet to her before jumping on. I wait until she scrambles behind me, and then start it up. Tires screeching, I take off, Willow's arms tucked tightly around my body. Leaning around the corner, I pull into a driveway, hiding behind a large shrub, and cut the engine. Twisting around, I fix my eyes on the road, spying through the branches as Byrns's car rolls by, his scowling face searching for us.

Willow's muffled giggles echo through the dark, and I bury my face into my arm to smother my own. Glancing over my shoulder, I catch the shadow of her face through the visor, mirth dancing in her eyes. As the rumble from Mason's engine fades, I start my bike and turn us toward home.

The night is quiet as we wind through neighborhoods, Willow's arms clamped tight around my waist. Her hand sneaks down, grazing my crotch as we cross the line into Reaper territory.

Grabbing her hand, I hold it to my cock, forcing her to stroke me, not that it takes much on my end. Her helmet thumps between my shoulder blades as I rev the bike, picking up speed, I flip the switch I had installed last week. Even over the wind and bike, I hear her squeal when the vibrations start up under her seat. A grin breaks free as I hit the gas again, causing the seat to pulse faster. As Willow's hips jump against mine, I ease off.

Coasting into my driveway, I pull around to the back and ease down a path leading into the trees. It's far enough from the other houses that the bike won't bother any of my neighbors this way. As soon as I kill the engine, Willow groans, a tinge of disappointment lacing the sound. Chuckling, I grip her leg as I get off, keeping her in place.

My fingers brush her throat as I unclip the helmet, her hair standing on end when I pull it off. Smoothing the strands down, she grins up at me, a wild spark in her eye. Just a few months ago she was terrified to get on my bike, but lately she's been begging to ride somewhere—anywhere. When I took my motorcycle into Gear's shop to get the enhancements put into her seat, she pouted for the whole two days from the passenger's seat of Blue's car.

I swing my leg over again, straddling the bike backward so I'm facing her before cupping her face.

"You really are a dream come true," I murmur.

She rolls her eyes, opening her mouth to deliver a smartass retort, probably, and I pull her mouth to mine. When she tries to scoot closer, though, I drop my hands to her waist, keeping her right where I want her. The huff she lets out when I pull back has me laughing.

Twisting, I turn the key just enough for the vibrator to start up again and her face transforms. She leans forward, dropping her head to my shoulder and letting out a breathless moan.

"Do you like my new toy?" I ask, skimming my hands under her shirt until my thumbs graze the sides of her tits through her bra.

A low hum is her only response as she squirms. Reaching around, I twist my fingers around the hook, giving me access to more of her smooth skin. Another moan leaves her when I roll her nipples between my fingers and she throws her head back, exposing her throat.

Latching onto the soft skin before pulling her mouth back to mine, a warm breeze rustles the leaves above our heads, sending a shiver through her. Her nails dig into my shoulders, a welcome sting of pain rushing through me. Grabbing her hips, I rub her back and forth along the seat until she's shuddering in my arms, her teeth sinking into my shoulder as she comes.

As her muscles ease, another quiver runs through her body, and she leans back to escape the vibrations. I could turn it off, but I like watching her fall apart.

"Hawk," she says breathlessly, grabbing my arms as I grip her waist.

"Hmm?" I tip her body forward until her clit hits the seat again, and she attempts to jerk away. "What did you need, Willow?"

"You. Please. I need—" her sentence ends with a groan as she battles me against her pleasure.

"Use your words, *mo dóchais*," I purr into her ear.

"I need you," she whines. I chuckle, tipping her back again to give her a small reprieve.

"Say it," I growl.

Her eyes meet mine, pleasure swimming within their depths. "I need your cock. Fuck me, Hawk. Now."

Her words are strong and clear, much more than they were when we met all those weeks ago. A shudder runs through me at how confident she's become. I lift her off the bike, setting her on her feet. Scrambling after her, I shuck my pants off and her giggle curls through the air, wrapping around my heart in the process.

"Something funny?" I ask, raising an eyebrow.

"Nothing, you just—" She smothers another laugh. "—don't have any pants on."

"It's the quickest way to get to my dick, Willow."

"But you have a shirt on."

She dissolves into laughter, and I scowl, stalking forward. Catching her around the waist, I hook my thumb into her pants and yank them down until they slide to her knees.

"There. Now we're both half naked."

I grin as she falls into my arms, and then lift her so she can shimmy her pants all the way off. Setting her back on the bike, she yelps before scooting back. I swing my leg over, facing her again and then snatch at her thighs to stop her from running away from the pleasure. When she squirms, she slips closer to me, sliding down the seat, and I plant my feet on the ground.

"Feet up, Willow," I command, and she raises an eyebrow. I lean closer. "Give me your ankles so I can fuck you properly, *mo dóchais*."

"And what if I don't?" she says, smirking.

"Do you really want to find out?"

Draping her arms over my shoulders, her fingers tug at the hair on the nape of my neck, sending a chill down my spine. A smile plays on her lips, joy reflected in her blue eyes, and I rest my forehead on hers. Tugging her hips forward, she slips further into my lap. I grip my cock, guiding myself into her wet pussy as she shudders, needy sounds falling from her lips.

"Willow," I whisper, waiting until her eyes meet mine, desire pooling in their depths. "I love you."

As I thrust into her, a gasp falls from her lips and her head drops, watching where we're connected. Finally, she lifts her feet to my thighs, the position forcing her to lie back. Reaching up, I roll her nipple between my fingers, and her pussy clenches around me.

"Legs around my waist," I grunt, and she wraps them around me, forcing me deeper into her.

Gripping her hips, I stand and surge into her, groaning when I'm finally fully seated. She jerks her hips and I thrust into her again, relishing the feeling of her warmth enveloping my cock. My tight grip is probably leaving bruises behind, not that she'll care. Last week I tried to apologize for one on her ass and she tore me a new one.

"Hawk," she gasps. "Harder."

She moans as I pound into her and I almost come when she slides her hands across her skin, squeezing her tits. A desperate noise leaves me when one hand moves to her clit. I can't pull my eyes away from the scene of her playing with herself while I fuck her. It's intoxicating.

Gritting my teeth, I slam my eyes shut. I'm close, but so is she. Her pussy is clinging to me, pulsing in time with my thrusts. Her voice whimpers my name as she cascades over the edge and I let go, following her into oblivion.

A cool summer breeze brushes across our damp skin and goosebumps appear on her body. Laying across her, I warm her skin with my own, kissing my way across her flushed chest. Reaching back, I blindly jab at the button to turn off the vibrating seat, and she huffs out a laugh as her pussy spasms again. I groan into her skin.

"Hawk," she murmurs, and I rest my chin on her chest. "You said it."

"*Mo dóchais,*" I breathe, bringing my lips to hers and kissing her gently. "You're everything I've ever hoped for. Did you doubt my love for you?"

Tears fill her eyes and I kiss them away, holding her as the sound of the summer night becomes the backdrop for our love.

* * *

Thank You

Thank you so much for reading Hawk and Willow's story! Not ready to leave the shadows of Synd behind?
Pre-order Mason's story-out June 2, 2023

If you'd like to hear about the other stories that have been living in my head, sign up for my newsletter, visit my website, or follow me on social media visit:

emiliaabraham.com

Special Thanks:
K.B. Barrett Designs-Cover Artist and Formatter
Emily Michel-Editor
Erenee-Beta Reader
Sapphire and Krysten-Omega Readers

ALSO BY THE AUTHOR

<u>Shadows of Synd:</u>

Under the Shadows

Book 1

Running From Shadows

Book 2

Becoming Shadows

Book 3

Shadows Within Us

Book 4 (May 2023)

<u>Ruins of Rima:</u>

Chasing Darkness (August 2023)

Charmed by Darkness (October 2023)

<u>Also by Emilia Abraham:</u>

Stuck at Sundown

ABOUT THE AUTHOR

After many years of dreaming of becoming a full-time writer, Emilia Abraham took the leap, bringing her words to print. From sweet contemporary romance to spicy why choose and everything in between, she focuses on the happily ever after.

Emilia lives in the Upper Midwest with her husband (who's probably sick of listening to her expound on fictional men) and three kids (who try to steal her post-it notes). When she's not writing, she enjoys reading, playing video games, and consuming copious amounts of energy drinks.

www.ingramcontent.com/pod-product-compliance
Lightning Source LLC
Chambersburg PA
CBHW021339310726
48971CB00001B/206